PEARL OF PIT LANE

When her mother dies in childbirth, Pearl Edwards is left in the care of her aunt, Annie Grafton. Annie loves. Pearl like her own daughter but it isn't easy to keep a roof over their heads and food on the table, so she supplements their meagre income by walking the pit lane, looking for men willing to pay for her company. As Pearl grows older she is unable to remain ignorant of Annie's profession. And when Pearl finds herself unexpectedly without work and their landlord raises the rent, it becomes clear they have few choices left and Annie is forced to ask Pearl the unthinkable. Rather than submit to life on the pit lane, Pearl runs away. She has nothing and nowhere to go, but Pearl is determined to survive on her own terms . . .

GLENDA YOUNG

◆——————

PEARL OF
PIT LANE

Complete and Unabridged

MAGNA
Leicester

First published in Great Britain in 2019 by
Headline Publishing Group
London

First Ulverscroft Edition
published 2020
by arrangement with
Headline Publishing Group
An Hachette UK Company
London

A catalogue record for this book is available
from the British Library.

ISBN 978–0–7505–4833–5

Published by
Ulverscroft Limited
Anstey, Leicestershire

Set by Words & Graphics Ltd.
Anstey, Leicestershire
Printed and bound in Great Britain by
TJ Books Limited., Padstow, Cornwall

Grace Emily Foster

Acknowledgements

My thanks go to: Ryhope Heritage Society, especially Rob Shepherd, Peter Hedley and Brian Ibinson; Sunderland Antiquarian Society, especially Norman Kirtlan, Linda King, Phil Curtis and Ron Lawson; all of the helpful staff at Sunderland Local Studies Centre and Sunderland City Library, and Allison Clarke for her support; Sunderland Museum & Winter Gardens, especially Marie Harrison and Janet Robinson for their invaluable help with research; Durham County Records Office; Beamish Museum; Reverend David Chadwick of St Paul's Church, Ryhope; Edward Keogh; Sharon Vincent for her knowledge of women's social history in Sunderland; Deborah Simmons for her help with the red feather hat; Beverley Ann Hopper; Paul Dunn for our chat over a coffee that changed everything; Martin Wallwork and Tony Kerr for their invaluable PR advice; staff at Sunderland Waterstones; Fiona Thompson at the *Sunderland Echo*. To my editor, Kate Byrne, at Headline, and my agent, Caroline Sheldon — two amazing women from whom I have learned a lot. And to Barry, for the love and support and endless cups of tea when I lock myself away to write.

A note on a fictional street name used in this novel

In all of my novels set in Ryhope in 1919 I try, where possible, to use the original street names. I am grateful to Durham County Records Office, who very kindly copied for me the Ordnance Survey Map of Ryhope from that era.

However, in *Pearl of Pit Lane*, my third novel set in the village of Ryhope in 1919, I have created a fictional street called Dawdon Street where some nefarious activity takes place!

1

The Promise

July 1919

'What are you doing sitting out in the rain?'

Pearl looked up into the face of her friend Joey, who was making his way towards her. As he walked, his bad foot dragged behind him. Pearl's skinny dog, Boot, lay on the wet ground at her feet, and when Pearl didn't reply to Joey's question, he raised his black head and nudged her hand with his nose.

'Annie's busy; she's dressmaking upstairs in our room. She wanted me out of the way,' Pearl said. She kept her gaze fixed on the ground, unable to face Joey when she was spinning him a lie. But how could she give him the honest reply he deserved? She couldn't tell anyone the truth. It was her and Annie's secret what happened in their room.

Joey pulled his thin jacket around him, but it proved useless against the rain. 'Shove along then,' he said, forcing his way on to the step.

Pearl moved to one side, letting her friend sit next to her. Rain dripped from the end of her nose. Her long auburn hair was plastered against her head, and her blouse and skirt were wet through. She wrapped her arms around her

1

knees and hugged them towards her.

'Annie's busy?' Joey repeated. 'What's so important that she won't let you stay inside on a day as wet as this?'

Pearl knew it would be a relief to tell someone, and with Joey being her best friend, there was no one better to confide in. So many times she'd wanted to tell him what was really going on, but she'd always held back out of respect for Annie's wishes. She didn't want to get her aunt into any kind of trouble. If she did tell, once the secret was out, there could be no taking it back.

The yard where Pearl and Joey sat belonged to landlord Bernie Pemberton. Bernie also owned the room above, where Pearl and Annie lived, and the haberdashery shop below, Pemberton's Goods, where Annie worked by day. But it was Annie's night-time work that Pearl was sworn to secrecy on.

'Isn't Annie working in the shop today then?' Joey asked. Pearl knew he'd keep on with the questions until she gave him a reply.

'It's early closing day,' she said. At least that bit was true, it *was* early closing day, although what came out of her mouth next was a line she had spun many times before. 'She says she needs all the space upstairs to spread the dressmaking material about.'

She looked at Joey's mucky face underneath his worn and frayed cap. He was a thin boy, small for his age, and two years younger than Pearl, who was almost sixteen. She was almost a woman, Aunt Annie kept telling her. Pearl understood only too well that her aunt meant

2

she was nearly of an age to do the same work as Annie did. But Annie wasn't talking about her shop work in Pemberton's Goods. She was referring to her second, secret job that she took on to earn extra cash, work that Pearl did not approve of and did not want at any cost. She'd seen the way Annie lived, taking men off the street to her room, and she knew that, whatever happened in her future, she herself wanted a life that didn't need to be kept secret. She wanted a life that wouldn't get her into trouble, one that meant she wouldn't need to hide from the coppers on their rounds like Annie had to do.

Pearl had been promised a job working behind the bar at the Colliery Inn as soon as she turned sixteen, and it was an offer she couldn't afford to turn down. Until then, she kept the room clean for her aunt, mended her clothes, and spent her free time making clippy mats from old scraps of rags. She'd even sold one of her mats in the shop. Annie had hung it up for sale and it had caught the eye of one of her customers.

Pearl hooked her arm through Joey's and the two of them huddled close. If anyone had seen them, if anyone had been daft enough to be walking by in the rain, they might have thought the pair were brother and sister, sitting on the doorstep with their skinny dog, waiting for their mam to come home. But the truth was that Pearl's only relation was her aunt, and the only person other than Pearl who cared about Joey was his mam, Kate Scotch, a short, bird-like woman not much taller than her son. His dad had run off before Joey was born.

'Were you going somewhere just now?' Pearl asked.

'The pit,' Joey replied. Pearl noticed the sadness in the way he said the two words. It was the same sadness that was always there now when he spoke of the place he used to work.

'Mam says I have to go and ask for my old job back. I've told her I've asked already, but she says I have to keep trying.' His voice trailed off.

'Do you want to go back?'

Joey reached down and stroked Boot behind his ears, the dog's favourite place. 'Mam says I have to.'

'I wouldn't want to go back after what happened,' Pearl said softly.

'Everyone says not to blame myself, Pearl, but I do. They say it was the pony's fault, but I should have been concentrating. If I'd been looking in the right direction like the gaffer taught me, I would have seen the coal tub coming loose. I just didn't see it, Pearl. It was my fault, I know it was.'

Pearl heard his voice break, it was a conversation they'd had many times since Joey's accident. He'd been working with a pit pony, which had been killed when one of the coal tubs fell from the track. Joey's life had been saved by a quick-thinking older lad who also worked on the tubs, but the accident had taken its toll and left him with an injured leg. Where once he would run through the back streets of Ryhope or kick stones along the cobbles, now he walked slowly, with a limp. It had taken its toll in deeper, unseen ways too. It was the nightmares he hated

4

most, seeing the dead body of the pony in his dreams.

As the two of them sat on the doorstep, the rain stepped up a notch and started hitting the ground faster, harder, like a song Pearl and Joey were getting used to hearing that had suddenly changed key.

'Can't you go inside at all?' Joey asked.

Pearl glanced up at the window, the curtains drawn in the middle of the day. 'Not yet,' she replied.

'What about the shop? Can't you wait in there until Annie's finished work?'

Pearl shook her head. 'I'm supposed to be in the village,' she said, remembering the task that Annie had sent her to do. She nodded towards Boot, who was lying on the ground, his dark velvet eyes keeping watch on her and Joey. 'Annie says I have to sell him.'

'Boot? No!' Joey cried. 'You've had him for ages, you can't just get rid of him.'

At the sound of his name, Boot stood to attention and shook himself from side to side, splattering rain against Pearl and Joey from his heavy wet coat.

Pearl shielded her face with her hands. 'Boot, stop it!' she scolded.

The dog waited for another command, but when none came, he laid his wet head on Pearl's knees.

'She says he costs too much to feed. We barely have enough food for the two of us most days. She reckons High Farm might buy him. He's a good ratter, and Ralphie, the farmer, could do with a dog like him.'

'Are you still working mornings at the farm?' Joey asked.

'Just until next week. Got myself another job as soon as I turn sixteen.' Pearl smiled. 'It's not much, just helping at the Colliery Inn — cleaning mainly, washing the pots and sweeping the yard — but they've offered a bit more money than the farm.'

Joey stroked Boot under his wet chin. 'Will you miss him if he goes?'

'Of course. But it's not as if he's really our dog; he just turned up one day and we've never been able to get rid of him.'

'We could walk down to High Farm now if you want. I'll come with you. Mam'll never know if I don't go to the pit. And you won't tell her, will you, Pearl?'

'Course not. You can trust me.'

'You asked if I wanted to go back to work there,' Joey began. 'And the truth is, I don't, not after the pony died.'

'But what'll you do for a job if you don't go back?'

'Maybe there'll be work at the farm,' Joey replied hopefully, but both he and Pearl knew that jobs in Ryhope were hard to come by. No matter how willing Joey was, his injured leg would go against him if he went up for jobs against stronger, bigger lads. And with soldiers returning from the war, Ryhope had plenty of big, strong lads being given a hero's welcome along with their pick of available work. Joey pushed his hands against the doorstep to help

6

him as he tried to stand. He still couldn't put much weight on his leg; the pain was too much to bear. He steadied himself against the brick wall.

'I know where we can go,' Pearl said, her face lighting up. 'We'll sit in the Co-op doorway; it'll be dry under the canopy. And when it stops raining, we'll walk down to High Farm.'

She grabbed Joey's arm and helped her friend gain his balance.

'Come on, Boot,' she commanded, and the dog followed as they headed from the yard into the lane. Joey lagged behind and Pearl slowed her pace to match his. She held out her arm to him. 'Want to hook on?'

Without a word, Joey slipped his arm through hers and Pearl supported him as he limped along. Boot scampered ahead of them, oblivious to the rain, while Pearl huddled inside her thin shawl and Joey pulled his cap down to shield his face as they walked along the back lane of Dawdon Street. The row of lime-washed cottages was rarely called by its full name by anyone who lived there. Being so close to the Ryhope Coal Company mines, Dawdon Street was simply one of the many ramshackle pit lanes.

★ ★ ★

Upstairs in the flat above the shop, Annie Grafton took the shillings offered to her by the man whose name she didn't know.

'Same time next week?' he asked.

'I don't keep an appointments book,' Annie

replied matter-of-factly. 'You know where to find me if you want me. I might be here when you come calling next.'

'Depends on how you feel, eh?' he smirked.

Annie kept silent. Whether she walked the pit lane or not depended on how broke she was. As the man bent to tie his shoelaces, she took a good look at him. It was her first proper inspection since he had taken up her services. His shoes had a shine to them that she didn't often see from the men she met in Ryhope. And his black suit and waistcoat weren't frayed like many she saw. He stood, straightened his tie and ran a hand through his thick dark hair. But Annie knew well enough not to ask any questions. The men who came to her were there for company, not conversation. She simply provided a service and was paid for her time; it was a matter of supply and demand. At least that was how she'd long ago squared her way to earn extra cash: it was a job that she turned to when she had to. Just a job.

'You'll see yourself out,' she said. It was a command rather than a question. Annie knew from experience that some of the men liked to loiter, treating her as if she were their girlfriend when she was anything but. She saw herself as a businesswoman who dictated her own terms. Apart from the hours she was contracted to work in the little haberdashery shop downstairs, her time was her own. She set the rules for the business she conducted upstairs, kept all the money she earned and worked only when she needed to. It was an arrangement that had suited her for years, since before Pearl was born.

As soon as she heard the door slam downstairs, she took the shillings and put them in her jar. It was filling up nicely but it was still nowhere near enough to pay what she owed. Even with her work in the haberdashery shop, her wages didn't cover her debts to her landlord and almost every shopkeeper on the colliery. And as if things weren't bad enough already, her landlord, Bernie Pemberton, was the same fella who owned the shop downstairs where she worked, making him her employer too.

Most of the shops on the colliery had been good enough to let Annie put groceries on the slate, allowing her to pay when she could. The problem was, she hadn't been able to pay anyone yet, and her credit had been withdrawn by most of the shops. First, though, there was the rent to find, for where would she and Pearl be without a roof over their heads? She had to take care of Pearl; it was what she'd promised her older sister Mary on the night she died, and she would never go back on her word. She knew that Pearl didn't approve of how she made her living, but what else could she do when there was so little money to be made in the shop? There were bills to be paid and two mouths to feed, as well as their greedy dog.

Pearl had grown into a young woman Annie was proud of, but she caught her niece looking at her sometimes in the same way that Mary used to do when they were girls. Pearl had Mary's looks about her. It was like looking into the past each time Annie looked at Pearl. Pearl had her mother's long auburn hair that parted in the middle and fell to her waist. She had the same pale skin as Mary, almost translucent; the same nose, the same rosebud mouth. But the similarities ended when it came to her eyes. Pearl's gaze held a hint of steel. When she was focused on something, concentrating on working on the colourful clippy mats, her eyes narrowed with determination in a way that Mary's never had.

* ★ ★

Annie reached for her sister's hand. It felt as light as air; cold, papery skin stretched taut on bony fingers.

'Promise me three things, Annie,' Mary said.

'I'll do anything for you. You know that.'

'Look after Pearl, won't you? Give her a home, Annie, please.'

Annie dipped her head to her sister's hand and gently kissed her cold skin.

'I'll love her as if she were my own.'

'The second thing I want more than anything in the world. Find a job, Annie. I beg you. A real job.'

It was a conversation they'd had many times in the past, and now, on her deathbed, Mary made her request for the final time.

'You know how hard it is . . . ' Annie began.

'Please, Annie. For Pearl's sake. Show her there's another way to survive. Teach her that there's a choice, another way to be a woman when she grows up. She doesn't have to sell

10

herself to men, not like you and I have had to do.'

Annie shifted her gaze from Mary's pale face, unable to look her in the eye, unable to promise that she could turn her life around, even for her dying sister.

'I'll try,' she whispered.

'No, Annie, I need you to promise. You can't deny me this, can you, not now?'

Despite her grief and sadness, Annie couldn't help but smile at Mary's words. Her bossy older sister was still calling the shots, even as she lay dying.

'I promise,' she said at last.

But she crossed her fingers as the words left her lips. She would try; that was all she could do. She knew that anything more might be beyond her. She thought perhaps Mary knew that too.

Mary rested her head against the pillow propped at her back. She closed her eyes. Annie sat for a while watching her sister, who was little more than skin and bones now. Her chest barely rose with each breath. It was some moments later when she opened her eyes again.

'There's one final thing,' she said. 'Promise me you'll tell Pearl who her dad is.'

'You know?' Annie whispered.

'I've always known. She's Edward's,' Mary said, her voice suddenly strong.

Annie bit her bottom lip and tried to stop her tears. The last thing she wanted was to cry in front of her sister, who was so close to death now.

'Are you sure?' she asked.

Mary swallowed hard, with difficulty. 'There was only ever Edward in the end.'

'Will I find him to tell him about her?' Annie asked.

'No.' Mary was firm. 'His family made their wishes known. They said I wasn't good enough for him, and he had to do as they bid. But I want my baby to know she was loved by both parents.'

'Of course,' Annie said.

A thin smile appeared on Mary's lips before her head sank back against her pillow and her eyes closed for the final time. Annie remained at her bedside, silent tears falling. She was still holding Mary's hand when Dr Anderson arrived, but he was too late to help. He laid his hand on her shoulder.

'Come on,' he said. 'The baby is awake and she needs you.'

Annie took one last look at her sister, then stood from her chair, grateful for Dr Anderson's arm, for her legs felt as if they had turned to stone. Mary's last words lodged in her heart.

'Will you name the child Mary, after your sister?' Dr Anderson asked.

'No. Mary has already named her Pearl, for our mother.'

'And will she take your surname? Pearl Grafton?'

Annie thought for a moment, remembering her promise to Mary that Pearl would always know who her dad was. She shook her head.

'No, she's Edward's . . . Pearl Edwards.'

★ ★ ★

'Pearl?' Annie called down the stairs. 'Pearl? Are you still out there? You can come up now, he's gone.'

She wasn't surprised when there was no reply. She knew Pearl wasn't daft enough to have waited outside in the rain. She'd have found shelter and warmth somewhere on the colliery, or she'd be at Joey's house; the two of them were inseparable. Annie wished she could let Pearl stay in the shop when she was working upstairs. But she had to lock up on early-closing day. She'd left her in there once, and Bernie Pemberton had found her and threatened Annie with the authorities, even though Pearl had been safe, warm and asleep. She'd never dared do it again.

When Pearl was a baby, she'd slept on a shelf on the landing, out of sight of Annie's callers. When she grew to be a toddler, Annie left her with any of her friends who wouldn't grumble too much about it, although she could never reveal the real reason she needed a babysitter. Only her friend Dorothy knew the truth, for she also worked the pit lane. Dorothy took Pearl in when she could, but when she had night-time work of her own, Annie was often left to beg favours from others. Whatever happened, she was determined to keep Pearl from the reality of how she earned her extra cash. But now Pearl was a young woman, almost sixteen, and she knew only too well what her aunt did to make money.

Annie stood in her bare feet, listening to the rain hammering against the window in the dark

13

room. She wondered if Pearl had managed to sell Boot as she'd asked her to do. What use did they have for the dog? If they could get money for it, all the better. They certainly couldn't afford to feed it any more.

She pulled at the bed sheets, straightening them as best she could. She turned the eiderdown the right way round and plumped up the pillows. The bed was so neat after she had finished that anyone looking at it would never have guessed what had just taken place in the room. With the bed tidied, she pulled her cotton housecoat about her slim waist and ran a comb through her long brown hair. It was as she began plaiting it that she felt a cold drip of water against the back of her neck.

'Flaming hell! Not again!' she cried.

She ran from the bedroom to the small alcove on the landing and pulled her cast-iron pan from a shelf. Back in the bedroom, she placed the pan on the floor where water was splashing on to the wooden boards. With the pan in place, the water fell with a dull *drip-drip* from the leak in the ceiling. But then she heard another dripping noise and looked up to see that a new leak had opened up.

'Heaven help us!' she yelled, fetching a brown earthen-ware bowl and positioning it next to the pan. She scanned the ceiling, ready to find another bowl if needed to stop the rain falling on to the bed or Pearl's corner of the room, where blankets and clothes were piled. On the floor next to the clothes was the clippy mat Pearl was working on. A large piece of hessian was

14

stretched taut on a wooden frame and dotted with blue and red strips of rags. Annie knew how heartbroken her niece would be if she came home to find it sodden after all the hard work she'd put in. But apart from the two leaks, the ceiling looked intact, for now.

Breathing a sigh of relief, she glanced out of the window, but all she could see was the dark sky. The best thing she could do would be to get the coal fire going, for even though it was summer, the rain made it feel like the darkest winter day.

She dressed quickly, pulling on a shapeless blue cotton dress and pushing her arms into the short sleeves. She was intent on heading out to the yard to bring in a bucket of coal. She'd need to bring in water too, to wash off the scent of the man with dark hair. He hadn't smelled earthy, like the miners who came to her did. Even after they'd bathed, their skin was still grimed with coal. Nor had he smelled clean and freshly scrubbed like the soldier who had come to her just the week before. She wondered if she'd see more soldiers now that the Great War was over. A smile played around her lips as she thought of the money soldiers might spend, and she wondered if she dared charge more.

She sat on the edge of her bed and pulled on her black boots. As she walked towards the door that led to the stairs, her boot heel became stuck in a hole in the floor.

'Damn thing!' she cried. She yanked her foot from the floorboard and made a mental note to remember to cover it with a blanket when she returned with coal and water. The hole in the floor was another problem that Bernie had ignored her requests to fix.

'I'll get on to it some time,' he said every time Annie brought up the problem.

'Actions speak louder than words,' Annie said each time he ignored her request.

★ ★ ★

Down at the Co-op, Pearl and Joey had been moved on from sheltering in the doorway.

'Get away now, the pair of you!' a stocky man yelled from inside the store. He was wearing a brown apron pulled tight across his bulging stomach. 'Get back up the colliery where you belong. Pit rats!'

'In here,' Pearl said as they left the doorway. She disappeared under a high archway and Joey followed. 'It leads to the stables at the back of the store. We can wait here; we won't be in anyone's way and no one will see us. We can stay here until it stops raining.'

Pearl, Joey and Boot stood under the archway and stared out at the rain. It was still coming down heavily, splashing up from the road. Joey turned and looked at the cobbled courtyard with its stables where the Co-op horses and delivery carts were housed.

'The horses here are looked after by the same vet who sees to the ponies at the pit,' he said. 'He was the vet who was called out when I had the accident.'

Pearl saw the sadness come over his face again. It happened each time he spoke of what

16

had happened at the pit some weeks ago. She'd noticed he'd lost his smile since then; it didn't come as readily as it once used to do.

'Aye, the vet's a decent fella, but he couldn't save Ned,' Joey continued.

It was the first time he had spoken the pony's name since the accident.

'You liked that pony a lot, didn't you?' Pearl asked.

Joey's face brightened for a moment. 'He was the best, everyone said so.' He turned his face away from Pearl. 'You know, they call pit ponies the workers who never go on strike. They never come to the surface, not even for a week's holiday in the summer. I asked one of the lads there once, Adam he was called, if I could take Ned up for a holiday, just for a day, so that he could graze on some grass and feel the sun on his back. But I was told no. It was daft really, as if a fourteen-year-old boy like me could have any say in how the pit is run.'

'At least you asked,' Pearl said. 'It's more than many would have done. Animals aren't daft, Joey; Ned would have known you liked him and that you would never have hurt him on purpose.'

'He'd wait for me every morning; he'd stand there and wait especially for me. He wouldn't let any of the other lads harness him. It had to be me. And he'd do tricks, Pearl, you should have seen him. He could pick up a water bottle with his teeth and drink the water right from it. And at bait time he'd wait for titbits the lads would throw down.'

'He sounds like a right character,' Pearl said.

17

She watched Joey's face, animated now as he talked about his pony.

Joey pushed his hand into his trouser pocket and brought out a folded piece of paper. He opened it up carefully, taking care not to tear it, and handed it to Pearl. She looked at the drawing of a pony's head, with big dark eyes and pointed ears. There was a sadness to the eyes that drew her attention. She'd had no idea that her friend was so talented. She'd thought she knew everything there was to know about Joey.

'Is this Ned?' she asked, astonished at the quality of the picture. 'Did you draw this?'

'I wanted to remember him, so I drew him. I keep him in my pocket for now and carry him around with me. Once I get a new job, I'll save up to buy a frame and put him on the wall at home if Mam says I can.'

Pearl looked again at the drawing then handed the paper back to Joey, who folded it carefully and returned it to his pocket.

'There was another good pony, Tarn,' he went on. 'Now he was an odd one. He wouldn't make a move on a morning until the lads sang a verse of 'Rule Britannia'.'

'You're kidding me?' Pearl laughed.

'I'm not. It's all true. Cross my heart. I wouldn't lie to you, Pearl.'

Pearl felt a stab at Joey's words. Her friend trusted her so much, yet she was still keeping the truth from him about her life with Annie. She wasn't sure how Joey would react if she told him. Boys were different, weren't they? Less understanding about the things that women had to do.

18

But he was Joey; they'd grown up together, he was as good as family. She could tell him, surely? He might understand and not judge Annie too harshly. But there was also a danger he might tell his mam, and who knew who else Kate Scotch might spill the secret to?

Outside the archway, the rain began to ease.

'Come on, let's get down to the farm. See if we can find you any work there and ask if they're interested in buying . . . ' Pearl stopped short of saying the dog's name and just nodded towards him. Joey understood.

'I'd take him in, but Mam's not keen on dogs,' he said.

Boot trotted in front of them as they headed down the colliery bank to the village.

Once they reached High Farm, Pearl's business with Ralphie Heddon, the farmer, was conducted briskly. Ralphie was a big fella with a thatch of straw-coloured hair. He was well-built and muscled, with a ruddy face from years spent working outdoors. He didn't hesitate to take Boot off Pearl's hands once she told him the dog was good at chasing rats. He had been at his wits' end over the last few weeks with rats in the barn. His own dog, Gem, was getting too old to chase anything now. He paid Pearl less than Annie had asked for, but it was cash nonetheless, and something was better than nothing. Boot sniffed at the unfamiliar farm scents before settling down at Pearl's feet.

'I brought my friend with me,' Pearl told Ralphie. She gently pushed Joey forward. Joey whipped off his cap. 'He's looking for work, and

I thought you might consider taking him on in my place.'

Joey stood as tall as he could. He pushed his good leg against the ground, squared his shoulders and stuck out his chest.

'Oh aye?' Ralphie said, appraising him, wondering how he could make best use of such a scrawny lad. 'Where have you worked before?'

'I was a tub putter at the pit,' Joey said. Then he remembered his mam's words about respecting his elders. 'Sir.'

'Have you ever worked with animals?' Ralphie asked him.

Joey gulped. 'Just the pit ponies, sir.'

The farmer thought for a while. 'How old are you, lad?'

'Fourteen.'

'And apart from your gammy leg there, are you fit and well? I saw you when you walked in; you were limping.'

'Pit accident,' was all Joey said by way of explanation. 'Other than that, I'm well. I might be little but I'm strong.'

A smile spread across Ralphie's round face. He needed a cheap and willing pair of hands on the farm to help his daft lump of a son, Ronnie. It wasn't work he could offer to any of the soldiers returning from war, who'd be affronted by the menial tasks and low pay. But Joey seemed keen, and if Pearl Edwards was vouching for him, that was all to the good. Ralphie had known Pearl's mam Mary before she passed away, and Pearl had been a good worker while she'd been helping at the farm.

20

'Well, I could do with an extra pair of hands around the place now that Pearl's leaving us,' Ralphie said. He eyed Joey from his boots up to his thin face and unruly brown hair. 'I can't pay much, mind. You'd be working in the dairy, stirring the milk and skimming it, cleaning the place out. Think you could manage it?'

Joey gripped his cap in his hands at his heart. 'I know I could. You won't be sorry if you take me on, mister.'

'He's a good worker,' Pearl chipped in. 'Honest, too.'

'And if I was to offer you the job, could you start tomorrow?' Ralphie asked.

Joey thought his heart would burst with pride. 'Yes, sir.'

Ralphie nodded slowly, thinking things over.

'Let's see you back here tomorrow morning at six o'clock. Don't be late. I'll start by showing you around the farm, and then you can help my son Ronnie feed the geese and hens and collect the eggs.'

Pearl nudged Joey with her elbow. Immediately Joey's hand shot out. Ralphie took it, shaking it heartily.

'Thank you,' Joey said. 'Thank you very much, sir.'

'Call me Ralphie, lad. *Sir* doesn't sit well with me.'

'Thank you, Ralphie,' Pearl said.

Ralphie walked towards Boot and gripped him by the scruff of the neck. Boot yelped and Pearl's stomach turned over. She wanted to say a proper goodbye to her dog, but the farmer was already yanking him away to the barn. He stopped when he saw Joey and Pearl were still there, and called out, 'Go on, the pair of you, let me get on with my work now the rain's stopped.'

As they walked away from the farm, Pearl gripped the coins Ralphie had given her in exchange for the dog. She turned to see Boot one final time, but he'd already gone.

'At least he'll be getting fed if he's catching rats,' Joey said, sensing Pearl's sadness. 'And there's plenty of space for him to run around here. The pit lane round Dawdon Street can't offer him that.'

'Will you keep your eye on him when you're at work, Joey? Will you watch out for him and give him a stroke from me? Scratch him behind his ears, he loves that.'

'Course I will.'

Pearl offered her arm. 'Want to hook on?'

Joey accepted Pearl's offer gratefully; his leg felt raw after the walk to the farm. They made their way slowly back to Dawdon Street, stopping now and then for Joey to rest. When they reached the back lane, he went off to tell his mam about his new job. Pearl glanced up at the bedroom window. The curtains were open, the sign that Annie was no longer at work.

She pushed the door open and climbed the stairs to their room. But when she reached the landing, a man was waiting there, a man she hadn't seen before. He looked rough and ready, his jacket torn and frayed, his face heavy with black stubble and his eyes paunchy from too much beer.

22

'Where is she?' he growled.

Pearl took a step backwards, keeping her distance, ready to flee down the stairs if she needed.

'How did you get in?' she demanded, sounding more assertive than she felt. Her legs were shaking from the shock of seeing a stranger in her home.

'Never mind that. Where's the woman?'

'She's not working today,' Pearl said firmly. She was surprised, though. Where on earth had Annie gone? 'You'd better leave.'

'I'm going nowhere.'

'Get out!' Pearl yelled. 'Get out now or — '

'Or what? You'll call the police? I don't think you'll be doing that, will you? Not if you want your dirty little secret kept under wraps. I know what goes on up here in your filthy knocking shop.' He eyed Pearl up and down. 'Well now. If I can't have the usual woman who works here, then I'll just have to have you.'

'Get out!' Pearl screamed, then she turned to run down the stairs, to get away as fast as she could. But the man was quicker than Pearl, his reflexes sharpened by his wicked desire and he grabbed her arm before she could flee. She struggled, punching him with her free hand, but it did little good, and as they fought, she landed heavily, twisting her back as she fell. She couldn't move, the pain pinned her to the stairs. She was powerless to do anything other than spit in the face of the man as he loomed over her, his hands already pulling at his trousers.

Just then, the door to the yard was flung open.

Pearl felt the cool air rush in and she screamed out for help.

'Get off her!' a voice roared from the bottom of the stairs.

Pearl knew immediately who it was. 'I said get off her! What the hell do you think you're doing?'

She felt the weight of the stranger ease from her body as he stood to deal with whoever was behind him. Joey was holding on to the wall, pulling himself up the stairs, and when he reached Pearl's attacker, he yanked him by his jacket and tried to pull him away from her. The man swung round, but when he saw it was just a boy challenging him, he simply laughed in Joey's face. He pushed Joey's shoulder hard, smashing him against the wall. Free of the man's grip, Pearl stood and moved backwards up the stairs as quickly as the pain in her back would allow. The man lunged for her again, but Joey was quicker than the fella had given him credit for, and he lashed out with a strong punch to the side of the man's face. Again he hit him, and again.

Pearl reached the alcove at the top of the stairs and searched in vain for Annie's cast-iron pan. She needed a weapon, anything she could use to show this fella she wasn't to be messed with. Her hands scrabbled on the shelf and landed on spoons and plates, but there was nothing heavy enough to use as a weapon or a show of strength. And then she found it, the wooden rolling pin. She gripped it tight in both hands, raised it high in the air and yelled for all she was worth.

'Get out of my house!'

24

Joey and the man both turned to see her standing at the top of the stairs. She looked fierce, her face contorted with anger, ready to lash out at this man who had made his way uninvited into her home.

'How dare you come in here and threaten me!' she yelled. 'How bloody dare you!'

With his attention focused on Pearl, the intruder never saw Joey's fist lash out again. It caught him hard on the cheek, and he stumbled, fell backwards and tumbled down the stairs. Pearl and Joey stood open-mouthed in shock, unable to speak, gazing down at the man who lay motionless at the bottom of the stairs.

2

Sweet Sixteen

'Is he dead?' Pearl whispered.

Joey saw a slight movement under the man's jacket. 'No,' he said, hardly daring to take his eyes off him. 'Who is he?'

'I don't know,' Pearl replied. She let the rolling pin drop and started walking down the stairs. As she neared him, the man groaned.

'What shall we do with him?' Joey whispered. 'Should I fetch the police?'

'No!' Pearl said quickly. She was only too aware that the last thing Annie would want when she returned from wherever she'd gone was the police asking questions.

The man groaned again. He was dazed but appeared not to be seriously hurt. Pearl and Joey watched as he tried to sit up. As he did so, a shadow darkened against the back door. Pearl breathed a sigh of relief when she saw Annie walking in.

'Jackson?' Annie gasped. She looked at Pearl. 'What's he doing here?'

'He was waiting upstairs when I came home from High Farm,' Pearl explained. 'I told him you weren't here and so he said he'd have me instead. If it hadn't been for Joey coming in . . . ' Her voice trailed off. 'Joey saved me.' She squeezed his hand.

'Mam wasn't in when I went home, so I came back to see Pearl,' Joey told Annie. 'And when I walked in the door I saw him standing over her, undoing his buttons.'

'You filthy beast!' Annie spat at Jackson. She grabbed his jacket lapels with both hands, heaved him to his feet, spun him round and chucked him out. He fell to the ground on all fours. In her rage, Annie kicked him up the backside and he fell forward on his face. Pearl and Joey squeezed each other's hands. Despite the horror of their earlier ordeal, the sight proved irresistible, and they gave in to their giggles.

'Don't you dare come here again, you hear me?' Annie yelled. She grabbed Jackson by his jacket, yanked him to his feet again and marched him out to the back lane. 'And good riddance!' she shouted.

Once she was sure Jackson had gone, she locked the back gate and rested her back against it, giving a long sigh of relief.

'You know him?' Pearl asked.

Annie quickly glanced at Joey before she replied. 'I know him. He's a bad sort who thinks the world owes him a living. Drunken scum, that's all he is.' She reached out and cupped Pearl's chin with her hand. 'Are you all right, love?' she asked. 'He didn't . . . .?'

Pearl shook her head. 'He wanted to, though. If it hadn't been for Joey . . .'

'It's my fault,' Annie said. 'I must have left the back door open when I went to the shop. Bernie Pemberton called by earlier, said he needed to do an inventory. I had to go and help him. I was

27

only gone five minutes, ten at most.'

'I'm fine, Annie,' Pearl said. 'Just a bit shaken, that's all.'

Annie glanced at Joey again. She knew she needed to give Pearl an explanation about Jackson. 'Joey, lad. Would you mind leaving me and Pearl on our own for a while?'

Joey put his hand to the wall to support himself. 'See you, Pearl,' he called as he walked out to the yard. 'See you, Annie.'

Pearl waved her friend goodbye, then watched as Annie unlocked the gate and followed Joey out of the yard. She glanced up and down the lane to make sure that Jackson had gone, then locked the gate again before heading inside.

'Sit down, Pearl. I need to tell you about that fella who was here,' she said when they were in their room with the door firmly closed.

'Who was he?'

Annie took a deep breath. 'A customer,' she said. She knew there was no point in lying to Pearl or sparing her any of the unsavoury details. She had to protect her niece from men like Jackson, and in order to keep her safe, she had to tell her everything she knew. 'He's one of the few bad 'uns I've come across. He . . . ' She paused and gave a little cough, bracing herself for what was to come. 'He beat me up once. Years ago, it was. I've managed to keep out of his way ever since. When I'm working the pit lane, if I see him coming, I turn and walk the other way. None of the girls want his money, none of them will be left alone with him. I'm not the only one he's turned violent with. But it's the first time he's

28

ever been in here since he left me black and blue. Oh, if only I'd locked the flaming door when I went out! I'm sorry, Pearl. Truly I am. The last thing I want is for you to get caught up in any kind of trouble because of the life I lead. I promised your mam I'd look after you, and heaven knows I try. But look what I've gone and done now.'

It was then that Pearl saw the cast-iron pan she had been looking for earlier. It was sitting on the bedroom floor, half full of rain water.

'I was ready to clobber him, Annie. If I'd got my hands on that pan, I would have smashed it over his head. But all I could find was the rolling pin. I think he was shocked when I yelled at him, and Joey was hitting him and . . . '

Annie drew Pearl towards her and put her arm around her shoulders. 'I'm sorry, love. I'll never let anything like this happen again.'

They sat in silence a few moments, holding each other.

'What did Bernie want?' Pearl asked. 'You said he was doing a stock take or something.'

'An inventory, he said. He was down there with another fella I've not seen before. He had a notepad, writing a list. Who knows what he's up to. Anyway, it's about time we started to think about what to have for tea.'

Annie headed to the alcove at the top of the stairs and stared at the empty shelves.

'We can have a whole load of nothing for starters. Followed by a dish full of nowt.'

Pearl rolled her eyes. 'Again? And what's for afters?'

'We've got a lovely big zero cake with a nil cream filling.'

'I'll have two of each please.' Pearl laughed.

Annie went to the window ledge where she kept her jar full of coins hidden behind the thin curtain. She picked it up, feeling the weight of it. 'I reckon there's enough in here to pay for a couple of fish suppers. What do you say?'

Pearl's face lit up at the thought. 'Do you want me to go and get them?'

Annie shook her head. 'You're going nowhere on your own. Not while Jackson is on the rampage. We'll go together and bring the fish and chips here.'

'Can I have plenty of vinegar and salt on mine?' Pearl asked.

'Salt and vinegar? If they sold gold and diamonds at Robson's chippy, I'd put those on for you instead,' Annie laughed. 'Listen, Pearl, I really am sorry about what happened with Jackson. I've never had bother like that before with any of the men who come here. It was a one-off and it'll never happen again, I promise.'

Pearl turned to look at her aunt. 'If we hadn't sold Boot, he would have gone for him and seen him off.'

'We had to sell him; you know we need the money. We had no choice, pet.'

Pearl dropped her gaze to the floor. 'Isn't it time to stop, Annie? Isn't it time to think about how else to pay the bills? If men like Jackson can come in here and take what they want, forcing themselves on us . . . I was scared. Really scared. If it hadn't been for Joey coming in, I dread to

30

think what might have happened.'

Annie put her arm around Pearl's shoulders again. 'Hey, lass. It's all right. You saw how I dealt with Jackson, kicking him out of the yard. He'll not be back to bother us again.'

'Promise?' asked Pearl.

Annie kissed the top of Pearl's head. 'I promise.' But she wished she felt more confident.

★ ★ ★

The following days were quiet and calm. Jackson's attack on Pearl had shaken Annie, and she stayed in each evening instead of walking the pit lane looking for business. Food was scarce, but she did what she could with the meagre rations she could afford.

Later that week, Bernie Pemberton came calling at the shop while Annie was working. Without a word, he set to measuring up and jotting numbers in his notepad, muttering under his breath. Bernie was a weasel of a man, with an oily way about him that Annie didn't like. She had little respect for him and refused from the off to call him Mr Pemberton; he was always Bernie to her. He had thick black hair swept back from his forehead and dark bushy eyebrows that rose at the ends, making him look as if he was questioning everything he saw. Annie demanded to know what he was up to, but he told her it was none of her business.

'My home's upstairs, Bernie, and my livelihood's down here. Of course it's my flaming business,' she retorted. She was angry that he was keeping things from her.

'You don't need to know, Annie, not yet,' was all he said in reply.

'Well while you're here, Bernie, how's about fixing a few things in the room above? I've been on at you for months asking you to sort things out.'

Bernie sank his skinny body into a wooden chair propped against the shop door. It was sunny outside and Annie left the chair there to keep the door open and let the warmth in. However, it also brought in noise and grime from the coal pit on the opposite side of Ryhope Street.

'There're leaks in the ceiling where the rain comes in. And a hole in the floorboard that I swear gets bigger every time I look at it.'

Bernie sighed. 'I'll sort it when I can.'

'When?' she asked him, infuriated.

'When you pay me the rent you owe. All of it.'

'I can't. You know I can't, not yet.'

'Then I'll take the money from your wages. You know I've got the power to do that.'

Annie felt her stomach turn over. This was a threat that Bernie had often made but never carried out. But now she was so deep in debt, she feared he might just go through with it.

He stood and kicked the chair away from the open door, letting it swing closed, then walked towards the wooden counter and leaned forward with his hands on the top of it. Annie felt his foul breath on her face.

'I heard you can afford pretty much anything you want, what with all the extra money you're making.'

Annie gasped. 'What do you mean?'

'You know full well what I mean,' he said, leering at her. 'I've been hearing things about you, Annie Grafton. There's not much goes on in Ryhope that I don't get to know about.'

She took a step back, away from his stinking breath.

'You've been selling more than just fancy goods from my shop, haven't you? I had a chat with an old pal of mine in the Albion Inn last week, and he told me what I'd long suspected. I'd heard things about you before and I chose not to believe them. But then I had a drink with Jackson last week, and . . .'

Annie squared her shoulders. 'Jackson? That drunken old fool? So what if I do offer myself for sale, eh? What's it to you? You don't pay me enough to live on, working here in your tatty little shop, and you charge me far too much rent for the grotty room upstairs. You pay me with one hand and take it away with the other. What's a girl to do? Am I supposed to live on fresh air and feed our Pearl too?'

Bernie licked his lips and leaned further towards her.

'And you can forget that for a start,' Annie hissed.

'Oh, it's not your womanly charms I'm interested in,' Bernie said. 'If you're making money using my premises for your illicit business, then I reckon I should get . . . ooh, let's think now . . . '

He went through the pretence of counting on his fingers, all the while leering at Annie. 'I reckon I should be getting a decent portion of whatever you're earning.'

'No chance,' Annie spat.

'I bet you haven't got a bully-boy to protect you, have you?'

Annie bit her lip. She'd heard of bully-boys, men who lived from the earnings of women who walked the streets at night in the East End of Sunderland. They took a cut from the women's money and in return offered them protection from men like Jackson. But Annie was damned if she was going to be controlled by a man, and she certainly wasn't about to pass on any of her earnings to anyone.

'You do know I enjoy a pint now and then with the chief inspector, don't you?' Bernie sneered. 'All it would take is one little word in his ear and he'd have you locked up.'

'That's blackmail!'

'I don't think you're in any position to tell me what is and isn't right,' Bernie grinned. 'And if you get banged up in a prison cell, your pretty little niece would be out on her ear, wouldn't she, with no one to protect her. But if you pay the rent you owe, Annie, I might be able to keep my mouth shut.'

Just then the shop door swung open. Annie's heart dropped when she saw Pearl walking in. Bernie pulled himself away from the counter and forced a smile.

'Morning, Miss Edwards.'

Annie felt bile rise in her throat as Bernie

addressed Pearl sweetly after the conversation they'd just had.

'Morning, Mr Pemberton,' Pearl replied. 'Have you come to mend the hole in our floorboard?'

Bernie glanced at Annie. 'I'll get on to it in due course,' he said. 'I was just chatting to your aunt here about business. I've made her a very attractive offer that she's going to be giving some thought to, isn't that right, Miss Grafton?'

Annie felt her heart hammer in her chest. 'Get out,' she said under her breath.

Bernie cupped a hand to his ear and a wicked grin spread across his face. 'Sorry, Annie? What was that?'

'You heard well enough. Get out.'

Bernie laughed in Annie's face then turned towards Pearl. 'I'll be seeing you both soon,' he said and then he swaggered out of the shop.

As soon as he'd gone, Annie laid both hands on the counter, steadying herself against the shock of his words.

'Is everything all right?' Pearl asked.

Annie bit her bottom lip. She was furious with the way the conversation had turned. How dare Jackson go around Ryhope telling everyone her business? How dare he!

'Annie?' Pearl asked again, concerned.

'Just a few problems, pet. Nothing to worry about,' Annie said at last, keeping her voice as even as she could. She would not be held to ransom by Bernie Pemberton of all people. If she had to pay the money she owed in order to keep him quiet, she'd do it somehow. The life she'd

35

made for herself and Pearl might have been littered with her own mistakes but she wasn't going to have anyone put them out on the streets. She'd promised Mary she'd look after Pearl, and while there was breath left in her body, that was what she would strive to do. She'd earn the rent money in the only way she knew how. And the next time she saw Jackson on the colliery, she was going to give him a piece of her mind.

She kept her eyes fixed on the counter top. 'Pearl?' Pearl looked at her. 'I'll be going out working tonight.'

Pearl's shoulders sank. She'd been looking forward to a quiet night in, just her and Annie.

'But I was hoping to do some work on my clippy mat,' she sighed.

'Not tonight, love,' Annie said. 'You could take your mat and work on it at Joey's house. I'm sure he'd be pleased to see you.'

Pearl sank into the wooden chair by the door. 'You don't even know what day it is, do you?' she said.

'Monday,' Annie quipped, quick as a flash.

'Monday the fourteenth of July,' Pearl replied, still waiting for the penny to drop.

Annie clapped a hand to her forehead and sighed.

'Oh love, I forgot. I clean forgot, what with my mind being on the rent money and all. I'm sorry, Pearl, truly I am.'

'Seems like you're always apologising for something these days, Annie.'

'I try my best, love, that's all I can do.' She

came out from behind the counter, walked towards Pearl and hugged her. 'Happy birthday, Pearl.' Then she took a step back and looked at her niece, really looked at her, all the way up from her worn black boots that let in the rain to the very top of her head. 'You look more like your mam every day,' she said, surprised to feel tears prick at her eyes. 'Sixteen years she's been gone, and it's like looking right at her when I look at you.'

Pearl hugged her tight. 'I was hoping we could stay in tonight, Annie, just the two of us.'

'I can't, love. I've got to work. I've got to get the rent paid and my debts cleared so I can start buying proper food from the colliery shops again. I promised your mam, Pearl. I promised I'd look after you, and I'm failing her now more than I've ever done before.'

'But I'll be starting my job at the Colliery Inn any day now,' Pearl said. 'Bobby Mac said I can start there as soon as I turned sixteen. I've let my job at High Farm go to Joey already. I'll go to the pub tomorrow to talk to Bobby.'

'Remember to keep on the right side of him, won't you?' Annie said. 'He's still getting over Ella's death. Grief can take a person a funny way, and there's no telling what might be going through his mind.'

'Of course,' replied Pearl. She glanced shyly up at her aunt. 'When I start work at the pub and we've got more money coming in, you won't have to walk the pit lane any more.'

Annie smiled down at her niece. 'Ah love, it's not as simple as that. It's not that I won't be

37

grateful for your earnings; heaven knows we could do with them to help keep us fed and watered. But I've let things slide with the rent for too long, and . . . ' she decided not to tell Pearl about Bernie's threat to turn her in to the police, 'and I need to get my debts cleared. The sooner that happens, the better things will be. You understand, Pearl, don't you?'

Pearl didn't reply; she didn't need to. She understood Annie's unpredictable way of life only too well.

★ ★ ★

That evening in their room, Annie readied herself for working the pit lane. As she got dressed, Pearl sat on the floor of their room with her clippy mat stretched on its frame. She worked quickly, taking scraps of rags from the bag, each one a different colour and texture, holding her progger with its sharp metal spike in her other hand. She used the progger to poke a hole in the hessian, through which she pushed one end of the scrap, then made a second hole close to the first and looped the scrap into that, pulling it tight. And so it went, until the hessian was covered in neat rows of rags. When it was finished, it was the underside of the hessian that would be displayed, with the closely woven rags providing a comfortable mat to walk on instead of the cold, bare floor.

'Looks pretty,' Annie said, nodding towards the mat as she worked.

Pearl glanced at her aunt. Annie had her little

finger stuck inside a lipstick tube, trying to find the nub of red left inside.

'So do you,' she replied.

'Got to use honey to catch bees.' Annie smiled. 'And the bigger the bee, the more he might pay.'

She had brushed her long hair out from the plait it had been tied up in all day, and the waves cascaded down her back. Her hair was a little too showy and her lips a little too red for Ryhope in daytime; if she turned up to work in Bernie's shop looking like that, she would be called a Jezebel, or worse. She leaned forward to the hearth, where the fire had burned itself out, and reached in with her fingertip, coating it with coal dust. Pearl watched, amazed as always at the way her aunt applied a tiny bit of ash to her eyelids, darkening them, disguising them. When she was done, Annie looked around the room, searching for something. 'Have you seen my hat?'

Pearl spotted it under Annie's bed. It was a small velvet hat that looked like an upturned pudding bowl. She picked it up, dusted it down and flung it through the air towards her aunt. Annie caught it with one hand and spun it around on her finger. 'Is my feather there too?'

Pearl peered under the bed again and caught sight of the little red feather. It was worn, tatty and missing most of its barbs. Wearing a red feather in a black hat as she walked the pit lane was the signal that Annie was available — at a price.

'It's here,' she said. She reached for it, pulled it out and handed it to Annie, who pushed it through a moth-eaten hole in the hat.

'Right. That's me ready for work. Are you going to Joey's house? We'll walk out together.'

Pearl stood, carrying her mat on its frame in one hand. In the other, she held her bag of scraps. She followed her aunt downstairs, and Annie made sure she locked the door that led up to their room.

'I'm not taking any chances,' she reassured Pearl. She kissed her niece, leaving a lipstick smudge of red on her cheek, and then the two women went their separate ways: Pearl turning right to head to Joey's house, and Annie going left to walk from the pit lane down to Sid's Corner.

The dark patch of ground, hidden from view from the main thoroughfare of Ryhope Street South, was tucked under a canopy of trees away from the prying eyes of those who came into the lane to fill jugs and buckets from the shared taps. A shop had stood there once, a tiny place selling tobacco and pipes, owned by Sidney Benton. And although it had closed when Sidney died and had stood empty since, the spot was still known as Sid's Corner. It was a place of secrets, where illicit business was conducted. Mothers whispered to their children never to go there at night-time, and any law-abiding, self-respecting resident of Ryhope stayed away after dark if they knew what was good for them.

When Annie reached the corner, another woman was already there. She smiled when she saw it was her friend Dorothy. She too was wearing a black hat with a red feather.

'Business all right, Dot?' Annie shouted.

'Not bad,' Dorothy replied.

Annie walked towards her and gave her a tight hug. Then she moved away to choose her spot under one of the trees, where she could keep her eye on the comings and goings.

★　★　★

Meanwhile, down the lane at Joey's house, it was his mam Kate who answered Pearl's knock. Kate was short, just like Joey, short and thin and she looked a lot younger than her years. She looked far too young to be a mam with her unlined face and sparkling clear blue eyes.

'Is Joey in, Mrs Scotch?'

'He's not, Pearl,' she replied. 'He's gone down to the Grand to see the film.'

The news surprised Pearl, for whenever Joey went to the cinema, he always invited her to go with him. She wondered why he'd kept that night's visit from her.

'Who's he gone with?' she asked.

'That lad from the farm he's working with, Ralphie's son.'

'Ronnie?'

'Aye, that's him.' Kate nodded at the frame in Pearl's hand. 'Working on another clippy mat?'

'I was going to do more of it tonight, with Joey,' Pearl said. Her shoulders drooped. If Joey wasn't at home, where was she supposed to spend the rest of the night while Annie was working? She couldn't go home until the bedroom curtains were open again, the sign all

41

was clear. Then she had an idea.

'Mrs Scotch?'

'What, love?'

'Can I leave my mat here while I go down to the Grand to find him?'

'Course you can, pet,' Kate said, taking the frame from her. 'He's not been gone long. If you run, you might catch him before the film starts.'

As Pearl dashed into the lane, she caught sight of her aunt leading a man in a shapeless brown jacket and trousers into their back yard. She ran straight past them. She ran past Dorothy too, all the way past the Co-op and down the colliery bank until the Grand Electric Cinema came into view, standing proud and solid, the curve of its roof welcoming all who entered. Ronnie was waiting outside. Pearl picked up her skirts with one hand so she could run faster. She saw Joey join Ronnie, and called out to him, but he couldn't hear her. By the time she reached the Grand, the two boys had disappeared inside.

She flew to the entrance. 'Joey!' she called into the dark of the cinema. Those sitting near the door turned to see what all the fuss was about. It was Ronnie who spotted her as he and Joey made their way to their seats. He nudged Joey in the ribs and nodded at the door. Joey glanced across and headed towards her.

'Why didn't you tell me you were coming to the film?' Pearl asked. 'You know we always do this together.'

'I'm here with Ronnie,' Joey replied. There was a defensive tone in his voice that Pearl had never heard before.

42

She took a step back, making room for those entering the cinema and heading for the rows of red velvet seats.

'But I haven't seen you in ages, not since you started work at the farm,' she said. 'I've just been up to yours and your mam said you were here.'

Joey cast a quick glance towards Ronnie, who was sitting eating a bag of sweets. He pushed his hand into his trouser pocket and pulled out a fistful of coins.

'Here, go and get yourself a ticket and come and sit with us,' he said.

Pearl's eyes widened when she saw the amount of money Joey put in her hand. It was enough to pay for three tickets, even four. She made her way to the booth and bought a ticket, then sidled her way along the row. She sat down and handed Joey the change, nodding to Ronnie on his other side. She knew Ronnie from her time working at High Farm but had never much liked him. He'd been lazy, always shirking or sleeping in the barn, leaving her to collect the eggs or sweep the dairy. She'd been polite to him, of course. After all, he was the farmer's son and Ralphie paid her wages. But in truth, she was a little afraid of him. He was a big clumsy lad, always stuffing his face with food, whether it was stottie bread or a bag of toffees. He and Joey made an odd-looking pair, with Joey so little and thin.

She settled into her seat. 'Thank you for buying my ticket, Joey,' she said.

'Thank you for buying my ticket, Joey,' Ronnie mimicked, and Joey burst out laughing. Pearl glared at Ronnie and felt her face burn. Was he

43

trying to humiliate her?

Just then the house lights dimmed and a lot of shushing went on along the rows. The pianist at the side of the stage struck up a chord as the film began, and for the next hour and a half, all three of them were lost in a make-believe world of American cowboys. When the film ended, they stood to leave and started shuffling along to the exit. But at the end of the row was a policeman. He looked like he was waiting for someone, and Pearl noticed his gaze was fixed firmly on the two boys.

'Joey Scotch?' he asked as they drew near. 'I want a word with you.'

Pearl noticed the fixed smile on the policeman's face. Other cinemagoers were turning to look at what was going on.

'Me? What have I done?' Joey said.

The policeman nodded behind him. 'And you, Ronnie Heddon, I want a word with you both.'

He stood to one side, letting the last of the audience members leave, until there was just Pearl, Joey and Ronnie left inside.

'Right then, lads,' he began. 'Where have you two been getting the money to pay for cinema tickets, eh?'

'We're both working . . . sir,' Joey said quickly.

The policeman eyed Ronnie, waiting for a response, but Ronnie was enjoying the last of his bag of toffees and his teeth were stuck together as he chewed.

'And all those sweets you've been buying: where do you get the money for them? I've seen the pair of you, I've had my eye on you both.

44

This is the second time you've been in here to see a film this week.'

Pearl's heart sank, hit with the double blow of discovering it was the second time that Joey hadn't invited her to the Grand.

'Turn your pockets out, both of you,' the policeman demanded.

Pearl watched as Joey and Ronnie emptied their trouser pockets. She knew that Joey had the change she'd handed him earlier, but she was shocked when he brought out three half-crowns as well. From Ronnie's pockets came even more money, along with four boiled mints and a bag of chocolate buttons.

'You earn this lot at the farm, then?' the policeman said, although the way he asked the question made it clear he was not expecting an answer. 'Maybe I should get myself a job there. Looks like you're both earning a small fortune.' He pointed his finger towards Joey's face and then at Ronnie's fat cheeks too. 'Now listen, the pair of you. I don't know what you're up to, but lads like you shouldn't be walking around with money like that. I'll be keeping my eye on you both, you hear me?'

Joey and Ronnie nodded sheepishly.

'Now go on, scarper. Get yourselves straight home.'

The policeman rubbed his chin as the two boys left. There had been reports of petty crime in the village, pop bottles being stolen. He'd been given descriptions of the culprits and they seemed to fit Joey Scotch and Ronnie Heddon, but he had no evidence to bring them in to the

45

station for a caution. Stealing pop bottles was nothing much in the scheme of things, not a high priority for the Ryhope Constabulary. But still, it was best to nip this sort of thing in the bud before it got out of hand.

Outside the cinema, the two boys said their goodbyes and Pearl and Joey headed up the colliery bank together. There were so many questions Pearl wanted to ask, but she didn't know where to start. They walked in silence for a while until she spoke at last.

'Do you see Boot at the farm? Is he all right?'

Joey shrugged. 'He's fine, Ralphie's happy with his ratting.'

Pearl cast a sidelong glance at her friend. 'Joey?'

'What?'

'What was the copper on about just now? Where's the money coming from?'

'It's my wages,' he said quickly.

They walked on in silence in the warmth of the summer night, Joey staring straight ahead, not looking at Pearl.

'Joey? You know I like coming to the films with you. I'll come next time if you like. I'm starting my new job and I can pay for my own ticket and — '

'We'll see, eh?' Joey said, cutting her short.

Pearl felt a lump in her throat. Something had changed between them, but what? Was it because of Ronnie, Joey's new friend? Was the older lad leading him astray?

When they reached the back lane at Dawdon Street, Pearl gave a quick glance at the window

46

and was relieved to see the bedroom curtains open.

'I'll come to yours and get my clippy mat back,' she said.

She followed Joey into his yard and was going to follow him into the kitchen, as she'd always done before, but Joey closed the door in her face. As she waited in the yard, trying to make sense of the changes in her friend, he reappeared with the mat in his hands and handed it to her.

'Is everything all right, Joey?' she asked him, but any reply he gave was lost as he closed the back door again, leaving her standing alone. She waited for a moment, wondering if she should bang on the door and demand to know what was wrong. But then she thought better of it. In her heart she felt hurt and angry. But in her head she knew they were growing up, and she had to accept they were growing apart. Both of them were working now; they were no longer children.

As she headed out to the back lane to walk the short distance home, a noise caught Pearl's attention: probably just a rat scurrying away, she thought. But then another noise came, as gentle as a breath or a sigh. She turned but saw no one behind her. In front of her the lane was empty too. She shook her head; she must be imagining things, the upset of the night with Joey causing her mind to play tricks. She headed into her yard and up the stairs to the room she shared with Annie.

Out on the back lane, a stocky man with a trimmed moustache stood hidden in the shadows, watching as Pearl headed indoors. He took one last look at the window above, then turned and walked away.

3

A Proposition

The next morning Pearl and Annie were getting ready for the day ahead. Annie was bringing in a bucket of water from the shared tap in the back lane. Pearl was sitting on the floor in the pile of old blankets that she used as her bed. Annie's bed was a big one, large enough for two, but as soon as Pearl was old enough to make sense of what her aunt did to earn extra cash, she had set up her own bed in the corner of the room. Oh, she missed the warmth and comfort of Annie's body beside her, but she relished the privacy of her own space.

Annie always made sure that any work she did with the men from the pit lane was never carried out in the dead of night. That way, once her paying customer had left, there was still time for the room to be tidied, cleaned and turned back into a respectable living space for her and Pearl. First of all she'd fling open the curtains to let Pearl know the coast was clear. Then she would throw open the tiny window that looked out across the workings of the coal mine, not to let in fresh air, because there was none, just the smoky pit air that hung in dark clouds, but to let out the stench of sweat that her paying clients often brought in on their skin. If she had been given

49

perfume by one of her men, she would sprinkle it on her pillow. Sometimes she even brought fresh flowers that she'd picked from the garden of one of the houses on the village green.

She did what she could to keep her life with Pearl separate from her pit lane work, but it wasn't easy in the cramped room the two women shared. For not only did Pearl and Annie sleep within the same four walls; they cooked over the coal fire and ate in front of it too. They washed in the milky light from the window, their bodies hidden behind the thin curtains. Against one wall of the room their clothes were piled tidily, and Pearl's clippy mats, of all colours and shapes, were dotted around the floor in a pretty mosaic, softening the jagged floorboards that Bernie Pemberton ignored their pleas to mend.

Where Pearl went when Annie worked in the evenings depended on who was at home elsewhere. Sometimes she went to Joey's house, to sit with him and his mam by the fire in their kitchen. She wondered now if she would be welcome there any more, with Joey acting so strangely towards her. Other times she went to Dorothy's house, if Dorothy wasn't working the lane. She would welcome Pearl in as one of her own, another to add to her own seven bairns. And there were times Pearl wanted to be alone and she would head to the welcome doors of St Paul's church and sit quietly in a pew at the back. She didn't go there to pray or out of any sense of religious duty, for none had been instilled in her as she grew up with Annie. But she felt at peace inside the church. More

50

importantly, she felt safe there.

Often Pearl would simply wander the streets of Ryhope to see what was going on. And if the Maling sisters, Sarah and Anne, were working on their large clippy mats in the back lane behind the miners' reading room, she'd sit on the ground and watch. The sisters were the oldest people Pearl knew, their faces wizened and shrunk, their bodies hunched and stooped. In bad weather they worked on their mats inside their house. But in good weather they brought their chairs into the back lane and sat with the frame stretched across their skirted knees. Pearl was entranced, watching as they worked their proggers into the hessian, pushing down and pulling up the cuttings of cloth until the whole frame was covered and a new mat was made. It was Sarah Maling herself who'd taught Pearl how to make her first mat. It was small, no bigger than a coal shovel blade. Now Pearl was making mats three times that size.

She turned when she heard a noise and saw Annie bringing in the bucket of water.

'You can get washed before me,' Annie said. 'And be sure to do behind your ears. You don't want to give Bobby Mac any cause for complaint about your appearance on your first day at the Colliery Inn.'

Pearl pulled her hair up with both hands and piled it high on her head. 'He's hardly going to look behind my ears, is he?' she laughed.

Annie gave her a look. 'You know what I mean. You need to scrub up as well as you can.'

'I'm only cleaning the place. I won't be on

51

show, you know, I'm not serving behind the bar.'

'Doesn't matter if you're the cleaner or the owner; you're my niece and you'll look presentable. It's your first day in a proper job. You're not down at the farm any more; you've got to look your best. Bobby Mac always turns himself out nicely in front of his customers, and he'll be expecting the same from his staff.'

Annie poured the water from the bucket into a pan by the fireside. Then she lifted the heavy pan with both hands and put it directly on the flames.

'It's warm outside,' she said, wiping her brow. 'Looks like it's set to be a lovely day.'

Once the water had warmed, she poured most of it into a large flat bowl and the two of them took it in turns to wash. The water left in the pan was boiled up for their breakfast tea. Annie went to the alcove at the top of the stairs that they used as their makeshift pantry. Apart from the cast-iron pan, the rolling pin and a few mismatched bowls, there were two plates, one with chips around the edge, and a few sticks of cutlery. Annie brought one of the plates out and delved into the enamel bread bin, finding the last piece of stottie bread. She tore it in two. It was better than nothing and would have to do for their breakfast, for there was precious little else. She finished getting ready, threw the last of her mug of tea down her throat, gave Pearl a kiss on the cheek and then went down to the shop.

Left alone in their room, Pearl gave herself another scrub behind her ears. She'd laughed at the notion of her new boss caring about her personal hygiene, but she might as well make the most of the luxury of warm water. She was excited and nervous at the same time about starting at the Colliery Inn. She'd never worked in a pub before, but Annie had somehow managed to sweet-talk Bobbie Mac into giving her a job there. She'd told Pearl that Bobby needed all the help he could get since Ella passed away.

All that Pearl knew of the Colliery Inn was what it looked like from the street. She'd heard it was the coal miners' favourite pub, being the closest to the pit and the quickest one to reach after a heavy shift was done. From the outside, it didn't look like much, just a small, poky place with a paned window at the front and a battered old door to one side. There was always noise coming from it whenever Pearl walked past, men's voices and laughter carried on the smoke of cigarettes and pipes. Sometimes there was singing from within; very rarely was it quiet. And its rowdy reputation meant that it was also the pub most likely to receive a visit from the Ryhope police.

It was said that the pub sold beer to lads who weren't old enough to shave, never mind drink. Pearl had heard tales from Joey too of the buying and selling of stolen goods that went on in the back room. The thought of Joey made her sad, and the previous night flooded back to her. Joey had another friend now in Ronnie and she had to accept that. But still, it hurt her that he had abandoned their friendship so quickly after starting his new job — the job she'd found for him too. Fancy him going to the films twice in one week without asking her along, when they'd always done everything together. She worried for him. Where was he getting all that spending money from? She was well aware of how much Ralphie Heddon paid for work at High Farm, and knew Joey must be getting the extra from somewhere else, but where?

She ran the brush through her long hair and set off down the stairs to the yard. At the bottom, she locked the door. Her key was on a long piece of string, which she looped over her head, pushing the key down inside her dress. Then she headed to Ryhope Street South and walked the short distance to the Colliery Inn. She was keen to start working again, and in a real job this time too. No more mucking out the hens at High Farm, no more shovelling straw from the barn. And no more doing twice the work she needed to do because Ralphie's lazy son would never pull his weight. She might only be helping out with the cleaning at the pub, but once Bobby Mac saw what a hard-working lass she was, she could easily end up with more responsibility. Why, she might even end up running the place — and wouldn't that be something?

She smiled at the thought of her and Annie with their own pub, living it up like two Lady Mucks, dispensing words of advice to all and sundry as they served beer to miners. No, not miners, Pearl decided. When she ran the Colliery Inn, she'd ban miners; they were too mucky by half.

She saw Dorothy walking towards her as her thoughts about running her own pub whirled in her mind. What if they only allowed women into their pub, she thought, women who could chat and drink, laugh and carry on and have fun. Women like Dorothy and Annie, who wouldn't have to walk the pit lane any more. Oh, the thought of it made Pearl smile. And what if she and Annie lived in the rooms above the pub, far away from Bernie Pemberton's greedy hands and the gaping hole in their floor . . . Her thoughts were cut short when Dorothy held out her arms and hugged Pearl to her.

'Good luck in your new job, flower,' she said.

'Did Annie tell you?'

'There's not much we don't tell each other, you know that.' Dorothy winked.

Pearl took a moment to ready herself and pushed her feet forward in her boots. She'd buy new boots, that was what she'd do, the minute she'd saved up enough money; new boots that didn't let in the rain. Above the front door of the Colliery Inn in tidy black letters were the names of the licensees: *Robert Henry MacDann & Ella Grace MacDann*. It was still too soon after Ella had passed; the brewery had yet to remove her name. Pearl took a deep breath, then pushed hard on the door, but it wouldn't budge; it was shut tight. She went to the window and peered inside, hoping to spot Bobby, to let him know she'd arrived and was ready to start work. But there was no one there. All she could see was a mess of a room with tables and chairs where they'd been left the night before. Empty glasses

55

stood on the tables and sawdust littered the floor. Pearl knocked again, harder this time. She heard a noise above as a window was pushed open.

'Who is it?' a voice called down.

She took a step back, shielded her eyes with her hand and looked up to see the hairy bare chest of Bobby Mac hanging out of the upstairs window. She gasped and brought her hand down to cover her eyes, then allowed herself to squint through her fingers and take in the sight of him. She'd never seen a naked man before. Bobby's black hairy chest was matched by the bushy black beard that all but covered the bottom half of his face. The only place he wasn't covered in hair was the top of his head, which was completely bald and round.

'It's me, Pearl Edwards. I've come to work for you,' she shouted.

Bobby scratched his chest and thought for a moment. 'Oh aye,' he grunted, and disappeared inside.

As Pearl waited at the door, her heart skipped a beat with the anxiety of what the day might bring. Would Bobby have her cleaning out the front room that she'd glimpsed through the window just now? Heavens, it could do with a good bottoming, she knew that just from the quick glimpse she'd had. It looked like there'd been a party in there, or maybe the Colliery Inn was always that scruffy? Eventually she heard a lock slide inside the pub doorway, then another. The door swung open and there was Bobby Mac standing in front of her, still without a shirt on, scratching his fat hairy belly. He put one hand to the door frame to steady himself.

'Pearl? Come in, lass,' he said.

Pearl followed him along a dark corridor. It was the smell that hit her first, the stench of beer soaked into the soul of the place. As she walked, her boots stuck to the floor. The corridor opened into a small, square room at the back. The light from the window rested on Bobby's hairy chest. He slumped into a chair and indicated for Pearl to take the one opposite. She sat as she was bid and held her hands in her lap, watching Bobby closely.

'I'm sorry, Pearl,' he said at last.

'Sorry? What for?'

'I should have told you yesterday. I should've and I didn't and now I feel awful about it, and I know Annie will have my guts for garters when she finds out about it and — '

'What is it?' Pearl asked.

Bobby tried to sit up straight in his chair, but the effort seemed to be too much for him and he ended up slumping forwards, cradling his head in his hands. Eventually he pushed himself up again and ran a hand through his thick beard. 'There's no easy way to tell you this, love, so I'm just going to come right out and say it.'

Pearl was starting to feel uneasy. 'What?'

'There's no job.'

She gripped her hands together. 'But you said — '

Bobby held up his hands in mock surrender. 'I know. I know what I said and I'm sorry, pet. But our Michael's come home sooner than expected

57

and he's going to be working here. Family comes first. It's more important than ever now that Ella's gone.'

Pearl was shocked to hear there was no job; saddened too — she'd been looking forward to starting work. But the thought of Michael back from the war, safe and sound, made a smile spread across her face.

'Micky Mac's back?' she cried.

Bobby laughed. 'Oh, don't let him hear you calling him that,' he said. 'He always hated that nickname. He's a grown man now, a soldier back from the front, and I couldn't be more proud of him. But I'm taking him on, Pearl, and I can't afford to employ the two of you.'

'But I gave up my job at High Farm to work here,' Pearl pleaded. 'You promised.'

'I'm sorry, lass, I really am.' He stood from the chair, and reached out to hold the back of it. When he was steady, he put a hand to his head. 'We did some celebrating last night when Michael got back. I think we'll all be suffering today.'

Pearl stood too, disappointed and angry at Bobby but also embarrassed at herself. All those silly thoughts she'd had just moments ago, walking up the colliery with dreams of running her own pub. And now here she was being given her marching orders from a job she hadn't even started. What would she tell Annie? Her aunt was relying on the extra money to pay the rent. What hope did she have of getting another job, no matter how menial? Any spare jobs would be going to the lads back from war.

'You understand, don't you, lass?' Bobby asked.

Pearl nodded. She understood only too well, but that didn't stop her stomach from tying itself in knots at the thought of having to tell Annie.

'Come on, I'll show you out,' Bobby said. But before he returned to the corridor that led to the front door, he disappeared behind the bar and brought out two bottles of Vaux stout. 'Here,' he said, handing the brown bottles to Pearl. She took one in each hand, surprised at how heavy they were. 'Give these to your aunt, tell her they're from me. And tell her that she's to call in any time and there's a free drink with her name on it behind the bar.'

Pearl walked down the colliery bank with the beer bottles in her hands. She felt sick with disappointment and her mind kept turning over how she would break the news to Annie. When she reached Pemberton's Goods, she walked slowly inside. Annie watched in amazement as Pearl plonked the two beer bottles on the counter.

'Bobby Mac sent these,' she said, and then she sank into the wooden chair by the door.

Annie eyed Pearl closely. 'Care to tell me why Bobby Mac is sending me gifts and what you're doing here in the shop when you should be at the pub?'

'Micky Mac's back,' Pearl replied.

Annie's face lit up. 'Michael? Oh, I heard he was coming home. Bobby must be over the moon.' She made the sign of the cross at her heart. 'Poor lad, though, he'll have come home

59

to find his mam dead of the Spanish flu. She was one of the good ones, was Ella.' She nodded towards the bottles. 'But what's Michael's return got to do with them and the fact that you're sitting here and not working up at the pub?'

'Bobby says he can't pay me now he's taking Michael on. There's no job.'

'But he promised!' Annie cried.

'Says he can't afford it. He seemed genuinely upset. Oh, and he said there's a free drink up at the pub for you too.'

'Did he now?' Annie huffed. 'Well, that's the least he can do, I'm sure. But next time I see Bobby-flaming-Mac, I'll be having words with him about this. He can't go promising one thing and doing another.'

She took the bottles and moved them off the counter. She didn't want any of her customers to see them when they came into the shop. The last thing she needed was for word to get around that she was taking gifts from Bobby Mac. She knew how gossip started in Ryhope; it wouldn't take much for rumours to spread, and she didn't want to do anything that would upset Bobby, not when he was still mourning his wife. Still, the news that Pearl wouldn't be bringing any money in was a severe blow.

She took a step back and stretched her arms to the counter top as thoughts whirled through her mind. She shot Pearl a look and then quickly looked away. She was certain that she could pay Bernie what she owed. But it would mean bringing Pearl down to Sid's Corner with her one night, and she still wasn't sure that she was ready to ask it of her. It would change her life for ever. Annie had wrestled with the dilemma for months. Was it really what she should ask of Pearl? Could she really go against the promise she'd made to Mary? Asking Pearl to work the pit lane was something she'd thought about many times in the past, though she had waited for her niece to turn sixteen before she gave it serious consideration. As Annie wrestled with her thoughts her empty stomach grumbled. Could she ask Pearl to work with her? *Should* she ask her? She'd told her sister, *promised* her, that she'd look after the girl as if she were her own. But if Pearl *was* her own child, her own flesh and blood, she'd feel better able to put such a notion to her. Men would pay good money for Pearl, with her translucent skin and her long auburn hair. Just a few nights might be all it would take for Annie to clear her debts, pay the rent and even afford ham for tea. They could start afresh, beholden to no one. But then she shook her head to get rid of the notion. She couldn't do that to the girl, she wouldn't; there must be another way. She closed her eyes tight against the image of Pearl waiting under a tree at Sid's Corner, wearing the red feather in her hat and smiling at strangers.

'No!' she cried.

Pearl turned, startled. 'What's wrong?'

Annie stood up straight and smoothed down the front of her skirt. 'Nothing,' she said, shaking her head. 'Just thinking of Bobby Mac, that's all. He shouldn't have gone back on his promise. Listen, Pearl, could you go upstairs and make us some tea? I'm gasping here. There should be enough heat left on the fire to warm up the kettle.'

Pearl left the shop and walked around the corner to the lane and in through the yard. She pulled the key on its string from under her dress and headed upstairs.

* * *

Once Pearl had left, Annie busied herself tidying the small wooden boxes that ran along the shelves. She knew exactly what was in each one, for this was her domain and it was ordered and smart; respectable in every way. The colours and quality of the materials and ribbons in the tiny haberdashery stood in sharp contrast to the bitter poverty of life in their room above. Annie kept the shop clean, and took pride in making it as welcoming as she could. When customers entered, the first thing that greeted them was the warm scent of dried lavender hanging in a bunch above the door. On the counter sat a straw basket of fat quarters, square off-cuts of material bundled up for sale. These too were scented with lavender bags that Annie made herself. Behind the counter on the wall at the end of the shelves hung one of Pearl's mats, made of clippings of blue and green.

Annie loved working in the little shop. She enjoyed handling the dress material, cutting through it with scissors, measuring with tape, and she was always precise and correct. It was a shop that many in Ryhope thought was too good for the colliery, sitting as it did opposite the filthy, noisy coal mine. But there was no other like it in the whole of the village. This meant that the ladies from the big houses around the green had to walk up the colliery bank, leaving their genteel surroundings behind, to buy their buttons and bows. It was either that or pay the expense of a tram fare to Sunderland and make a trip to the more expensive Binns store. The shop was Annie's world, but there was just one problem with it, which could be summed up in just two words: Bernie Pemberton.

The sight of Pearl coming in with mugs of tea pulled Annie from her thoughts.

'I've just passed Bernie on the street,' Pearl said, nodding down the colliery bank. 'He was standing chatting, said he'd be up here any minute. Says he wants a word with you about something.'

Annie took her mug from Pearl's hand and stood it carefully on a straw mat on the counter. 'Did he say what about?' she asked. Pearl shook her head.

It was only a minute or so later that the landlord appeared in the shop doorway. 'Morning, Annie,' he said. 'Morning, Pearl.'

'Morning, Bernie,' Annie replied. She kept her tone level, for heaven only knew what news he was bringing with him this time. She glanced at Pearl, ready to send her out of the shop if Bernie brought up the matter of him taking a cut from her earnings from working the pit lane again. She stood with her hands on the counter as if ready for combat. In her chair by the door, Pearl took a sip of tea and watched.

'What brings you in here this morning, Bernie?' Annie asked. She didn't trust him one bit and never had. He'd always underpaid her wages and overcharged her the rent on her room, she knew that. But as a single woman with a bairn, she'd had little choice. She was grateful for a roof over her head and a job in the shop.

Bernie thrust his hand into his jacket pocket and brought out a folded sheet of paper, which he slid across the counter towards Annie. She didn't touch it.

'What's this?'

'I'll be straight with you, Annie. I've been doing some thinking, taking care of my assets. I met with my financial adviser the other week.'

Annie snorted with laughter. 'Financial adviser? When did you get to be Mr Money Bags?'

An evil grin played around Bernie's lips. 'He's saying I should put the rent up.'

Annie gasped with the shock of his words and her hand flew to her heart. How on earth was she going to manage to pay him even more money when she was already in so much debt?

'Well, you know me, Annie, I wouldn't normally do these things,' he continued. 'But when my business adviser tells me I should increase your rent, then that's what I'm going to do.'

'You can't, Bernie!'

He leaned across the counter, his foul breath whispering against Annie's skin. 'Oh, I think I can. Unless you'd like me to take payment from

64

you the other way we talked about?'

Annie took a step away. She glanced at Pearl to see if she was listening, knowing full well that the lass never missed a thing; she was far too clever for that. 'Get out,' she hissed.

'Are you throwing me out of my own shop?' He laughed, then picked up the letter from the counter and waved it in Annie's face, taunting her. 'It's all there, in black and white. Read it and see how much the rent's going up. Oh, and you'll find a repayment schedule listed on it too for the back rent you owe. As I said, Annie, I hate doing this to you, but it's all the work of my adviser.'

Annie stood straight behind the counter. She was aware that Pearl was watching, and wouldn't allow herself to look as weak as she felt, not in front of her niece. 'You know I can't pay more,' she said.

Bernie sucked his teeth. 'Well now. There's a paragraph in that letter all about the seven-day notice period you'll need to give if you want to move out. The choice is yours, Annie. Pay up or get out. It's as simple as that. And of course, if you move out, it goes without saying that you'll lose your job too. I can't have someone working here who doesn't live above the shop. Got to protect my property. Who knows what kind of bad 'uns roam the pit lane at night?'

Pearl jumped up from her seat. 'Has Annie ever given you cause for complaint?' she demanded. 'In all the years she's worked here in your shop, in all the years we've lived above, have we ever given you any problems? Have we

65

caused you bother, had the police to the door, or caused the neighbours to complain?'

Annie listened open-mouthed as Pearl continued haranguing Bernie.

'No! We've never given you a peep of trouble in all the time we've lived here. We've kept this place clean and tidy, we scrub every inch of it, upstairs and down, once a week without fail. *And* we have to put up with rain pouring in from the ceiling above and a hole in the floor that we've got to stuff an old blanket in so that our feet don't go through. How would your business adviser react if we fell and hurt ourselves because of your negligence? Has he even seen the state of upstairs? It's not fit to house a dog, never mind me and Annie. We've got nowhere to cook, nowhere to wash, no privacy, just four walls and a rotten ceiling that stink like something's died.'

Bernie opened his mouth to reply, but Pearl wasn't finished with him yet.

'And you come in here and tell us we have to pay more for the privilege of living in such a scruff hole? It's extortion, Bernie Pemberton. You should be ashamed of yourself!'

Bernie glanced from Pearl to Annie and back again. He gripped the lapels of his jacket as he addressed them both. 'It's all there in the letter,' he said. And with that, he turned and walked away.

Pearl ran behind the counter straight into Annie's arms. 'What'll we do?' she whispered. 'We can't pay him any more than we do already. He'll chuck us out on our backsides and we've

66

nowhere to go. Seven days, he said, seven days is all we have.'

Annie hugged her niece tight. 'We won't have to leave, love, not if we don't want to.'

Pearl pulled back and looked deep into Annie's eyes. 'What do you mean?'

Annie's heart pounded as she realised there was nothing else for it. It was time to tell her niece the idea that had been on her mind. 'I mean there's a way out; a way to clear the debt I owe Bernie and the debts I owe the shops on the colliery, and maybe even a way to move out of our grotty room.'

'But how? I don't understand,' Pearl said, confused.

'If I told you that you could help, would you do it?' Annie asked.

'Course I would,' Pearl replied quickly. 'You know I would. What is it, Annie? Tell me.'

Annie glanced out of the shop window at the passers-by on Ryhope Street South. She moved the chair, closed the shop door and slid the bolt to lock it. Then she pulled down the blind at the window, casting a shadow over her niece.

'Come and sit down,' she said gently. 'There's something I need to ask you.'

4

The Peace Parade

Pearl felt a rage burn inside her as Annie's words sank in.

'I won't do it!'

She leapt from the chair and ran to the door, but Annie reached it first and put her back against it. She knew she'd gone too far, she knew she shouldn't have asked her, but what else was there to do? She was desperate.

'Please,' she begged. 'Just think about it, love.'

'No!' Pearl cried. She tried to slide the bolt open, but Annie wouldn't budge. She caught Pearl's hands and held them tight, forcing her niece to look straight at her.

'Listen, Pearl. You've heard all I've had to say, I've told you the thoughts I've been having. All I ask is that you think about it too, get used to the idea.'

'Never!' Pearl spat as she struggled against Annie's grip.

Annie let go of her hands. Pearl took a step away and began pacing the floor of the small shop like a caged animal. Every now and then she glared at her aunt, furious with her.

'Put me to work on the pit lane, would you? Is that all you think I'm worth?'

'Oh, I know exactly what you're worth,' Annie

said quietly. 'Why else do you think I suggested it?'

Pearl strode back and forth, her heart thumping with anger.

'It's not *all* about sex, if that's what you're thinking,' Annie said at last.

Pearl's eyes flashed. 'Of course it's all about sex!' she yelled. 'Do you expect me to believe you get paid for playing tiddly winks?'

A smile played around Annie's lips and she turned her face away so that Pearl couldn't see. 'No, love, listen,' she said at last, her tone softening. 'What I mean is that it's not all about men like Jackson, not all about men with no respect for us girls who work the pit lane.'

'Respect?' Pearl was unconvinced. 'Do you think anyone in Ryhope respects any of you tarts who strut about Sid's Corner?'

Annie's hand shot out and she slapped Pearl's face hard. Pearl stood still, shocked and speechless. Her hand flew to her cheek, cradling it, as the pain flared beneath her eye. Both women realised they'd overstepped the mark, crossed an invisible boundary between them. Annie moved to hug Pearl, but Pearl pulled back, still holding her stinging cheek.

'Don't you ever call me a tart again, you hear?' Annie whispered. She was deeply hurt; it was not something Pearl had ever called her before. It was a word that had never been used between them, even when gossiping about women they knew. Pearl nodded and sniffed back her tears. 'My work at Sid's Corner and in the lane helps put food in our bellies and clothes on our backs.

And if you do it too . . . why, it could pay off our debts and get us out of trouble. I can't do it on my own any more, Pearl. I need you to consider joining me. I'm not asking you to do it day in, day out. Just now and then, just when we need to.'

'Like now,' Pearl added.

'Yes, like now,' Annie said. 'You'll get used to it, Pearl. Your first time, I'll find you someone gentle, someone easy, I promise. There's a fella from the village, he comes to me regular — '

Pearl covered her ears with both hands. 'No!' she cried.

Annie stepped towards her. 'Listen to me.' Pearl let her hands fall to her sides. 'He comes to me, but not for sex, Pearl, not for that.'

Tears began to fall down Pearl's face and Annie gently brushed them away with her fingers.

'I bathe him. He comes to me for a bath and that's all there is to it.'

'That's all?'

Annie nodded. 'He doesn't even touch me. The hardest part is bringing in all the buckets of water from the back lane to warm up on the fire. I've another man who comes to me to talk, just talk. He talks and he cries and he gets rid of all this emotion that builds up inside him, and yet you see him on the street and he's one of the hardest fellas in Ryhope. No one would know what he's really like inside. But I know.'

'He cries?' Pearl asked, surprised. 'So you bathe them and you talk to them . . . but what about the others?'

Annie shrugged. 'Then there's sex. It's up the stairs, do the business, take his money, send him out. As simple and straightforward as that. Takes no more than ten, fifteen minutes. Some of them like a bit of a cuddle afterwards, but that's rare. And if they do, you charge more.'

Pearl thought for a moment, but then shook her head. 'No. I won't do it.'

Annie dropped her gaze and laid her hands at her heart. 'I just hope your mam forgives me for this,' she whispered. She lifted her eyes to meet her niece's and swallowed hard. 'I'm no tart, Pearl,' she said. 'You hear me? I'm a working woman doing all I can to stay one step ahead of being chucked out on to the street. Me and your mam, we had no education or training when we were girls. We weren't given any help or support to get us into work; no one wanted the Grafton girls, not even to work in service. We were just two scruffy colliery kids and our parents didn't care if we roamed the streets instead of going to school. Grandma Grafton was a drunk, and your grandad was never at home, always travelling somewhere, away for days, never with an explanation as to where he'd been.

'We had no guidance, your mam and me. There was only one profession open to girls like us. And I'm not proud of it, I'll tell you now. But do you know what? There's no overheads to pay, no boss to report to, and it's immediate cash. It's the difference between starving or both of us eating. Do you understand what I'm saying, Pearl? It's the difference between life and death.'

Pearl blinked back her tears 'What's all this

71

got to do with Mam? Why are you mentioning her now?'

'You've always known your mam worked when she had to, just like me,' Annie said. 'I've never kept that from you. That's why I never want to hear you use that word again, you hear? Because if you use it against me, you're using it against your own mam, my sister, and I won't have her spoken of that way.'

Pearl sank into the wooden chair. Annie could tell she was hurting; she could see the tears in her eyes. This wasn't the way she had planned to tell Pearl about what might lie ahead for her. But then planning had never been one of her strengths.

There was a knock at the door. Without even looking to see who it was, Annie yelled out: 'We're shut!'

Pearl dropped her head and closed her eyes. She gripped her hands together in her lap. Annie put her arm around the girl's shoulders.

'It's our only way out.'

'And if I don't do it?' Pearl asked.

'If you don't do it, we'll have to move out,' Annie said matter-of-factly. She'd given it much thought, preparing herself for the worst. 'We'll move out of the room above the shop and I'll lose my job, that goes without saying. There's the Salvation Army we can turn to in Sunderland, or — '

'I'll do it,' Pearl said quietly, too quietly for Annie to hear. She looked up into her aunt's eyes. 'I'll do it,' she said again, louder.

Annie dropped to her haunches in front of the

chair and took Pearl's hands in hers. 'Are you sure?'

Pearl nodded.

'Good lass.' She breathed a sigh of relief. 'I'll keep you safe, you know that.'

Pearl managed a weak smile. 'When?' she asked.

'We've got seven days, Bernie Pemberton said, so we should start at Sid's Corner as soon as we can. How about tonight? Dorothy sometimes uses a room upstairs at the Blue Bell, and slips the landlord a little cash. I'll ask if you can have the room tonight. Unless you'd rather use ours?'

'No,' Pearl said forcefully. She couldn't bear the thought of using either Annie's bed or her own.

'Well then, I'll make enquiries at the pub, see how much they charge.'

Pearl bit her lip. 'Then all I have to do is lie back and think of England?'

'No, lass,' Annie said, shaking her head. 'Lie back and think of the fish and chip supper you'll have in your belly afterwards, or the ham you'll have in your stottie bread for your dinner tomorrow, or the breakfast of fresh eggs you'll have every day for a week. And of the home we'll be able to keep, ragged floorboards and all, until we can afford to move out.'

As she hugged Pearl tight, Annie thought of her sister and the promise she'd made to her as she lay dying. She raised her eyes heavenwards.

'Forgive me, Mary,' she whispered. 'Please.'

★ ★ ★

73

Later that day, after Annie had finished work and locked up the shop, she and Pearl sat on the bed together.

'You'll be needing this,' Annie said. She held out a small black cloche hat. Pearl took it from her aunt's hands and held it carefully. Black threads hung around the bottom where the hem had come loose. 'It'll not bite you,' Annie smiled. 'Put it on. It's an old one of mine.'

Pearl did as she was told, pulling the hat down over her auburn hair. Annie gave her an appraising look.

'Not too tight?'

Pearl shook her head.

'It looks all right on you,' Annie said. 'But there's one thing missing.'

She opened her handbag and pulled out a feather. It was as red as the berries on winter trees, as scarlet as blood in the snow. Pearl took it and held it on her palm. It weighed nothing. When she closed her eyes, she couldn't feel it; it was as if she held air in her hand. It wasn't an old, battered feather like the one Annie wore. This one was new, the barbs lying flat in the same direction, with no gaps. The bottom of the shaft was fluffy and downy.

'Those fluffy bits at the bottom are for warming the bird's skin, not for flight,' Annie explained. 'That's why they look different to the rest.'

'Where did you get it from? It's brand new,' Pearl said.

'I had some downstairs in the shop; they've been in the back of a drawer for ages. No one

74

round here wants to pin red feathers in their hats any more, not now they've become the uniform of the Sunderland tart.'

Pearl gasped. 'You said we weren't to use that word again.'

'See? It's a word that stings, isn't it?' Annie said sharply. 'But it's true. Folk see a woman wearing a red feather in a black hat and they assume only one thing.'

She found a pin in her handbag and leaned across to Pearl. 'Give it here,' she said. Pearl handed over the feather and sat in silence as Annie pinned it to her hat. 'I think you're just about ready,' she said.

Pearl sat quietly on the bed as Annie bustled around the room. She watched as Annie sat on the splintered floorboards in front of the fireplace, dusting ash to her eyes.

'Come on, I'll do yours,' Annie said when she saw her watching. Without a word, Pearl walked across and knelt beside her aunt.

'Close your eyes,' Annie said.

Pearl allowed Annie's expert fingers to apply the coal dust to her left eyelid and then to her right. Then she felt Annie's hand tilt her chin gently, moving her face this way and that, inspecting her.

'Make sure you wash it off when you're finished tonight,' she said. 'Don't leave it on overnight; you'll look a right state in the morning.'

She pulled her handbag towards her and rummaged inside until she found what she needed. Her one and only lipstick had long ago

75

lost its lid and was no more than a blackened metal container with a nub of red inside.

'Stay still, Pearl, and push your lips together.'

Pearl closed her eyes again, not wanting to see what Annie was doing. Wearing the black hat was bad enough; she was keenly aware of the display of it. And now it had the red feather pinned to it, the sign that she was ready for work, the work she swore she'd never do. But if her mam had done it, then where was the shame in her doing it too? Just once or twice, Annie had told her, that was all. Just enough to clear their debts and pay the rent. Nothing more.

Lost in her thoughts, she felt a tugging at her bottom lip. Annie's little finger had managed to find some colour in the lipstick container, and she painted Pearl's lips before doing her own. Then she threw the lipstick back into her bag and reached for Pearl's hands.

'You ready?' she asked.

Pearl didn't reply. She touched her hat and her fingers worked around until they found the feather. She felt sick to her stomach, a mixture of nerves about what was to come and resentment towards Annie for putting her in this position. She felt angry with herself for not having the courage to stand up to her aunt; with Bobby Mac for whipping away the job he'd promised her; with Joey for palling up with Ronnie. But most of all she was angry at the world. For if the world was fair, she wouldn't be forced out to work the pit lane.

She swallowed hard and looked at Annie waiting by the door, ready to go to work.

'Well, are you coming? Or are you going to sit there all night?' Annie asked her.

Pearl didn't answer. She stood, pulled her thin jacket around her and followed her aunt into the lane.

* * *

'Business should be good tonight, Annie!' a voice called out.

Pearl and Annie turned to see Dorothy bustling towards them. She was a short, dumpy woman with curly brown hair that she wore tucked under her hat. There was a look of something decent, respectable about her, and she wore good sturdy shoes that were shined to perfection. Her bairns were always clean and tidy too, and if anyone in Ryhope knew what Dorothy did after a hard day's work cleaning at the asylum, they couldn't complain that she didn't look after herself and her bairns.

Pearl and Annie waited, and the three women set off together. Dorothy linked her arm through Pearl's and pulled her towards her.

'Don't be nervous,' she whispered. 'We'll keep you safe, don't worry.'

'Why do you reckon business will be good, Dot?' Annie asked.

'It's the Peace Parade tomorrow,' Dorothy replied. 'Fellas will be getting in the mood for drinking and celebrating all day. With a bit of luck they might have money to celebrate the way we like them to, eh, Annie?'

The Peace Parade! With everything else on

Annie's mind, she'd forgotten all about it. Just then a gate was flung open in the back lane and Bobby Mac came wandering out of the Colliery Inn yard in nothing but his vest and trousers.

'Evening, ladies,' he smiled when he saw them. He raised his hand as if to doff an invisible cap, and the gesture made Annie smile.

Pearl shrank back behind her aunt. She was hoping not to see anyone she knew tonight of all nights. She still felt too nervous to speak, her legs were shaking and she clung on for dear life to Dorothy's arm.

'You all right, Annie?' Bobby called as the women walked past.

'I'm canny, Bobby. Apart from you taking back your promise of a job to our Pearl.'

'I'll make it up to you,' he said.

'Aye, that's what they all say,' Annie sighed.

Bobby turned and went back into the yard, and the women walked on.

'I reckon he fancies you,' Dorothy laughed.

'Me?' Annie squealed. 'I don't think so, Dot. Anyway, it's not been five minutes since Ella passed on. He'll not be casting his eye at another woman yet.'

Pearl's stomach tightened as they walked further and Sid's Corner came into view. Two women were waiting there already.

'See, told you tonight would be busy,' Dorothy said, nodding towards the pair. 'I'll see you later, Annie. Pearl, look after yourself.' And with that, she walked away, leaving Annie and Pearl by a high stone wall.

Annie turned her back to the women already

waiting and issued instructions to Pearl.

'This is what we'll do. When I see a fella I know can be trusted, one who'll not put too many demands on you, I'll give you the nod and you can go with him to the Blue Bell. They're keeping the room up there for you tonight. Just sort out the payment with John at the bar. Okay, love?'

Pearl bit her lip. 'What if I'm approached by a fella who can't be trusted, one you don't know?' she asked.

'I'll wait for you to go first,' Annie explained. 'Only when I know you've gone to the Blue Bell with a decent fella will I go off with . . . well, what I mean is, only then will I go to work. Do you understand?'

Pearl nodded sullenly. Annie gently lifted her chin. 'Eh, lass. You don't half look like your mam, you know. With your dark eyes and your red lips, you're her double. I won't let you get into any trouble. I promised her I'd look after you and that's what I'm going to do. Now then, go and stand over there.' She pointed to a spot against the wall where Dorothy and the other women were chatting. 'I'll stay here to keep an eye on you, and Dorothy will look out for you too.'

Pearl did as she was told and walked to the wall, keeping her gaze firmly fixed on the ground. She was afraid that if she looked up, she'd spy a man coming towards her, a man who would take her to the Blue Bell. Her stomach rumbled with hunger. There'd been nothing in the pantry, nothing at all, and she and Annie had gone without eating again. She glanced from under her hat towards Annie, who gave her a reassuring smile. But Pearl didn't feel reassured. She felt sick, and had to lean against the wall for support.

'What's she doing here?' a voice called out.

Pearl looked up and saw the two women she'd noticed earlier walking fast towards her.

'Oi! You! What do you think you're doing?' one of them called.

Pearl's heart raced and she looked across at Annie, who was talking and laughing with an older man. It was like watching an actress in a play; Annie was pretending to be someone else, someone different. Pearl stood transfixed, watching this version of her aunt she'd never seen before, until she was brought out of her reverie by the arrival of the two women.

'Who do you think you are, working our corner?' the first woman demanded. She was taller than Pearl, older too. She stood with her hands on her hips, glaring at Pearl, waiting for an answer.

'Well?'

Annie appeared at Pearl's side, and Pearl noticed the man she'd been talking to waiting for her across the lane. She glanced at him and saw the pink of his tongue working its way around his lips.

'Bet you'd rather be an old man's darling than a young man's plaything,' he shouted when he caught her watching him. Annie ignored him and turned her attention to the women who had accosted Pearl.

80

'Come on now, Peg, leave the lass alone,' she said. 'We all had to start somewhere, didn't we?'

'Get her out of here,' the woman snarled. 'She's not coming in here taking our business. It's not right.'

'Not right!' the second woman echoed.

Pearl tried to stand as tall as she could. In truth, she was relieved, hoping that Peg would force Annie to send her home. But Annie had other ideas. She pushed herself in between Pearl and Peg and poked Peg hard in the chest.

'Peg Tindall, there's business enough to be had here, so leave the lass alone.' She looked at the second woman who was standing behind Peg. 'Worried about the competition, the pair of you?'

Peg reached around Annie and as quick as a flash whipped the black hat from Pearl's head and threw it to the ground.

'Get her away,' she snarled. 'We've earned our right to work here. She hasn't.'

Annie didn't budge. Instead she turned her head and whispered to Pearl, 'Go home.'

Pearl didn't need to be told twice. She ran like the clappers all the way up the back lane, but just as she was about to turn into the safety of her yard, a man stepped out of the shadows towards her. She recognised the torn and frayed jacket first, and knew immediately who it was. Jackson.

'How much you charging?' he sneered, his words thick and slurred.

He reached a hand to pull at Pearl's jacket, but in his drunken stupor he missed, and slid to the ground, his head slumped to one side. Pearl ran quickly into the yard, her heart going crazy in her chest. She poked a finger down inside her boot and pulled out her door key. Once inside, she locked the door behind her, for she knew that wherever Annie ended up working that night, it wouldn't be in their room, not when she knew Pearl was there.

She washed her face, scrubbed the coal dust from her eyes and the fatty taste from her lips, then changed into her nightgown and slid under a blanket in her bed on the floor. She was calm now, safe. The door was locked and she was alone. The sick feeling she'd had in the pit of her stomach started to disappear, only to be replaced by something more familiar when she remembered how hungry she was.

Reaching under Annie's bed, she pulled out her clippy mat frame. She sat up cross-legged in her blankets and laid the frame across her knees, with her bag of scraps to one side. Slowly she started poking the coloured rags through the hessian with her wood and metal progger held tightly in her hand. She worked until the light was too dim to carry on and her eyes began to feel heavy. Then she slid her mat and bag of scraps back under the bed and settled in her blankets. She knew better than to fall asleep, though, for Annie would be banging on the back door when she'd finished work, demanding Pearl open up and let her in.

★ ★ ★

The next morning Pearl was woken by noises outside on the street. She stood, sleepy and tired, and pulled back the curtain to see what was going on. Ryhope Street South was abuzz with activity. Men were carrying tables and chairs from pubs and houses into the street, lining them up along the pavement. It was then she remembered that today was the day of the Ryhope Peace Parade.

She turned round and saw that Annie's bed was empty; she must have already left for work, leaving Pearl to sleep off the horror of the previous night. She knew her aunt would want to talk to her about what had happened, and dreaded what she might say. She guessed that Annie would insist on putting her back to work at Sid's Corner, whatever Peg Tindall and her friend might have said. She shivered at the thought. And Jackson had been there too last night, even if he'd been too drunk to grab her this time. She needed to let Annie know about that. Her heart felt heavy with sadness as she ran through the events of the night.

A noise outside caught her ear and she glanced to see the preparations for the parade. She hoped it would bring a little cheer to her soul. The parade made her think of Joey. They'd talked about it for weeks, about joining in with the floats and marching with the bands. But she hadn't seen Joey for days and wasn't sure what he wanted any more. Well, there was only one way to find out.

After she was dressed, Pearl ran from the room, out through the yard, into the back lane and along to Joey's house. It was Joey's mam who answered the door, and she told Pearl that Joey was at work. Pearl was about to turn and head down to High Farm when Kate Scotch put her hand on her shoulder.

'Are you all right, Pearl? You're looking a bit pale this morning, pet.'

Pearl put her hand to her stomach. 'Just hungry,' she said. She decided to keep quiet about what had happened the night before.

'Come in,' Kate said. 'I've got stottie fresh out of the oven. You can tear a handful off, it'll keep you going.'

Pearl accepted the bread gratefully. She took a careful bite from it under Kate's watchful eye, and then headed back to the lane. Only when she was out of sight did she scoff the remainder greedily; she couldn't get it into her mouth fast enough. She glanced back occasionally to ensure she hadn't been followed. She didn't want Kate to find her gorging on the bread and spreading gossip about Annie not being able to feed her.

When she had finished eating, she set off down the colliery bank, past the pubs and shops with their coloured bunting fluttering in the summer breeze. She ran past the Co-op and the rhubarb field. She ran past St Paul's church, where she saw Reverend Daye, the vicar, stringing a line of Union flags around a tree in the churchyard. When she reached the village green, she slowed to a walk, taking in the sight of it all done up for a celebration the likes of which Ryhope had never seen. Flags and banners were flying high from the Albion Inn and the Farmers'

Club. The big houses around the green had their windows flung open and coloured cloth draped from inside to the gardens below. Ryhope was ready to celebrate those who had returned from the Great War and to remember those who had not.

As soon as Pearl stepped on to the worn stones that paved the yard at High Farm, a familiar sound greeted her. It was Boot, barking madly. He came running towards her, running rings around her, his tail wagging so hard that his backside almost lifted off the ground in his joy at seeing her again. Pearl got down on her haunches and waited for him to settle. His tail was whipping about madly, but finally he became still and dropped his head into her lap, letting her stroke behind his ears.

'How are you, boy?' she said, nuzzling her face into his neck. 'They treating you all right here? They looking after you, eh?'

'What do you want?'

Pearl looked up into the fat face of Ronnie Heddon.

'Boot!' he ordered. 'Here!'

The dog obediently made its way to his side. Pearl stood and scanned the yard, hoping to catch sight of Joey. Ronnie was an idle lump and little more, but she wanted to be polite to him; they were both Joey's friends, after all.

'I've come to see Joey,' she said.

'He's not here.'

'But his mam said — '

'Don't care what his mam said. I'm telling you he's not here.'

A crashing noise behind Ronnie startled Boot. Pearl looked in the direction the noise had come from and saw Joey pushing a wheelbarrow full of what looked like cow manure.

'He's there, you big liar!' she said.

'Joey!' Ronnie called in a sing-song voice. 'Your girlfriend's here to see you.'

Pearl felt her face redden with anger. 'Shut up, Ronnie! We're just friends.'

Joey let the wheelbarrow drop. He wiped his hands on his trousers, pulled his cap down over his eyes and walked slowly towards them, dragging his bad leg. He stood close to Ronnie.

'Pearl,' he said, giving her a curt nod.

'I was wondering if you were coming to the Peace Parade today,' she said, locking eyes with him for just a second before Joey pulled his gaze away. She wished Ronnie wasn't there. She wanted to talk to Joey on his own; it felt like ages since they'd had a chat together. But Ronnie showed no sign of budging. He was chewing, his fat cheeks working their way around something inside his greedy mouth.

'I'm going with Ronnie and my mates,' Joey said, with no apology to Pearl that he was reneging on their long-standing arrangement to attend the parade together. Neither did he extend an invitation to her to join them.

'I thought *I* was your mate,' Pearl said firmly. 'Can't I come with you?'

Joey dropped his gaze to the flagstones when he gave his reply. 'I'm going with the lads, like. It's just us.'

'Aye, no girls,' added Ronnie.

86

Pearl looked Ronnie straight in the eye. 'I wasn't talking to you, Ronnie Heddon.'

'What do you want to hang around with lads for anyway?' Ronnie asked. His words came out slowly, as if he was thinking up each one a split second before it left his lips. 'Joey's with me now. He's *my* friend and there's a group of us going to the parade together. It's all arranged.'

Pearl bit the inside of her mouth. 'Joey?'

This time Joey raised his head and pushed his shoulders back. 'I'm going with Ronnie and his mates.' Without another word, he turned and walked back to the barrow.

'You heard him, now get lost,' Ronnie told her.

Pearl waited a few moments, hoping Joey might change his mind. She wanted things back the way they used to be. Why did people have to change? What had happened to make Joey turn against her? But he carried on with his work, studiously avoiding her gaze.

'You still here?' Ronnie sneered when she didn't move.

Without a word, Pearl turned towards the road. Boot began to follow her; she could hear him whimpering behind her.

'Boot! Stay!' Ronnie commanded as Pearl carried on walking away.

⋆   ⋆   ⋆

Ryhope's Peace Parade went by in a blur of clapping and singing and the stirring sounds of the colliery brass band. Soldiers marched from the Colliery Inn at the top of the bank all the way down to the village. Pearl watched them go by in their uniforms, their arms swinging and their legs in step. She noticed one of them in particular, who was staring right at her even as the rest of the men faced forwards. He was a stocky man with a trimmed moustache, a lieutenant leading what was left of his platoon. So intense was his gaze that Pearl turned her face away, embarrassed by the man's curious attention.

She saw Bobby Mac dancing in the street with his son Michael, the two of them tipsy on ale and laughing and carrying on with everyone around them. She saw Joey's mam Kate waving a Union flag, but there was no sign of Joey at all.

Annie had closed the shop at noon and made her way to the packed pavements, searching for Pearl. She found her sitting on a kerbstone, enjoying the parade's sights and sounds, grateful to have her mind taken off how hungry she was. In almost two days all that she had eaten was the handful of bread from Kate Scotch.

'You all right, girl?' Annie asked. She sat on the kerb next to her. Around them the celebrations continued, the drinking went on, the singing and laughing drowning out Annie's words so that only Pearl could hear her. 'You hungry?'

Pearl nodded.

'Fancy eating fish and chips on the village green?' She patted her skirt pocket. 'Might as well spend last night's earnings.'

Pearl shot her aunt a look. As much as she loved Annie, there were times when she really despaired. 'We should be keeping it to pay the bills. What about the rent?'

Annie simply shrugged. 'What about our starving stomachs?'

The two of them stood, and Pearl linked her arm through her aunt's as they pushed their way through the crowd.

'Look, Pearl, we need to try again tonight,' Annie told her.

Pearl's heart dropped. She had hoped Annie might have changed her mind about putting her back to work. But what other choice did she have?

'I've smoothed things over with Peg and her mate. They'll not bother you again.'

'Does it have to be tonight?' Pearl asked. Ryhope was celebrating; she wanted to be part of it, to enjoy it, to soak it all in. Instead, her stomach was turning with anxiety at what lay ahead.

'Could be a good earner,' Annie replied. 'Look around, Pearl. See how much the men are drinking? Drink loosens tongues in the women, gets them gossiping and crying. In the men, drink loosens wallets. Sid's Corner will be busy. Peg and her friend won't have time to give you any grief. And I'll be there keeping an eye on you. We're one day closer to Bernie Pemberton's deadline for paying back the debt. One day closer to losing our home. Please say you'll give it another try.'

Pearl knew she had to do it. There was no other way. Losing their home was unthinkable. She'd plucked up the courage to go out to Sid's

Corner the night before. Surely she could do it again. She pulled Annie close as they walked to the village, giving her the answer she needed.

★ ★ ★

That evening, Annie and Pearl went through the same routine as before. Annie made up Pearl's face with coal dust and lipstick, and Pearl pulled on her hat with the red feather pinned to it. Then the two women headed out. The warmth of the July day hung in the air as they made their way to Sid's Corner.

Annie positioned Pearl in a well-lit spot where she could keep her eye on her. A couple of men came up to Pearl, chatting casually as if they were noting the weather, but Annie knew what they would be saying. They'd want to know her price and if she had a room. Pearl glanced over at her each time a man approached, but Annie shook her head. No, not that one, not him. She knew them both, knew them to be unsuitable for her niece's first time. She dismissed the same men when they came to her after being refused by Pearl. She needed to wait until Pearl had secured her own business, with someone Annie considered right, before she went to work herself.

As she had predicted, Sid's Corner was busy with men walking from the noisy, decorated streets of the Peace Parade into the quiet hush of the lane. A noise caught her attention, and she glanced over to see a couple of lads, just kids, walking down towards the corner. As they came closer, she could make out just how young they were, both of them skinny, with spots on their necks. They were egging each other on to approach Annie.

'You ask her,' she heard the taller of the pair say.

'I'm not asking her. You do it. You said you'd do it.'

She smiled as they approached her. She couldn't believe what she was seeing, and had to force herself not to laugh at these lads pretending to be men of the world.

'How much, missus?' the taller one plucked up the courage to ask. He blushed red as Annie eyed him up and down.

'It's not for us, missus. Honest. It's for our mate. It's his first time, like.'

'Oh aye? And where's your mate?'

'In the Colliery Inn. We're to go and get him when we've sorted things here and paid you. We've all chipped in. He won the short straw.'

Annie thought for a second. 'His first time, you say?'

The tall lad nodded eagerly. 'Aye.'

Annie indicated Pearl. 'What about her? Will he like her?'

The boy glanced at Pearl and nodded eagerly.

From across the lane, Pearl was watching with interest. Just what was Annie up to?

The lads disappeared the way they'd come, laughing and pushing each other, running to the pub where their friend was awaiting his fate. Annie walked across to Pearl. 'I think we've found you someone. He's young, probably your

91

age if those two idiots that were just here are anything to go by. It's his first time. You'll be learning together. You can use the room upstairs at the Blue Bell; I've squared things with them for tonight.' Then, secure in the knowledge that Pearl would be safe with the young first-timer, she found her own business and disappeared up the lane.

Pearl waited for the lad to arrive. But it was a whole group that came this time, five of them, and they were walking slowly, as if something or someone was slowing them down. She gasped when she saw them, and turned her back to them, cowering by the wall as she waited nervously for a tap on the shoulder from the lad who'd been chosen to go with her.

After a moment, she stiffened, her senses heightened, and then she heard footsteps coming towards her. Except it wasn't footsteps, not really. It was the step and scrape of someone with a limp, one bad foot dragging behind the other. Her blood ran cold. She forced herself to turn — and came face to face with Joey.

5

No Going Back

It was hard to say which of them got the bigger shock.

'Pearl?' Joey slurred. He tried to focus. He knew he shouldn't have had so much to drink, but Ronnie and his mates had laughed at him when he said he didn't want any more. And now the beer was making him see things that weren't there. This couldn't be Pearl in front of him, not Pearl. He reached an arm to the wall to steady himself, gave his head a shake and looked again at the girl. This time there was no mistaking the features of his friend.

'Joey! Get away, I'm working.'

'It's really you, isn't it?' he giggled.

'Course it's me,' she replied sharply. 'You need to go.'

Pearl looked across the lane, hoping to see Annie. But Annie was nowhere to be found. She didn't know what she'd been expecting from her first night working, but it hadn't been this. It certainly hadn't been Joey.

'What are you doing here?' she asked.

'I could ask you the same question,' Joey smirked. 'You didn't tell me you were working as a —'

Pearl raised a hand. 'Don't say it. Don't use

93

that word about me.'

Joey's head dropped forward and his eyes closed. 'I feel sick, Pearl,' he said. 'Really sick.'

All around them men were prowling, eyeing up the women waiting for business. They no longer looked Pearl's way when they saw Joey standing with her. But Pearl saw them, saw the hunger in their eyes, the way they appraised each woman, eyeing them up and down. They scared her. Without Annie keeping watch on her, she felt frightened and vulnerable, even with Joey next to her.

'I need to get out of here,' she muttered under her breath. She ripped the black hat off her head. 'Are you coming?'

Joey nodded sheepishly. 'Where will we go?'

'We'll walk to the beach, get some sea air. It might help sober you up.'

Joey straightened, filling his lungs with the night's warm, mucky air.

'Want to hook on?' Pearl asked, offering her arm. In her other hand she carried her hat, with its red feather pinned to the side.

Slowly the pair of them headed away from Sid's Corner, out of the pit lane and on to the road. They walked in silence for a while, until Joey's nausea left him.

'I didn't like it much you know, drinking the beer,' he said.

'Then why did you do it?'

'It was Ronnie, he made me. Said it'd make a man of me. I was the youngest one there tonight. His mates all clubbed together to give me some money to send me down the back lane to find a . . .'

94

Pearl shot him a look.

' . . . to find a woman to be with. They thought it was a right laugh and I was too drunk to care. I must have had three pints. I've never drunk so much in my life.'

'What happened to the money? Have you still got it on you?'

Joey shook his head. 'The lads gave it to Annie.'

Pearl was relieved to hear that; at least Annie would have a little extra in her pocket to help with what she owed.

They walked in silence to the village green, where the pubs were doing a roaring trade with those still celebrating after the parade. Down past the cattle market they went, past the Railway Inn, and across the road to the track that led down to the beach. It was getting dark now and the moon cast a silvery glow on the sea. The tide was as far out as Pearl had seen it, and the whole beach was calm and still. There was no one else there, just rocks and cliffs and a wide expanse of sand.

'Come on,' she said, helping Joey clamber down to the sand. 'We'll find a rock to sit on.'

'In the dark?' he asked. Pearl noticed the tremor in his voice and realised he must still be finding it hard to cope after his accident.

'You'll be fine,' she smiled. 'The moon's lighting up the sea, and I'm here, aren't I?'

She didn't walk as far out on the dark sands as she wanted to, but hung back near the track, only too aware now of her friend's fears. She saw a large flat rock ahead.

'Here, this one will do,' she said.

Joey sat heavily, breathing deeply, trying to calm himself. Pearl sat next to him. She took off her boots, revelling in the touch of the damp sand on her bare feet. Ahead of them was the dark horizon, where an indigo sky met the black of the sea, and above it, the moon's silver light. Pearl looked up and saw a star, then another. The sea swished softly as the waves broke. She breathed in the salty night air as she pushed her toes into the sand.

'You feeling better now?' she asked. 'You're probably going to have a hangover tomorrow.'

Joey laughed. 'I've always wondered what a hangover would be like. I suppose there's a first time for everything.'

Pearl was staring out to sea and missed the look that Joey gave her.

'Were you going to do it?' he asked hesitantly. 'You know, tonight, on the pit lane? Were you going to go with a fella?'

Pearl sighed and felt tears spring to her eyes. She'd had so many confusing, hurtful thoughts about the work Annie was forcing her to do, and no one to talk to about it. She was afraid that if she started to talk to Joey, she might not be able to stop. She swallowed the lump in her throat before she allowed herself to speak. And there, in the silence of the night, with the only sound the soft rolling of the tide, she began to unburden herself to her friend. She told him about Annie's debt and Bernie Pemberton's demand for the rent. She told him how hungry she was, how she and Annie were living hand to mouth. She told

96

him how much she loved Annie, that she was like a mother to her. But she was angry with her too, bitter that Annie had allowed her debts to spiral and that she was being forced to work to pay for those mistakes.

Joey sat in silence, letting her speak, letting her words sink in. He was hearing for the first time about Annie's way of life. Pieces of Pearl's life began to make sense to him; how she wasn't allowed into the room when Annie was dressmaking. Except she hadn't been dressmaking at all.

As they talked, Pearl dropped her black hat to the ground and kicked sand over the top of it, hiding it. She never wanted to see it again.

'Why didn't you tell me any of this before?' Joey said at last.

'I couldn't betray Annie,' Pearl said. 'I would never have done that. And lately, I haven't seen you. You've changed, Joey, since you started work at High Farm. I know you're Ronnie's friend now, but you can still be my friend too, can't you?'

'Course I can,' he said.

'I've missed you. I had no one to talk to. I didn't even have Boot to tell my secrets to.'

'He's enjoying being at the farm,' said Joey.

'What about you?'

'I guess so.' He shrugged. 'I'm learning stuff. Ronnie says he'll teach me how to be a man.'

'Just watch what you're doing with him,' Pearl warned. 'He's a lazy so-and-so and he'll have you doing his work for him if you're not careful.'

'He's all right. I can handle him.'

Pearl hesitated for a moment. 'What happened, Joey? Those nights when you went to see the films with Ronnie, where did the money come from?'

Joey picked up a stone and threw it as far as he could. They heard it land with a dull thud in the sand.

'It was stolen, wasn't it?'

Joey looked at her. 'Not really.' He turned away from her gaze and looked out to the black horizon as he began to explain. 'Ronnie showed me how to do it. Easy pickings really. We nicked empty pop bottles from round the back of the Italian ice cream shop.'

Pearl gasped. 'You stole from Alzoni's?'

'Well . . . we took the bottles from the back and in through the front door, and the old woman that works there, she didn't know what we were up to and gave us money for them. We did it a few times a week, always when she was in the shop alone.'

'Oh Joey,' Pearl sighed. 'That's not you, you're no thief. What were you thinking?'

Joey shrugged. 'It was easy money, that's all, to help Mam buy coal and food.'

'To buy yourself sweets, you mean. Come on, Joey, this is me you're talking to. I can see right through you.'

Joey hung his head. 'Shouldn't have done it, I know. I feel bad for the old woman. She doesn't even speak English, did you know? She just saw the bottles, knew she had to give us money for them and didn't ask any questions.'

'You're not still doing it, are you?'

98

'Nah, I think I'll leave Ronnie Heddon and his mates to make their own mistakes after tonight's fiasco. I want nothing to do with them any more.'

'Are you still doing your drawings?' Pearl asked.

'Sometimes,' Joey replied. 'I like to remember Ned and I draw him from memory pretty good now. Mam let me nail one of the pictures to my wall. What about you? Do you still make your mats?'

'Annie's got one up for sale in Bernie's shop,' Pearl said proudly, but then her voice faltered. 'No one wants to buy it, though.'

Another silence sat between them until Joey finally made a move. 'We should be going now, it's late,' he said. He put his hands to the rock and started to push himself up.

Pearl stayed where she was. 'I'm not going.'

'You have to. You've got to go home. Annie will be worried if you stay out all night.'

Pearl shook her head. 'She won't miss me. I'll be one less mouth to feed, that's all. The only thing she'll miss is the chance to get me out on the pit lane to earn money to pay her debts. It's not fair, and I won't do it!'

'Then come and stay at ours,' Joey said. 'Mam won't mind. We can make a bed for you on the kitchen floor.'

'No, Joey. I can't impose on your mam. It's too close to home. Annie will find out I'm there and she'll drag me back home.'

'Where will you go?' he asked her. 'You can't stay here all night.'

'Can't I?' Pearl said, challenging her friend.

'It's not safe, Pearl, it's dark.'

Pearl got up slowly from the rock. She held out her arm to support Joey and the two of them walked back up the track through the cliffs.

When they reached the village green, it was quiet. The Peace Parade celebrations were over and the pubs were shutting up for the night. They walked past the village school towards the church. Pearl saw a flickering light from inside the door, and an idea came to her.

'I'm going to stay here,' she said.

'In the church? Are you sure?'

'I'm certain. It'll be warm and dry inside.'

'The vicar will find you and chuck you out.'

'I'll hide.'

'And tomorrow?'

'Tomorrow I'm going to ask in the village, see if anyone's got a job. I'll take anything. Even cleaning up pig muck at High Farm is better than working the pit lane. I'll send money up to Annie to help clear her bills, but I'm not going back. My mind's made up.'

Joey gently planted a kiss on her cheek. 'If I see Annie, I'll tell her not to worry. I'll tell her you're safe.'

'But don't tell her where I am, please,' begged Pearl. 'She'll try to make me go back, and I won't. It's time I stood on my own two feet. I'll get Annie her money, I'll make sure of it, but I'm going to do it my way, whatever it takes.'

As Joey walked away, Pearl squared her shoulders and pushed her feet forward in her boots. Then she took a step up the path towards the open church door.

★ ★ ★

Just before midnight, Reverend Daye walked into the church, as was his routine. Before he locked the church at night, he always made sure that no one was left inside. He'd sometimes found drunkards slumped in the pews and had to encourage them to leave before he could bolt the door. Other times he'd found mourners after a funeral who hadn't wanted to go home. He would sit with them and offer words of comfort. But as he did his rounds at midnight on the night of the Peace Parade, the church was empty, or at least he thought it was. He blew out the candles and locked the door with the heavy key. Then he made his way home to the vicarage for a mug of tea and a slice of fruit cake baked for him by one of his parishioners.

At the back of the church, Pearl breathed a sigh of relief. She'd crouched down behind the pew at the very back of the church when she'd heard the vicar's footsteps, and watched as he walked around collecting hymn books into a pile, humming a tune to himself that she didn't recognise. She held her breath, waiting for him to leave, hoping he wouldn't spot her. Because if he found her and turned her out, she didn't know where she would go. Her mind was made up now: she would not go back to the room she shared with Annie while there was a chance that her aunt would put her back on the pit lane. When Reverend Daye turned to leave the church, he gave one final glance around and Pearl kept as still as she could, hardly daring to

101

breathe. At last she heard the key turn in the lock.

Moonlight filtered through the windows of the church, lighting up the stained glass as if an oil lamp had been placed behind them. Pearl walked towards a window depicting Christ with a child on his knee. It wasn't high up like some of the windows; this one was her own height, in a corner of the church. She looked at Christ's ruby-red robe embellished with gold. He looked nice, she decided. He had a calm face, although he looked rather sad. But the child sitting on his knee looked happy to be there, and protected. She took comfort from the image and allowed herself to feel safe inside the darkening church.

She made herself comfortable underneath the window of Christ and the child, collecting the little cushions from the pews to create a makeshift bed. She shivered and pulled her jacket tight, then leaned back on the cushions and gazed around the vast space of the church, where colours from moonlight on glass shone against the stone walls. She thought of her aunt and hoped that Joey had told her she was safe and that Annie had no reason to worry. Then she closed her eyes and lost herself to the silence and stillness of the night.

Her sleep lasted all of five minutes. For at midnight, the bells of St Paul's rang out loudly from the tower above her head. They rang again at one a.m., at two and at three. Pearl slept fitfully, snatching sleep where she could. When the bells rang out at six the next morning, she was already awake. She scurried about the church, putting the cushions back in the pews, tidying the corner where she'd slept, trying to leave no trace. And then she began to panic. She was locked inside the church; how was she to leave? What if Reverend Daye didn't come that day, what then? What was she thinking of, running away from Annie? She paced the stone floor, her mind spinning with worry as she tried to put her thoughts in order.

She was stopped in her tracks when she heard the key turn in the lock and the hinges squeak as the door opened. Startled, Pearl looked right and left, trying to find somewhere to hide before Reverend Daye found her. She ran up the aisle of the church, as quick as she could, before the vicar came in from the entry hall. She thought she hadn't been seen. The church organ stood at the top of the aisle and she crouched at the side of it. She tried to keep her breathing calm, she was scared. What would the vicar do if he found her? Would he march her back to Annie's care? Pearl peeked around the side of the organ and saw Reverend Daye go about his business in the church. She watched as he took a seat in the very front pew and dropped his head in prayer. Pearl's heart hammered as she watched him. Her gaze flickered to the open church door. Could she run for it and leave while he had his eyes closed? But just then, he began to speak.

'O Lord,' he said loudly. 'Help me to keep careful watch on any stray members of my flock.'

Pearl didn't see him open one eye and glance in her direction.

'Help me to guide them and advise them.

103

Help me to offer them comfort and to soothe their wretched souls. Help me to ease whatever ails them. And help me, O Lord, to provide a roof over their heads whenever it is needed. Amen.'

He stood and gave a little cough before sitting back down again. He bowed his head and closed one eye again, keeping his gaze on the organ as he went on.

'One more thing, O Lord. Help me prepare a breakfast of eggs and ham and a nice cup of tea for whoever might need it. With your guidance, let me bring the breakfast to our church in twenty minutes' time.' And with that, he stood and walked out.

Pearl didn't move. She was stunned by the vicar's words. He must have known she was there. She began to inch her way out from behind the organ, glancing around her as she moved forward, terrified that he would come back and throw her out. Yet his words, if indeed they had been aimed at her, were kind; he had sounded forgiving, not angry. She walked to the front pew where Reverend Daye had been sitting just minutes before and sat in the same spot, her stomach gnawing with hunger.

Twenty minutes later, true to his word, the vicar returned. In one hand he carried a plate of food and in the other a hot mug of tea.

'Good morning!' he beamed as he entered the church.

Pearl jumped from her seat. 'I'm sorry, Vicar, I'm really sorry. I was just — '

'Beautiful morning, isn't it?' He held out the

plate and cup. 'Please sit, my dear. I expect you'd like something to eat.'

Pearl took the food and drink gratefully. She sat down, laid the plate on her knee and sipped the hot tea. She waited to be told off, but the vicar didn't say a word. He simply smiled warmly as she tucked into the thick ham and the eggs that had been scrambled with creamy milk. Only when she had finished did he finally speak.

'Is there anyone you would like me to contact to let them know you're safe?'

'Annie Grafton,' Pearl said quickly. 'She's my aunt. I live with her. Well, I used to. But I don't any more.'

'Annie Grafton?' The vicar thought for a moment. 'She had a sister, Mary, is that right?'

'Mary was my mam, she died after she gave birth to me,' Pearl said.

The vicar's eyes twinkled. 'Ah, the Grafton girls. I remember them well. A couple of unruly . . . ' He glanced at Pearl. 'A couple of enthusiastic, energetic girls, I seem to recall, when they were younger, of course.'

'Annie doesn't come to church,' Pearl said. 'She lives up on the colliery, works in Bernie Pemberton's shop.'

'Yes, I know the place. Up by the Colliery Inn.'

Pearl dropped her gaze to the stone floor. 'I'm sorry, Vicar. I didn't mean to trespass, but I had nowhere else to go.'

'You can't go back to live with your aunt?'

Pearl shook her head. 'No. She wants me to . . . ' She raised her eyes to look at the vicar's

105

kind face. She thought he had a look of the man in the stained-glass window. Only there was no sadness in the vicar's face the way there was in Christ's captured in glass. Could she tell him about Annie and the work she'd been forced to do? He'd mentioned her mam; perhaps he knew how she had earned her living before she passed away. Could she trust him? Who else could she trust if not a man of God? But her loyalty to Annie meant she couldn't tell anyone, not even Reverend Daye.

'No, I can't go back,' she said.

'Then I'll make sure that a message is given to Annie Grafton,' he said kindly. 'And who will I say it's from?'

'I'm Pearl Edwards,' she replied.

The vicar took a moment to let the name sink in. He rubbed his chin and thought for a moment, remembering the man who had visited him just a week before. He had been a soldier, a lieutenant no less, back from the war, who had asked him in the strictest confidence for his advice on finding someone in Ryhope, a young woman by the name of Pearl. But hadn't he said her surname might be Grafton? How confusing this all was.

'Well, Pearl Edwards. Allow me to offer you the refuge of St Paul's if you should ever need it again,' he said. 'But before I send you on your way, for I've a wedding to prepare for inside the church today, let me offer you the use of the facilities at the vicarage.' He waved a hand towards Pearl's face, streaked with coal dust from where Annie had coloured her eyes the night before. 'My housekeeper can help you prepare for the day ahead and all it may bring.'

'Thank you, Vicar,' Pearl said, grateful beyond words for his help, and for not judging her or telling her off.

'Then come with me now and I'll instruct her to help you as best she can.'

And with that, the vicar and Pearl left the church and headed towards the vicarage.

★ ★ ★

The vicar's housekeeper, an elderly, no-nonsense woman called Joan Kelly, helped Pearl wash the coal dust from her eyes. She asked Pearl no questions; she simply got on with the task Reverend Daye had asked of her. Once Pearl was ready to face the day, the vicar walked her to the front door and laid a hand on her shoulder.

'I hope you can make peace with your aunt and return home where you belong,' he told her kindly. Pearl smiled at his words, thanked him and stepped outside.

The vicarage path meandered through the graveyard to the front of the church. Once she reached the pavement, Pearl hesitated. If she turned right, she could walk up the colliery bank, past the pubs and the shops, past the coal mine and the air filled with dust. Her heart wanted so much to turn that way and go home. But she knew that if she did, it meant walking back to Sid's Corner. No, that was not the direction she wanted to take. Instead, she turned left. Her mind was made up. She would not go

107

back to the hovel of a room she shared with Annie and the dangers of a life working on the pit lane. Annie would worry, of course she would, but Joey and the vicar would pass on Pearl's messages that she was safe.

She walked slowly towards the school and turned the corner to the village green. In the early morning sunlight, Ryhope was coming to life, shaking itself off after a day spent celebrating the Peace Parade. Remnants of bunting and flags were strewn on the green and paper streamers hung limply from trees, fluttering in a gentle breeze. She carried on to High Farm, the only other place she knew well. She'd had a thought she might ask Ralphie Heddon if he had any more work. She'd do anything, she'd tell him, going over the words in her head. She'd clean the pigs, swill the yard, she'd do all the jobs that she knew lazy Ronnie hated doing. She'd even put up with Ronnie's nasty comments and idle ways if it meant she was earning money to pay her way, to buy food to eat. Where she would stay that night, or the next, or the one after, she wouldn't let herself think about just yet. What she needed first was a job, and she'd knock on the door of every pub and shop in the village until she found a way to earn cash.

But when she reached High Farm, Ralphie simply shook his head. He had Joey working there now, hadn't he? 'Try the Albion Inn,' he suggested. He gave Pearl a look, taking in her ragged jacket, her dress crumpled from where she had slept in it, and her worn boots with the holes that let in water when it rained. 'You might want to smarten yourself up first, lass, if you're going looking for work,' he said gently.

Pearl stood for a moment letting the horrible truth of her situation sink in. She had no clean clothes to change into, not even a spare pair of drawers. She had no money, no food. What hope was there for her? What was she thinking, that she could survive like a tinker, robbing food and sleeping rough? It wasn't too late to head home. Annie would take her in with open arms and a welcoming heart.

She glanced across the village green to the imposing sight of the Albion Inn, and her heart pounded in her chest. Going back to Annie was the easy option, the coward's way out, and Pearl Edwards was no coward. She was standing up for herself, finally. Ralphie had advised her to try the Albion Inn and that was what she would do. But could she really walk into a place like that and ask for work? They wouldn't know just by looking at her that she could do heavy lifting. They wouldn't know how dedicated she could be, how polite and engaging. All they'd see would be a scruffy colliery kid, just as Ralphie had seen moments before. All kinds of thoughts ran through her mind. She was still tempted to run home to Annie, but she also knew she had to stand by what she believed. She had to do what was right, and working the pit lane wasn't it.

She felt the sun on the top of her head and lifted her face to the sky. The warmth spread across her brow and cheeks. It had been cold in the church overnight and she was grateful for the sun's rays to warm her. She took off her jacket

109

and tied it tight around her waist. It covered the worst of the creases in her dress. She ran her fingers through her hair. She was just about to set off towards the Albion Inn when she felt something nudge at the back of her knees. She spun round, startled, then overjoyed when she saw what it was.

'Boot!' she cried. She put her hands to the dog's head and scratched behind his ears. 'How you doing, boy? How's my Boot?'

She stood and glanced about for Ralphie or Ronnie, expecting one of them to be looking for the missing dog. But there was no sign of either.

'Come on, boy,' she urged, and headed back through the farm gates with Boot at her side. She called out, but there was no reply. She even banged on the farmhouse door, but still no one came.

'What am I going to do with you?' she said to the dog. Boot twitched his head to one side and his tail wagged so hard that his back end was in danger of lifting from the ground.

Pearl called once more for Ralphie and Ronnie, but her shouts were met with silence. She should leave Boot in the yard. He wasn't her dog any more. But he'd already followed her out once, and when she walked away a second time, he followed again. This time, she let him walk beside her. She felt safe with the dog at her side, and every now and then she reached down to scratch him behind the ears. He looked fatter, she noticed, stockier than he'd ever been while he lived with Pearl and Annie.

'You been eating lots of rats, Boot?' she asked

110

as they walked to the Albion Inn. At the door of the pub, she held her hand in front of his nose. 'Stay!' she commanded. Boot sat obediently.

Pearl took a tentative step into the pub. Despite the sunshine outside, it was dark and cold. Her footsteps echoed on the wooden floor and there was not a soul to be seen.

'Hello?' she called nervously. 'Is anyone there?'

She heard footsteps, and a woman appeared through a doorway. She was carrying a crate filled with bottles. Her auburn hair was piled on top of her head and wisps were escaping around her face. Behind one ear was tucked a pencil. Pearl took a step backwards, ready to flee. She was unsure what sort of welcome she would be given. The woman looked up and caught sight of her. The crate of bottles rattled down to the bar top.

'Eeh, lass, you gave us a fright. How long have you been standing there?'

'I've just come in,' Pearl said quietly. 'I'm looking for work, and I wondered if you had any jobs going. I'll turn my hand to anything. I'll do cleaning or — '

But even as Pearl's words left her, the woman was shaking her head, causing more wisps to break free from the knot at the back of her head.

'I'm sorry, pet,' she said kindly. 'There's nothing going. It's just me and my husband running the place, and when we're busy, we've got a local lass called Dinah who comes and helps out.' She leaned across the bar and held out her hand towards Pearl. 'I'm Hetty Burdon, pet. What's your name?'

111

'Pearl Edwards.'

Hetty smiled at her. 'That's a bonny name.' She eyed Pearl closely. 'You're not from the village, are you? Don't think I've seen you before.'

'I live up the colliery,' Pearl said quickly. 'I've worked at High Farm, though. I can lift stuff, do heavy work. I'll do anything, Mrs Burdon. Please . . .'

'Sorry, lass,' Hetty replied. She pulled the pencil from behind her ear and laid it on the bar top next to a pad of lined paper.

'I wish I could help, but like I say, there's no work here. You could try the Railway Inn across yonder. Ask for Molly Teasdale behind the bar; she's the woman who runs the place. She might have something going.'

Pearl thanked her and left. She blinked against the light as she emerged from the pub. As soon as Boot saw her, he stood to attention and followed as she headed towards the Railway Inn. But the story there was the same. Molly Teasdale was kind with her words but there was no work to give.

Pearl headed back to the village green. The streamers that had hung from the trees earlier had now been taken down, and the banners and flags tidied away. The sun was high now and the day hot. She walked to the drinking trough at the edge of the green, hoping there would be water she could sip. Boot followed at her side. She cupped her hands and lowered them into the trough, bringing the cold water to her lips, while the dog stuck his head in, soaking his face, ears

112

and neck. When she had drunk her fill, she sat on the grass in the shade of a tree, watching people as they walked by. Around the green stood the big houses, some with three or four floors and showy bay windows. She saw the expanse of Ryhope Grange, where the manager of the Ryhope Coal Company and his family lived. She saw the gardens in front of the house where bushes of blue hydrangeas frilled through black iron gates.

Boot lay on the grass at her side. She stroked the dog's head as her mind whirred with worry. She needed a job and she needed a home, but how was she to get either? All she had were the clothes on her back and, for now at least, Boot's protection. She couldn't return to the church; she knew in her heart it would be wrong to take advantage of the vicar's kindness. She needed to find her own way. But without money for food or a bed for the night, what was she to do?

She settled her back against the tree, allowing herself to rest until the turn of the hour. When she heard the bells of St Paul's, she'd continue her search for work. But the lack of sleep from her night in the church caught up with her and she began to feel tired, not just behind her eyes, but throughout her whole body. Slowly her eyelids drooped, her eyes closed, and sleep took her. And while she rested, a man walked towards her.

Boot sniffed the air as the stranger approached. The man came closer. Boot stood to all fours, bared his teeth and growled a warning. Only then did the man walk away, leaving Pearl undisturbed and unaware.

6

Change of Heart

Pearl slept from late morning into early afternoon. When she finally woke, it was as if she was waking from a dream, and it took her a few moments to remember all that had happened. She was sitting under a tree on a warm and sunny village green with Boot by her side. If she closed her eyes, would this dream end? Would she wake up on the pit lane with coal dust smeared on her eyes and greedy men eyeing her, asking how much she charged? But when she breathed in the clean village air, she knew it was no dream. There was a contentment when she woke, a sense of escape and release from the world Annie was dragging her into. But those feelings were clouded by anxiety, worries about how she would feed herself and where she would sleep that night.

'Come on, Boot,' she called. 'We've got to get you back to High Farm before Ralphie comes looking. He'll not be happy if he thinks I've stolen you.'

Pearl and Boot walked the short distance to High Farm, and she was pleased to see Joey there, working in the yard. Joey's face lit up when he spotted her. He looked as happy as Pearl felt about the two of them being friends again.

'How's your hangover?' Pearl asked.

114

Joey put his hand to his forehead. 'I'm never drinking again.'

'I've brought Boot back; he followed me to the village green,' Pearl explained.

Joey opened his mouth to say something, but thought better of it when he saw Ronnie lumbering over. The tubby lad grabbed Boot by the scruff of the neck and marched the dog away. Boot yelped in pain as he was dragged along.

'Hey! Be careful with him,' Pearl cried.

Ronnie stopped and glared at her. 'Be careful with him? You must be joking. He's been eating our bloody chickens and Dad wants him shot.'

Pearl and Joey exchanged a look.

'Did you know about this?' Pearl asked.

Joey shook his head. 'No, honest I didn't.'

Pearl ran after Ronnie and tried to yank his hand from Boot's neck, but his grip was too strong. He held tight to the dog. Boot started growling as he tried to twist his body free.

'Give him here, he's my dog,' Pearl demanded.

'We bought him off you, remember?' Ronnie sneered.

'Give him to me! I won't let you shoot him.'

Ronnie laughed. 'And how are you going to stop me?'

Pearl was so incensed that she kicked Ronnie hard in the shin. Her aim was spot on, and he cried out in pain and let go of the dog. Boot stood and barked until Pearl called for him and they ran from the yard. Joey watched the scene unfold, trying not to laugh at Ronnie, who was sitting on his backside inspecting his leg. He raised his hand to wave goodbye to Pearl just as

115

Ronnie looked up at him.

'Get on with your work,' he growled.

★ ★ ★

Pearl carried on with her job search and headed to the cattle market, but her request brought her nothing there either. In truth, she was a little relieved, because not only did she know nothing about livestock, but the market scared her a little, with its overbearing stench. And she wasn't fond of cows. She didn't trust their placid faces and big velvet eyes, their calm countenance at odds with their bulk and power. She'd heard they could even crush a person to death.

She called at more pubs, the Wellington Inn and the Prince of Wales, but the answer in both was the same. There was no work, not even cleaning, and even if there was, it would go to someone stronger, bigger and older, preferably a soldier returned from the war. What use did they have for a slip of a lass like her? Wouldn't she be better off at home? they asked, but only Pearl knew the truth. She walked no further up the colliery, wanting to keep her distance from Annie and the life that awaited her there. She would stick to the village. It was far enough away, for now.

She crossed the road from the Wellington Inn and came to Alzoni's ice cream shop. She paused and looked in through windows decorated with slogans advertising chocolates and cocoa. She'd never been inside, for Annie had never had the means to pay for ices and sweets. The tiny ice cream parlour was the most exotic shop in the village, owned by an Italian family who had made Ryhope their home. Could she go in there? she wondered. Did she dare? Well, when it came to either plucking up the courage to ask for a job or starving for the rest of the day, she knew she didn't have any choice.

She pushed open the heavy green door and walked inside with Boot following behind. The shop was cool and dark and a wonderful smell greeted her. It was a sweet smell like nothing she had known before. It wasn't sickly sweet like the perfume Annie sometimes wore. It was sweet in a way that made her want to stick out her tongue and taste the air. The walls were lined with dark wooden shelves, on which sat fat-bellied glass jars filled with sweets. One jar held red jellies, another striped mints. Some jars held sugar powders of pink and cream, others red and green lollipops. And at the very back of the shop was the counter where ice creams were sold. Behind the counter was a doorway that Pearl had heard tell led to a room where the ice cream was made by Carlo Alzoni, the owner's son.

'Out!' a voice rasped from the darkness.

Pearl started. She looked around the shop again but couldn't see anyone.

'Dog! Out!' the harsh voice called again.

As her eyes became accustomed to the gloom, she saw an old woman sitting behind the ice cream counter. She was knitting furiously, her fingers flying across needles and wool.

'No dog!' the old woman called.

Pearl shooed Boot out and closed the door

117

against him, then walked towards the old lady. She was dressed in black from head to toe. Every inch of her was covered. She wore a black scarf over wiry white hair and her body was draped in a black jerkin and skirt. The only exposed parts of her skin were her face and her hands. Pearl watched as the woman's fingers worked their way across the needles and white wool, a sharp contrast against her black clothes. She saw the shape of a tiny white jacket, baby clothes being formed. The woman turned her dark lined face to Pearl.

'What?' she demanded.

'I've come looking for work,' Pearl said with as much confidence as she could muster. She wondered if the old lady was the same one Joey had taken money from in exchange for the stolen pop bottles.

'Carlo!' the woman yelled, and returned to her knitting, leaving Pearl waiting at the counter wondering what to do next.

Within seconds, a tall, slim young man appeared. He had dark hair clipped short around his ears. He nodded at Pearl and then addressed the old lady.

'Nonna?'

The woman replied in a language Pearl did not understand. Carlo turned his attention to her.

'Ice cream, miss?'

'No, I'm seeking work,' Pearl said. Once she began, the words tumbled from her. 'I was hoping you might have something I could do. I can lift heavy boxes. I worked at High Farm; the

118

farmer there will put in a word for me if you ask him. I can sew and make clippy mats. I could serve your ice cream, I could clean and I'd — '

Carlo smiled at her. 'I'm sorry. We have no jobs here. My *nonna*, my grandma, she employs only her sons and grandsons in her little shop. It's a family business, you see.'

Pearl's shoulders drooped and she turned to walk away.

'Just a minute,' Carlo said. He beckoned her back to the counter and pointed at a large white ice box.

'Strawberry or vanilla, which one would you like?'

Pearl smiled weakly. 'Thank you, but I can't. I have no money.'

'It's on me,' Carlo said. 'You look as if you could do with cheering up.'

The old woman barked something at her grandson. Pearl couldn't tell what had been said, but she understood the tone of the woman's words. She was clearly not happy about ice cream being given for free. Pearl paid her no mind, and returned Carlo's warm smile.

'Strawberry, please,' she said. As she waited for Carlo to hand her the ice cream in a paper cone, the inside of her mouth prickled with anticipation. She'd never eaten ice cream before, and to be given a free one, and a strawberry one too, was beyond anything she could have imagined.

'Lick it slowly,' Carlo said as he handed her the cone. 'And don't bite with your teeth, it will hurt.'

Pearl thanked him profusely.

119

'And good luck with your job-hunting,' Carlo said as she walked from the shop. '*Ciao, bella!*'

Out on the street, Pearl held the cone in her hand and turned it this way and that, watching as the ice cream began to soften in the heat of the sun. She stuck her tongue out and licked it as Carlo had told her. Again she licked, and again, until her mouth was full of the sweet taste. She sat down on the kerb with Boot by her side and savoured every mouthful, turning the cone to stop the ice cream from running on to her hand. Boot watched her closely, waiting for a taste of whatever she was eating, but he was disappointed as she finished every last bit.

They walked back to the village and Pearl stood at the gates of Ryhope Grange, trying to pluck up the courage to go inside to ask for work. But when the housekeeper spied her waiting there, she shooed her away like a dog. There was only one shop left to try, Watson's Grocers, but when Pearl reached the door, she saw the *Closed* sign. She stared at it, her stomach sinking at the thought that she was no nearer to finding a job or to knowing where she would spend the night.

As she stood there wondering what to do, she heard a voice, then another, two men talking and laughing behind the low wall at the back of the shop. She inched forward to see who was there, but when she reached the yard, the men had gone inside, leaving the back door ajar. Over the wall Pearl could see boxes of fruit — apples, pears, bunches of dark cherries. Her mouth watered at the sight of such bounty. She didn't

120

know when she would eat next. Would they miss a handful of cherries, she wondered, or one apple? She cast a quick glance at the door before clambering over the wall and scurrying to the boxes. She bent low and scooped an apple into her pocket. She was just about to do the same with a bunch of cherries when she felt a heavy hand on her shoulder.

'And what do you think *you're* doing?' a woman's voice demanded.

Pearl froze.

'Stand up, girl,' the woman said. 'Stand up and look at me!'

Pearl did as she was told, and as she stood, the apple fell and rolled across the ground, bumping over uneven stones. Suddenly her chin was gripped and her face was tilted sharply upwards, taking her by surprise. Because of the woman's harsh tone, Pearl was expecting a harridan, but the woman in front of her had a soft face with pleasing features, and her smooth brown hair was swept back neatly from her face. Yet despite her attractive looks, her grey-blue eyes held a glint of something dangerous, malicious. They flashed at Pearl, ready for a fight. Her lips were pursed, ready to unleash a torrent of anger at the thieving girl she'd found in her yard.

'Look at me when I'm talking to you!' she barked.

Pearl tried hard to control the flash of anger that shot through her. How dare the woman touch her face in this way? She took a step backwards, trying to compose herself, to offer up an excuse, a reason for stealing the fruit. But the

121

woman grabbed her dress, bringing her towards her again. They were so close their noses almost touched, and Pearl could smell the woman's rose-water cologne. She held her breath, afraid that the woman would hit her. From the corner of her eye she saw a man appear. He had thick white hair, round wire glasses and a little white beard. The woman saw him too and dropped her hands, letting Pearl go.

'Renee? What are you doing, love?' he asked.

The woman kept her gaze firmly on Pearl as she answered. 'Caught her stealing,' she hissed.

Pearl glanced at the man. He was dressed in a grey woollen jacket, white shirt and black tie. Around his waist was a grocer's apron that reached down to his boots. He turned to look at Pearl.

'Stealing, eh? And what do you have to say for yourself?'

Pearl felt both pairs of eyes bore into her. She knew there was no point in lying; she'd been caught red-handed after all.

'I'm hungry, with no money for food,' she explained. 'I saw the fruit and I thought you might not miss one apple.'

The man smiled at her. 'Well, it *is* just one apple. I suppose we could — '

But his words were lost, for at that moment the woman struck Pearl hard across the cheek with her open hand. Pearl cried out in pain and cradled her face. She was shocked, too, for whatever she had expected for stealing an apple, it hadn't been this. She gasped, and tears sprang to her eyes.

'Renee!' the man called sharply. He took hold

122

of the woman's hands. 'You've gone too far. Leave the lass alone. What the devil's got into you, woman?'

'I won't have riff-raff stealing from us, James,' Renee spat. 'We've spent years working hard here and I'm not having the likes of her ruining us, do you hear?'

The man sighed heavily. 'I know, dear,' he said gently. 'Now come on, let's get you inside and I'll deal with the lass.'

He offered his arm to Renee and led her inside. Pearl waited in the yard, unsure of what to do. The fallen apple lay at her feet and she wanted very much to pick it up. A moment later, the man reappeared.

'I'm sorry about that,' he said. 'My wife gets a little . . . ' he searched for the kindest word, 'a little upset at times. But you shouldn't have stolen from us.'

'I know, and I'm sorry,' said Pearl. She was surprised to hear the man refer to the woman as his wife, for he appeared many years her senior.

He pointed towards Pearl's face, which was stinging from Renee's slap. 'Does it hurt?'

'Just a little.'

'You say you have no money for food, is that right?' he asked.

'None.'

He thought for a moment and ran his fingers through his little white beard. He had a kind face, Pearl thought. A pair of blue eyes twinkled from behind his glasses.

Just then Boot's head and front paws appeared over the wall.

'Get down, Boot,' she hissed, but he paid her no heed and leapt over into the yard.

'Is that dog yours?' the man asked.

Pearl hesitated, not wanting to reveal that she had stolen back her own dog. 'Sort of. He worked with me at High Farm. He's a good ratter.'

The man raised his eyebrows, clearly interested to know more. 'Is he now? Well, we sometimes get rats here at night. I've had to chase them off with a stick before now. I've often thought a dog might help keep them away.' He leaned in conspiratorially towards Pearl and whispered, 'Mind you, I could probably set Renee on them and they'd scarper pretty quick.' He chuckled at his own remark.

'I know he'd work as a guard dog,' Pearl said quickly, although the truth was that Boot was as soft as an old teddy bear, without a bad bone in him. But she'd seen the way he'd reacted earlier when Ronnie had grabbed him by the scruff of the neck. And hadn't Ronnie said that he'd been killing chickens too? 'I'm sure he'd see off rats for you.'

'Then the dog stays,' the man said, full of business now. 'How much do you want for him?'

Pearl glanced at Boot, who was lying on the ground with his tongue out, panting. She thought for a moment, taking her time to reply. She crossed her arms tight in front of her, not to ward off any chill but to give her strength for the words that were about to leave her lips.

'You can have the dog for free,' she said firmly. 'On one condition.'

'Oh, aye?' he replied, intrigued.

Pearl stood up straight and pushed her shoulders back, copying the stance she'd often seen Annie take in the shop when she was negotiating with a customer.

'If you take the dog, then you take me as well and give me a job. I work hard, I'm a grafter. Ask anyone, they'll tell you.'

'You have no work, nothing at all?'

Pearl shook her head.

The man nodded towards the fruit. There were four wooden boxes, filled with apples, pears and cherries. 'All right. Could you lift those? All of them at the same time?'

She looked at the boxes. 'I think so,' she said at last.

'Go on then,' he said. 'I could do with a bit of help in the shop, truth be told. But you need to prove you've got the strength for it first.'

Pearl braced herself and bent her knees, just as Ralphie had taught her to do when she shifted farm equipment for him. She worked her hands under the box of pears and placed it carefully on top of the cherries so as not to damage the fruit. Then she picked up a box of apples and set it on top of the pears before lifting the final box of apples into place. She had made a strong construction and she knew it wouldn't move when she lifted it. That's if, of course, she could. She pushed her hands underneath the tower of boxes and slowly, carefully raised herself to a standing position while tilting the boxes so that they rested against her chest.

The man stood with his hands on his hips,

admiring the strength of the girl. He was impressed not just by her physical prowess but by the way she had stood tall and held her own against Renee. Not many people had the nerve to stand up to his wife in that way.

'Now walk the length of the yard and put the boxes down again,' he told her. 'Do it carefully; I'll be watching.'

Pearl did as instructed and walked to where a crate of empty pop bottles stood. Once the boxes were safely on the ground, the man walked towards her and held out his hand.

'Well, there's a thing! Turns out you're true to your word. You're a grafter indeed and there's a job here if you'd like it.' He shook Pearl's hand. 'I'm Jim, Jim Watson, and you've already met my wife Renee. Our son Billy works with us; it's a family business, like.'

'But what about your wife?' Pearl asked. 'I don't think I made a good impression on her just now.' In truth, she was a little afraid of having to face Renee again. But she knew that wouldn't stop her from taking up the offer of a job.

'What's your name, lass?' Jim asked her.

'It's Pearl Edwards, Mr Watson.'

Jim laughed. 'The vicar's the only person who calls me Mr Watson, and Renee's the only one to use my Sunday name of James. Same as she calls our son William. To everyone else we're just Jim and Billy. Renee gets these airs and graces about her, fancy stuff, you know. But don't you worry about her, just leave her to me. You'll be working with me and Billy, fetching and carrying stuff at first, until we see how you get on. Then we might

126

have you serving in the shop if you fit in well.'

'Thank you,' Pearl said.

Jim eyed her worn boots. 'Are you a colliery lass?' he asked. 'Live up by the pit?'

Pearl shifted uncomfortably under his appraising gaze. 'I used to live with my aunt, but things turned difficult and now I'm . . .'

Jim waited for her to finish her tale, to find out more about the girl who was going to be working for him, but Pearl faltered.

'You're what, lass? What is it?' he asked gently.

Pearl stared straight at him. There was no point in hiding the truth, not if she was going to be working in his shop. If he didn't like what he heard, she'd just have to move on, sleep down on the beach and worry about what tomorrow would bring.

'I've got nowhere to live,' she said at last.

Jim scratched his head. 'Well now, there's a thing,' he said. 'You can't go back home to your aunt?'

Pearl bit her lip, because there was her dilemma. She *could* go back to Annie's, and she knew she'd be received with open arms. But they were arms that would fling her out on to the pit lane after they'd hugged her close. She'd go back there only as a last resort. While there was still a chance for her to make a life away from the pit lane, she was going to take it. But having nowhere to spend the night was a major concern.

She looked at Jim's worn and lined face, his little white beard and his sparkly eyes behind his glasses. There was warmth in his expression and in his character. She smiled as appealingly as she could, knowing she mustn't overdo it. She didn't want him to think she was playing him for a fool when she had already figured he was anything but.

'No, I can't go back,' she said.

'Then you're to stay with us,' Jim declared. His eyes darted from left to right as he thought through his plan. 'Yes, you can stay here, we'll look after you. We've got a tiny room up the stairs that's used for storage, but if your dog here . . . what did you call him?'

'Boot.'

'Yes, well, now that old Boot's here to keep the rats from the yard, we can bring some of the boxes from upstairs down here. You can have the attic room, lass. It'll work out, I'm sure of it. Mind you, I'll have to pay you a little less in your wages, for room and board and whatnot. That sound all right to you, Pearl Edwards?'

Pearl was so happy she thrust out her hand towards Jim and they exchanged another handshake. 'It sounds perfect,' she said. 'And you're sure your wife won't mind me moving in?'

'I've told you, lass. Leave her to me.'

Pearl bent to where Boot was sprawled on the ground. 'You hear that, Boot? We're going to live here, both of us.'

Jim reached to the box of apples and handed one to Pearl. He gave another to Boot, who sniffed at it then patted it around with his paws before crunching the sweet, juicy fruit.

'When would you like me to start?' Pearl asked.

128

'We rise at four in the morning,' Jim said. 'You can help us open up, and go with Billy to get the fruit from the market at Hendon. You'll get on with him fine. He's a hard-working lad and he'll show you the ropes. Now come on, follow me inside and you can help me clear the attic room and create a bit of space for yourself.'

Pearl fizzed with a mix of emotion that she tried to make sense of. She felt relieved, excited and nervous. But she didn't feel afraid. She didn't feel the need to run back to Annie any more; there was no need to go back now. She had her own job and a room in a house in the village. It was more than she could ever have dreamed of, and she knew she had to make the most of it, whatever it might bring. There was no going back to Dawdon Street, no going back to the pit lane and Sid's Corner. No going back to Annie . . .

She felt something harden inside her. She would always love Annie, always. But could she ever trust her again like she used to? She felt differently towards her aunt since she'd put her to work on the lane. She'd make sure that money from her wages at the grocery shop was sent up to Annie to help clear her bills. She'd do that much at least. She could give the money to Joey when she saw him at High Farm, and he could tell Annie that Pearl was safe and happy. That was all she needed to know.

Pearl followed Jim into the shop trying to make sense of all that had happened. She'd been given a job and a home, and had bartered away a dog she didn't rightly own. She'd stood up to

129

Renee Watson and held her nerve without retaliating when she'd been slapped. She had demonstrated her strength to Renee's husband. She had even been given a free breakfast by the vicar, and eaten her first ice cream. All things considered, her first day away from Dawdon Street hadn't turned out so bad after all.

Inside the shop there was a sweet and tangy scent that became stronger the further she entered. It was polish, Pearl realised as she saw the shine on the wooden counter that ran around the shop. Lemon polish. The shop was neat and tidy, with boxes lined up on gleaming shelves. Biscuits were arranged in glass-fronted cases next to tins of corned beef and boxes of starch. There were cigarettes for sale along with tobacco and pipes. Bags of dried goods lined the shelves: butter beans and lentils, barley and peas, sago, loose coffee and tea. And on the counter top directly in front of the door was a set of weighing scales. These too were shined to perfection. Pearl looked around her in awe. She'd never seen so much food.

Jim Watson waved his arm in the air. 'Welcome to our little shop,' he said kindly. 'Do you think you'll enjoy working here, Pearl?'

'I know I will,' she replied, happy beyond words.

Boot had followed Pearl in from the yard, but as soon as Jim saw him, he shook his head.

'Best to keep the dog outside, lass. It'll not be good for business; folk don't like to see a dog near fresh food. I'll have enough on my plate trying to explain all of this to Renee as it is,

130

never mind getting her to accept a dog indoors. It'll be all right sleeping in the yard, won't it?'

Pearl walked Boot back to the yard and he gave a soft whine when the door closed against him. Jim pointed to a wall that had empty wooden boxes on its shelves.

'That's where the fresh fruit and vegetables go when we bring them in from the market. Everything else comes in from the wholesaler. We're cheaper than the Co-op, so people like to come in here and spend their cash. Course, we can't offer the dividend like the Co-op does.'

'Of course,' Pearl replied in what she hoped was the right tone, because she had no clue what a dividend was. Annie had never been able to afford to shop at the Co-op.

Her eye was taken by boxes of chocolates and sweets, bags of broken toffee next to sultanas, raisins and rice. Her stomach rumbled as Jim led her through a doorway that led up a steep flight of stairs.

'Come on,' he said. 'Let me show you your new home.'

⋆   ⋆   ⋆

For the rest of the day the two of them worked together, clearing the room at the top of the building that was to become Pearl's. It was filled from floor to ceiling with boxes holding tins and packets, some of which had been nibbled by mice or rats. Up and down the two flights of stairs Pearl and Jim went with boxes in their arms, lining them up in the narrow passageway

131

that led from the back of the shop to the yard where Boot lay chewing his apple. When at last the little attic room was empty, Jim declared it fit for a queen.

'As long as the queen doesn't mind a bit of dust and muck.' He winked at Pearl. 'You can clean it up as you settle in,' he said. 'Bit of elbow grease, that's all it needs.'

Pearl glanced around the tiny space. There were mouse droppings along the skirting boards, and cobwebs hung black from above. But there was a window that looked out over fields at the back, and a door that she could close against the world. It was a room with a view, her own private space, a safe haven, something she'd never had before. She would clean it until it sparkled, she thought.

'I expect you'll be wanting some blankets, a pillow, that kind of thing,' Jim said distractedly. He lifted his glasses from his face and rubbed each lens on his shirt. 'Listen, lass. I might be gone a while. I'm going to have to square all this with Renee. And I'm guessing she might have something to say.' He chuckled and shot a mischievous look towards Pearl. 'But it's my shop and I always get my own way. Still, as I say, I might be gone a while. Probably best that you stay here until I give the all-clear.'

Pearl looked out of the window and saw Boot in the yard. She breathed a long, slow sigh of relief. It felt strange standing in the unfamiliar room. It was a mess, but it wasn't anything she couldn't put right. She thought of Jim's kindness and the rudeness of his wife, and wondered what would be said between them. She sank to the bare floorboards with her back against the door, propping it open, and waited.

It was hard to know how much time had passed when she finally heard footsteps on the bare wooden stairs. She stood, expecting to see Jim again, terrified of hearing that Renee had forced him to throw her out. But it wasn't Jim this time. It was another man, younger, taller, broader about the shoulders. He had the same kind face as Jim, but unlined, and fuller about the cheeks; the same sparkling blue eyes, though they were not hidden behind glasses. His dark hair was cut short, tidy around his face. He was dressed in a loose brown shirt tucked into black trousers, and on his feet were black, sturdy boots. He was older than Joey, she guessed, even older than Pearl herself; perhaps the same age as Bobby Mac's son Michael.

He paused when he reached the top of the stairs. Pearl jumped to her feet when she saw him. 'Billy Watson, nice to meet you,' he said, thrusting out his hand. He had the same friendly way about him as Jim, she noticed. She liked the way her small hand fitted inside, and she enjoyed the warmth of his touch. It was silly and she knew it, because they'd only just met, yet her heart was beating nineteen to the dozen.

'Pearl Edwards,' she replied. 'I think I'm your new lodger. That's if . . . ' She stopped herself from saying anything about Billy's mam Renee.

'No ifs or buts about it,' Billy said. 'Dad managed to talk Mam round. I've been sent up to see if you'd like tea with us downstairs. It's

133

nothing fancy, just a plate of beef and potatoes, with apple crumble for afters. That sound all right to you?'

'All right? It sounds like heaven,' Pearl replied.

Billy's boots clattered on the wooden stairs as he went back down. Pearl waited a moment, steadying herself with her hands behind her back, resting against the wall. There had been something about Billy Watson's smile that she'd liked, a gentleness in the way he'd spoken to her, a friendliness she'd never known. Oh, it wasn't like being friends with Joey; they'd grown up together and he was more like a brother to her. No, Billy wasn't a boy like Joey. He was a man. But he wasn't like any of the men she'd seen with Annie hanging around the pit lane. There was something good, honest and solid about Billy.

She gave her head a shake and told herself not to be silly. But if anyone had seen her there, they would have noticed the blush in her cheeks and the fire in her eyes. They would have realised what Pearl did not yet understand: that she was smitten. And though she didn't know it, from that very first meeting, Billy Watson was smitten too.

7

News

Pearl settled into life at Watson's Grocers with ease. She sought out Joey at High Farm and asked him to bring her as many of her clothes as he could from Annie's room. Joey was nervous about coming between Annie and Pearl. He didn't want to be seen to be taking sides in a family feud he knew little about, but he finally agreed to Pearl's request after she begged him to help.

Pearl was happy at Watson's and enjoyed working for Jim and learning from him. She got on well with Jim and he treated her with respect in the shop. He quickly learned what a hard worker she was, as content to fetch and carry heavy boxes as she was to pass the time of day with his customers. And having her in the shop meant he could take the occasional break too.

But it was Billy's company that Pearl enjoyed most. Since the first moment she'd met him, she had wanted nothing more than to spend time with him. She felt safe in his company, safe and warm and completely herself. She took any excuse to stand next to him, their arms almost touching, as they worked behind the counter. But any romantic notions she might have had towards him came to nothing, for he seemed not to be interested in her that way. He told her he admired her strength when they worked at the market, lugging sacks of potatoes to the small van with *Watson's Grocers* emblazoned in green. He told her that her presence cheered up the shop and their customers had passed comment on her smile and her winning ways. But he never once told her that he liked her in the same way she felt about him.

Pearl kept her feelings to herself, resigned to nothing more than Billy's friendship. But still something hurt within her, something she couldn't express. All she knew was that she wanted to be alone with him. She wanted to tell him about her clippy mats, to talk about Joey and his pit pony. She even wanted to tell him the real reason she left Dawdon Street. But their conversations were confined to the size of potatoes and the price of leeks.

★ ★ ★

Although Pearl woke every morning looking forward to her day working with the Watson men, her relationship with Renee was strained. Pearl tried her best to be polite, but Renee proved herself as difficult a woman as Pearl feared. It was clear Renee did not approve of her husband's decision to take Pearl on in the shop. And for a colliery lass like Pearl to be living in Renee's house, even if it was just the attic room, was too much for Renee to bear. She saw it as a blow to her dignity that her husband had overridden her wishes. The slum pit lanes of the

136

colliery with the air thick with coal dust were where Renee herself had grown up, and she was determined to have nothing to do with them again. She had put her foot down when Billy had wanted to follow his friends to work at the pit. No son of hers was going to be a coal miner, not while she had an ounce of breath left in her.

Jim couldn't blame Renee for wanting the best for herself and their son, but there were times when he wished she could be content with what she had. Instead, she was always wanting more than he could provide for her; something better. And now she was channelling her desire through their son, even managing to inveigle her way into the doctor's house for a drink with his wife and daughter. Jim knew Sylvia, the doctor's daughter, or at least he knew of her. She worked as the receptionist in her father's practice on Stockton Road. And what he knew of her he didn't like. She was bonny enough, with her curled fair hair and clear skin, but he'd never once seen the lass crack a smile. Not even while she was tending to the poorly patients who arrived at the surgery. Was he really going to end up with someone as unfriendly as that for his daughter-in-law? Well, if Renee had her way about it, he knew there would be little choice.

★   ★   ★

The Watsons lived above the shop. It was a simple arrangement of two bedrooms, one for Jim and Renee and the other for Billy. A third room, overlooking the street, held two armchairs and a sofa, a side table and dresser, all in dark polished wood. Pearl noticed the same scent of lemon polish in the room she'd first noticed in the shop below. The living room was spartan and as neat as a pin. In one corner was a table and four chairs. It was always set with four plates, four knives and forks. A tiny kitchen that was less of a room and more a pantry with a worktop and coal fire was situated beyond.

One evening as the four of them sat down to a meal of panackelty stew, Billy pulled out a chair for Pearl. She thought her heart would burst as she took her place at the table next to him. She smiled her thanks, but Billy seemed not to notice.

Her attention snapped back to the panackelty on her plate when Renee took her seat at the table.

'William, you'll accompany me to the doctor's house this evening after dinner,' she instructed her son.

Pearl lifted her spoon to her mouth, savouring the potatoes, onions and beef. She didn't notice Billy stiffen at his mother's words.

'Do I have to?' he mumbled.

Jim shot his wife a look. He wasn't at all happy about Renee dragging the lad off to the doctor's house. He knew what Renee was up to, and he didn't approve. He concentrated on his stew.

'And you'll be cleaning the pots tonight while William and I are out.'

Pearl was surprised to realise Renee was addressing her directly, for it wasn't something she usually did.

'I will, Mrs Watson, of course.'

★ ★ ★

Later that evening, Pearl boiled water on the fire to wash the dinner pots and pans. There was a bustle of activity in the living room and she positioned herself so that she could see what was going on. When she'd heard talk of the doctor's house, she'd assumed that either Billy or Renee was ill. But it seemed to be something different going on, something that had put a spring in Renee's step. She had her best hat on, a small brown velvet one that sat low over her eyes, and was dressed in her good shoes with heels, stockings too. And when Billy came to join his mother, Pearl couldn't believe her eyes. Gone was the grocer's apron, the baggy trousers and the loose cotton shirt. In their place were smart black trousers and a jacket with a white shirt and tie.

'William, come here, let me do your tie properly,' Renee called. Billy walked towards his mam and lifted his chin. Pearl saw him run a finger around the inside of his collar and pull it from his neck.

'I don't feel right in this,' he complained.

'Well, you look right and that's all that matters,' Renee huffed.

Jim was sitting on the sofa reading the day's *Sunderland Echo*. He peered across the top of his newspaper at his wife and son. He couldn't hold his tongue any longer.

'I wish you'd leave the lad alone, Renee. I'm sure he can make his own decisions. He's a man now, not your little boy any more.'

Renee chose to ignore the remark. She

139

brushed her hand along the shoulder of her son's jacket, gathered her handbag and marched towards the door. 'William, we're leaving now. Come!' she ordered.

Billy and his dad exchanged a smile before Billy followed his mam. As they headed into the yard, Pearl heard Boot barking.

'That dog doesn't like Renee,' Jim laughed. He stood, folded his newspaper and walked into the tiny kitchen, where Pearl was on her knees scrubbing dinner plates in a flat metal dish on the floor. 'I was just saying, your dog hasn't taken to Renee very well,' he said. The lines around his eyes creased as he smiled.

'I'll take him for a walk later,' Pearl said. 'If you know what time Mrs Watson is due back, I'll make sure I walk him then so he doesn't bark at her when she returns.'

Jim looked at the clock on the living room mantelpiece. 'I'd give them an hour or so. The wife's got it into her head that the doctor's daughter is a good match for Billy. I just wish she'd let him choose who he wants to go courting with. But no, she's determined to send him up in the world. Being a grocer isn't good enough for Renee, you see. But she's his mother, what say do I have?' He sighed and returned to the sofa, where he picked up his newspaper and sank back with his feet up, something Pearl never saw him do when Renee was in the house.

Left alone in the kitchen, Pearl let Jim's words sink in. Now it made sense why Billy was dressed up to go and see the doctor. Renee was trying to marry her son off to a well-to-do family. Pearl

140

felt a heat rise in her cheeks. How could she have been so stupid? There she was, thinking that he might be interested in a colliery kid like her, when he could have his pick of Ryhope's young women. She was embarrassed and disappointed, angry at herself for even thinking she could be anything more than friends with Billy Watson. She returned to the task in front of her and scrubbed the pots with a little more vigour than before.

* * *

As the days turned, Pearl began to think of Watson's Grocers as her home. When she had an hour free, she went to see Joey at High Farm, this time to hand over money for him to take to Annie. She wasn't ready yet to forgive Annie and visit herself.

'She misses you, Pearl,' he told her. 'Mind you, she's getting friendly with Bobby Mac; I've seen them chatting in the yard at the Colliery Inn.'

'I miss her too, but . . . ' Pearl thought of Billy and a warmth spread inside her. She thought of the kindness Jim had shown her, and although Renee did little to hide her disdain for Pearl, at least she fed her well. Tea was served with vegetables, and there was always a dessert of fresh fruit.

'But you're not coming back, are you?' Joey said.

Pearl shook her head. 'I've got my job now, a new home.'

'Do you need more clothes bringing?'

141

'I don't have any more,' she replied. 'You brought them all before. But tell Annie . . . tell her I'll keep sending money to help pay her debts. It'll keep Bernie Pemberton off her back. He won't throw her out while she's paying at least something towards the rent.' Pearl hoped that even a wily rascal like Bernie Pemberton had a heart somewhere deep down.

'I've seen Jackson, you know,' Joey said.

'Where? In the back lane?'

Joey shrugged. 'He says he might have some work for me.'

'Ah Joey, you can't be serious? And after you knocked him down the stairs?' Pearl cried. 'You mean he's willing to help you find work after what you did to him?'

Joey looked down at his feet. 'He says I've got a bit of strength about me, for a little 'un. And he says he'll pay me good money. All I'd be doing is a bit of running for him to the bookies.'

'Putting bets on? You're not old enough! If the coppers catch you, they'll have you in the cells.'

'I'm just thinking about it,' Joey said quietly. 'Mam's not well; she's had to leave her cleaning job at the Co-op. We need the money.'

Pearl leaned towards Joey and kissed him on the cheek. She watched as he dropped the coins she'd given him into his trouser pocket and then she walked away.

★ ★ ★

Pearl was working alone at the counter, weighing loose leaf tea on the polished brass scales. As she

142

lifted the scale to fill a paper bag with tea, she breathed in the earthy aroma. She carefully folded the top of the bag in the way Jim had shown her, rang up the amount in the till and took payment. Just as she was saying farewell to her customer, a familiar figure appeared at the door.

'Hello, Pearl,' Annie smiled.

Without stopping to think, Pearl ran from behind the counter and flung herself into her aunt's arms. They stood together in the middle of the shop for what seemed like a lifetime, hugging each other to within an inch of their lives.

'I've missed you so much, pet,' Annie said.

Pearl was torn. She had missed Annie too, and was hurting without her. But she had hardened towards her aunt after being put to work on the pit lane. Would things ever be the same between them?

Billy walked in from the yard, and as soon as Annie saw him, she let go of Pearl.

'I'm just here to see my niece,' she explained. 'I won't be taking up too much of her time.'

Billy looked at the two women and saw tears in Pearl's eyes. 'You all right, Pearl?' he asked.

Annie noticed the touch of concern in the boy's words, and she pulled Pearl to her again. 'Course she's all right, aren't you, love?'

Pearl nodded and wiped away a tear. 'I miss you, Annie, but I'm doing all right,' she said, the words coming out of her with urgency. She wanted to let Annie know all that had happened. 'Got a good job here and it comes with my own room up above. I've even got Boot back; he's

143

working as the rat-catcher out the back.'

'I've heard all about it from Joey; he keeps me up to date,' Annie said. She nodded towards Billy. 'You Watsons taking good care of my girl, I hope?'

'We're doing our best,' Billy replied. He held out his hand. 'Billy Watson,' he said.

'Annie Grafton. Pearl's aunt,' she replied.

'Look, Mrs Grafton — ' he began.

'It's Miss. I never married,' Annie interrupted. 'Never met a man I liked enough to want to spend my life with.'

'Miss Grafton, Pearl should be getting back to work now. If Mam comes in and finds she's not behind the counter, she'll not be happy.'

Annie held up her hands in surrender. 'I'm going, lad, don't worry.' She hugged Pearl again and kissed her on both cheeks. 'You're looking well, lass,' she said, appraising her. 'Filling out. Must be all the fresh veg, eh?'

Pearl walked her to the door. 'How are things, Annie? Did you pay Bernie's rent? Has Joey been giving you the money I've been sending up?'

'Don't worry about me, love. Bobby Mac's loaned me money to get me out of a hole.'

Pearl's heart sank. 'A loan? And what's he charging you on that?'

'Nothing, pet. He's given it to me, says I'm to pay him back when I'm able. It means Bernie's off my back. I've just got my bills to pay. Should be back in the black before long. Oh, and you'll never guess . . . '

'What?'

'Your clippy mat's been sold from the shop.'

144

Pearl beamed; this was good news indeed. 'The blue and green one with the white stripes?'

'The very same,' said Annie.

'Who bought it? Anyone we know?'

Annie shook her head. 'Some little fella, never seen him before. He didn't talk much. I tried asking him if it was a present for his wife or daughter, but he didn't stop to chat. He was very businesslike about the whole thing, to be honest.' She delved into her handbag. 'I've got the money here for you.'

'Keep it,' Pearl said forcefully. 'Put it towards paying your bills, or paying back Bobby Mac.'

Annie stood for a moment, humbled by her niece's generosity. 'Are you sure, pet? I know how much hard work went into that mat.'

'I'm sure,' Pearl said. She kissed her aunt on the cheek. 'Annie?'

'What, love?'

'Joey's told me about Jackson, that he's asked him to run to the bookies for him.'

Annie's shoulders dropped and her gaze fell to the floor. 'It's money for the lad, Pearl. Joey has to take his chances where he can. We all do.' She glanced towards Billy, who was placing brown eggs from an old box into a gingham-lined basket. 'Anyway, I'd better go,' she said. 'I don't want to be getting you into trouble with Mrs Watson.'

'Annie, could I . . . could I come up to Dawdon Street some time and pick up my clippy frame? I've still got a mat to finish and then you could put it up for sale in the shop.'

'You know you can come any time,' Annie

145

replied, but then she thought better of it. 'Well, maybe not this evening, I'll be working. Probably best if you come during the day, just in case I'm out on the lane.'

'But I can't come during the day; I'm working here,' Pearl sighed. 'Maybe I could ask Joey to collect it instead.'

'We'll work something out, pet. Don't we always?' And with that, Annie was gone.

Pearl stood at the door and watched as her aunt walked away up the colliery bank, back to Sid's Corner and the women working the pit lane. She wanted to run after her, to link her arm through hers and walk home to all that was familiar. But she stood firm, knowing that as much as she loved Annie, she had a better life with the Watsons. Her reverie was cut short by Billy.

'Did I hear you say you needed something collecting from your aunt?' he asked. 'Sorry, I didn't mean to pry, but I couldn't help overhearing. I could collect it for you in the van, if you like.'

'It's nothing important, just my clippy frame,' Pearl said, turning from the door and heading back behind the counter.

'You make clippy mats?' Billy asked, surprised. He realised there was a lot he didn't know about Pearl, and he wanted to learn more. 'There's some skill in making those things, isn't there? Bet you need the patience of a saint to sit and poke all the scraps through with that tiny little stick.'

'The little stick's called a progger,' Pearl laughed. 'But thank you for the offer of

146

collecting it for me. It's in Annie's room, above the shop where she works: Pemberton's Goods, on the colliery.'

'Is that the little shop that sells dress materials, the one by the Colliery Inn? I'll call next time I drive past, as I've to go to Silksworth for eggs.'

'I thought Watson's eggs came from High Farm?' Pearl said.

'They used to, but they've got a shortage at the minute.' Billy shrugged. 'Something to do with their hen and chicken stock being low. Some of them were killed, I heard. Probably a fox made its way in.'

Pearl turned away, knowing full well that Boot had been responsible.

'Has Dad ever said anything about giving you a day off?' Billy asked.

'I already get Sunday afternoons off, so I wasn't expecting anything more,' Pearl replied.

'Ah, but Sundays aren't your day off, not really. Mam keeps you busy with the cleaning most of the day.'

'I don't mind,' Pearl replied quickly. 'It's the least I can do to help pay for my bed and board. She's looking after me well, Billy. I don't mind the chores.'

Billy stretched his arms to the counter top and placed his hands flat as if he was preparing himself to say something. But then he thought better of it, dropped his gaze and stared at the polished wood. Pearl watched him, aware of the familiar heat rising in her face. To spare her blushes, she busied herself untying a sack of dried butter beans, then, using a wooden scoop,

147

began to transfer the beans into jars decorated with the Watson Grocer's logo in green.

* * *

When Sunday morning dawned, Pearl woke in her makeshift bed on the floor of her tiny room. There was no need to get up early on a Sunday, for the whole household rested. It was the only time the Watson house wasn't a bustle of activity. As she lay in bed, Pearl watched the light streaming in through the window, dancing on the wall above her bed, throwing shadows that twisted and turned. She thought about Annie and wondered what she'd be doing. She thought about Joey and wondered if he was working with Jackson. She'd rather he spent his time with that daft lump Ronnie Heddon than have him scavenging with Jackson. But she didn't hold any sway over Joey, she knew that. He had to find his own way and make his own mistakes, just as she had to do.

She thought of her morning ahead, the luxury of having the whole house to herself while the Watsons were at church. After they left, she'd wash the breakfast dishes before scrubbing the kitchen with scalding water and a stiff brush. Then she'd clean the living room, dusting and polishing. Renee often stroked her finger along the furniture after Pearl had finished, to be sure that everything had been done to her exacting standards. Then downstairs to the shop she would go with Renee's lemon polish, to shine up the counter top and shelves and scrub the shop floor. The yard would be swilled next, and if she was quick, she'd have a few minutes to enjoy the quiet of the house before the Watsons returned from St Paul's.

As she lay planning her day ahead, Jim's voice called up the stairs. 'Pearl! Breakfast!'

She leapt out of bed, threw on her clothes, pushed her feet into her boots and ran her fingers through her hair. She ran down the stairs to where the breakfast table was set in the corner of the living room.

'Must you make such a clatter, girl?' Renee said sharply. 'How many times do I have to tell you to walk down the stairs, not run?'

'Sorry, Mrs Watson,' Pearl said. She strode towards the table and sat down between Jim and Billy, bidding them good morning. Billy didn't reply; he was too busy eating a link of the butcher's best sausage that Renee had fried with eggs. There was a fried egg on toasted bread for Pearl, along with a mug of steaming hot tea. Renee brought her own plate to the table, set it down and slid on to the chair opposite.

'Now remember, William,' she said, addressing her son, 'you're to take Sylvia to the vicar's talk this evening at the church.'

'Yes, Mam,' Billy said without looking up.

'She'll be at the service this morning, and you're to say good morning to her and greet her family too.'

As Renee cut into her sausage and eggs, Pearl noticed Jim and Billy exchange a look.

'And you'll sit next to her at church, but keep a respectable distance. I don't want her mother and father passing comment where it's not needed.'

149

Billy paused with a forkful of sausage mid-air. 'Yes, Mam.'

'The lad knows what he's doing, Renee,' Jim said. 'Leave him be and let him enjoy his breakfast.'

Renee slammed her knife and fork to the table. 'Leave him be? James! This is important to me, to all of us. We could very well end up having the doctor's family as our in-laws. Certain protocols need to be applied. I've worked for months to get us this far!'

Gently Jim covered one of Renee's hands with his own. 'Steady on now, let's not get carried away. We don't want to be talking about weddings and in-laws. The lad hasn't even been on a proper date with Sylvia yet.'

Billy stood and his chair scraped behind him. Jim and Renee looked at him in surprise.

'Will you stop talking about me as if I'm not even here!' he said. 'Both of you!' He glared at his mam before picking up the last piece of sausage from his plate with his fingers and storming from the room.

Renee turned to her husband. 'Now look what you've gone and done,' she sniffed.

The rest of the breakfast was eaten in silence.

* * *

As Pearl was cleaning the breakfast pots in the kitchen, she spotted Billy in the parlour in his suit and tie, looking handsome and smart. Her stomach turned over with disappointment and embarrassment. How could she ever have

150

thought he might be interested in someone like her? She couldn't compete with Dr Anderson's daughter. She wasn't rich, for a start. She wasn't beautiful either, or at least no one had ever told her she was. And yet hadn't there been a moment in the shop earlier that week? The way he'd looked at her when he'd asked her about having a day off from the shop. It was as if he'd wanted to say something, ask her a question, but no words had left his lips. And he'd promised to collect her clippy mat from Annie, hadn't he? What if he did want to be more than just friends?

No, she mustn't think that. The proof was there in front of her, Billy dressed in his Sunday best, waiting to head to church with his parents. He'd be sitting next to Sylvia, perhaps even taking her hand, offering her a hymn book, giving her a sly look when he should have his eyes closed for prayers. And he'd be courting her that very night, accompanying her to the vicar's talk. What hope did Pearl have of competing in that world when she knew nothing of the rules, the regulations and the . . . What was it Renee had said earlier? The protocols.

She sighed and went back to scrubbing bits of burnt sausage from the frying pan. With her head down, lost in her chores, she didn't notice the look Billy gave her as he went out; nor did she see the sadness in his eyes.

When she heard the door slam at the bottom of the stairs, she breathed a sigh of relief and began to sing, a tune that Annie had taught her when she was a child. And with each verse and every chorus, she worked harder at her chores.

151

She polished the living room, cleaned the landing, then made her way downstairs to make a start on the shop. When all was done, she swilled out the yard, cleaned the outside netty and then fed Boot. As she sat on the doorstep in the summer sunshine, the dog walked towards her, dropped his head into her lap and gave a satisfied whine as she scratched him behind his ears.

★   ★   ★

The next day, Pearl was working in the shop, filling the wooden boxes with turnips and parsnips that Billy had brought back from the market. Once he had lugged in the last sack of vegetables, he disappeared back to the van.

'Got you this,' he said when he returned. He handed Pearl her half-finished clippy mat on its frame, holding it as carefully as a priceless work of art.

Pearl brushed the soil from her hands, rubbing them against her apron, then took the frame from him, holding it gently by the edges.

'But how . . . when . . . ?' she stammered.

'Called in at Annie's shop, like I said I would, on the way back from collecting the eggs.'

'Oh Billy!' she cried. She wanted to throw her arms around him to say thank you for his thoughtfulness, but she didn't move; she couldn't do anything other than stare at the frame.

'She said you'd be needing this too,' he said, swinging a small linen bag of clippings towards her. 'She's put your little stick . . . I mean your

152

progger in there as well.'

Just then, Renee entered. Pearl had been so lost in the excitement of Billy's kind gesture that she hadn't heard her footsteps on the stairs.

'I don't pay you to stand around, girl,' she said. 'Back to work. And put that dreadful mat away.'

'Yes, Mrs Watson,' Pearl said. She walked around the counter and slid the clippy frame and the bag safely out of sight. 'I'll take it up to my room at the first opportunity.'

Renee didn't reply. 'William?' she barked. 'I'm off to see Mrs Anderson this morning to discuss last night. I'm hopeful of another date for you and Sylvia; perhaps a dinner at the doctor's house if we're lucky. Who knows, there might even be talk of an engagement soon.' And with that, she swanned out of the shop, leaving a scent of rose water in her wake.

Billy stood in silence watching his mam leave. Suddenly he patted his jacket pocket.

'Almost forgot.' He smiled at Pearl. 'I bought something for you. Your aunt had them in a box on the counter in her shop when I was there this morning. Selling them off cheap, she said. She had them in all colours and I couldn't resist. I thought you might like it for your room.'

He opened his hand and there in his palm was a feather. A single red feather. Pearl froze. She couldn't speak. Was this some kind of sick joke? But one look at Billy's face showed he was serious. There was a sparkle in his eyes and a smile on his lips. He was holding his hand out towards her, waiting for her to take the gift,

153

hoping she would approve.

'Don't you like it?' he said anxiously.

Pearl stared in shock. Then she flew at Billy's hand, grabbed the feather and ran out into the yard. She stood with her back against the brick wall, calming herself, taking deep breaths of the soft morning air. She was furious with Annie. How could she have let him pick the red one? How dare she?

Billy had followed her out to the yard. They stood in silence, looking out towards the fields. Neither of them so much as glanced at the other. Slowly, haltingly, Billy found the words he needed and apologised to Pearl. He'd never meant to upset her, he explained. It was the last thing he'd wanted to do. In turn, Pearl apologised for overreacting and thanked him for being so thoughtful as to buy her a gift. But she couldn't offer any explanation for her behaviour, for how could she tell him the significance of the red feather?

'It reminded me of Annie and my old home up on Dawdon Street,' she said softly. 'I think maybe there's a little bit of my heart that wants to return.' She hated not telling him the whole truth, and had to bite her lip to stop herself from saying more.

The two of them stood a while longer in silence. Finally Billy spoke.

'If I asked Dad if we could have an afternoon off together, would you come for a walk?'

'With you?' Pearl asked, surprised. She turned to look at him, but Billy was still staring ahead.

'We could go to the beach, before the autumn sets in.'

Pearl turned back to look at the fields. The two of them were standing side by side, almost touching, close enough to hear the other breathing. She wondered if Billy could hear her heart beating, for it was going wild in her chest.

'I'd like that,' she said. 'I'd like it very much.'

★ ★ ★

Billy spoke to his dad one evening after Renee had gone to bed claiming a headache. Jim knew there was more to his son's words than wanting to give Pearl a break from the shop. He asked Billy if he knew what he was doing, if he was sure that stepping out with Pearl was what he really wanted to do.

'I like her, Dad,' Billy said. 'There's something about her; she's got spirit, you know?'

Jim nodded. Oh, he knew. He'd seen it that very first day when she stole an apple from the yard. It was why he'd given her the job and offered her a home too.

'She works hard and isn't afraid of putting her back into things in the shop,' Billy continued. 'And when we're at the market, she talks to the stallholders like they're old friends. She even managed to get us a better price on potatoes than we've ever had before.'

Jim laughed when he heard that. 'Old George? She's never talked him into dropping his prices, has she?'

'She charmed his socks off, Dad,' Billy said, remembering the exchange between Pearl and one of the most irascible men at the market. 'I'm still not entirely sure how she did it.'

'Well, I've seen the way you two work together in the shop, and the way she's brought a kind of peace to this place. Even your mother's calmed down a little; I reckon having Pearl here to help with the cleaning has done her the world of good. She's out more with her friends in fancy places these days, mind you. But I'm not complaining if it keeps her happy.'

'What'll you tell her, Dad? About me and Pearl, I mean?'

Jim took his glasses off and rubbed each lens slowly against his cotton shirt. A mischievous glint played in his sparkling blue eyes.

'I'll tell her the whole sugar-coated truth. And by the time I've finished spinning her a tale, she'll think it was her own idea for you and Pearl to step out together.'

But Billy wasn't convinced. 'Are you sure? She's expecting me to take Sylvia Anderson out again; she's got it all planned. But I can't be doing with a woman like Sylvia. Could you really see me living a hoity-toity life in the doctor's house? I'm a Watson, Dad. A grocer. My place is here with you and Mam.'

Jim looked at his strong, strapping son and thought his heart would burst with pride.

'Well, Billy. I'm expecting your mam to kick up a stink when I tell her you're intending to step out with Pearl. But don't worry. Just leave your mam to me.'

8

Secrets

Jim stood back from the counter and adjusted his glasses. He allowed himself a smile of satisfaction as he admired his handwriting on a small chalkboard: *This shop rat free 14 days.*

Renee bustled into the shop. When she saw what her husband had written, she was horrified. 'Must we really advertise such a thing?' she bristled.

'It's something to be proud of,' Jim beamed. 'Taking on that dog was one of the best things we ever did.'

'But it's so common, James,' she said. 'No other shop puts the notion of vermin into their customers' minds when they arrive. It's not the sort of thing our customers want to see.'

Jim shook his head. He didn't like to disagree with Renee; it usually ended in her sulking for days. He preferred a straightforward life and he'd learned to keep quiet when Renee got the wind up about something. But on this he knew he was right, and he was determined to make his point.

'I think you'll find it's exactly the sort of thing our customers want to see when they come in. It says we keep a clean shop. Hygienic,' he said firmly.

Renee snapped her gaze towards her husband.

157

'Our customers want fresh produce at good prices,' she said sharply. 'They do *not* want to be reminded of rats from the sewers. When I come back, I want that chalkboard to be gone.'

'Come back? Where are you off to this time?' It was then that Jim noticed his wife was wearing her best hat. Dressed like that, he knew there was only one place she could be headed. 'You'll be off doing more meddling in our son's love life then?'

Renee straightened her hat and tucked escaping wisps of brown hair behind her ears. As she did so, James suddenly saw the girl he'd fallen in love with all those years ago. It was there in the way her fingers fluttered to her face. And he saw it again when her gaze fell as she arranged her hat. Everyone had said he was too old for her, and for a long time he'd believed them. Perhaps he *was* too old and set in his ways. But back then, the age difference hadn't mattered; Renee had been as much in love with James Watson as he was with her. Now, though, with Jim's aches and pains becoming more noticeable, and Renee's frustration with her life stuck in the grocer's shop, he wondered if they'd done the right thing after all.

He glanced at his wife again, saw the softness in her face and the light in her eyes, and his heart ached for the woman he'd married. But then Renee straightened her back and pulled her handbag close to her, and in that moment the warmth and magic of Jim's memories left him. When had she changed? he wondered. When had the girl he'd fallen in love with become the hardened woman in front of him now? He often wondered if he was to blame somehow, for dedicating his life to the little shop. Renee had always had her sights set higher, on a better life elsewhere.

'Meddling?' she barked. 'I'll have you know I'm working as hard as I can to secure William the best possible match for his future.'

'I just wish you'd leave the lad alone,' Jim replied. He remembered what Billy had confided to him about Pearl. And although Jim had promised his son that he'd speak to Renee about the subject, he'd not yet been able to pick the right moment. He'd be crushing her dreams and he knew he'd have to pick his words carefully. This needed some thinking through.

'And if I do that?' Renee continued, breaking into Jim's thoughts. 'If I don't find the right woman for him, what then? Is he to end up a grocer for the rest of his life?' She pointed at the chalkboard on the counter top. 'Updating all and sundry on rats?'

Jim knew from experience that if he let Renee say her piece, she'd eventually run out of steam. But she was far from finished yet. She leaned across the counter and poked him in the chest. 'Is our son to end up like *you*? Stuck there like a bottle of milk behind a counter in a back-street shop?'

Jim felt heat rise in his face. 'What's got into you, woman?' he asked. His voice was tinged with sadness.

Renee dropped her gaze. She knew she had gone too far. Jim waited for her to apologise, but

159

she said no more. Instead, she walked towards the door. She was intent on heading to the doctor's house, where she had invited herself to morning coffee with his wife and daughter. She reached out and pulled the door open. Jim cleared his throat.

'I'd like to remind you, Renee Watson, that the clothes on your back and that fancy hat on your head have been paid for by a grocer.'

Renee stiffened. She was holding so tight to the doorknob that her knuckles turned white.

'The food in your belly and the cotton sheets on your bed, all of it comes from being a grocer. That van outside? We're one of the few lucky enough to afford a vehicle in Ryhope. It all comes from the earnings my family have built up in this little shop. There's no shame in what I do and what I hope our son will take on after me. I'm proud of Watson's Grocers. This line of work was good enough for my parents and there's no reason on this earth why it'll not be good enough for our son.'

'It will never be good enough,' Renee whispered under her breath, and then she disappeared out into the street.

Left alone in the shop, Jim reached his hands to the counter and took a deep breath. He and Renee had been happy together once. But working in the grocer's shop had hardened her. He knew it wasn't what she'd wanted; it wasn't fancy enough for her with her big ideas. Many times she'd suggested selling up and moving out, but Jim had stood firm. He was a Watson, and Watsons were grocers. When they were first wed,

160

the little shop brought in enough money to keep them both fed and clothed. And when Renee fell pregnant with Billy, Jim had wanted nothing more than for his son and heir to take on the shop as soon as he was old enough. But Renee had other ideas, fancy ideas above her station. She wanted the world on a stick for her baby boy, not a poky little shop in a mucky pit village.

That was when the rot had set in. Jim was content with his lot, but Renee wanted to change their lives, *improve* them, she said. Jim adored his baby son and loved his wife. How could that be improved? It was a question he'd often asked. Renee would turn away from him to look out of their living room window, giving him no reply. But with that look, that turn of her head, she told him everything she wanted him to know. She wanted to move away from Ryhope, from the coalmining village she'd been brought up in. She wanted to move away from the people she knew, to make acquaintance instead with the likes of those who lived in the posh areas of Sunderland such as Roker or Ashbrooke. She wanted to be anywhere but Ryhope, and yet she was trapped because Jim would not budge. The shop was a Watson shop, as he often reminded Renee. It was Watson money, his money; he held the purse strings. And as long as he was in charge of the finances, he would not be selling up and moving on. Oh, he still loved Renee and thought the world of her, yet he longed for the softness he knew she kept hidden inside.

When Jim heard the clatter of footsteps coming down the stairs, he busied himself

161

arranging a pile of red and white onions into a striped display. He smiled when he saw Billy, ready for work with his apron tied around his waist.

'Has Mam left already?' Billy asked. 'Have you managed to speak to her yet about me taking Pearl out one day?'

Jim shook his head. 'Listen, son. I've been thinking.' He chose his words carefully. 'I don't think we should tell your mam anything. The less she knows, the better it'll be.'

'But she's still trying to fix me up with Sylvia. I don't want her to end up looking a fool in front of the doctor and his family.'

'No, lad. I won't let your mam be taken for a fool, not by anyone. But neither will I send you into a marriage you don't want. You and Pearl should seize your opportunity. Take some time out this Sunday afternoon with her, see how you get along. And if things work out between you, if there's a chance it might get serious, come back and we'll talk again. Leave your mam to me, and when the moment's right, when you know for sure in your heart about Pearl, then I'll say my piece.'

★ ★ ★

On Sunday, the Watsons headed to church as they did each week. Renee was all of a flutter, ensuring that Billy's tie was straight and his shirt was clean. Each time Sylvia's name was uttered, his heart sank.

From her spot in the kitchen where she was

162

cleaning the floor, Pearl watched as Billy slid his arms into his black jacket and Renee brushed imaginary dust from his shoulders.

'Aren't you rushing things a little with the Andersons, Mam?' he asked quietly. 'Sylvia and I hardly know each other and you're already talking about a wedding.'

'The lad's got a point,' Jim chipped in, relieved that his son had spoken up again.

'I need time to think, Mam,' Billy continued. He raised his eyes and glanced towards Pearl in the kitchen. It was a look that did not go unnoticed by Renee. 'I need to know if Sylvia is the right woman for me.'

Renee glared at Pearl before addressing her son. 'Of course she's the right woman for you. I won't hear another word about it.'

Billy took a step away from his mam as she fussed over him, and Renee's hands dropped to her sides. 'Mam, please,' he begged. 'I need to clear my head. I was thinking . . . I was hoping I might go for a walk to the beach, take some sea air after church. It'll give me time to think. It's all moving too fast.'

'Then you can take Sylvia with you,' Renee smiled. 'That's an excellent idea.'

'No, Mam,' Billy said firmly. 'I want to go on my own.'

This time Renee missed the look that passed between Billy and Pearl. Pearl felt her face grow hot and she busied herself with the mop and bucket. Jim's ears pricked up. He was proud of Billy for standing up to Renee. But he also knew that it would take a lot more work from both him

163

and Billy to get Renee to back down over the wedding plans.

After the church service ended, Billy bade a polite farewell to Dr Anderson and his wife. Sylvia waited expectantly for him to say a private word to her too. But she was confused when he headed away after giving just a brief nod and a polite goodbye.

'He's not feeling so good,' Renee said by way of explanation.

Sylvia watched as he disappeared out of sight. 'Will we see him this evening at the house, as planned?' she asked.

'You can count on it,' Renee said through gritted teeth.

★ ★ ★

When Billy reached the beach, Pearl was waiting, sitting on a large flat rock with her legs stretched in front of her. She waved when she saw him and Billy was surprised by how much his heart leapt at the sight. He ran along the sand and sat beside her on the rock.

The tide was out and the expanse of sand lay ahead. The heat of high summer had now gone and there was a coolness to the day. Clouds scudded above them and a brisk wind whipped Pearl's hair. She turned to Billy with a wide smile. 'I wasn't sure you'd come.'

'I wasn't sure you'd be here.'

'I wouldn't have missed it for the world,' she said, looking out to where the grey sea met the clouded sky. 'It's nice, just the two of us.'

164

Billy pointed towards the stack rocks along the beach. 'Shall we walk there and back? And we can talk, if you'd like.'

He offered his hand to help her from the rock, although Pearl could have stood perfectly easily on her own. She held on to it for a little longer than needed, delighting in the touch of his skin. They walked in silence at first, squashing stones underfoot into the damp sand.

'I want to apologise, Billy,' she said at last. 'For the way I reacted when you gave me the red feather.'

Billy listened in silence as Pearl confided to him about the meaning of the gift he'd bought in all innocence. She told him everything, all about Annie and Sid's Corner. She told him about being forced to work the pit lane. She told him about Joey and Kate Scotch, and about how she'd saved Boot from being shot at the farm. The words tumbled from her; she wanted no barriers. If they were to be friends, or maybe more, there could be no secrets between them.

'What I don't understand is why Annie gave you the red feather when she knew it was a gift for me,' Pearl said. 'She had other colours there; why the red one, I wonder?'

Billy turned towards her and placed his strong hands on her shoulders. A shiver ran down Pearl's spine at his touch.

'You mustn't blame your aunt. It was me who chose the red one,' he said. 'Annie tried to persuade me not to take it, and I didn't know why. She even offered me two white ones for the price of one red. But I thought the red was the

165

prettiest, I thought you'd like it the best. I convinced her to let me buy it. I had no other intention. I didn't know what it meant, Pearl. You must believe me.'

'I do believe you,' she said, gazing into his eyes.

Billy's kiss caressed Pearl's lips, softly, gently, not asking for anything in return. Pearl felt light-headed, and pushed her feet hard into the sand to steady her legs. This wasn't a kiss like she'd ever had before. She'd been kissed on the cheek by Annie and Dorothy. She'd been kissed on the lips by Joey once when they were younger, playing in Joey's back yard. But this was something else, something that sent shivers right through her. She reached for Billy's waist with both hands and pulled him towards her. Their lips pressed tight together for what seemed a long time. Finally Billy stepped back, but he held Pearl's gaze.

'You've been honest with me, Pearl. And I thank you for it.'

'You're not shocked? About Annie?'

He shook his head. 'Not shocked. No . . . I mean, I've heard that women do it, you know, to make money. But I've never met one before.'

'You've never met a woman?' Pearl teased.

'No, I mean a — '

'Don't say it,' Pearl said. 'Don't use the word. It's not what Annie is, it's not *who* she is. She just needs to make extra money now and then to pay her bills. That's all any of them do it for.'

'I guess we all have to make a living, whatever way we can.'

166

Pearl breathed a sigh of relief.

'Now I need to be honest with you,' he said.

'What about?'

'Sylvia Anderson.'

Pearl looked down at the sand. 'You're going to marry her, aren't you?' she asked, dreading the reply. Would this be her only moment of happiness with Billy, one short walk on the beach? One short and yet wonderful kiss?

'I can't marry her,' he said quietly. 'Not when I have feelings for someone else.'

Pearl's heart skipped a beat. Was it too much to dare to hope? 'Who, Billy?' she whispered.

Her question was answered by the sweet taste of Billy's lips again. This time Pearl pressed hard against his body. She wanted more and longed for the touch of his skin. Billy took her hand and they walked further along the beach. They left the stack rocks behind and headed to a cave in the cliffs. Nothing needed to be said between them; they both knew what they wanted. It was cold in the cave, but quiet away from the wind. They were hidden, out of sight of anyone walking past. Billy pulled Pearl gently to the damp sand, and she fell to his side. She was happy, relieved to finally give in to the feelings she'd had for him since the day they'd first met. Soon they were wrapped around each other's bodies, lost in their own world. Outside the cave, seagulls flew overhead and the sea gently rolled to the shore.

★　★　★

In the rooms above Watson's shop, after dinner had been eaten, Renee took out her darning and Jim settled on the sofa reading the previous day's *Sunderland Echo*.

'House seems quiet without William, doesn't it?' Renee said. 'Wonder what's so special that he took off after church without a word to poor Sylvia?'

Jim rustled his newspaper and laid it on his lap. 'Leave the lad alone, love,' he said. 'I've told you before, he's a grown man. He's got to have his own life. If he wants to go out for the afternoon . . . '

'With *her*?' Renee asked without looking up from her needlework.

'It's none of our business who he's with,' Jim replied. He lifted his newspaper, putting an end, he hoped, to any more questions from his wife.

Renee had by now been told by Jim that Billy and Pearl were friendly, although she had her suspicions that there was more to their friendship than Jim was letting on. She was right. They were much more than friends. Over the coming weeks, they spent as much time together as they could. They worked happily at the shop counter, smiling and chatting. And when there was a quiet moment in the shop, with no danger of Renee or Jim walking in, they exchanged gentle kisses. They shared an hour each Sunday afternoon and spent it walking on the beach.

Their feelings for each other grew, and Pearl was happier than ever. Billy was happy too, or so he told her. But she noticed a sadness about him; something about their relationship troubled

168

him. It was his mam, he finally told her one quiet afternoon in the shop. Renee was still forging ahead, making plans for an engagement party for Billy and Sylvia. He had repeatedly told her that he had no feelings for the girl and had begged her to call it all off. But still she ploughed on, convinced that she knew what was best. Jim had kept quiet, reluctant to invoke Renee's sharp tongue and dark moods.

At first Pearl took Billy's feelings to heart and was considerate of them. She told him she understood; that things would find a way of working out. Besides which, she didn't want to push Billy into telling his mam the truth before there was something for her to know. She was only too aware that if Renee were to discover how close the two of them were, she'd be furious. She didn't want to do anything to rock the boat and lose not only Billy, but her job and home too, so she kept her thoughts to herself.

For a few weeks she suffered the torture of Billy meeting Sylvia one evening a week, and again at Sunday church. Each time he visited the Anderson house he was chaperoned by Renee. And each time he left Pearl, he told her again it was her that he loved. Only her. But Annie's words rang in Pearl's head, the phrase she often used in Bernie's shop. *Actions speak louder than words*. Surely if Billy meant what he said, then he'd speak to his mam and put an end to talk of engagements and weddings. And there was Sylvia herself; it wasn't fair on her. How would she feel when the truth came out, as it surely would in time?

169

After a sleepless night, Pearl finally decided to tackle Billy. She chose her moment carefully. Billy was driving the van to the market early one September morning, and Pearl was beside him in the passenger seat. This was the perfect opportunity to share the words she had rehearsed many times in her head. But as the van rattled and bounced its way along Ryhope Road to Sunderland, Pearl began to feel queasy. She cracked open the tiny window and a blast of cold air rushed in. Billy shot her a look before returning his concentration to the road.

'That breeze feels a bit nippy,' he said, but Pearl didn't close the window. She breathed deeply, gulping down fresh air, trying to quell the rising nausea. She felt her face flame hot and closed her eyes, swallowing hard. Billy kept driving, unaware that anything was wrong, and slowly she began to feel better. As she snapped the window shut, a wave of tiredness came over her, and the beginnings of a headache. She hadn't eaten breakfast, had declined Jim's offer of stewed apples. Perhaps that was what was causing the nausea. But the thought of eating brought the sick feeling on again.

As soon as they reached the market and Billy pulled the van to a stop, Pearl leapt out. She breathed deeply, over and over, taking in the morning air. But it did little to help. The market sat by the River Wear on the edge of Sunderland's shipbuilding yards, and the stench from the murky depths was strong. Pearl covered her nose and breathed through her fingers. Billy was already walking ahead, intent on carrying out the business of the day. Normally Pearl would be with him, striding alongside, calling out to the traders, wishing them good morning. But today she walked slowly behind, taking shallow breaths, trying to quell the sickness. She knew she still needed to speak to Billy about his mam, but not today, not when she was feeling like this. She would bide her time until another, brighter day.

★ ★ ★

While Pearl and Billy were at the market, Jim opened up the shop. He took a small rag and rubbed at the chalkboard on the counter top. Then he chalked up the new tally: *This shop rat free 63 days.*

The board remained a bone of contention between him and Renee. Renee had thrown it out to the bin they kept in the yard, but Jim had returned it indoors. He was intent on asserting himself, and although it was just a small victory, the chalkboard with its tally filled him with pride.

He picked up a couple of pears and went through to the yard. Boot walked up to him, rubbing his head along Jim's outstretched hand. Renee disapproved of him feeding the dog. She complained that he might as well throw fruit into the street. But Jim knew how much Boot enjoyed the sweet crunch of apples and pears, and felt the animal deserved a treat. Still, he was careful not to let Renee catch him. If she did, she'd only complain, and Jim had enough on his mind without risking the wrath of his wife.

He was worried about Billy. He'd seen the way he was becoming more friendly with Pearl. He'd even walked in on them kissing behind the counter one day, and had caught them holding hands when they thought no one was looking. And yet Renee was still intent on visiting the Andersons and pushing ahead with a wedding Billy didn't want. Jim had tried many times to sit down with Renee and talk to her about it, to beg her to stop her plans. But each time he'd only got as far as gentle remarks, a hint that what she was doing was wrong. And each time, Renee brushed his words off as if she was brushing dust off her coat. She was determined to match the Watsons with the Andersons.

Yet in all her meetings and chats with the doctor's wife and Sylvia, not once did Renee invite the Andersons to her own home. She visited the doctor's house often, but she was determined that they should never have even a glimpse of her life at Watson's Grocers. In comparison to the doctor's house, with its over-stuffed furniture and even a maid, the rooms above the shop looked like squalor of the worst kind — but only to Renee's eyes. To Jim it was his little palace, the home he'd worked hard to keep every day of his life.

Jim was lost in his thoughts when he heard a sound outside. It was Billy and Pearl arriving back from the market. He smiled when he saw them both, but then he noticed that Pearl looked pale. He remembered that she'd not taken breakfast earlier.

172

'You all right, dear?' he asked.

Pearl nodded and busied herself bringing turnips from the van. Jim decided not to ask any more questions, and went to help.

★ ★ ★

The day passed as most days did at Watson's Grocers. Pearl and Billy worked behind the counter as Jim pottered about, as was his way now. Since Pearl had started working there, he had allowed himself the luxury of cutting down his hours in the shop. Instead he worked on the easy jobs in the yard, tidying boxes, or simply arranging items on shelves. His eyes weren't what they once were and he found it increasingly difficult to see. His knees weren't good either. He'd always had problems with them, after an illness in childhood that had left him with aches and pains.

He liked how Billy and Pearl worked together, industrious and happy. Pearl was always welcoming to the customers, always with a ready smile, and he thanked his lucky stars that he had taken her on. But that day, he noticed that she was withdrawn and quiet, and not as cheery as usual. Later, she took him to one side to ask if she could be excused.

'I just need some fresh air,' she explained.

Jim patted her hand. He knew she must feel really poorly to ask for a break as it was an unusual request from the girl. 'Take as much time as you need,' he replied. 'You're looking a little done in.'

Pearl headed to her room to collect her jacket, then headed out through the yard rather than through the shop, where Billy and Jim were serving customers. When Boot saw her, he trotted to her side, ready to follow her to the road. She turned and put her hand in front of the dog's face.

'Stay!' she commanded, and he slunk away to his corner of the yard.

Pearl was still feeling queasy; she hadn't felt right all day. She hadn't eaten anything either, for just the thought of food made her stomach turn over. What had really shocked her, though, was what she had seen on the chalkboard on the counter just now. Seeing the number of days had made her think of what should have happened to her body in the weeks that had passed.

She headed towards the village green, intent on walking to the beach. She needed to be alone, to make sense of the thoughts running wild in her head. As she walked past St Paul's church, she counted the days since the first time she'd lain with Billy in the cave. The dates didn't add up; it didn't make sense. Her body should have been doing what it had done monthly since she'd turned thirteen. And yet there'd been nothing; just the sickness that morning and an awful queasy taste in her mouth.

Ahead of her she saw a familiar figure walking on the other side of the green. Her heart rose at the sight of the dumpy woman with curly brown hair, and she walked quickly, trying to catch up.

'Dorothy!' she called when at last she was close enough for the woman to hear.

174

Dorothy swung round and her face lit up when she saw Pearl. She opened her arms and Pearl fell into them, grateful for the warmth of the hug. Dorothy finally let her go and looked her up and down.

'How are you doing, pet?' she asked, and then, without waiting for an answer: 'You're looking a bit peaky if you ask me.'

Pearl's hand flew to her face. 'Am I?'

Dorothy eyed her keenly. 'You feeling all right?'

Pearl hesitated. She needed to tell someone. She needed to know what was going on inside her; she needed confirmation of what she dreaded might be true. She'd lived with Annie long enough to hear gossip about women who got themselves into trouble. But she never would have believed, not for one minute, that one of those women would be her.

'Come on, pet,' Dorothy said. She hooked her arm through Pearl's and set off walking again, more slowly this time, towards the Albion Inn.

Hetty Burdon was behind the bar, working a glass cloth around a jug. Her auburn hair was piled high on her head and there was a red pencil tucked behind her right ear.

'We're not open yet, Dot,' she called.

'I know,' Dorothy said. 'But the lass isn't well. Any chance we could just sit for a while until she pulls herself together?'

Hetty nodded towards a table in the corner of the room. She was sure she'd seen the young girl before. It took her a few moments to remember that the lass had come in asking for work some time ago. With a sigh, she shook her head and

175

returned to her glass work. It wasn't her business, but if the girl was being looked after by Dorothy Marshall, it seemed she might have found work, and not the sort Hetty approved of. But then who was she to judge? She knew that if she ever found herself in a position where she was desperate for work and she only had one way to make cash, she'd do exactly what Dorothy Marshall did on the pit lane rather than starve.

As Dorothy and Pearl took their seats, a short woman with dark hair bustled into view. In one hand she carried a tin bucket sloshing with water and in the other she held a wet cloth. A dirty feather duster poked from her apron pocket.

'How am I supposed to clean in here with you two sitting there?' she huffed when she saw the women.

'Lil!' Hetty called. 'Just work around them; they'll not be long. Finish that room and you can go. We're all done now.'

Lil shot a look at Dorothy and Pearl and sniffed loudly to let them know they were in her way. She took pride in her work and didn't like interruptions to her cleaning routine.

Hetty brought a glass of water and placed it on the table in front of Pearl. 'I can only give you ten minutes, Dot. If Jack comes down and finds I've let people in before we're open, he'll not be happy.'

'Thanks, Hetty,' Dorothy said. 'We'll be gone soon, I promise.'

Lil carried on cleaning. As she worked, she tried to pretend she wasn't interested in listening to what Dorothy and Pearl were whispering

176

about. But she knew of Dorothy's reputation working the pit lane. And she knew who Pearl was too; she'd seen her in Watson's, and had also spotted her walking past the pub on her way to the beach with the grocer's son.

Her curiosity and well-trained ear for listening in on other people's business got the better of her, and with each swipe of her feather duster she inched closer to the two women. Finally, she began to hear fragments of conversation. The word *pregnant* was whispered, the word *baby* said in a hushed tone. And when Lil finally heard whose baby it was, she allowed herself a secret smile. Oh, this was gossip and a half, she thought with a delicious shiver. In fact, it was the best bit of gossip she'd heard in a long time. She couldn't wait to get home to tell her husband Bob all about it. But the more Lil thought about it, the more she realised that there was someone else she would deliver the news to first.

177

9

Gossip

The two women left the Albion Inn arm in arm.

'You need to eat, pet,' Dorothy said. 'We'll walk to the Railway Inn. I've heard they've got a girl in there, Sadie, who's baking pies for the pub to sell.'

'I don't want to keep you,' Pearl said. 'You've been too kind already.'

'I'll hear no more about it,' Dorothy said firmly. 'I'm not leaving until I know you're not going to pass out or throw up. I was only calling to see an old friend who lives behind the railway station, I wasn't doing anything important.'

'What'll you tell Annie when you get home?' Pearl asked. She was afraid of what her aunt would have to say.

Dorothy turned towards her. 'Oh lass. Me and Annie have been best friends since we were girls. Annie, me and your mam, we were like the three wise monkeys. We were always together. They used to call me the third Grafton girl. What I'm saying, love, is that I'd find it hard to keep this a secret from Annie. You know that, don't you?'

Pearl nodded and felt tears spring behind her eyes. Dorothy softened when she saw her look of distress.

'Don't worry, love. This is *your* secret,' she

said. 'I'll keep quiet about it, but you know what Ryhope's like. Gossip spreads quick here, and if you don't tell Annie and someone sees you with a bairn in your belly . . . '

'Will she be disappointed in me, Dorothy?'

Dorothy pulled Pearl to her. 'No, lass. No one could ever be disappointed in a lovely girl like you. Now come on, let's get something warm inside you. We'll talk more once we're in the pub.'

At the Railway Inn, Pearl and Dorothy shared a plate of beef pie and sliced potatoes. The landlady, Molly Teasdale, knew only too well the sort of woman Dorothy Marshall was, and she didn't want her beloved pub turned into a knocking shop. And so, as the pair huddled together whispering in a corner, Molly kept a watchful eye on them both.

★ ★ ★

Later, up at Watson's Grocers, Renee was furious to find Pearl was away from the shop.

'What do you mean, she's gone for a walk?' she demanded. 'We're paying that lass to work for us, not wander the streets. You already give her too much time off. She's been taking liberties with her Sunday afternoons too, gadding about heaven knows where.'

'Sunday afternoons are the only time the lass has to herself,' Jim said. 'And today she wasn't feeling well. I said she could go and get some fresh air and come back when she felt better.'

'You'll be docking her wages, I trust.'

179

'Come on, love, have a heart,' Jim said, although he knew Renee's heart had been well and truly buried for years. He glanced at his wife, who was bristling with fury, and decided to say nothing more.

'I thought the point of taking her on was so that you could ease up down here,' Renee reminded her husband. 'You're not getting any younger, you know. Besides which, there's a mountain of little jobs you promised to do upstairs. None of them are getting done if you're down here working . . . ' She raised her eyebrows at her husband. 'Are they?'

'Look, love — ' Jim started to say, but his words were cut short when a small, thin woman bustled into the shop. She wore a dark green coat with a black scarf tucked tidily into the collar, and an old green hat that sat askew on her head.

'Afternoon, Lil!' Jim called out cheerily. Renee pressed her lips into a forced smile. She wasn't keen on Lil Mahone. As far as she was concerned, Lil was the worst kind of gossip Ryhope had.

'What can I get for you today?' Jim smiled. 'And how's your Bob doing? We've got some smashing leeks in if you fancy making him a leek pudding for tea tonight. They're not as big as the ones the lads grow up at the allotments, but they're strong-flavoured.'

'Oh, I've got every faith that your leeks are as good as you say. But it's not you I've come to see, Mr Watson,' Lil said, nodding towards Renee. 'It's her.'

180

Renee's hand flew to her chest. 'Me? What on earth . . . I mean, how can I help you, Mrs Mahone?'

Lil glanced from Renee to Jim and back again. 'I need a word with you, Mrs Watson. In private.'

'I'll be out the back,' Jim said. Whatever it was that women got to chatting about when they were together was no concern of his. He wanted no part of it, wasn't even the slightest bit curious. Still, he couldn't help thinking it just a tiny bit odd that someone like Lil Mahone would want to speak to Renee. He couldn't for the life of him imagine what they might have in common. He went out to the yard to help Billy, who was supposed to be tidying and cleaning. But when he got there, he found his son playing with Boot. Billy was rolling an apple and the daft dog was running after it, retrieving it for Billy to roll again.

Inside the shop, Lil stood with her arms crossed. A small black handbag hung from her wrist. She nodded towards the shop door. 'You might want to lock that. I don't think you'll want anyone walking in and hearing what I've got to say.'

There was something about her tone of voice that made Renee do as Lil requested. She slid the bolt, pulled the blind and turned the sign to *Closed*. Then she walked back behind the counter, putting as much distance as she could between herself and Lil Mahone.

'Young Pearl not here today?' Lil said. A wicked smile slid across her lips and it didn't go unnoticed. Renee placed her hands on the

181

counter top and leaned towards the other woman.

'Out with it,' she said.

Lil looked around the shop and her eyes fell on the leeks Jim had mentioned. They did indeed look good. She wondered what else she might take with her after she'd said her piece. She let her gaze fall on a basket of onions, then raised her head and locked eyes with Renee. The two women stared hard at each other for what seemed like a lifetime.

'I hear she's expecting a baby,' Lil said.

It took a few moments for the words to make sense to Renee. She tried to form a reply, her mouth working, her mind bursting with questions. She gripped the counter and forced her feet hard against the floor. Lil's gaze didn't waver. She watched as the news sank in and waited for Renee to speak.

'What else do you know?' Renee managed at last. Her voice came in a whisper as she forced the words out. She felt a heat in her face and her heart began to pound. She dreaded what Lil was going to tell her, for why else would the woman be there other than to drip poison of the worst kind in her ear? She swallowed hard.

Renee straightened her back and pushed a wisp of hair behind her ear.

'Spit it out, woman,' Renee barked.

Lil stood firm. 'I hear . . . well, I hear the baby will be your grandchild.'

Renee gasped. She wanted to lash out, to stop any more lies coming from the woman's lips. How dare Lil come in here and slander her son?

How dare she? She reached for a tin on the counter. In her anger, she was ready to throw it, to hurt Lil, to make sure she couldn't spread any more evil lies. But she knew, oh she knew only too well, that Lil's words had every chance of being true. She'd seen the way Billy and Pearl were with each other, always chatting and smiling. She'd tried to deny what she had witnessed with her own eyes because it was a truth she didn't want to acknowledge. She'd done her best to ignore Jim's words when he'd tried to raise the subject. But there could be no denying this, the gossip that had been brought into her shop.

'Where did you hear this?' she hissed.

'I'd rather not reveal my sources, Mrs Watson,' Lil smirked.

Renee swallowed hard as the bile rose in her throat. 'If — and I repeat, *if* — this is true, did your source tell you whether my son knows of this news?'

Lil thought back to Dorothy and Pearl whispering in the Albion Inn. 'I couldn't say for sure, but I'd lay a bet that he's ignorant of the truth.' She stared hard at Renee before delivering her killer stroke. 'That is, he's ignorant so far. But you know how fast gossip travels in Ryhope. I'm sure you wouldn't want him becoming appraised of the news, would you?'

'What do you want, Lil?' Renee hissed. 'Money? Is that it?'

'You're a clever woman, Mrs Watson,' Lil said calmly. 'I knew I was right to come to you first.'

'So you've told no one else?'

'Not yet. And I'd be happy to keep the secret

for you, but you're right, there is something I want in exchange.' Lil pointed at the basket of eggs on the counter. 'I'll take half a dozen brown, half a dozen white, and I'll have some of those leeks your husband mentioned and a bag of onions too.'

Renee glared at her. 'You're making a shopping list? Are you mad, woman?'

'Oh, I think you'll find I'm anything but, Mrs Watson,' Lil replied. 'But I am as poor as a church mouse. Those of us who live on the pit lanes don't have much, and we'll take anything for nothing where we can. You should know, Renee Kearney as was. You were one of us once, not so long ago.'

She took a step towards the counter and saw tears in Renee's eyes. But she knew she couldn't back down now, not when she was so close to getting what she needed. She'd known the gossip she'd overheard in the Albion Inn had currency. It had taken her the short walk to Watson's shop to work out how she could spend it best.

'And so I'll take what I can here. Once a week I'll call in and do my weekly grocery shopping. I'll not embarrass you in front of your husband or your son, Mrs Watson. I'll only come in when I see you behind the counter. You give me my fruit and veg for free, or I'll tell my friend Em about your Billy and Pearl having a baby. And Em's a terrible gossip. Once I tell her, I can't be held responsible for what might happen with the news.' She took another step. 'The whole of Ryhope will know. And here's me thinking Billy was courting the doctor's daughter. Am I right?

184

Yet he managed to get Pearl Edwards pregnant. You do know her aunt brought her up, don't you?'

'What's that got to do with anything?'

A wicked smile lit up Lil's face. 'You don't know, do you? Annie Grafton is a common tart. Ask anyone up the pit lane.'

Renee put her hands over her ears. The blunt words were too much to bear. Her mind spun with thoughts of the doctor's wife and what she would say if she found out about any of this — about Pearl, the baby, Annie. She'd lose the Andersons' patronage, she'd lose Sylvia, she'd lose her passport away from Watson's. In her panic, her heart screamed and her breath came out of her thick and fast.

'Get out!' she hissed. She wanted to scream, to let rip with her anger, but one glance at the door to the yard reminded her that her husband and son were out there, and she didn't want either of them to know what had been said.

Lil stood firm. 'Not without taking my groceries.'

Renee took a deep breath, then walked from behind the counter. She gathered an armful of leeks and onions and threw them into a bag. She picked up an egg.

'Six white, six brown, remember,' Lil said, eyeing the basket.

Renee placed the eggs into the bag and thrust it towards Lil. Then she stormed to the shop door, slid the bolt and pulled the door wide. Lil walked towards it, but before she could leave the shop, Renee put her arm across the doorway to block her exit.

'You breathe a word of any of this, just one word, and you'll regret it.'

Lil swallowed hard. 'Nice doing business with you,' she said before ducking under Renee's arm and out into the street.

As she walked up the colliery, leaving Watson's Grocers behind, Lil felt her legs shaking. She'd had to hold her nerve there and it hadn't been easy. But she'd been surprised at how quickly Mrs Watson had given in to her demands. She'd been expecting a fight. News of who'd got who pregnant in Ryhope was bread and butter to Lil. She received and passed on gossip like this all the time. But this was special, it was worth something. And she was spot on in her thinking that it was news the grocer's wife wouldn't want making public. The further she walked, the more the relief spread through Lil Mahone's skinny body. For the first time in a long time, she and Bob would eat well tonight, maybe even a leek pudding for tea.

Back at the shop, Jim was shocked by the state of his wife. Had she been crying?

'I'm going upstairs for a lie-down,' she told him. 'I'm not feeling so good.'

Without waiting for a response, she took herself to bed, where she lay on top of the eiderdown with much on her mind. Downstairs, Billy and Jim went back to work.

'Have you had a word with her yet, Dad?' Billy asked. 'I mean, about me and Pearl?'

Jim shook his head. 'Not yet, son, but I will. Just give me time, lad. Give me time.'

★　★　★

Later, in the rooms above Watson's, Jim paced the living room floor.

'Renee, there's something you need to know,' he muttered. He walked from the bay window to the wall and back again. 'Now, you're not going to like what you're about to hear, and I suggest you sit down and brace yourself.'

He shook his head. No, that wasn't right. He gave it another try.

'Renee, love. I know you've been worrying about William and his future. And so have I. We both want the best for him, but I can't have you meddling in things that don't concern you.'

He sank into the armchair in front of the window and banged his fist against a cushion.

'God damn it!' he cried. He'd worked himself up into a state rehearsing what he was planning to say. But no matter how he tried to phrase it, the words wouldn't come out right.

At that moment, Renee walked into the room. She looked better now, Jim thought, less red in the face, more calm than she'd seemed earlier in the shop.

'Did I hear you taking the Lord's name in vain there, James Watson?'

Jim gazed out of the window, over the rooftops and chimney pots of the lime-washed cottages squashed into rows. He didn't want to hurt Renee; that was the last thing he wanted. But he had to put his foot down. He couldn't bear to see her steamroll their son into a marriage he didn't want.

187

'Renee . . . ' he began. 'Sit down a minute, would you?'

Renee shot him a look. 'Are you feeling all right?'

'Just sit down, please. I've got something I want to talk to you about.'

'If it's about that chalkboard downstairs, I've already told you my feelings on it, James. It doesn't seem right to let people know we ever had a rat problem.'

'Renee, will you sit?' Jim said, louder this time.

Renee took a seat at the end of the sofa and turned her attention to her husband. 'Come on then, out with it,' she said.

Jim cleared his throat and began. And once he'd started, he knew there was no point in leaving any detail unsaid.

Renee's face dropped and her mouth opened in shock as her husband's words sank in. Twice in one day she'd been dealt the same blow, confirmation of the fears she'd harboured for weeks.

'You've got to let the lad live his life as he wants to, love,' Jim said finally. 'Things might not work out with him and Pearl, but we have to give them a chance. We can't force him into marrying someone he doesn't even know, not when he has feelings for someone else. And even if it isn't Pearl he ends up with, if it *is* Sylvia, then it has to be his own choice, Renee, you must see that, surely?'

Jim had expected fireworks, a furious explosion of shouting and crying. But instead Renee listened in silence, the wind knocked out of her sails for the second time that day. Finally, she rose from the sofa, walked towards the armchair where Jim sat and stood in front of him with her hands on her hips.

'You've said your piece, James. And I've listened. But with every last breath in me, I will not be swayed from my plans to better the life of my son.'

'*Our* son,' Jim chipped in. 'Renee, I beg you, love. Think of Billy's happiness. Are you really going to push him into a marriage he doesn't want? To live a life where he'll suffocate under airs and graces he doesn't understand?'

'You'd rather he marry that scruff of a lass from the colliery?' Renee hissed. She thought about Lil Mahone and the poison of her words that had been brought to her door. And now there was this news from Jim . . . It was too much to bear and she stormed from the living room.

Jim heard their bedroom door slam shut. He'd give her a few moments, as he always did when she got this way. She would cry, rid herself of the worst of the anger. Only then would he allow himself to enter their bedroom and hold her in his arms to calm her. He couldn't allow her to marry their son off to a lass Billy wasn't keen on. Especially when there was someone he liked instead. Oh, he knew Pearl wasn't to Renee's taste — she thought her common and nowhere near good enough for her son. But Jim liked the girl, and if Billy was keen on her, then that was all right by him.

He walked to the small kitchen and pulled a bottle of Scotch from the back of a cupboard. He

189

poured himself a tot, downed it in one and then headed across the landing to his wife.

★ ★ ★

After the shop closed for the day, Billy and Pearl sat at the table with Jim. Renee was nowhere to be seen. Jim explained her absence to Pearl and Billy by way of a little white lie.

'She's not feeling well,' he said, glancing at Billy. Nothing more was said, not while Pearl was at the table. Jim thought it best not to burden the girl while there was still a chance that he might be able to talk Renee into seeing sense.

As they ate slices of jellied pork pie and drank mugs of tea, Billy and Pearl smiled shyly at each other. Pearl was feeling brighter now, hungry too. She knew she'd have to break her news to Billy, but when? When Billy thought his dad wasn't looking, he reached under the tablecloth and brushed Pearl's knee. Her heart leapt at his touch and she held tight to his hand.

After the meal, Pearl cleaned the dishes in the kitchen before disappearing to her room to work on her clippy mat. Downstairs, Billy and his dad sat together in the quiet of the living room. The only sound came from the clock on the mantelpiece.

'If Mam's poorly, does it mean I won't have to visit Dr Anderson's tonight?' Billy asked hopefully. But Jim shook his head.

'No, lad, your mam wants you to go without her. It's all been arranged; you can't let them down.'

'But Dad — '

'No, Billy. They'll be expecting you.' Jim took off his glasses and wiped the lenses on his cotton shirt. 'I suggest you go, and if you can, start cooling things with Sylvia, if that's really what you want to do.'

He replied without hesitation. 'It is, Dad.'

'Then do it as politely as you can,' Jim instructed. 'Be a man about it. Be respectful to Sylvia and to her mam and dad. Tell them you're not ready for marriage. Tell Sylvia you've given it a lot of consideration, that you've thought of little else. Tell them you've got your apprentice-ship to serve in the grocery before you can think about getting engaged.'

'Thanks, Dad,' Billy said. 'I will.'

★ ★ ★

When Billy left to walk to the Andersons' house, Pearl was still in her room, sitting on the floor beneath the window, working on her mat under the glow of an oil lamp. She pushed the progger through the hessian and wondered if Annie might be able to sell the mat in the shop the same way she'd sold the last. She pulled the progger out and wondered where her mat that had been sold had gone. Whose bare feet was it protecting from a cold floor? She thought about Billy, about their afternoons at the beach when they had given themselves to each other. A delicious shiver ran up her spine at the thought of Billy's broad shoulders, his muscled arms and the gentleness of his touch.

Her fingers worked quickly, pulling the brightly coloured scraps from her bag and threading them into the hessian. The whole effect was pleasing, creative, a mesh of brown and blue. The work calmed her mind and brought focus to the reality of her situation. She was pregnant with Billy's child. Pregnant. The word hung heavy in her heart; she wasn't sure how to feel, or what words she would need to tell Billy. She still hadn't spoken to him about Sylvia; the opportunity to tackle him on the subject had passed her by after the morning sickness caught her unawares. And now this, a baby! Oh heavens, what a mess it all was. She would need to pick her moment carefully to tell him everything that was on her mind. Maybe they could talk the next time they visited the beach. What would happen then, she didn't know. But if he felt the same way about her as she felt about him . . . He'd told her so already, hadn't he? They'd talked of their hopes for the future, of Billy wanting to run the shop. Of Pearl wanting to work at his side. He had even offered to teach her to drive the van. There was so much to look forward to. Who was to stop them being together and in love? But still she felt sick with anxiety at the thought of revealing her news.

As she worked, she heard a door slam on the floor below. She paused with her progger mid-air. She heard footsteps coming up the stairs to her room. Her heart jumped, stiffened when she heard the clipped sounds of a woman's boot on the bare treads. There was only one person it could be.

Renee burst into the room without knocking. 'Get out,' she hissed.

Pearl pulled her clippy mat towards her as if to protect herself. Renee bent to the floor, where Pearl's clothes lay in a neat pile. She picked them up and threw them at Pearl.

'Get out, now. Or I'll do something I'll regret.'

Pearl scrambled to her feet. She was scared, confused, her heart racing. Had Renee somehow discovered the life that Annie led? Had she found out that Pearl had been forced to work at Sid's Corner? Was that why she was telling her to leave? She couldn't have found out about the baby; it was impossible, only Dorothy knew.

'But why?' Pearl asked.

'You know why,' Renee spat. 'Think you can come into my home, get your feet under my table and steal my son away?'

'No, Mrs Watson. No!' Pearl cried.

Renee's face was flushed and she glared at Pearl with her eyes full of hatred. 'You've chosen the wrong family to mess with. You're not getting my son. Now get out and take your belongings with you.'

As scared as she was, Pearl stood her ground, determined not to give in without a fight. 'You can't throw me out!' she cried.

'I can do what the hell I want, girl.'

'What does Mr Watson have to say about this?' Pearl demanded. Her words came out more assertively than she felt. 'And what does Billy have to say?'

An evil smile played around Renee's lips. 'William is with the Andersons this evening,

193

where he should be.'

Pearl's heart dropped. She needed to speak to Billy; she had to tell him her news. Had she left things too late? Might she really lose him to Sylvia after all? She struggled to comprehend what was going on, what Renee was doing in her room. Where was Mr Watson? She shook her head. No . . . no, this couldn't be happening. It was a bad dream she would wake from. But Renee's words continued to bite.

'And my husband has taken a stroll, not that it is any concern of yours. You might have fooled him, but you won't fool me. I want you gone before they get back. Now gather your stuff and go!'

Renee stood tapping her foot angrily against the bare floorboards. She glared at Pearl with a hatred she had never felt before. This young girl, coming into her home, disrupting everything. Well, she wasn't going to have it. She'd worked damned hard on getting herself invited to Mrs Anderson's coffee mornings and charity events. She'd always kept her eye on the prize, knowing that the doctor's daughter was the perfect age for Billy. And now that prize was well within her grasp, she wasn't prepared to let anyone spoil things, certainly not a girl from the pit lane. She would not let her son become stuck in the claustrophobic world of the grocer's shop in the same way that she had.

'I've nowhere to go,' Pearl said, hoping for a tiny bit of kindness from Renee. But she was to be disappointed, for Renee was not changing her mind.

'You were homeless when you moved in here,' she said without emotion. 'You've lived on the streets once; you can do it again. Now hurry up, girl.'

Pearl bundled her clothes together in a cotton bag, together with her clippy mat scraps, and tucked the frame under her arm. She then followed Renee down the stairs, biting back the tears that threatened to fall. Whatever happened, she was determined not to show how much she was hurting. For she knew that if she showed weakness, Renee would think it a fight she had won.

At the bottom of the stairs, Renee held the back door to the yard open and nodded her head towards Pearl.

'Out,' she said, dismissing her as if she were a dog.

Once Pearl was in the yard, the back door banged shut and she heard the bolt slide across. She was locked out, with nowhere to live and no money for food. She swallowed hard, desperate not to cry. She caught sight of Boot lying asleep behind a pile of wooden boxes.

'Boot! Come!' she called, and at the sound of her voice, the dog's eyes opened wide. He leapt to his feet and trotted alongside her as she left Watson's Grocers behind.

Her first thought was to run back to Annie, but it was evening and there was every chance that Annie would be working to pay off Bobby Mac's loan. Besides, Pearl felt embarrassed at being thrown out of her job and her home. How would she explain it to Annie? And now, with a

195

baby on the way, she'd be returning with news that Annie wouldn't want to hear. Her aunt would see the child as just another mouth to feed, and one she could ill afford. No, she couldn't return there, but if not there, where *could* she go? She thought of St Paul's church, where the doors would be unlocked until midnight. She was reluctant to return — she didn't want to take the vicar's kindness for granted — but it would be safe there, she knew. Or perhaps she'd head to the beach, to the shelter of a cave, the same cave where she and Billy had spent time together on Sunday afternoons. But what if the tide was in and the waves were crashing at the cliffs?

Her mind whirled with anxiety. She was so lost in her thoughts as she headed to the green that she never noticed a movement in the shadows behind her.

★ ★ ★

A man was following Pearl, walking on the other side of the road. If anyone had seen him, they would have thought him a gentleman out for a stroll. They might have guessed him to be on his way to the cinema to meet a lady friend. Or heading to the Albion Inn, where he would take a glass of ale before retiring for the night. No one could have known his true intent. Boot never sniffed him out either, as the man was too far away for the dog to detect his scent.

The man kept a safe distance behind Pearl. He saw that she was carrying something large, a cumbersome item she had to keep lifting up under her arm. In her other hand she carried a blue cotton bag, and he wondered what it contained. He kept his eye on the dog at her side, aware that if he got too close to the girl, the animal might growl and cause a fuss, intent on protecting its owner.

He watched as Pearl walked to the village green and sat against the stone trough in the cold evening air. He hung back at the entrance to the cattle market, unseen, in the dark of a doorway. After a while, he walked to the Albion Inn, where he took a pint of Vaux stout from Hetty Burdon. It was the man's hat Hetty noticed first, for it wasn't the usual flat cap that the men of Ryhope wore. It was a black bowler, clean too. The man removed his hat and jacket, then positioned himself in a seat by the window. From his vantage point, he kept a watchful eye on Pearl.

★ ★ ★

Pearl settled as comfortably as she could with her back against the trough, and Boot laid his head in her lap. She stroked his ears to calm her mind as a million thoughts whirled around it. She thought of walking to the doctor's house, demanding to see Billy. She would have it out with him, ask him to choose between her and Sylvia, to put her out of this misery she felt herself in. She had to know one way or another. But then she thought better of it. As Renee had said, Billy had gone willingly to meet Sylvia. It

197

seemed as if his choice had been made. Annie had always said that actions spoke louder than words. But hadn't Billy told her during their afternoons at the beach that his heart was with her, not Sylvia? It was too hurtful to think that he had lied, but she didn't know what else to think. She had no one to talk to about any of the whole tangled mess and her thoughts ran confused in her mind.

She sat in the quiet of the night, thinking of Billy and Jim and Renee. She thought of Joey, who she missed more than anyone. But even if Joey was here now, she knew she wouldn't be able to tell him what had happened. He wouldn't understand, he was still too young for such things.

She heard the bells of St Paul's toll the hour. Her eyes closed and her head nodded forward. Boot's eyes closed too, and his tail twitched as his dreams took him under.

While they were sleeping, the man left the Albion Inn and walked towards the trough. He approached carefully, aware that any sharp movement or noise might wake Pearl — or worse, the dog. He looked from left to right to be certain no one was about, and then moved closer. Keeping his eyes fixed on Pearl, he gingerly lifted the clippy mat frame and placed something underneath it. Then he turned and walked briskly away, heading to Stockton Road, where he had parked his car.

As he strode up the main road, he saw the doctor's house ahead of him, with light from the windows spilling on to the pavement. The sound

198

of voices caught his ear as he approached, and he turned to look. The front door was open and two women stood in a lit hallway. The younger woman was pretty, with fair hair, the other more plump around the face. Both were waving goodbye to a broad-shouldered young man with dark hair. He caught the name *Billy* on the wind as the women said their farewells. Then the door closed against the night, and Billy walked towards him on the pavement.

The man raised his hat. 'Evening, sir,' he said.

Billy smiled at the stranger. 'Evening,' he replied.

The men passed each other and Billy thought no more about the polite man in the hat. He had more than enough on his mind already. He didn't want to hurt his mam, but he needed to tell her the truth about his feelings for Pearl before he broke things off with Sylvia. He hadn't cooled things with Sylvia that night as his dad had advised him to do. The opportunity hadn't arisen, as her mother had sat with them all night. But he couldn't marry Sylvia, not in a million years, not when he had feelings for Pearl. And now that he'd experienced passion with Pearl too, there could be no going back. He wanted her more than ever.

How hard could it be to sit down with his mam and talk? Billy sighed as he walked. He knew exactly how hard it would be. His mam would be furious, especially after all the work she'd done in securing him a place at the doctor's table. He'd never gone up against her before, but he knew what her reaction would be.

199

He'd seen her take out her fury on other people, not least his poor dad. Sometimes she even fought with the customers at the shop when they complained the eggs weren't fresh, or the onions too expensive. He'd never had the nerve to defy her before, but this time he needed to.

He was determined to get home as quickly as he could. His walking pace turned into a run. He wanted to hold Pearl again, to tell her how much he loved her. He wanted to wrap his arms around her and cover her sweet face in kisses. It was Pearl he loved, only Pearl. Since the first moment he'd met her, he'd known. Since he'd introduced himself in her attic room, he'd felt it with his heart and his mind. And after their afternoons at the beach, he felt it with his body too. He ran faster now, determined to take Pearl by the hand, stand firm, be a man and tell his mam the truth.

10

Home

Billy ran the rest of the way home, his heart pounding with excitement about declaring his love for Pearl. When he reached the yard of the shop, he stood for a moment to gather his breath, and as he did so, he realised that Boot hadn't come to greet him. He didn't give it another thought as he let himself in and walked up the stairs. In the living room, Jim was in his armchair reading the *Sunderland Echo* and Renee was on the sofa darning socks. But Billy didn't stop to call out hello or announce his return. He carried on straight up to the attic.

'Pearl!' he called as he ran. 'Pearl!'

Renee froze at the sound of her son's voice, and laid down her darning on the sofa. She heard Billy's footsteps running down the stairs and then he flew into the living room.

'Where is she?' he asked. He was still panting from the exertion of his run from the doctor's house. 'Where's Pearl? Has she taken Boot for a walk?'

Jim lowered his newspaper. 'Sit down, son,' he said sternly. 'Your mam's got something she needs to tell you about the lass.'

'Mam? What is it?' Billy asked. His heart was still beating wildly; he was desperate to know what was going on. 'What's happened? Is she hurt?'

'Have a seat, lad,' Jim said.

Billy pulled a chair from the table and sat sideways, holding the back of the chair with one hand. 'Mam?'

Renee looked her son straight in the eye. 'Pearl's gone,' she said. There was not a trace of emotion in her voice.

Billy swung his gaze to Jim. 'Dad? Is this true?'

Jim nodded.

'No!' Billy yelled. 'No! And you just let her go? Why didn't you try to stop her?'

'Son, I wasn't here when she left. I'd gone out for a breath of fresh air.'

Billy felt his face turn hot and his whole body fill with anger. He jumped from his seat. 'I'll get her back. She'll listen to me.'

'Sit down, son,' Jim said.

Billy knew from his dad's tone of voice that there was something serious going on. He sat, his whole body slumped forward, and he locked eyes with Renee. 'Mam? Where's she gone?'

Renee braced herself. She didn't like having to lie to her son and her husband. Dishonesty wasn't something that came easily to her, and she hated to see Billy upset. But this was for his own good; he'd see that in the end. 'She said her position here was no longer tenable,' she began.

'Tenable? Pearl said that?' Billy asked, confused. It wasn't a word he'd ever heard her use.

'Words to that effect,' Renee continued, remembering to stick to the lie she'd created.

202

'She said she was missing her old life up at the colliery and wanted to go back to her aunt.'

Billy shook his head as if to remove the words from his mind. 'No, that can't be right. She was happy here, she told me.'

'She's gone, lad,' Jim said softly. 'Whatever her reason, whatever she told your mam, I'm afraid the truth of it is that she's gone.' He glared at his wife. 'We've lost one of the best workers we ever had in this shop. She pulled her weight more than anyone who's worked downstairs, apart from me and Billy.'

'You know a grocer's life was never my calling,' Renee sniffed.

'Aye, but you've lived off a grocer's money all these years, haven't you?' Jim said. Then he rattled his newspaper and held it up in front of his face again, putting an end to further talk.

'I'm going after her,' Billy said, leaping up.

'No, son. You're not,' Renee said firmly. She stood from the sofa and walked towards him. She reached up and put her hand on her son's broad shoulder, and gently but firmly pushed him back into his seat. 'She said you weren't to follow her. Under any circumstances.'

'But, Mam . . .'

Renee could see the tears in her son's eyes. She knew his heart was breaking, and despite everything, she felt herself moved. She hated to see him so upset, but she knew she had to stand firm on this. It was all for the best, for the good of the future of the Watsons.

'Things will work out, you'll see,' she said, stroking his hair. 'You've got Sylvia, and your whole life ahead of you.'

Billy put his head in his hands. 'But I don't love Sylvia, Mam.'

Jim peered across the top of his newspaper at the scene unfolding in front of him. Renee took her hand away from Billy's shoulder.

'Of course you love her,' she said. 'And I won't hear another word about it.'

Billy stood, his bulk towering over Renee. 'It's Pearl I want, Mam, not Sylvia. That's what I wanted to tell you both tonight.'

'If Pearl wanted to be with you, she'd be here right now,' Renee said. 'She wouldn't have done a flit while you were out. She didn't even have the decency to tell you face to face.'

Billy held up his hand. 'Don't say another word.' And with that, he turned and walked to his bedroom.

He locked the door and threw himself on to his bed, where he lay trying to work out what he'd done wrong that would have made Pearl up and leave without a word. Had he said something to upset her? Had she lied to him about her feelings for him? His thoughts tormented him, and every time he thought of Pearl, his heart broke a little more. When Renee knocked at his door to offer him supper, he ignored her.

Renee bustled in the kitchen preparing a supper of stottie bread with ham for her and Jim. When she brought the food into the living room, her husband looked her in the eye.

'I don't know what's gone on today, but I'll tell you this. If I find out you had anything to do with that lass leaving . . . that you forced her out

204

of our son's life, I'll — '

'What, James?' Renee sneered. 'What *will* you do? Go and stand behind your counter downstairs polishing your chalkboard?'

Jim slammed the plate of food on to the table in front of him and stormed from the room, leaving Renee to eat her supper alone.

★ ★ ★

Meanwhile, down at the village green, Hetty and Jack Burdon were nearing the end of a busy night at the bar.

'Time, gentlemen, please!' Jack called. His voice echoed around the pub as Hetty began to gather glasses from tables. Within minutes, the noise and chatter had died away as customers bade each other goodnight. Hetty was just about to lock the front door against the cold autumn night when she spotted a dog beside the horse trough on the village green. She looked again, and saw a girl there with the dog.

'Jack!' she called. 'I won't be a minute, just nipping out for some air.'

Without waiting for her husband's reply, she walked sharply across the road to the green. Her footsteps woke the dog, which raised its eyes and sniffed the air. Sensing no danger, it remained silent.

'Good dog. Good boy,' Hetty said calmly as she neared them both. She gasped when she saw the girl's face. It was the same girl who'd been in the Albion Inn with Dorothy Marshall. The girl who had come calling asking for work. Hetty

205

bent low and shook her arm. She tried to remember her name. Was it Pauline? No . . . that wasn't right. She remembered thinking it a pretty name. Pearl, that was it.

'Pearl . . . ' she said. 'Pearl, wake up. You can't sleep here. You'll catch your death.'

Pearl's eyes slowly opened. She was groggy and confused. 'Billy?' she whispered.

'No, love, it's Hetty from the Albion Inn. Wake up, Pearl, there's a good girl.'

It took Pearl a few moments to realise what was happening and who Hetty was. She looked around her, taking in the village green. Her back was hurting where she'd rested against the stone trough, and her legs were stiff. She was cold, too. But it was the heartache over Billy that was the worst pain of all. She moved slowly and Hetty helped her to stand, holding tight to her arm.

'Let me take you to the Albion Inn, get you indoors,' Hetty said.

'But my dog . . . '

'It can come too,' Hetty replied, although what Jack would have to say on the matter wasn't worth thinking about, as he detested dogs. Holding Pearl by the arm, she walked her to the edge of the green, but then suddenly Pearl pulled back.

'My mat!' she cried. She went back to pick up the mat frame that she'd propped against the trough, picking up her bag of scraps and clothes too.

As Pearl lifted the frame from the ground, Hetty saw a glint of silver nestled in the grass, illuminated by the street lamp above. It was four

206

coins by the look of things, four crowns. So that was what the girl had been doing. She must have been so desperate for a job, she'd taken work with Dorothy on the pit lane.

'Is that money yours?' she asked Pearl, pointing towards it.

Pearl stared at the coins, confused. She looked at Hetty. 'No . . . it's not mine. It wasn't there when I sat down. I don't know where it's come from.'

Hetty picked up the coins and handed them to the girl, who stared at them blankly, trying to make sense of it.

'No need to explain, love,' she said. 'I'm not a judgemental woman, although there are plenty in Ryhope who are. How you earn your cash is your business.'

'But it's not mine,' Pearl insisted.

'Shush, pet. Come on, let's get you indoors. I can't have you sleeping outside all night, it's not right. You can spend the night in the pub; it'll be on the floor of the bar, but you'll be comfortable enough. Though it's just for one night, you hear?'

Pearl struggled to take in what was going on. She lifted the clippy mat frame and positioned it under her free arm. In her other hand she held her bag tight. 'Thank you,' she whispered.

★ ★ ★

The next morning, Hetty slid a plate of fried mushrooms and stottie bread across the bar to Pearl. Pearl sat on a stool with a mug of tea and

207

the breakfast in front of her. The sight of the food made her feel queasy again, but she knew she had to eat something. She needed the strength to cope with whatever the day would bring. Hetty's husband Jack muttered darkly behind the bar about his wife taking in waifs and strays. But each time he complained, Hetty told him to hush and told Pearl to pay him no heed.

Boot was given a dish of water, which he lapped up greedily, and Pearl fed him bits of stottie bread too. After she'd finished eating, Hetty gave her a hug and told her to keep her hand tight on her money. The four crowns bothered Pearl and made her uneasy. Just where had they come from? She knew they hadn't been there when she'd sat down at the horse trough; she'd have spotted them for sure. What if the money was stolen? And now that it was in her bag, did that make her a thief?

As Pearl headed from the Albion Inn with Boot at her side, her bag in her hand and her clippy mat under her arm, Hetty stood at the door and watched her go.

'Poor love,' she said out loud.

'Poor love, my backside!' Jack Burdon growled. 'She knew you were a soft touch, Hetty. She'll be back for more of your charity, just you mark my words.'

Hetty ignored her husband's moaning and watched Pearl and the dog disappear. 'No,' she said, too softly for Jack to hear, 'I don't think she will be back.' There was something about the girl; she'd felt it the first time she'd met her, when she'd come into the Albion Inn looking for

208

work. 'There's a rod of steel running through that lass. Whatever happens to her, she'll cope,' she said, but Jack just grunted in reply. Hetty hoped to high heaven she was right.

★ ★ ★

Pearl walked along Ryhope Street South until she came to St Paul's. She glanced at the huge clock above the church door. It was still early. Dare she go to Watson's Grocers and demand to see Billy? She needed to know what on earth was going on. But she dismissed the thought as soon as it arrived. She knew exactly what was going on, for hadn't Renee taken great pleasure in telling her? Billy wanted Sylvia, not her. His actions had proved that his words to her had been a lie. Well, Pearl wouldn't beg. She didn't have much but she did have her pride. No matter how heartbroken she felt over Billy, how hurt she was inside, she knew she would never plead for his love.

She paused a moment, listening to birdsong from the trees in the church grounds, a sweet chirrup in the cold morning air. As she shivered in her thin jacket, she noticed the church door was ajar.

'Boot, come,' she commanded. She pushed open the iron gate and walked up the path. All she wanted to do was find some warmth for a while; to sit in silence to think and to plan. As well as her heartache over Billy's betrayal, she had her baby to think about, and then there was the mystery of the money to solve. Her mind whirred with anxiety and she began to feel queasy again.

Leaving Boot to sniff around the churchyard, she stepped into the church porch, and stopped. There were voices coming from inside, a man and a woman. She recognised both of them immediately. The man was Reverend Daye and the woman . . . Pearl's heart skipped a beat . . . the woman was Annie. She tiptoed to the door and peered around it. There they were, sitting together on a pew at the front. Annie had her back to Pearl, turned to face Reverend Daye. Pearl jumped back. What on earth was her aunt doing there? She never came to church!

The voices continued, and Pearl heard Reverend Daye calming Annie, telling her all would be well. Pearl was panicked. She looked around the porch. To her left was a narrow opening in the wall just wide enough for one person. She peered inside and saw a flight of steps that curled up to the bell tower. Quickly she scrambled up until she knew she was out of sight. It was dusty on the stairs, and the dust caught in her throat. She covered her mouth with both hands and breathed through her fingers. Then she gasped. Her clippy mat! Her bag! She'd left them in the porch.

She heard a shuffling noise, footsteps, then Annie's voice loud and clear. 'Thank you, Vicar.'

'Any time, my dear,' Reverend Daye replied.

'I miss her so much. I miss her more every day.'

Pearl pressed her back against the wall, her breath caught in her throat. Annie and the vicar

210

were right at the bottom of the stairs.

'And I love her as if she were my own, I always have. I've never been blessed with children, Vicar. I've never had a fella stick around long enough to care. But I can't go dragging her back to my life up there, can I? I've got nothing to offer her. I can't afford to feed her or keep her. I can't even offer her a safe place to lay her head. She's better off without me.'

The vicar's eye was taken by an unusual item in the porch. He was sure it hadn't been there when he'd opened the church earlier. It seemed to be a mat of some kind, propped against the stone wall. He snapped his attention back to Annie, who hadn't seen it; she was still deep in her sorrow, blaming herself for the loss of her niece. He took one of her small, warm hands in his own.

'And remember, Annie,' he continued, 'I'm here if you need to talk at any time. You know you'll be welcome here and you'll never be judged.'

'He that is without sin, let him cast the first stone. Isn't that right, Vicar?' Annie said softly.

'Indeed, it is written in John, Chapter 8. But also remember, in that same chapter, 'And Jesus said unto her, Neither do I condemn thee: go, and sin no more.''

Annie laughed. 'Well, I'll try my best, Vicar.'

'That's all I can hope for, my dear.'

Annie walked from the church leaving Reverend Daye standing looking out to the churchyard. He listened to the birdsong, and the rustling of the leaves in the autumn wind. He looked at the

211

mat again and thought it curious that someone would leave it there. Then he saw the sprinkling of dust at the bottom of the steps leading up to the bell tower.

'You can come down now,' he called.

The vicar's voice curled up the stairs to where Pearl sat rigid. She gasped, then reached a hand to the chalky wall at her side and waited, silent, hardly daring to move. But there had been something warm in the words, something welcoming and calm that soothed her. Slowly she slid one foot forward, then the other. Step by step she made her way down the stairs. When she reached the bottom, she saw the vicar with her clippy mat frame in his hands.

'Beautiful work,' he said, keeping his eyes on the mat as Pearl inched closer to him. 'You've a real talent.'

'How did you know where I was?' she asked softly.

The vicar turned to her. 'Oh, I know all the hiding places in my church. I sometimes use them myself.' He smiled at his own little joke.

'My aunt Annie was here . . . ' Pearl began.

The vicar handed her the frame. 'Indeed she was, child,' he replied.

Pearl looked into his face. 'Do you think . . . do you think if I was to visit her, she'd welcome me back?'

'I know she would,' he replied. He didn't want to break the confidence of the talk he'd shared with Annie, but he felt sure he could say that much at least. It was not for him to become tangled in the mysteries of the lives of his

212

parishioners. He thought of the ex-soldier who had visited him some time ago, asking about Pearl. The man had spoken in earnest and in the strictest of confidence. With that knowledge, the vicar secretly welcomed the idea of the girl heading home. There were more people in her life who cared about her than she knew.

Pearl had been moved by Annie's words, touched to hear her aunt speak of her in that way to the vicar. The tiny part of her heart that had frozen towards Annie since she'd been forced to work the pit lane began to thaw.

'Is it possible to forgive someone even when you know what they've done is wrong? What I mean is . . . if someone did something wrong, but you understood their reason for doing it, can you forgive them?'

'Well, my child,' the vicar replied. 'One of the most celebrated forgiveness texts in the Bible is when Jesus prayed from the cross: 'Father, forgive them; for they do not know what they are doing.'' He hoped the quote might ease the girl's mind.

'I might ask Annie if she'd welcome me home,' Pearl said.

'Then you should. In fact, if you run, you might catch her.'

Pearl gathered her bag to her and thanked the vicar. She rounded up Boot from behind the church and walked quickly down the path to the road. The vicar stood at the door and watched her leave. Pearl turned and waved when she reached the pavement.

'Ah! Another lost sheep returns to the fold,'

Reverend Daye whispered as he waved back. He turned back into the church. He'd left his diary behind on the pew and he needed to check it for the day ahead. There was the morning Eucharist to prepare for, then his rounds in the afternoon visiting parishioners too old or frail to walk to church. And that evening there was something he was looking forward to a great deal: a wedding to discuss between two of Ryhope's finest families.

Pearl started to run, which wasn't easy with the mat frame under her arm.

'Annie!' she called. 'Annie!'

Boot began to bark, and Annie turned around to see what the fuss was about. When she saw Pearl running towards her, she flung her arms open to her niece. Pearl fell into her embrace and let her mat and bag fall. Boot ran rings around the two women as if herding them together. Annie stood back from Pearl and took in the sight of her. With both hands she smoothed Pearl's hair and brought her niece's face to her to kiss her on the cheek.

'Oh love! What a surprise!' she said. She tried choking back the tears that rose inside her, but then thought better of it and simply let them fall. Pearl too was crying as the two women hugged.

'Where are you off to? On a mission for the grocer?' Annie asked, wiping her hand across her eyes.

Pearl shook her head. 'I want to come home,' she said. She held tight to Annie's hands, waiting for her reply.

For a moment, Annie couldn't speak.

214

'No more running away?' she said at last. 'You had me worried sick when you disappeared without a word before.'

'I was scared, Annie. Being put to work on the pit lane, it's not what I want to do, ever.'

'I know, love. But I didn't think we had any other choice. You see that, don't you?'

Pearl nodded and her gaze fell to the ground. 'I've got something to tell you.'

Annie placed her hand under her niece's chin and gently lifted her face so that they were facing each other. 'Bad news or good?'

Pearl thought of Billy, her heart still breaking over his betrayal. She thought of Renee, who had cruelly thrown her out on the street.

'Mostly bad,' she said. She felt the hot sting of tears behind her eyes again.

Annie bent to the ground and picked up the frame and Pearl's bag.

'Come on, let's get you home. I've got to start work soon at Bernie's; you can tell me all about it as we walk.' She cast a glance behind her. 'See you've brought Boot back with you,' she said.

Pearl kept quiet. She didn't want Annie to know yet that it wasn't just Boot she was bringing to her door to feed, but a baby too.

'I saw you in church earlier,' she said, changing the subject. 'I was hiding in the bell tower.' She remembered the dust from the steps and wiped her hands across the back of her skirt. 'What were you doing there, Annie? You never go apart from the Christmas Eve carol service, and that's just because you hate to miss out on Ryhope's social event of the year.'

Annie bit her tongue. She couldn't tell Pearl that she and the vicar had been discussing the soldier who had come asking questions about Pearl. She'd been sworn to secrecy and so she crossed her fingers against the lie she was about to tell. 'Dorothy told me she'd seen you in the village and I thought maybe you'd used the church as a refuge,' she said quickly. 'She said you were looking the worse for wear. I was worried about you, Pearl. I asked the vicar if he would keep an eye on you if he saw you, to let me know how you were. I couldn't call at the grocer's again.'

'Did Dorothy tell you anything else?' Pearl asked. She wondered if the secret about her baby had been shared.

'No, love, nothing. Just that you were feeling poorly.'

Pearl breathed a sigh of relief. She wanted to tell Annie about the baby herself and in her own way. She planned to break the news gently in the quiet of their room.

The two women headed up the colliery, past the shops and the pubs, the Co-op and the miners' hall. As they walked, Pearl told Annie all about life at Watson's Grocers. She told her about Sylvia and the engagement that Renee was determined to arrange. She told her about saving Boot from being shot at High Farm. And she told her about meeting Joey once a week at the farm, where she handed over money from her wages for him to pass on to Annie.

'He did at first, love, but I haven't seen Joey for weeks now; no one has,' Annie said.

Pearl felt a hardness inside her. If Joey hadn't

been handing the money over, then where had it gone? 'I'll talk to him,' she said, determined to find out the truth.

'You'll have to find him first,' Annie said. 'He's running around with Jackson these days; the two of them have become as thick as thieves.'

★　★　★

By the time they reached Bernie Pemberton's shop, Pearl had revealed much of her life to her aunt. But there was still the news about her baby to share. And she had not asked yet about the money Annie owed, about her debts to the shops and the loan from Bobby Mac. All that would come in time, once she was settled in.

'Still got your key to our room, love?' Annie asked as she headed to the door of Bernie's shop.

Pearl delved into her bag and her fingers hit something solid. The money! The four crowns that had appeared at her side the night before. She brought the coins out of her bag along with her key. Annie stared hard at the riches.

'But there's twenty shillings there, Pearl, a whole pound!' Her eyes widened. 'Did Billy give it to you? Oh, you haven't stolen it, Pearl. Tell me you haven't.'

Pearl shot her aunt a look. 'Of course I haven't stolen it. The truth is, I don't know where it came from. I fell asleep on the green last night, and when I woke up, the coins were at my side.'

Annie reached to touch the coins, but Pearl snapped her hand closed. 'Probably best if you look after them, you're right,' Annie said with a

217

resigned air. 'I'm useless with money, I think we can both agree on that. Anyway, listen, love, I've got to get to work, or Bernie will dock my wages.'

Pearl kissed her aunt on the cheek. 'We'll talk more tonight,' she said. 'There's still something I need you to know.'

'Whatever it is we'll get through it,' Annie said. 'Don't we always?'

Pearl and Boot left Annie at the shop and walked to the back lane. Pearl lifted the sneck on the gate and stepped into the familiar yard. Boot walked around, sniffing, before cocking his leg in a corner. Pearl climbed the stairs with the dog following. She held her breath to help quell her nerves as she pushed open the door.

The room was tidy and clean, and Pearl was grateful for that. But there was a smell, a sour odour of damp, that caught in her throat. It was a smell that hadn't been there before. She looked up at the ceiling and saw black mould growing where the roof had let in the rain. But everything else looked the same. Annie's bed was made up with the old green eiderdown. The hole in the floor was still there, gaping wide as ever. It was as if Pearl had never been away, as if time had stood still. And yet . . . so much had happened in the short months she'd been gone. The room seemed enclosed to her after the freedom of Watson's shop.

Pearl stood with her mat and her bag, looking around, drinking it all in. She was home. But while the room might have been the same, she knew that she had changed. It was a different

218

Pearl who stood there, a wiser Pearl. No longer the young girl who had been forced out to work the pit lane. She had learned lessons in the time she'd been gone. She'd learned of love and friendship. Working at Watson's, she'd visited places that she'd never known existed; met more people at the market and in Ryhope village than she ever had living on the colliery. Her world had opened up, and she felt stronger for it. But she had learned of heartache too. It was overwhelming, all-consuming, and she could think of little else, especially with Billy's baby inside her. She wondered if the pain of losing Billy would ever truly leave.

★   ★   ★

Pearl slept much of the day, making up for the lack of sleep on the floor of the Albion Inn the previous night. When she woke, she headed to see Joey's mam, but Kate Scotch still wasn't well. She told Pearl she was suffering the after-effects of a flu that she couldn't seem to shake. And when Pearl asked about Joey, Kate's face took on a hardened look.

'He's with that bloody Jackson all the time. Stays out most nights and doesn't come home till the small hours. The fella's a bad influence on him, but Joey's old enough to do what he likes. I just hope he doesn't turn out like his dad.'

Walking home along the back lane with Boot trotting behind her, Pearl ran into Bobby Mac, who was working in the yard of the Colliery Inn. He called out when he saw her, saying how glad

Annie must be to have her back. 'And give her my regards when you see her,' he added.

Seeing Bobby reminded Pearl that she had to speak to Annie about the money he'd loaned her. Perhaps one or more of the crowns could go some way to paying him back. There was so much to talk to her aunt about, Pearl hardly knew where to start.

★ ★ ★

That evening, Annie climbed the stairs to their room, tired after a day spent at work. When she pushed the door open, she couldn't believe her eyes. Not only had Pearl got the fire going, but she was cooking there too. A wonderful smell hit Annie as soon as she walked through the door. She looked at Pearl, sitting by the fire, stirring a spoon around Annie's pan.

'Carrot soup,' Pearl explained. 'I made it myself. Jim Watson taught me. And I bought some stottie to go with it.'

Annie sank on to her bed, grateful beyond words.

'How can you afford it? And the coal, lass. How did you pay for it? I haven't been able to have the fire on in weeks.'

'I spent one of the crowns,' Pearl replied. She kept a careful eye on the soup, making sure it didn't catch and burn.

Just then there was a clatter of footsteps running up the stairs to their room. Both women turned in surprise when Dorothy burst in. She ran immediately to Pearl, covering her face in kisses.

220

'Oh pet. I've just bumped into Bobby Mac and he told me you were back.'

'And what were you doing talking to Bobby?' Annie bristled.

Dorothy began to laugh. 'Ooh, get you! Jealous, are you?'

Annie felt her face turning hot and she busied herself gathering bowls and spoons for the soup.

'Something smells good in here,' Dorothy said, eyeing the pan of soup greedily. 'Got any going spare?'

Pearl and Annie exchanged a look that didn't go unnoticed by Dorothy.

'Oh, don't worry, I won't stop if I'm not wanted,' she said.

'You can have some, course you can,' Pearl said.

'We've only got two bowls, Dot,' Annie said. 'You'll have to have yours in a mug.'

As Annie went to fetch a mug from the pantry, Dorothy sat cross-legged on the floor beside Pearl.

'Have you told her yet?' she whispered.

Annie's sharp ears missed nothing. 'Told me what?'

Dorothy laid her arm across Pearl's shoulders. 'Will you tell her, or should I?'

'Pearl, what's going on?' Annie said.

Pearl stood with the pan of hot soup in her hand. She poured the chunky orange liquid into the bowls and the mug. Curls of steam escaped into the room. Her words came slowly at first, hesitantly, as she revealed how much she'd loved Billy and, with a crack in her voice, how much

221

she loved him still. She told of her heartbreak at finding out he'd gone to be with Sylvia instead of standing up to his mam. And then she told Annie about Billy's child inside her.

Annie sat open-mouthed, unable to comprehend what she was hearing. 'How are we to look after a child?' she asked at last. 'Here? In this room? With that flaming hole in the floorboards and the rain coming through the roof? We can barely afford to eat and we can't afford coal. We can't — '

'You can,' Dorothy said firmly, looking from Annie to Pearl. 'Now listen, the pair of you. If I can bring up seven bairns on my own in that rat-hole of a house along the pit lane, then two strong lasses like you can bring up a baby in here.'

Pearl and Annie were chastised by Dorothy's outburst. They sipped at their soup. It was too hot to eat yet, but the smell was so delicious they suffered the burning on their tongues in exchange for the wonderful taste.

'You out working tonight?' Dorothy asked Annie.

Annie glanced at her niece. 'Not tonight,' she replied. 'Pearl and I have got some catching-up to do.'

Dorothy took the mug home to share the soup with her bairns, leaving Pearl and Annie eating in silence, with Boot watching and hoping for scraps.

★ ★ ★

222

Over the coming days, Pearl kept herself busy and tried to occupy her mind. Bobby Mac even gave her a few hours' work in the Colliery Inn, cleaning the bar and the yard. His son had got himself a job in Grangetown — a proper job, he'd told his dad. It just about broke Bobby's heart that Michael didn't want to follow in his footsteps running the pub, but Pearl was grateful for the work and the cash.

The days passed easily through the autumn into the cold weeks of winter. With Pearl's shifts at the Colliery Inn and the crowns in her pocket, she could now buy food for her and Annie. And with Annie's debts cushioned by Bobby Mac's loan, the fire burned to keep them both warm. Bobby was in no hurry to have his money back, he often told Annie, and she took comfort from that. In fact, she was more grateful to him than he would ever know, for it meant that she would no longer need to work the pit lane.

There was money too from the sale of Pearl's clippy mats from Pemberton's Goods, which they gave Bernie towards the rent. Bernie wasn't happy that there was still an amount outstanding, but as long as Annie kept giving him something each week, no matter how small, to pay it off, he didn't complain too much. He could be a nasty piece of work when he wanted to be, but he also knew how much of a grafter Annie was in his shop and how the customers enjoyed spending time there, and spending their cash. He was happy to let her run the place as she saw fit and knew that if he turned her out of her room, he'd lose one of the best workers he'd ever had.

During those frosty weeks of winter, Pearl's belly began to swell, and by mid December she was three months gone. One night, Annie climbed to their room at the end of another long day at the shop and flung down the day's *Sunderland Echo* on her bed.

'There's something in here I think you should see,' she said. 'Bottom of page thirty-two.'

Pearl picked up the paper and thumbed through until she reached the page Annie had suggested she read. It was the page for births, weddings and deaths and she knew immediately the news it contained. Her eyes scanned the notices until she saw it for herself. There it was, in black and white, the announcement of an engagement between William James Watson and Sylvia May Anderson. The wedding was to take place in June of the following year.

★ ★ ★

At Watson's Grocers, Jim picked up his chalkboard from the counter. Without Boot, Watson's was no longer rat-free. And without Pearl, the air in the shop hung heavy with gloom and despair.

224

11

Christmas

Christmas Eve dawned bright and frosty, with a cloudless eggshell-blue sky. It was bitterly cold, and ice gripped the inside of the window in Pearl and Annie's room. Annie got the fire roaring within minutes of getting out of bed. It had all been prepared the night before: an old copy of the *Sunderland Echo* had been rolled into long sausage shapes, then tied into loose knots and placed in the hearth. On top of the paper, chopped sticks of wood had been placed, and then a shovelful of coal went on last. The paper at the bottom was set on fire first, and once the flames took hold, they licked the wood and coal.

With the fire burning, water could be warmed for washing and boiled for drinking, and breakfast could be cooked: oats with milk and a tiny bit of sugar that Annie could now afford. With Pearl's cleaning job at the Colliery Inn, the mysterious crowns that had turned up and Bobby Mac's loan, Annie had paid her debts to the colliery shops. She was welcomed back at them all, as long as she had cash in her purse; the one thing she wasn't allowed any more was the luxury to buy goods on tick. Now that her finances were finally settling, she was even able to start paying back Bobby Mac's loan.

'Ah, you shouldn't bother,' he'd tell her when she'd call in at the Colliery Inn with a handful of coins.

But Annie knew she should. If it hadn't been for Bobby's kindness, she dreaded to think where she would have ended up. He'd saved her from being thrown on to the streets, and he'd saved her from having to work on the pit lane through the winter too. Annie's priority now was looking after Pearl, preparing for the months ahead with the baby. She had smothered Pearl with love and affection when she'd first moved back to Dawdon Street. She could tell her niece had a sadness about her; the grocer's lad, Billy, had clearly meant the world to her. She heard Pearl crying from her bed in the dark of the night when she thought Annie was sleeping.

Over the weeks, Pearl had pulled herself round, though Annie knew it hadn't been easy. She was brighter now, but Annie knew she was still hurt over Billy and she worried about when the baby came, for it would be a constant reminder of the lad. Annie had only met Billy twice, but she'd liked what she'd seen. The first time was the day she'd gone to visit Pearl at the grocer's shop. He was there behind the counter and they'd chatted briefly. The second time was when he'd visited the shop to collect Pearl's clippy mat and frame. Whilst there, he'd had his eye taken by the tray of feathers for sale. Annie had tried very hard to dissuade him from taking the red one, but Billy was a man who had made up his mind, and he wouldn't be swayed. He knew nothing of the significance of the red feather; he kept saying how pretty it was and how much Pearl would love it. On the whole, Annie felt that he'd had a nice way about him, polite but not posh, and charming but not oily the way some men could be.

As the fire crackled in the hearth, Annie stirred the pan of oats. Pearl roused herself from her bed, but seemed to be taking longer than usual to stand up from the floor. Annie left the pan on the fire to help her niece when she saw her struggling.

'We're going to have to swap beds, pet,' she said. 'We can't have you sleeping on the floor in your condition.'

Pearl started to object, but Annie wouldn't hear of it.

'We'll start tonight. You have the big bed and I'll take the floor.'

'We could share the bed,' Pearl said. Now that Annie was no longer working the pit lane and bringing customers back to their room, she was happy to suggest this. She was surprised when Annie burst out laughing.

'What? With the way you snore? I'd never get a minute's sleep!'

'I don't snore,' Pearl teased.

'Oh, you do. You're as noisy as the winding gears at the pit,' Annie said, kissing her niece on the cheek. 'Now come on, breakfast's almost ready. And I've got the kettle on to boil for some tea.'

Pearl pulled a blanket around her shoulders and shuffled across the room to sit on Annie's bed. The heat from the coal fire went right into her; she relished the feel of it warming her skin. 'What'll we do tomorrow, Annie?' she asked.

'For Christmas Day, you mean? Well . . . ' Annie thought for a moment. Their options weren't exactly limitless, but they had been given a choice, one that Annie hadn't shared yet with Pearl. 'We could go up to the Colliery Inn,' she offered.

Pearl wrinkled her nose. 'Spend Christmas Day in the same pub I spend all my time cleaning?'

Annie stirred the porridge a little faster, working the wooden spoon around the pan as she explained. 'Bobby Mac's invited us up, both of us, like. He's offered to share his Christmas dinner.' She turned to look at Pearl. 'That's if we want to go, of course.'

'And do we want to go?' Pearl laughed.

'It beats sitting here trying not to fall down a hole in the floorboards. The truth of it is, I don't think Bobby wants to be on his own his first Christmas without Ella. The poor fella's still struggling without her. Not that he'd tell anyone, but I know. There's a look in his eye when he talks about her still. Anyway, I think it's just as much for his benefit as ours that he's invited us. What do you reckon, Pearl?'

'Will Michael be there too?'

Annie shook her head. She lifted the pan from the fire and poured the hot oats and milk into their bowls. 'He's got himself a new girlfriend. Bobby says he's going to be spending Christmas Day with her family up on Brick Row.'

Pearl raised her eyebrows. 'The brick houses by the pit?'

228

'Aye, her dad's a gaffer with the Ryhope Coal Company.'

'So it'd just be us three tomorrow, if we go?' Pearl asked.

'If we go, yes. We don't have to. I wouldn't want you to feel obliged. But it might be nice, eh? Bit of goose, a few potatoes, nice bit of sage and onion stuffing, a spot of Christmas pudding. What do you say?'

Pearl let the blanket drop as she began to feel the heat from the fire. She took the bowl of oats Annie offered. 'Are you sure there's no other reason you want to spend time with Bobby Mac?' she asked.

'Eeh, I don't know what you could possibly mean,' Annie replied, dismissing Pearl's question with a wave of her hand. But Pearl saw the smile that played on her aunt's lips and knew exactly where they would be spending Christmas Day.

★ ★ ★

That evening, Pearl and Annie put on their coats and hats for the walk to St Paul's church. The carol service was not to be missed. It was one of the social highlights of the year, which almost everyone in Ryhope attended, whether they were regular churchgoers or not. Folk flocked from the village and the colliery, and the church was packed to the rafters. But just before Pearl and Annie reached the church gate, Pearl froze. She reached for Annie's hand.

'I can't . . . ' she said.

'What it is?' asked Annie.

Pearl nodded ahead to where a group of people were gathered at the church door, waiting to file inside. Annie looked, desperate to see what had upset Pearl. She couldn't make anything out at first — it was just a sea of faces under hats — but then she recognised Billy. At his side was a tall, slim young woman with a serious face, light hair and fair skin. They were being ushered inside the church by a woman Pearl recognised as Renee. Billy looked downcast, his gaze fixed firmly on the ground.

'Look, love, just because Billy and Sylvia are at the service, it doesn't mean you can't go in too.'

'But — '

'No buts, Pearl, you hear me? You're going to hold your head high and walk in. You've got every right to be there. They're no better than you and — '

'No,' Pearl said firmly.

She turned around and headed back along the pavement, retracing her steps. Annie ran to catch up with her, and when she reached her, she threw her arm around her niece. She pulled Pearl towards her and they walked home in silence.

★ ★ ★

The next morning, when Pearl woke, it took her a few moments to realise where she was. She knew she was at home in the room above the shop, but her view was different. She sat up, looking around from her new position in Annie's bed.

'Annie!' she called out. 'Did you sleep well down there?'

Annie groaned in reply, letting Pearl know exactly how she'd slept. 'My poor back,' she complained. 'I don't know how you did it all those years.'

'And I don't know how you managed to sleep in this bed. It's far too soft and squishy.'

Their exchange was cut short by a loud banging downstairs. Annie pulled her housecoat over her nightdress and headed to the landing, where Boot lay curled asleep. She walked down the steps to the yard and called out demanding to know who was there.

'It's me!' Dorothy replied.

'Well, I didn't think it was flamin' Father Christmas, did I?' Annie laughed when she opened the gate.

'Merry Christmas, love,' Dorothy said. The two women kissed. 'Brought you a present.'

'Oh Dorothy, you didn't? I haven't bought anything for you. You know I'm trying to pay Bobby Mac his loan back.'

'Don't worry, I didn't pay for it. I got it free off a fella.'

Annie ran up the stairs with Dorothy following. By now, Pearl was up and getting the fire going in the hearth.

'Merry Christmas, Pearl,' Dorothy said cheerfully. 'Brought you something to celebrate the day.' She opened her arms to reveal a parcel wrapped clumsily in newspaper. She placed it carefully on the green eiderdown.

'What is it?' Pearl asked.

231

Dorothy looked from Pearl to Annie and back again. There was a mischievous glint in her eye. 'You're going to have to open it and find out,' she laughed. 'And when you do, you can tell me what to do with it, because I haven't got a bloody clue!'

The three women stared at the bundle on the bed. It was the size of a loaf of bread, but thinner and rounder.

'Is it alive?' Annie asked, eyeing it suspiciously.

'I don't think so,' Dorothy replied.

Pearl nudged her aunt. 'Open it.'

Annie eyed the package suspiciously and didn't make a move.

'Apparently you can eat it,' Dorothy announced.

'Get away with you!' Annie cried in surprise.

'Well, that's what I was told. My fella gave me one last night as a Christmas gift. Says he saw one when he was overseas in the war but he'd never seen one in England before. Thought I might like it, he said. He brought me two. I wanted you to open yours, see if you knew what to do with it.'

'It's foreign?' Annie cried.

Pearl took a step forward. 'I'll open it,' she said.

She pulled the parcel to her. She was surprised to feel it was heavier than it looked. She tore at the newspaper, gently at first and then with more force, until the most peculiar-looking thing appeared.

'What on earth is it?' Annie asked. She gingerly reached her hand towards it and ran her fingers around the prickles and bumps. On the top of it — or was it the bottom? — spiky green

232

leaves sprouted. With Pearl and Dorothy watching closely, she picked it up from Pearl's lap and held it in both hands.

'Well I never,' she said. 'It's heavy, too. Come on, Dot, put me out of my misery and let me know what the devil it is.'

Dorothy crossed her arms in front of her and said proudly, 'It's pined apple. But it looks like no apple I've ever seen before.'

'It's called a pineapple,' Pearl corrected her.

'You know what this is?' Annie asked.

'I've heard of them. When I was working at Watson's and I'd go to the market with . . .' She stopped and took a deep breath. 'I heard about them at the market, but I've never seen one before.' She took the pineapple from Annie's hands. 'It's beautiful, isn't it?' she said, admiring it.

Annie wrinkled her nose. 'I'm not so sure about that. How are we meant to eat it with the prickles on the skin? And what about the leaves sprouting from the top? What are we supposed to do with them?'

'Well, that's what I've been wondering,' Dorothy replied. 'I was hoping you might know.'

'I think we're supposed to cut into it,' Pearl explained, remembering what she'd heard about the exotic fruit when she'd been at the market with Billy.

'Annie, get a knife,' Dorothy ordered.

Annie walked to the pantry and came back with her sharpest knife. Pearl laid the pineapple on its sheets of newspaper on the wooden floor. All three of them crouched down around it,

Annie poised with the knife in her hand.

'I'll take the leaves off first,' she said. 'Or do you think we're supposed to eat them?'

Dorothy shook her head and tutted. 'Who knows which bits we can eat?'

'It's not poisonous, is it, Pearl?' Annie asked.

'They wouldn't be selling them on the market if they were,' Pearl replied. 'I remember they used to cost a bob or two. There's not much call for them in Sunderland, so the market rarely had them for sale.'

Annie brought the knife to where the leaves joined the fruit. It was tougher than she'd imagined, and she ended up having to saw at it.

'What now?' she asked Pearl once she'd removed the leaves.

'Try slicing through the middle.'

She held tight to one end of the pineapple to stop it rolling away, then pressed down on the hard skin and the knife slid inside. It was the smell that hit them first, the sweet, sugary tang released into the air. Pearl felt her mouth water as the pineapple split in two.

'It's yellow!' Dorothy cried. 'It's bright yellow inside!'

Pearl picked up one half of the pineapple and put her tongue to the fruit as Annie and Dorothy watched.

'Well?' Annie asked.

'It tastes almost as sweet as it smells,' Pearl announced.

Dorothy breathed a sigh of relief. 'Oh thank heavens for that. Right, well, I've got to get back to the bairns. Looks like we're having pineapple for breakfast over there.'

'Give them a kiss from us,' Annie said.

Once Dorothy had gone, Pearl and Annie were left with the pineapple between them.

'What shall we do with it?' Pearl asked.

Annie eyed the fruit, wondering where to make her next incision with the knife. 'Maybe we can take some to Bobby Mac's.'

A smile played around Pearl's lips. 'Or we could have it for breakfast,' she said.

Annie paused with the knife in her hand. She was studying the fruit from all angles, wondering how best to get the skin off. 'Oh, I don't see why not,' she laughed. 'It's Christmas after all, and if we can't treat ourselves to a bit of luxury today, then when can we?'

After the pineapple had been stripped of its skin, Annie chopped the fruit into chunks and she and Pearl ate half for breakfast. It was like nothing they'd tasted before. It set their tongues fizzing. The unusual taste made them wince at first before the sweetness of the fruit came through.

'If this is what foreign food's like, I think I could get used to it,' Annie smiled.

★   ★   ★

Christmas Day went by in a blur. Christmas dinner with Bobby Mac in his kitchen at the Colliery Inn was a lot nicer than either Annie or Pearl had expected. Bobby proved himself a surprisingly competent cook, and even laid on ginger wine for Annie while he brought in beer

235

for himself from the bar. Boot had been invited too and sat underneath the table, greedily lapping a bowl of gravy. Bobby's son Michael and his new girlfriend Veeda surprised them all by calling in after dinner.

'I couldn't not come, Dad,' Michael explained, giving his dad a hug. 'Not on your first Christmas Day without Mam.'

'I know, son, I know,' Bobby said softly. 'And I'm glad you're here to join us, you and Veeda. It's good to see you both.'

The five of them sat happily around the table, drinking and chatting and wearing paper hats. Pearl was in awe of Veeda and kept casting shy glances towards her. Michael's girlfriend was older than Pearl; she wore powder on her face, her brown hair was softly curled and her lips were cherry red. She wore a pretty blue blouse with a lacy collar and Pearl felt the shabbiness of her own clothes in comparison. She wondered what Veeda made of her and Annie. But she needn't have worried. Veeda was kind to her, asking when her baby was due and if there was anything she could do to help in the run-up to the birth. She had a calm manner about her, in the way she spoke and the way she moved, and Pearl watched in awe at Veeda's beauty and grace. She could see why Michael had fallen for her and she wondered if she and Veeda might become friends.

After dinner had been cleared and the washing-up done, Pearl and Annie headed back to their room. It was warm inside as they'd left the fire burning, and with their bellies full, they lay down side by side on the bed to rest. Annie held Pearl's hand.

'It'll be all right, you know. When the baby comes, we'll manage. You'll see.'

Pearl stared up at the ceiling, counting the cracks. The last thing she wanted to do was think of the future — her future — without Billy. Seeing him at the carol service with Sylvia had upset her, the two of them looking cosy with their families around. She wasn't jealous of Sylvia — she didn't even know the girl — but she was angry with Billy. She felt a fool, too. How could she have believed his words about love as they lay together in the cave on the beach?

'Will we call to see Kate Scotch this evening?' she asked Annie, changing the subject.

'Good idea. I've been wondering how she's doing,' Annie replied.

Pearl felt her eyes growing heavy and she let them fall closed. She wanted to check on Kate to see how she was and to wish her a merry Christmas. But she was also worried about Joey and wanted to find out what he was up to these days. Since she'd moved back to live with Annie, she'd seen little of her friend.

After their afternoon nap, Pearl and Annie readied themselves for the short walk to Kate's house.

'Let's take her some pineapple,' Annie said.

'Might do her the world of good if she's still not feeling right,' Pearl agreed.

The two of them bustled along the back lane arm in arm. The rooftops of the lime-washed cottages sagged and the windows were smeared with coal dust and grime. Kate's house was no better than any of the rest, as dirty and dingy as them all. Annie rapped at the back door, but when it opened, it was Joey who stood there. Pearl gasped in horror when she saw her friend. Gone was the fresh-faced boy she had grown up with. In his place stood a gangly, skinny lad with a black eye that was yellowing down the side of his face. Where his hands gripped the door, Pearl saw dirty fingernails bitten to the quick.

'Merry Christmas, Joey.'

He didn't move, and neither did he reply.

'We've come to see your mam,' Annie said. She waited for him to invite them in.

'How've you been, Joey?' Pearl asked softly. 'What happened to your face?'

'Nowt,' he spat.

Without another word, he pulled the door open and stood to one side. Pearl noticed immediately that his bad leg was playing him up worse than ever; he moved heavily, as if in more pain than before.

'Mam's in bed,' he said.

'She still not well?' Annie asked.

Joey bit his lip and gave the tiniest shake of his head.

'Has the doctor been to see her?'

But Annie knew the answer to her own question. The moon's silvery glow coming in through the window illuminated the ruinous state of Kate's kitchen. There was no money for coal to burn on the fire, and none for food either, by the look of things. There would

238

certainly be none to pay a doctor's bill.

'Does your mam still use the back bedroom?' Annie asked. Without waiting for a reply, she was already heading up the stairs to see Kate.

Left alone in the kitchen, Pearl and Joey eyed each other suspiciously.

'Can I sit down?' Pearl asked. Despite the afternoon nap, she was still feeling tired. Joey pulled a chair from the table and she sank gratefully into it. He pulled another chair for himself, and they sat facing each other with the table in between.

'You all right?' she asked him.

Joey looked her straight in the eye, challenging her as he gave his answer. 'What's it to you?'

'Cut it out, Joey. It's me you're talking to, remember? You might act the hard lad with Ronnie Heddon at High Farm and with Jackson . . .'

At the mention of Jackson's name, Joey turned his head away.

' . . . but I know you better than anyone. I know the real Joey's still in there under all that swagger. The Joey I grew up with, the Joey who's my friend.'

Joey stared at the floor.

'I've been worried about you.'

'Worried? About me?' he huffed. 'Pull the other one. No one cares about me.'

Pearl looked at the bruising around his eye and down his cheek. Caught in the moonlight, his face took on a deathly glow.

'Who gave you the shiner?' she asked.

Joey didn't answer.

'Was it Jackson?'

He kept his gaze firmly fixed on the floor. In the silence, they could hear Annie's footsteps walking across the bare floor above them as she tended to Kate.

'We got caught . . . ' Joey began hesitantly, but once he started, the words came tumbling out. 'We were nicking beer bottles from the back of the Prince of Wales. And we got caught and Jackson ran, I mean, he just left me. I couldn't run, not with my leg the way it is, and before I knew what was going on I was being yanked around by my ear. I was crying, Pearl, I was begging the fella to let me go, but . . . ' he turned his face to Pearl's and she saw that his eyes were rimmed with tears, 'he called the police. I was given a warning. Had to spend the night in the cells. Jackson got off scot-free. He said if I ever mention his name to the cops, he'll come after me again. My life wouldn't be worth living if he found out I'd snitched.'

'And was he the one who hit you?'

Joey nodded. 'I tried to fight him off, but you've seen the size of him. What use am I up against someone like him?'

Pearl was furious. Joey might not have the courage to report Jackson to the police, but someone ought to . . . and why not her? She wouldn't need to mention Joey's name, and she wouldn't let him know what she was planning. The less he knew, the better. Men like Jackson needed to be punished for their crimes. He'd been getting away with his violence and thieving long enough.

'Joey, I know you're not a bad lad. But I still

240

don't understand what you were doing hanging around with someone like Jackson in the first place.'

'He said he'd look after me, didn't he? When I worked at the pit, the fellas used to watch out for me, but I've no one to do that now.' He gave a huff of ill temper. 'The pit. It's got a lot to answer for. I could run and play and be a normal lad before the accident. And now? I'm useless, that's what. Down the pit, lads work with their dads. They follow their father's profession. How can I amount to anything when I don't even know who my father is? I've got no dad to follow, no one to look up to, no one to ask for advice.'

Pearl reached across the table and held tight to Joey's hand. 'We've got each other, Joey,' she whispered. 'And at least you've got your mam.'

Joey's eyes glistened with tears. 'I'm sorry, Pearl, I didn't mean anything by that. Here's me going on, and there's you . . . '

Pearl shrugged. 'Little orphan Pearl, you mean? I never think of myself as an orphan, you know that. All I've ever known is Annie. She might not be perfect, but she does her best.' A shiver ran down her spine as the words left her lips. She thought about the night she and Joey had met on the pit lane when Annie sent her to work. 'Well, she does her best most of the time,' she said softly. She looked Joey hard in the eye. 'What happened to the money? The money I was giving you each week from my wages at Watson's that you were supposed to be handing to Annie?'

'Needed it for food, for coal,' he said softly. He lifted his eyes to meet Pearl's. 'I'm sorry.'

241

She squeezed his hand. 'Annie will look after your mam now,' she said. 'And we can give you some coal. It's freezing in here; you need to get the fire burning.'

They fell into silence again, then Joey said, 'What about you? Why aren't you down at Watson's?'

Pearl took a deep breath. 'I'm going to have a baby,' she said.

Joey slid his hand free from hers. 'A baby?' he whispered. 'But how?' Then he caught himself, and laughed.

'I think we both know how,' Pearl said, joining in with the laughter. 'Everything we used to whisper about at school, it all turned out to be true.'

'But I mean . . . who? Who's the dad, Pearl?'

'Promise not to tell anyone?'

Joey made the sign of the cross at his heart. 'Cross my heart and hope to die, stick a needle in my eye.'

Pearl smiled; it was a phrase they had used many times as children.

'Billy Watson,' she said.

Joey's eyes grew wide. 'The grocer's lad?'

Pearl nodded.

'Why isn't he here, then?' Joey demanded, his tone firm. 'Why aren't you with him on Christmas Day of all days?'

'He doesn't know I'm pregnant,' Pearl said. 'He's engaged to someone else. It's what he wanted. I wasn't going to chase after someone who got rid of me like an old shoe.'

Joey stroked her hand. 'You know what we are, don't you?'

'What?'

'We're just a couple of pit rats.'

Pearl gave a cheeky wink. 'And we should be very proud of that, too.'

Joey laughed bitterly. 'Proud? I've got no money, Mam's ill and I can't afford the doctor. I've got no job, no mates — '

'No job? But I thought you were working at High Farm?'

Joey hung his head in shame. 'They caught me stealing. Just a couple of hens it was at first. Jackson said he could sell anything I could get my hands on. Then I started taking eggs, for Mam, like. But Ronnie caught me and sacked me on the spot.'

'Oh Joey. What are we going to do with you, eh?'

'I've been shovelling muck this week. You know that girl who runs the rag and bone round with her horse and cart?'

'Meg Sutcliffe?'

'That's her. I've been following her old horse every time I see it in Ryhope. I shovel up the muck and sell it as manure to the gardeners who work in the houses on the green.'

'It can't pay much.'

Joey shook his head and another silence sat between them. Above them they heard the murmur of Kate and Annie's voices. Joey shifted in his seat and opened his mouth as if to say something, but then snapped it closed again.

'Come on, out with it,' Pearl said. 'I know you, Joey Scotch. It's not like you to keep quiet when you've got something to say.'

'It's daft; you'll think I'm barmy.'

'I won't, go on.'

'Do you believe in ghosts, Pearl?'

Pearl began to say that she didn't believe in anything she couldn't prove was real, but Joey interrupted her and started talking again.

'I think I see things sometimes, I think there's someone from the other side trying to make contact.'

Pearl bit down on her tongue to stop herself from laughing. Joey looked so earnest that she resolved to take him seriously. Whatever he thought he had seen had clearly frightened him.

'I see shadows, you know? As if someone is walking past the window in the lane, peering into our kitchen. He wears a hat and he's got a round face. But when I run outside to see who it is, there's no one there.'

'How many times have you seen it?' Pearl asked.

'Three times,' Joey said. 'Always in the night, never during the day.'

'And does it speak to you?'

Joey shook his head. 'No, it's just shadows.'

'Could be the moonlight playing tricks,' Pearl suggested, trying to make sense of it. 'Could be a drunkard walking past, checking to see if he's got the right house before he barges through the door.'

'No, it's not like that,' Joey said. 'I get . . . scared about it, Pearl. After my accident, things changed. I'm scared of the dark now. It's stupid, I know.'

'It's not stupid, you mustn't think that. Anyone who went through what you did would feel the same.'

'Are you saying you think it *might* be a ghost?'

Pearl shrugged. 'Ask it to come in next time,' she smiled.

Joey laughed, the joyful sound she knew so well. But then he put his hand to the bruises on his face.

'Don't make me laugh,' he said. 'It hurts.'

'Are you still doing your drawings?' Pearl asked.

Joey stood and limped heavily from the kitchen. He returned a few moments later with rough sheets of paper in his hand. He handed them to Pearl and she lifted the first one to catch the moonlight coming in through the window. At first glance it appeared nothing more than scribble on the page, lines and circles as if from a child's hand. But when she continued looking, she saw Joey's artistic talent there.

'It's Ned,' Joey said. 'My pony.'

Pearl didn't need the explanation. Once her eyes focused on the whirls of pencil on the page, she saw the pony's face clearly, his furry ears and velvet eyes. She flicked through the pages; all of them showed the same pony, drawn from different angles. Each one was more detailed and beautiful than the last.

'Could I keep one?' she asked.

'Of course,' Joey said. 'I've got loads more upstairs.'

Pearl leafed through the drawings and pulled out one to take home with her. As she did so, they heard footsteps coming down the stairs.

'Your mam's settled for the night,' Annie said. 'It's all we can do for now; we'll see how she is in

245

the morning. She says you're to come home with us.'

'No.' Joey shook his head firmly. 'I'm not leaving her. I'm not going anywhere.'

'Then you need the fire on, lad,' Annie said. 'Come and collect a bucket of coal from our yard, and we'll give you some food too. We've got stottie and ham you can have.'

Pearl reached across to Joey and planted a kiss on his face, taking care to avoid his bruises.

12

Birthday

The year turned and life went on at Dawdon Street. In the early weeks of 1920, gales battered the roof over Pearl and Annie's room, letting in even more rain. Yet again Bernie Pemberton avoided being drawn into conversation about fixing it. Annie threatened to report him, but to whom she had no idea. Bernie knew they were empty threats and simply laughed off her complaints.

As the weeks turned into months and winter turned from spring to early summer, Pearl grew heavy with her baby. She worked on her clippy mats, creating another two that Annie sold from the shop. The second mat had been bought by an older woman who had come into the shop to buy ribbon. When she'd spotted the mat behind the counter, she had asked to see it. She had run her hands over it, turned it over to check the workmanship and Pearl's even stitches edged around the hessian. Annie had expected to have to haggle, but like the first mat, it had been sold at the asking price. The sale of the third mat was just as straightforward. This time it had been a younger woman, who had admired the red and green pattern that Pearl had created.

Annie had tried her best to find out more

about these customers, but all three had refused to be drawn into any kind of conversation. She had thought it odd, but quickly shrugged the feeling off as she pocketed the cash for Pearl. After her years working on the pit lane of Ryhope, Annie Grafton had learned many things. She knew from experience that there was nothing so unusual as folk — and as the seasons turned to a warm day in June, she was about to find out just how peculiar some people could be.

★ ★ ★

'I've been given to understand you sell ribbons, is that correct?'

Annie stared hard at the customer who had walked into her shop. She didn't much like the woman's sharp tone, but managed to force a smile through gritted teeth. 'That's correct, madam.' Annie glanced at the woman's hat, with its neat stitching around the edge and decorative bow at the side. It wasn't the sort of hat a miner's wife could afford, she knew that for sure. Her trained eye took in the black coat with its fur collar that must surely be uncomfortably warm for the summer day. It was clear that the woman was wearing it for show.

'Well?' the customer barked. Her grey-blue eyes flashed with a glint of steel.

Annie shook herself out of her reverie. She didn't want to come across as being nosy, but she hadn't met such a rude customer in a very long time and was still trying to figure her out. 'Ribbons, you say?' she said politely.

248

'Blue, as light as you have it, and about two inches wide,' the woman replied. 'It's to decorate the hat I plan to wear at my son's wedding.'

Annie reached behind the counter to where rows of flat, narrow black boxes sat neatly on the shelves. She pulled one of them to her and placed it on the counter. Nestled inside were ribbons in shades from the indigo of midnight through to a blue so light that at first glance it appeared white. The customer ran her hand through the box, taking out the paler colours she preferred and holding up a length from each spool to examine them.

Annie was curious. 'Will your son's wedding take place here in Ryhope?'

The customer kept her gaze on the ribbons as she replied. 'Yes, at St Paul's church. Of course, I would have preferred him to be wed in town, at the Minster. It only seems right for a family of our standing to be granted the privilege of using Sunderland's most glorious church, but — '

'Your family?' Annie asked.

The woman glared at her, furious at being interrupted. 'But it is the wish of the bride's family to hold the wedding in Ryhope. And one must do as the bride's family wish at times such as these, don't you think?'

'You would have preferred the Minster?' Annie said, eyeing the customer, wondering how much she dare ask.

'Heavens, yes!' she replied. She rolled her eyes heaven-wards. 'But as much as my husband is a hard-working forward-thinking businessman, we have to do as the doctor and his wife prefer.'

Annie's heart missed a beat. 'Your son is marrying Dr Anderson's daughter?'

'Sylvia. That's right. She's a marvellous girl, just lovely. And a perfect match for William, if I do say so myself.'

Annie took a long breath to steady herself. She spread her hands on the counter to stop them from shaking. So this was Billy's mam, standing right in front of her. This was the woman Pearl had told her about, the one who'd thrown her out on to the streets. Annie hoped Bobby Mac was keeping Pearl busy at the Colliery Inn. She couldn't bear the thought of her niece walking into the shop to find herself face to face with the woman she despised.

'I'll take a yard of this one,' Mrs Watson said, delving into her handbag to find her purse.

Annie pulled herself together; she wasn't going to give the woman the pleasure of seeing her upset. She cut the ribbon to length, pulled a sheet of mauve tissue from a shelf and carefully wrapped the purchase.

'I hope your son will be very happy with Sylvia,' she said as she worked. 'It sounds as if they deserve each other.' Then she stopped what she was doing, and pretended to think for a moment. 'Oh . . . but I'm sure I heard that your son Billy . . . '

'His name is William,' the woman snapped.

' . . . was courting another girl. A pretty girl, so I heard, with auburn hair.'

Mrs Watson bristled and gathered herself to her full height, which was still a good few inches shorter than Annie. 'My son . . . ' she began in a whisper before her voice rose and gathered strength. 'My William is not the sort of young man I appreciate hearing gossip about on the colliery. It's true he had a young friend such as you mention, but she was not of our class and there was certainly no romance. Now, if you have nothing better to do than repeat idle chatter about other people, I'll take my business elsewhere!'

Annie wasn't going to let her off the hook that easily. The sale of the expensive ribbon, and a whole yard of it too, wasn't one she was willing to lose. 'I'm sorry if I've offended you, Mrs Watson. It's none of my business, you're right.' She held out her hand. 'That'll be two shillings, please.'

The woman's eyebrows shot up in shock. 'Two whole shillings just for that?'

'It's the best we offer here at Pemberton's,' Annie lied. 'Direct from the fashion houses of Paris.'

Mrs Watson narrowed her eyes. 'Direct from Paris?'

Annie was enjoying herself now and determined to have a bit of fun with the woman who had caused Pearl so much pain. 'From the banks of the Seine all the way to Ryhope pit. It's the very latest à la mode with the Frenchies.' She leaned in conspiratorially across the counter. 'Mr Pemberton goes to France on buying trips and hand-picked this very ribbon himself.'

'He did?' Mrs Watson whispered.

Annie tapped the side of her nose. 'You can't go around telling people that. He doesn't like it

251

to get out, you know. But when you wear this on your hat for your son's wedding, you'll be the talk of the village. It's not everyone who could carry off this colour, Mrs Watson. But I've a feeling you'll manage it well.'

The woman raked in her purse and handed over some coins. 'French ribbon, you say?' she mused. She gave a little cough. 'You know, I was told by my mother that I have some French in my blood.'

'You do?' Annie exclaimed, trying not to laugh. 'There you go, then, that's the perfect ribbon for you.'

'My name, you see, the way it's spelled . . . R . . . e . . . n . . . e . . . e.'

'Oh!' said Annie, pretending to be impressed.

'Of course, Ryhope folk don't know that it's French. I mean, why would they? Most of them have travelled no further than the nearest pub. But my grandfather travelled.'

'He did?'

'Oh yes. He went to France. And so you see, the correct way to pronounce my name is not Ree-nee but Re-nay.'

'Renay,' Annie repeated in her best voice. 'Yes, it's certainly got a ring to it. And of course this ribbon you're buying . . . well, it's not just French, Mrs Watson . . . or Renay, if I may. It's Parisian!'

Biting her tongue to stop herself from giggling, Annie rang the sale through the till and pulled out one of the white paper bags with the Pemberton logo printed on it. She was just about to slip the wrapped ribbon into the bag when something caught Renee's eye at the other end of the shop.

'How much are your feathers?' she asked.

Annie glanced at the box of feathers sitting on the counter. Renee walked towards it. Without waiting for a reply, she reached into the box and pulled out a handful of red feathers.

'Why, these would be perfect for decoration at the wedding reception,' she enthused.

Annie thought for a moment and wondered if she could allow herself to let the woman buy them. It would be revenge of a sort, for there would be some men amongst the wedding guests who would know their meaning. But could she really be so cruel as to allow that to happen? It was tempting, but if she turned Mrs Watson into a laughing stock at her son's wedding, it might backfire. And if Bernie Pemberton found out, she might even get the sack. No, Annie had already had her fun at the woman's expense with the farce of the French ribbon. She strode across to her and snatched the box from the counter.

'Those are not for sale,' she said firmly. She slid the box out of sight and thrust the bag of ribbon towards Renee. 'Good day to you.'

Mrs Watson took the bag from Annie's hand and left the shop without another word, letting the door slam shut behind her. As soon as she had gone, Annie sank on to the wooden chair by the door, smiling at the thought of the woman boasting to all and sundry how she'd bought French ribbon on Ryhope colliery bank. For there was no doubt that she was the sort who wanted to be admired and envied; Annie had

253

learned that in the short time Renee had been in the shop. As she ran over the exchange that had just taken place, she started laughing. She was still chuckling a few moments later when the door opened and Pearl walked in. Framed in the shop doorway, with the summer sunshine behind her, she'd never looked more bonny. Her pregnancy had made her bloom.

'You look happy,' Pearl said, noting the playful smile on Annie's face.

'And you look beautiful,' Annie replied. She stood to greet her niece and kiss her on the cheek. 'Here, I've got you a bag of scraps for your mats, there are some bonny colours inside.'

Pearl took the bag gratefully.

'I've had a bit of a morning with a tricky customer,' Annie said.

'Anyone I know?'

Annie had decided to keep quiet about Renee's visit, as she didn't want to bring up the matter of Billy's wedding. It had been months since Pearl had left Watson's Grocers, but Annie knew she still carried the pain.

'No one you need to be concerned about,' she said.

Pearl put her hands to her back and stretched upwards.

'Baby giving you a bit of gyp?' Annie asked.

'Think it's trying to play a game of football in there,' Pearl said.

Annie offered the chair and Pearl sank into it gratefully.

'I was thinking we might invite Bobby Mac for tea tonight,' Annie said. 'And Michael if he wants to come. Veeda too, and Joey, if you'd like.'

'Invite them to our room? What on earth for?'

'Just a spot of tea, love. Don't you think we could do with a treat, just this once?'

Pearl stared at her aunt as if she was mad. 'We can't have guests in our room; we've got nowhere to put them. And there's that flaming hole in the floorboards and the stain on the wall from where the rain's leaked in. We can't let people like Veeda see how we live.'

But Annie was not to be dissuaded. 'What about just Joey, then? He's been in before; he knows exactly what it's like.'

'Just you, me and Joey? You promise you'll invite no one else?'

Annie gave a mischievous smile. 'How about Dorothy?'

'All right then, just the four of us,' Pearl agreed. 'But there's something I need to do first.'

Annie raised her eyebrows. 'Oh aye, and what's that?'

'I'll be back soon,' Pearl said as she disappeared out of the door.

Pearl walked down the colliery bank all the way to the Grand Cinema. It was the closest she'd come to Watson's Grocers since Renee had thrown her out. She kept her fingers crossed she wouldn't see Billy or Jim, or worse, Renee. She thought it unlikely, however, as she knew the Watsons would be working in the shop. She looked across the road at Ryhope police station, and her heart skipped a beat. It was a visit she'd been planning to make for some months ever since she'd seen Joey with his black eye. Yet with the baby on her mind, and settling back in to her room at Annie's, time had slipped by, weeks had turned into months and now here she was, no closer to telling the police what she knew about Jackson. Well, it was time she told them now.

She'd never been into the police station before. She glanced around, her heart hammering, terrified in case Jackson was on the prowl and spotted her going inside. At the entrance to the brick building, she took a deep breath. She knew she was doing the right thing. Jackson had to be brought to justice, and she would tell the police all she knew.

* * *

When Pearl returned from her mission at teatime, she and Annie set about putting a thin scraping of ham paste on triangles of stottie. They set the small table using an old blanket as a tablecloth. On the blanket Pearl placed a plate of sandwiches and a beef and onion pie bought from the Forester's Arms, alongside four juicy jam tarts. The jam was as red as could be, enclosed in thin pastry. When all the food was laid out, she allowed herself a smile of satisfaction.

As Pearl and Annie prepared the food, Boot whined on the landing until Annie had heard enough and shooed him away. The dog slunk to a corner of the yard and chewed on an old bone Bobby Mac had thrown over the wall.

First to arrive for the tea was Joey. Pearl was pleased to see her friend again, but kept tight-lipped about her visit to the police station earlier.

'What you been up to?' she asked him. She didn't want to appear nosy and tried to keep her tone casual. 'You back working anywhere?'

Joey shrugged. 'Doing a bit of this and that.'

He didn't mention Jackson and so she didn't ask, but the man's name hung between them, keeping them from being as honest with each other as Pearl would have liked.

'Where?'

'Here and there.'

Pearl laughed. 'Come on, Joey. It's me you're talking to. How's your mam doing?'

Joey's face flickered with the briefest of smiles. 'She's been out of bed this week, I think it's the warm weather, makes it easier for her. She sends her love.'

Pearl reached to touch Joey's arm, but he flinched and pulled away. That was when she noticed the bruises on his arms. 'Who did that to you?' she asked him.

Joey hung his head. 'No one. I fell.'

Pearl knew then, in an instant, that she'd done the right thing in visiting the police station. But she would keep it a secret from Joey for fear that it would put him in more danger with Jackson if he knew the truth.

She caught him staring at her stomach, the baby bump obvious under her clothes. She'd grown so big that she'd had to start wearing some of Annie's things. She felt a twinge in her back again, the same pain as earlier, and stretched upwards to ease herself.

257

'When's it due?' Joey asked, still staring at Pearl's stomach.

'The doctor reckons a couple of weeks to go.'

'You've seen Dr Anderson?'

Pearl shook her head furiously. 'No, I couldn't go there. I couldn't risk bumping into Billy or Sylvia. I've seen the other doctor, the one up at Silksworth. It's a bit of a walk to get there, but it keeps me clear of going past Watson's Grocers too.'

'You've still not seen Billy, then?'

'I told you I wasn't going to run after him, didn't I? I meant what I said. Why would I give him a second chance to hurt me? He made his position clear: his life is with Sylvia. They're getting married soon anyway.'

'Don't you want him at all, Pearl?' Joey asked.

She couldn't look her friend in the eye. 'He means nothing to me now.'

Joey listened carefully to Pearl's words and heard a sadness in the way she spoke, a sadness he understood only too well. He knew Pearl better than she guessed, for hadn't he grown up with her? Hadn't he been her only friend? He knew better than anyone that the words coming from her lips belied the feelings she harboured inside.

Outside on the landing there was an almighty clatter, and a cry went up. Annie pulled the door open and saw Dorothy scuttling away down the stairs. She appeared to be chasing something that was bumping down the steps. Annie followed her friend down into the yard to find Boot sniffing at what looked like a ball. Dorothy

258

walked over to it, picked it up and held it aloft.

'Got you, you little bugger!' she cried.

'What the devil is that?' Annie asked as the two of them returned upstairs.

'Ah, you'll have to wait and see. Got it off my fella, the one who brought the pined apples at Christmas, remember?'

Annie opened her mouth in surprise and stared for a long time at her friend.

'You're still with the same fella?'

Dorothy shrugged. 'He treats me well, why shouldn't I be?'

'What about working the lane?' Annie asked. 'Are you still — '

Dorothy cut her short. 'I stopped not long after you. I mean, if I need it, it's there, but my fella's looking after me and the bairns for now.'

'What's he called then, this fella of yours? Anyone we know?'

Dorothy's eyes twinkled with mischief. 'He might be,' she laughed.

'Who is it, Dorothy?' Pearl asked.

'Tommy Surtees,' Dorothy said proudly.

The name meant nothing to Pearl, but Annie burst out laughing. 'Little Tommy we used to go to school with? That Tommy Surtees? The one with the funny eye? We always used to think he was winking at us, do you remember?'

Dorothy bristled before she replied. 'Well, his eye's all right now, otherwise he wouldn't have been able to sign up to serve with the Durham Light Infantry. But yes, it's the same Tommy Surtees.'

'Well I never,' Annie said, shaking her head in

disbelief. 'Little Tommy Surtees.' She nudged Dorothy playfully in the ribs, but Dorothy only gave a hard stare in return. There was silence between them for a few moments, a tension so thick it hung in the air waiting to be sliced open. It was Dorothy who spoke first.

'He did have a funny eye, didn't he?' she said, and then she and Annie burst out laughing together, holding on to each other until their giggles subsided. Pearl and Joey exchanged a look, and Joey whirled his forefinger at the side of his head.

'Crackers, the pair of them,' he whispered.

'Sorry, pet,' Dorothy said to Pearl. 'Here, this is for us to have with our tea.' She held out her hand, and Pearl peered at the round object in her palm. It was the size of an orange, but it was a peculiar dark red colour, almost purple and it had hard wrinkled skin.

'Can I eat it?'

'You'll need to cut it open first,' Dorothy replied. 'But you don't cut it into chunks, not like we did with the pined apple.'

'Pineapple,' Pearl laughed. Then she gasped as a pain shot through her, all the way up her back. It gripped her sides and her hands flew to her stomach. She rocked slowly back and forth, waiting for it to release its grip.

Dorothy knelt on the floor beside her. 'Breathe, Pearl. Breathe in long and hard.' She put her hand to Pearl's brow. 'When's it due?' she asked.

Pearl couldn't speak for the spasms of pain that sliced through her.

'Couple of weeks,' Annie replied.

'Might be coming a little early,' Dorothy said matter-of-factly. 'Happened to me with three of mine. The other four came on time.'

Pearl slumped forward, the pain finally leaving her.

'Get her some water,' Dorothy ordered, and Annie did as she was bid.

Pearl sipped at the water and gradually sat upright. All the time this had been going on, Joey had been watching, his attention focused on his friend. Pearl looked into his concerned eyes, then at Annie and Dorothy.

'I'm fine,' she said softly. 'I feel all right now, honestly.' She shuffled across the floor to rest her back against the bed, and smiled at Dorothy, who still held tight to the strange object. 'Is that really for me?' she asked.

Dorothy handed over the fruit and Pearl sniffed it then gave it a shake. It didn't seem to have juice inside it in the way she knew coconuts did. She'd seen coconuts on the market when she'd been there with Billy. But she'd never seen one of these strange fruits before and had no idea what it was.

'It's a Malaga pomegranate!' Dorothy announced, her chest swelling with pride. 'Tommy says he used to eat them when he was abroad. His brother's over in South Shields and they get these fruit and veg on the docks, so he bundled up a couple and passed them on. We ate one of them the other night, so I know what to do with it. Give it here.'

Annie went to get her sharp knife and handed

261

it to Dorothy, who sliced the fruit through. Joey, Pearl and Annie leaned in to take a look.

'Cor blimey!' Joey breathed.

'It's beautiful,' Pearl said.

'Are you sure we can eat this?' Annie asked.

Dorothy cut each half into quarters and then pulled back the skin, exposing the scarlet fruit.

'They're like little gems, rubies,' Pearl exclaimed.

'Pick one,' Dorothy said. 'Pick one, close your eyes and pop it in your mouth.'

Pearl did as Dorothy instructed and crunched down on the tiny piece of red fruit. As the sweet, sugary taste hit her tongue, she opened her eyes wide.

'It really is something else,' she said. 'Try a bit, Annie, and you, Joey.'

Annie and Joey each tried one of the exotic red seeds. Soon all four of them were picking at the fruit. When they'd finished, Annie put the kettle on the fire and Joey sat cross-legged on the floor. Dorothy took the jam tart Annie offered and placed it in her skirt pocket before leaving as noisily as she'd arrived, her boots clattering on the stairs.

With tea made in the pot, Pearl, Annie and Joey tucked into the sandwiches and pie. Pearl tried a couple of times to engage Joey in conversation, curious to know what he was up to with his days. But Joey remained tight-lipped and so she didn't push him for answers. She knew only too well that if he wanted to keep something to himself, he would guard it with a passion in his heart. He wouldn't react well to her pushing and poking him for news.

She thought again about her visit to the police, and wondered briefly if she was wise to keep it a secret after all. Perhaps she should tell Joey what she'd done? But she changed her mind as soon as the thought entered her head. She knew Joey wouldn't be happy that she'd got involved, and wouldn't understand that all she wanted to do was protect him. It was on the tip of her tongue to ask him about Jackson, but she let the subject drop. Joey had a haunted look about him these days; he was all skin and bone, his face sunken and sallow. And he appeared nervous too, twitchy, not the Joey she'd once known who always had a ready smile on his lips. She decided to ask him about something she knew he liked.

'Done any more drawings of your pony?'

His face lit up. Bingo, Pearl had guessed right. She'd known this would get him talking.

'A few,' he replied. 'Mam puts them on the windowsill in the kitchen so she can see them when she looks out the window.'

The mention of the kitchen window started Pearl wondering if Joey had seen his ghost again. She was just about to ask him when Annie announced she was going down to the shop.

'I've forgotten to lock the safe. Bernie will kill me if he finds out.' She grabbed her keys from the drawer in the pantry and hurried down the stairs.

Pearl and Joey sat together picking at the remains of the pomegranate. But then another spasm of pain cramped Pearl's body, and this time it seemed to be everywhere, gripping her relentlessly. She yelled as hard as she could. Joey pulled himself up in alarm, using the support of Pearl's bed. Pearl could hardly breathe properly, never mind speak, but she managed to force out the same two words over and over again.

'Get Annie!' she yelled. 'Get Annie!'

Joey stood rooted to the spot. He couldn't leave his friend when she was like this, clearly in agony. And what if it was the baby coming, what then? He didn't know what to do. He stood dithering for a minute. What if he left and she died? He'd have it on his conscience for ever.

'Get Annie!' Pearl screamed again.

Joey made up his mind. He moved as quickly as his bad leg allowed, barely stopping for breath, half running, half limping out of the yard and into the lane. Boot was sleeping when he hurried past, and lazily opened his eyes as Joey headed towards the shop, yelling for Annie at the top of his voice.

Meanwhile, in the room above, Pearl was in shock and pain. This wasn't supposed to happen yet, she thought; she still had two weeks left, the doctor had said so. Tears streamed down her cheeks as she called out for Annie. She was scared and hurting and she felt frightened and alone. It was only minutes, but it felt like a lifetime before she heard Annie's boots clatter on the stairs.

Annie flew into the room to find Pearl lying on the floor with water pooled on the wooden boards beneath her. She got down on her knees with not a clue what to do. She wasn't a mother herself; she didn't know how to bring a child into the world.

'Get Dorothy!' she yelled to Joey, who had followed her up the stairs. Panicked, Joey flew down the stairs again as fast as he could, paying his own pain no heed. He had to reach Dorothy, to bring her, to tell her the baby was coming.

Dorothy received the summons with stoicism. She pulled towels from her cupboards along with a bottle of bathing disinfectant and a very sharp knife to cut the cord. Only when she was sure she had all she needed did she run to Annie's room. When she flew into the yard, Boot raised his eyes at the noise before settling himself back to sleep.

With Annie and Dorothy tending to Pearl, Joey stood for a moment in the back lane to catch his breath. His chest heaved from the exertion of running up and down the stairs. The pain from his leg was throbbing all the way up to his hip. But he knew that whatever he was feeling, whatever pain he was suffering, it was nothing compared to what Pearl was going through.

He made his way into the yard and looked through the open door. He didn't dare go up there. He didn't want to see Pearl all bloodied and torn with the baby coming from her. He'd heard enough in the school yard from his friends to know what happened; and from his time at High Farm when he'd watched a calf come into the world he remembered the blood and mucus clinging to spindly legs and bone. His stomach turned and he sank heavily on to the bottom step. He'd keep guard there for Pearl; that was the least he could do. He'd stop anyone walking in from the lane.

Sitting on the step with his head in his hands, he heard Pearl. She was groaning at first and Joey thought she sounded angry. The groaning turned louder, fiercer, and then she was screaming. He winced. Crossing the fingers on both hands, he willed all his good luck to his friend. He heard Annie's voice, gentle and encouraging, telling Pearl everything was going to be fine. And then he heard Dorothy, firmer, telling Pearl to keep pushing, keep breathing. He heard Dorothy direct Annie to get water, to spread towels on the floor. And then it was Pearl again, crying harder, screaming, yelling. Would it ever end? Joey couldn't take it any more; every time Pearl cried out, the sound pierced his heart. He wanted to run . . . to run upstairs and hold Pearl's hand, to tell her he would always be there for her, always be her friend. And he wanted to run far away too, to get away from the cries and the pain and the horror of whatever was going on up there.

Still keeping his fingers crossed, he pressed his hands to his ears to block out the screams, but they were still there, still in his head, and then he was underground again, with the ponies, with Ned, and he was being crushed by the coal tubs in the darkness of the pit. Tears ran down his face and he closed his eyes to let them fall. When he opened them again, Boot was standing right in front of him, the dog's velvet eyes staring up into his own. Boot's tail wagged and he laid his head on Joey's lap.

There was silence from upstairs. Total silence. Joey gasped and held his breath, listening. And then it came, the unmistakable cry of a newborn baby. He allowed himself a smile as relief flooded through his body. He wanted to run up and see Pearl, but he knew he wouldn't be welcome in the room up above until she was decent. He wondered how best to help her; there must be something he could do, surely? He thought of her sadness when she'd talked of Billy, and in that moment, he was filled with certainty. He didn't need to mull his idea over. He didn't need to ask Pearl, for he had never felt more sure of anything before.

'Come on, Boot,' he said.

Boot stretched his front legs along the ground and gave himself a shake. Joey closed the back door and shut the gate before he headed into the lane. The pain in his leg raged as he walked, but he was determined to get to his destination as quickly as he could.

It took him the best part of an hour to reach Watson's. On the pavement outside the shop, he gathered his breath.

'Boot, stay,' he ordered and the dog sat next to the wall.

Joey pushed at the door where a *Closed* sign hung. Through the glass pane in the door he saw two faces turn towards him from behind the counter. One was an older man with a tidy white beard and small round glasses. The other was a younger man.

'Billy Watson?' he yelled through the glass.

Billy walked towards the door and unlocked it.

'That's me,' Billy replied. 'How can I help?'

'I've come to give you some news.'

13

Reunion

Billy flew from behind the counter. Jim looked on with his mouth hanging open.

'I've got to go to her, Dad,' Billy yelled.

'Course you do, son,' Jim replied, but his words were lost as Billy was already storming from the shop.

'Run, Billy! Run!' Joey urged.

Billy didn't need any encouragement. With his apron flying, he pounded up the colliery. In his blind panic he forgot about the grocery van that would have got him there quicker than his legs could carry him. The adrenaline surged through him, propelling him on. He ran past the Co-op and the rhubarb field, past the miners' hall and the colliery pubs. And as he ran, his heart beat wildly. Could it really be true, the news that the young lad had brought? Pearl had mentioned her friend Joey to Billy many times while she'd lived at Watson's. There was no need to doubt the boy's words, was there? There would be time for questions later. All Billy wanted more than anything, all he'd ever wanted since the night his mam told him she'd gone, was to see Pearl again.

In the months without Pearl, Billy had been forced into Sylvia's arms. Their wedding invitations had been sent and new hats had been bought. He'd accepted that Sylvia was his destiny, but only because he'd been forced to accept that Pearl no longer loved him. And now this bombshell had exploded at his feet. Pearl had been pregnant with his child all this time. How could he have not known? How could the news have been kept from him?

As Billy ran, the blood rushed in his head in a white-hot rage. All he could think of was Pearl. His beautiful Pearl, a girl like no other he'd met. She might not have the grace of the doctor's daughter, nor the manners or style. Her clothes might be worn and shabby, but she had a heart the size of Ryhope itself. Sylvia was no match for Pearl, no matter how expensive her clothes or how fragrant her cologne. Oh, she had a good heart and a pretty face, even if she rarely cracked a smile, but she would never be the girl Billy wanted her to be. She would never be Pearl.

He had loved Pearl from the moment he'd met her, and had never stopped. There had been nights when he'd cried himself to sleep after she'd left without a word of goodbye. He'd wanted to visit her, but his mam was firm on the matter, and even his dad too.

'She's gone, lad,' Jim would say with a resigned air. 'You've got to let her go and get on with your own life.'

But Billy had been lost without Pearl, rudderless, steered into Sylvia's arms by his manipulative mam.

He ran on, his heart pounding, not once stopping for breath. The Forester's Arms pub came into sight, then the Colliery Inn. Next to it was Pemberton's Goods. He ran to the shop door, pushed at it but found it locked.

'Pearl!' he yelled, banging on the wood with his fists. 'Annie!' He looked at the grimed windows above. 'Pearl!' he yelled again. He cupped his hands to his mouth and shouted up to the windows, but there was no movement. He looked from left to right, hoping to see someone he could ask where he'd find the entrance to Pearl and Annie's room, but all he could see was two women gossiping on the street, one with a basket on her arm, the other with a child at her hip.

The main road dipped down to the village and Billy peered down its length, but there was no sign of Joey. He remembered the lad limping when he'd come into the shop to give him the news. If he was lame, he would likely be making his slow way up the bank. Out on the horizon, the ocean twinkled with diamonds as the sun danced on the sea. Billy saw the spire of St Paul's reaching up to white strips of cloud.

He allowed himself a few minutes to fully catch his breath and focus his mind. Of course! There was only one way into Pearl's home if the shop door was locked! He walked up the bank a little further, feeling the heat in his body after his run. When he'd passed the Colliery Inn, he turned left and headed into Dawdon Street. He gasped in shock when he saw what lay ahead. It was the same view down the bank as he'd taken in just minutes before. He saw the same church spire and the same sparkling sea but it was now framed by a dark, dirty pathway. An unmade road ran the length of the row of tiny houses squashed together. Cobblestones were missing, and rainwater and mud puddled in black holes. Was this the pit lane where Pearl said Annie had offered her for sale? Billy had seen nothing like it. It was decrepit and forlorn, a cold, uninviting place. There were no trees to be seen, no greenery of any kind, just roofs with missing tiles, broken windows, and stones strewn on the ground. He stepped over a steaming pile of horse muck.

'Get off it, lad!' a voice called out behind him. 'I saw it first!'

He swung round to see a man in a shabby jacket and flat cap running towards him, waving a shovel in the air. Billy leapt to one side, ready to fight if necessary. He didn't know what rules existed in the colliery back lanes, but he was damned if he would let anything stop him reaching Pearl. But when the man drew near, he simply shovelled up the muck.

'It'll bring my leeks on a treat, this will. Pure gold.' He smiled at Billy, then turned and disappeared from wherever he had come from, carrying the manure as carefully as if he'd shovelled up precious gems.

Billy looked at the window above the yard next to the Colliery Inn. She'd still be in bed, wouldn't she, after giving birth? She'd be getting tended to by a doctor, surely? The thought shot a bolt of fear through him. What if Sylvia's dad, Dr Anderson, was there? What then? Billy squared his shoulders. He'd deal with whatever came next. He'd take the consequences. Nothing could stop him from finding Pearl.

He pushed tentatively at the rotting wooden gate. It swung open at his touch and he peered into the yard. A tin bath hung on a hook against the wall and a chewed meat bone sat underneath. He inched past the metal poss tub used for washing clothes, and was about to open the back door before remembering his manners. He was desperate to see Pearl but he knew he couldn't just barge in. He banged at the door with his fist and waited. There was no answer, no sound from within, and so he tried again, harder this time, more insistent. At last the door flew open and he found himself face to face with the woman he recognised as Pearl's aunt. She was not pleased to see him.

'What the hell do you think you're doing here?'

'I need to see her, please, Annie. I've just found out about the baby. I need to see her.'

Annie stood firm and crossed her arms, blocking the doorway. There was a cry from behind her, another cry, louder, followed by wailing.

'I need to see my baby, Annie. Please let me in,' he begged.

Annie bit her lip.

'Who is it?' a woman's voice called down the stairs.

Annie didn't turn; she just stared straight at Billy's face. He felt as if she was staring right into his soul. 'Stay there,' she hissed, and closed the door, leaving him standing in the yard. He took a deep breath, but the foul air of the back lane caught in his throat.

It felt like a lifetime that he waited there, wondering if the door would be opened again. When it swung wide a second time, a woman Billy hadn't seen before stood there.

'Are you the nurse?' he asked urgently.

The woman didn't answer. She just jerked her head to one side, indicating that he should enter. 'She's upstairs, but go easy. She says she'll see you for five minutes, to hear what you've got to say for yourself. Five minutes, you hear? And not a minute more.'

Billy followed her up the stairs, the treads creaking under his feet. It smelled damp, he thought, damp mixed with a rotten smell that he couldn't place. When they reached the landing, the woman stood to one side.

'Five minutes,' she reminded him.

Billy gulped. His legs turned to jelly. Somehow he managed to put one foot in front of the other to propel his body into the room. The smell of damp was stronger in there, and the first thing that caught his eye was the black mould growing on the wall. The other smell was there too, heady, powerful, unpleasant, and he realised it was coming from a mound of bloodied cloths on the floor. He glanced around. Thin faded curtains hung at the windows, and he was shocked to see a gaping hole in the floorboards beside the fireplace. He'd never seen anything like this room in all of his eighteen years. He was appalled at the sight of it, sickened to the stomach at the thought that Pearl had chosen to live here rather than in the small, clean attic above the grocer's. She really must hate him, and yet what had he done to deserve it? That was a question he'd wrestled with for months.

He took another step. Annie was standing in front of him with her arms crossed and lips pursed. But there was no sign of Pearl. He took another step, and there to his right, behind the open door, he saw the foot of a bed covered in a green eiderdown. He didn't dare look. The second woman came into the room after him and moved next to Annie. The two of them stood glaring at him, both of them with their arms crossed, silently warning him not to say or do the wrong thing.

His eyes flicked to the right, and there she was, sitting up in the bed, her legs covered with the green eiderdown. She looked tired and worn, but Billy thought she had never looked more beautiful. In her arms was her child, their child, a tiny pink baby with the bonniest little face he'd ever seen. His heart dropped into his boots. He couldn't speak. He looked at Pearl and they locked eyes for a second before she pulled her gaze away.

'I want to speak to him alone,' she said to the two women.

'Are you sure, pet?' Annie asked.

'I'm sure.'

The second woman gathered up the bloodied towels and sheets. 'I'll bring some barley broth over for you later,' she said.

Annie followed her out of the room, but before she left, she paused at Billy's side and whispered in his ear. 'You upset her and you'll have me to deal with, you hear? And when she's said her piece and asks you to leave, you leave.'

Billy swallowed hard. 'I will,' he whispered back.

And with that, Annie was gone, pulling the door closed behind her, leaving Pearl and Billy to talk.

There was too much to say . . . so much that neither of them knew where to start. The words hung between them in the foul damp air of the room.

'Pull that chair out, sit yourself down,' Pearl said at last.

Billy looked to where she indicated. He stepped over the hole in the floor and lifted the chair to her bedside.

'The woman . . . ' he began hesitantly, afraid of the sound of his own voice, afraid that it might hurt the baby or upset Pearl. But he had to speak, he had to. 'The woman with the dark hair, she said you'd give me five minutes. I'm grateful, Pearl, I swear.'

'Who told you about the baby?' she asked, staring ahead at the window, where the remains of the daylight struggled to fight their way in.

'Joey,' he said.

Pearl laid her head against the pillow propped up at her back. 'Joey,' she breathed.

Billy forced himself to carry on. 'Are you well, Pearl?' he asked somewhat stiffly. He held his hands in his lap and tried to sit still while every fibre of his being was screaming at him to lean across the bed and kiss Pearl. 'And the child?'

She smiled at him then. 'It's a boy,' she said. 'You have a son.'

'We have a son,' he replied.

'I don't know why you'd want anything to do with him. You discarded me quickly enough. What use have I got for a dad like you for my bairn?'

Her words found their target and stung Billy deep. He was confused. What did she mean by *discarded* when it was she who had run out on him? He glanced at his son, but all he could see was a tiny pink face peeking from a tightly wrapped shawl. The baby's eyes were screwed shut.

'And is he well?' he dared to ask.

'Yes, he's well. Ten fingers, ten toes and a tiny little you-know-what.'

Billy laughed at Pearl's words and they shared a smile before falling silent again. This time Pearl turned her face towards him and they looked deep into each other's eyes for a very long time.

'You've got three minutes left, Billy,' she said seriously. 'Is there anything else you want to say while you're here? Anything about a woman called Sylvia Anderson, perhaps?'

'Sylvia? I don't want Sylvia. I've never wanted her. I've only ever wanted you, Pearl.'

'You must have known where I was,' she said softly. 'How could you not have known I was back here with Annie? Yet you never came calling, not once. Don't tell me you wanted me, Billy. If you'd wanted me, you'd have come for me. Actions speak louder than words, remember.'

She stared straight ahead again, willing herself not to cry.

Billy shook his head, confused. 'But you were the one who left me! You told Mam you were going back to Annie's because you didn't want to live down at Watson's any more. You told her you were finished with your life there, finished with me. You said you wanted to come back to the colliery. You said — '

Pearl cut him short. 'I didn't, Billy. I never said any of that, not one single word.'

Billy rocked back in his chair. 'What?'

Slowly, hesitantly, Pearl began to unwind the threads of the past as she told Billy the real reason she'd left. And each time she mentioned Renee's name, Billy winced. It was painful for him to hear the selfish and wicked things his mam had been capable of. He thought of the lost months without Pearl, wasting time with Sylvia, and his anger began to grow. He hated to hear how upset Pearl had been, how distraught at thinking he didn't love her or want her. He shook his head and cried: 'No! No!' as she carried on with her tale.

When she had finished speaking, he reached across the eiderdown and she slowly offered her hand. He raised her fingers to his lips and kissed them gently, then laid her hand against the side of his face. Pearl looked at him, really looked at him this time, and she knew he wasn't lying about what his mam had said. She knew it was Billy, her Billy, sitting there. It was as if the last few months hadn't happened, didn't matter. Time simply melted away. Tears began to fall down Billy's face and on to Pearl's fingertips.

'I can't hate her, Pearl,' he sobbed. 'She's my

mother and I can't hate her, but I'll never forgive her for this.'

Pearl kissed the top of the baby's head. 'She only wanted the best for her son. I understand that more now than I ever could before.'

'Can you see a life for the three of us, Pearl?' he asked.

She gave a tiny nod and choked back the lump in her throat. 'But what about your mam? What about Sylvia?'

Billy thought for a moment. 'Leave them to me, they're not your problem.'

'Please be gentle with Sylvia's heart,' Pearl said. 'She's not to blame for any of this.'

Billy wiped the back of his hand across his eyes and sat up straight in the chair. 'I'll call the wedding off immediately. Mam's going to swear blue murder, I know it, but I can't live a lie, Pearl. Marrying Sylvia is the only thing she's been talking of for months; it's going to ruin her. But rather her than me. I've got to stand up to her, no matter how much it hurts. I'll go and speak to Mam and Dad now. I'll tell them about you, Pearl, about the baby, about how I really feel. I had it planned you know, that night you disappeared; I was ready to tell Mam everything about us. But when I came home you had gone and I . . . ' He stopped himself. He didn't want to tell Pearl about the nights he'd cried after she'd left; he didn't want to break down in front of her and their baby. ' . . . and the next thing I know I'm being shoved about like a prize pig backwards and forwards to Dr Anderson's house to court his flaming daughter.'

'You need to learn to stand up to your mam, Billy. I can help you. Let me come with you when you speak to her; we'll do it together. In a few days I'll be up and about. We'll take the baby with us.'

Billy shook his head. 'No, I've got to do this alone, Pearl. But I *will* stand up to her, just you wait and see.'

★ ★ ★

Outside on the landing, Annie and Dorothy were huddled together with their ears pressed up against the door.

'His five minutes is up,' Dorothy whispered. 'I say we go in and chuck him out.'

Annie shook her head. 'No. Let's give them a few minutes more.'

When the door flew open without warning, the two women almost fell flat on their faces. Pearl and Billy burst out laughing as the pair stumbled into the room. They gathered themselves, but Pearl could see a blush rising on her aunt's face at being caught out.

'Right then. I'll be taking my leave,' Billy said.

'Not yet, Billy,' Pearl said. 'There's something you've forgotten to do.' She beckoned him back to her bedside. 'You haven't said hello to your son.'

Billy leaned down to the tiny bundle in Pearl's arms and kissed the top of the baby's head. 'Hello, little one,' he said softly.

Pearl looked deep into his eyes. 'I'll be seeing you, Billy Watson,' she whispered.

He bent low and kissed her on the lips. 'What will we call him?' he asked.

'I'm too tired to think of that now,' she replied.

Billy pulled back from the bed. 'I'm sorry, of course. I must let you rest.' He glanced at Annie and Dorothy. 'Thank you for letting me see her.' And with that, he was gone, away down the stairs, through the yard and out to the mucky pit lane.

After he'd left, Annie and Dorothy sat on the edge of Pearl's bed.

'How much did you hear?' Pearl asked.

Annie and Dorothy exchanged a sly look.

'Enough to know you've got a good fella there,' Annie said. 'I thought he had something special about him the first time I met him, and I think the same now. Sounds like his mam's got a lot to answer for, though.'

'I'll deal with her in my own time,' Pearl said. 'But for now, all I want to do is sleep, just like this little one.'

★ ★ ★

As Pearl rested in her bed with the baby at her side, Annie and Dorothy worked to get the coal fire going.

'Gorgeous little baby, isn't he?' Annie said.

'Beautiful,' Dorothy agreed. 'Makes me all broody seeing them that little.' She cast a look at her friend. 'You were lucky you never got caught in the family way, but then you didn't want any of your own, did you?'

'It never worked out, Dot. Never found a fella I wanted to spend my time with. Jackson, the men on the lane . . . what hope have I ever had of meeting someone nice? Besides which, I always had Pearl. And look how that's turned out.'

'She's a grand lass,' Dorothy said.

'Aye, she is. But I'm flaming useless. I got myself deep into debt, and then I tried to use her as a way to solve my problems. I promised Mary I'd look after her, but I feel like I've let her down at every step.'

Dorothy squeezed her friend's hand. 'I suppose her having the little 'un makes you like a grandmother now. Granny Annie!' She nudged her in the ribs.

'What do you suppose he'll grow up to be?' Annie wondered. 'Wonder if he'll always live in Ryhope, like we have, or if he'll travel further afield.'

'What, all the way to Silksworth, you mean?' Dorothy smiled.

'Well, at least he won't have to go to war when he's older; that's something, I suppose.' Annie sighed. 'All them young lads killed at the front fighting for king and country, it's a crying shame. A nation's shame. They've called the Great War the war to end all wars, and so help me, I hope that's true. I'd hate to think of Pearl's little 'un being brought into a world where we might see killing on that scale again.'

Dorothy sat quietly for a while, watching the flames lick around the newspaper and sticks in the fire. 'What do you think she'll call him? She's hardly got any fellas to use as role models, has she?'

'She's got Billy, of course, and there's Joey. I don't think she knows many other lads she'd want to name her baby after. Just Bobby Mac and Michael. Oh, and she knows the vicar.'

'What's his first name?' Dorothy asked.

Annie thought for a moment. 'Do you know, I've got no idea! I always call him Reverend Daye or just Vicar. I never think of him as having a first name. Do you?'

'We need to get Pearl out knocking on doors,' Dorothy said. 'We've got to get her to at least three houses with her new bairn. She's to ask for salt, bread and water so that her little 'un will never know hunger or thirst in his life.'

'Oh Dot, no! Not them daft superstitions. They went out of fashion years ago. Old wives' tales, they are, nothing more.'

'That's as may be,' Dorothy said, 'but there's plenty of old wives in Ryhope who set store by them. You can get all sorts out of old wives if you go knocking on doors with a newborn in your arms. You wouldn't believe the things I was given when I had mine. I got a whole fruit cake from one of the houses on the village green once.'

* * *

Billy walked down the colliery bank deep in thought. Just that morning he'd woken up with Pearl on his mind and in his heart, as always. He'd wondered how she was and what she was doing; the pain of losing her had never fully

282

gone. And now here he was, the very same day, and his whole world had been turned upside down. He didn't know where to begin to put things in order. But he knew he'd have to speak to his mam. He needed to be strong and firm. He knew he mustn't lose his temper; she was his mother after all. His dad would be on his side. He'd always liked Pearl and had never gone along with Renee's plans for Billy to marry Sylvia. But he'd never firmly opposed them either, preferring a quiet life instead of incurring his wife's wrath.

Billy thought of Pearl's room with its rotten, rancid smell and the gaping hole in the floor. How could anyone live like that? He'd heard of slum landlords who rented out rooms in a ruinous state, but this was the first time he'd seen anything like it. He determined to find a wooden board and fix the hole in the floor for them. He'd ask his dad for advice on mending the roof to stop the damp getting worse. And what then, he thought, what then? Would he and Pearl live together with the baby? He needed to get her and the child out of that room, away from the horrors of the pit lane.

But all that would come in time. To know that Pearl loved him, had always loved him, filled his heart with joy. He would take things one step at a time. As he walked, he ordered his thoughts. He'd speak to his mam and dad first, then he must speak to Sylvia and, as Pearl had advised him, be as gentle as he could. Whatever happened, the wedding needed to be called off. He'd take the blame and the gossip that was sure to fly about. He'd take it all, for it meant that he and Pearl were together. Nothing else mattered now, nothing at all.

When he reached the village green, he saw the Albion Inn ahead. He was tempted to go in for a drink. He needed the courage before confronting his mam, the kind of courage that could come only from inside a whisky glass. The bells of St Paul's rang the evening hour long and loud. Who'd have thought it? Billy Watson, a dad! The thought made him crave a drink more than ever, and he headed into the pub. He was greeted with a smile from Hetty Burdon.

'What'll it be, Billy? Your dad joining you tonight?'

'Scotch, please, Hetty,' he replied. 'And no, I'm on my own. I'm just after a quiet drink.'

Hetty eyed her customer as she took the whisky bottle down from the shelf. She'd never known Billy drink anything stronger than a pint of Vaux ale. But she didn't pry. If she'd learned one thing in her years running the Albion Inn, it was that if customers wanted to chat, they would chat. And if they wanted to keep themselves to themselves, the last thing they needed or wanted was her or Jack prying into their business.

Billy paid for his drink and took himself to a quiet corner, where he sat at a table alone. He held the glass in both hands and swirled the amber liquid before lifting it to his lips. In truth, he wasn't a great lover of whisky, and the spirit burned his throat as he drank. But he needed something to dull the shock of the day, and what a day it had turned out to be. He was elated, overjoyed at having Pearl back in his life. But he knew he had a hard task ahead confronting his mam, and a difficult meeting with Sylvia. And then there was the baby, his baby, and his future with Pearl.

He took another sip from the glass, and this time the whisky slipped down more easily now his throat had been numbed to the burn. He glanced around the pub and saw a man sitting alone. There was a familiar look about him — something about the trimmed moustache and auburn hair that Billy recognised — but he couldn't place him. On the table in front of him was a folded copy of the day's *Sunderland Echo*, and next to it, the gentleman's hat. For he was a gentleman, Billy decided, taking in the pressed trousers and shined shoes the man was wearing.

The stranger looked up, caught Billy staring at him and raised his glass in his direction. 'Penny for them, son?'

'Sorry,' Billy muttered, embarrassed. 'I was just wondering . . . you're not from round here, are you? I don't think I've seen you before, but there's something familiar about you. I was trying to place you.'

The man picked up his pint glass, hat and newspaper and walked across to Billy's table. 'Mind if I join you?'

Billy nodded his assent.

'Whisky, is it? At this hour?' The man smiled. 'You've either got a guilty conscience or there's something on your mind.'

Billy leaned back in his chair. It was a relief to be able to speak to someone, and who better

285

than a stranger who wouldn't judge? He began slowly, putting into words everything that had happened. The man listened patiently without interrupting, nodding at the appropriate times and wincing when he heard the part that Renee had played.

'She might disinherit me, you know,' Billy explained. 'When she finds out the truth about me and Pearl, there's every chance she'll do what she can to make sure the shop doesn't come my way when Dad retires.'

'Your own mother would do that?' the man asked, shocked.

'Wouldn't put it past her,' Billy replied. 'Now that I know what she's capable of, nothing would surprise me.'

'If you ever find yourself in need of work, lad, seek me out. Hetty Burdon will tell you how to find me. Or ask the vicar, he knows me too.'

When Billy reached the end of his story, the man insisted on buying him another drink. 'To wet the baby's head,' he said.

But Billy knew that if he stayed for a second drink, there was every danger he'd want to stay for a third. And he needed to keep his wits about him for when he returned home to tackle his mam. He had plenty to say to her and didn't want to be slurring his words. He thanked the man for listening, for not judging, and then took his leave.

After he'd gone, the man walked to the bar and ordered himself a whisky.

'What is it with all you Scotch drinkers tonight?' Hetty joked. 'Are you celebrating

286

something I've not been told about?'

'Something like that,' the man replied with a curious smile.

Outside the Albion Inn, the cool evening air brushed Billy's face. He realised he had not asked the name of the man he'd just been speaking to, and neither had it been offered. He thought of Pearl again, lying with their child at her breast, the tiny baby who belonged to them both. He took a few deep breaths to steady himself against the effects of the whisky. It had only been a tot, not enough to make him drunk. But it was enough to put fire in his belly so that he could give vent to his feelings to his mam as soon as he got home.

When he reached the grocer's shop, it looked dark and deserted, and he realised that his dad had finished locking up against the lateness of the day. He pushed the door, just to check, and was surprised when it opened at his touch. He stepped inside.

'Dad?' he called.

There was no answer, not a sound.

'Dad?' he called again.

It was most unlike his dad to leave the shop door open. Once they closed up, the door was bolted and the family went upstairs to their rooms.

Despite the dark, Billy knew the layout of the shop like the back of his hand. He stepped to the right and held tight to the counter to help guide his way. And that was when he saw it . . . the body of a man sprawled on the floor. He gasped with shock. Was it an intruder who had fallen? he wondered. He inched forward.

'You there!' he yelled as assertively as he could.

But there was no response.

Just then, something caught his eye: a glint of glass. A pair of glasses had skittered across the floor where the man had fallen. A pair of small, round, wire-framed glasses exactly like the ones his dad wore.

14

Redemption

The truth of it hit Billy hard and a cry left his body that he didn't know he was capable of. He flew to the man's side, searching for a breath in his dad's body that he prayed was still inside.

'Dad!'

He shook Jim's arm, but there was no response. Gently he slid his strong arms under his dad's body and rolled him on to his side.

'Come on, Dad,' he said, his voice choked with emotion. 'Come on now.'

There was a moan, a soft cry of pain as a breath left Jim's lips. 'Knee,' he whispered. 'My knee, it gave way.'

Billy breathed a sigh of relief at hearing his dad's voice, and a tremor of emotion ran through him. 'Do you think you can move, Dad?'

Jim gave the slightest nod. 'Help me, son.'

Billy eased his dad into a sitting position and slowly pulled him along the floor to rest his back against the shop wall.

'How long have you been lying there?' he asked.

'It happened not long after you left. My knee cracked and I went down like a sack of spuds. Think I banged my head.'

Billy picked up the glasses from the floor and slipped the thin wires over his dad's ears. He thought for a moment. He didn't want to leave his dad on his own in the darkened shop, but he knew he needed to be looked at by the doctor.

'Where's Mam?'

'Where do you think?' Jim sighed.

'You didn't tell her the news about Pearl?' Billy asked.

Jim shook his head. 'No, son. I've barely seen her today. But never mind your mother, how's the baby, did you see it? How's Pearl?'

Father and son sat together on the floor, looking through the glass door to the street.

'He's a beauty dad, a right bobby dazzler. And Pearl's tired but well.'

'Think you two can put things right between you?' Jim asked.

'I hope so, Dad,' Billy said. 'Now listen, I'm going to go and get the doctor.'

'No, son. I'll be all right,' Jim insisted.

Billy knew his dad hated anyone fussing over him and so was firm in his reply. 'Dad, we've got to get you seen to. You can't stay here all night. You'll need carrying upstairs. I can't do it on my own.'

'Oh, all right,' Jim said, no longer trying to hide the irritation he felt towards his body failing on him.

Billy made sure his dad was comfortable, then drove as fast as he could to Dr Anderson's house. Any anxiety he felt about bumping into Sylvia there was overshadowed by the desperate need to get help. He'd always seemed indestructible, had Jim Watson, everyone said so. He'd spent a lifetime lugging heavy sacks of vegetables

290

and boxes of fruit. And all those stairs he'd walked up and down between the shop and their home had made him as fit as a fiddle. Yet there he was now, sitting on the floor of the shop he'd taken over as a lad from his own father, unable to move an inch.

Billy reached the doctor's house within minutes. He rapped hard at the door. It was Dr Anderson himself who answered.

'Ah, Billy!' he said cheerfully. 'Come to visit Sylvia, have you? I'm afraid she's with friends this evening in Ashbrooke.'

The words rushed out of Billy about his dad and his knee, about his fall and the bang to his head. Even as he was speaking, Dr Anderson was pushing his arms into his jacket and picking up his black bag.

Billy's arrival had stirred interest in the front parlour, where the doctor's wife and Renee were chatting. When Renee was told who was at the door and what his business was, her hand flew to her heart.

'I must go to James,' she told Mrs Anderson as she collected her coat and bag and jumped into the passenger seat of the grocery van next to Billy. The doctor took his own car.

When they reached the shop, Jim was in exactly the same spot Billy had left him.

'Come on then, fella, let's have a look at this knee,' Dr Anderson said.

Billy lit an oil lamp so the doctor could see what he was doing. Dr Anderson poked, prodded and wrapped bandages around Jim's bad leg.

'How is he, Doctor?' Renee asked, choking back the worry of what she would do if she ever had to cope without Jim. She had come to depend on him more than she would ever admit. In that moment, she thought her husband had never looked so frail and old. As she studied the lines etched on his face, he caught her looking and smiled, his lips turning up slightly. And in that moment, she knew she loved him more than she had done in years.

Billy heard the break in his mam's voice, her tone heavy with concern, and saw the genuine worry etched on her face. She looked older, too, he thought, and vulnerable. And his mam was a woman Billy would never have described as vulnerable.

'Oh, he'll live,' Dr Anderson smiled. 'We just need to get him upstairs. No working for at least a week, maybe two. I want this knee rested before he puts weight on it again. Now, about the bang on your head you told Billy you'd had. Any headache?'

Jim shook his head.

'Double vision?'

'No.'

The doctor held his hand in front of Jim's face. 'How many fingers am I holding up?'

'Three potatoes and a carrot,' Jim replied.

The doctor's eyes opened wide.

'Just kidding,' Jim said. 'I can see the fingers, all four of them.'

Satisfied that his patient wasn't seriously injured, the doctor packed his bag. 'I'll be back in the morning to take another look at you.'

'I'll look after him, Doctor, rest assured,' Renee said. 'It's my duty as his wife, the one thing I can do.'

Again Billy heard the tremor in his mam's voice, so unlike anything he'd heard in years. A memory rushed back from his childhood, a birthday party with Renee smiling and laughing. It lasted just a second, before disappearing as quickly as it had arrived.

Billy took one of his dad's arms and the doctor took the other. Together they lifted Jim from the floor and carefully, slowly, made their way up the stairs, squashed tightly into the stairwell.

'Put him in our bedroom,' Renee called as she followed them.

'No, don't,' Jim said, with as much force as he could muster. 'Put me on the sofa, make a bed for me there. I'm no invalid yet.'

Renee went to fetch blankets and a pillow, and as she did so, Billy took Dr Anderson to one side.

'Would you stay for a drink, Doctor?' he asked. 'There's something I need to talk to you about.'

He turned to his mam, who was fussing over his dad, tucking blankets around him in the same way she used to do to Billy himself as a child. The anger he'd felt towards her earlier had turned into something else now, something he wasn't sure how to deal with. He saw the look on her face as she tended to his dad, her husband, the man she had devoted her life to. He knew that now was not the time to have words. When Billy had seen his dad lying on the shop floor, he'd feared the worst. He knew now more than ever that his parents meant the world to him. Instead of unleashing his anger and losing his temper, he had to make his mam understand that Pearl was a part of his world, and always would be.

'Are you sure, son?' Jim asked, fully aware of what was on Billy's mind.

'I'm sure,' he replied.

Billy poured a tot of whisky for the doctor and another for his dad, who said it would help with the shock of the fall.

'I'll take a drink, son,' Renee said.

Billy glanced at his mam; he'd never known her drink before.

'Your dad's accident has shaken me up,' she explained.

He was about to pour himself a tot too, but stopped before the amber liquid left the bottle. He wanted to keep his wits about him when he broke the news about Pearl.

When everyone was seated with their glass in their hand, Jim gave his son a silent signal — just a nod of the head — and Billy began to tell them about the day's events. Dr Anderson's features remained impassive, professional to the last, as he took it all in, while across the room, the colour drained from Renee's face. The truth about Pearl was out at last, Billy's feelings revealed.

No one spoke for a long time after he'd finished. The news sat heavy in the room.

Renee swallowed hard. An icy trickle ran through her heart and she decided there and then that she would not under any circumstances reveal that she had known Pearl was pregnant on the night she threw her out. She understood how close she had already come to ruining her relationship with Billy; she couldn't take the chance of making things worse. She must never let this secret be known and vowed to herself that she would take it to the grave.

Renee knew she had been lucky that night. Jim's fall had given her a scare. It had forced her to realise that life without him would be no life at all. He was the one who held the purse strings after all; she would be lost without his support. But it was more than just money, much more. She had only her husband and her son in her life; her sharp tongue had driven her friends away. Jim's frailty and his fall had frightened her. What if it heralded something much worse? A life without him didn't bear thinking about.

'I'll speak to Sylvia, of course,' Billy said, addressing the doctor. 'And I'll do all I can to cover the costs incurred for preparation for the wedding.'

Was he mistaken, or did the twitch of a smile play on the doctor's lips? Billy wasn't aware of the relief that was flooding through Dr Anderson's body. He'd never wanted Sylvia married off; that had been his wife's plan. And now his hopes of having her go to medical school in the same way that her brothers had done might finally come true.

'Leave the finances to me, lad,' he said. 'But yes, you need to speak to my daughter and offer her a full explanation, and an apology too. Sylvia's tougher than she looks; this won't break her, you know that.' As he stood to take his leave, he turned back to Billy. 'Pearl Edwards, you say, above Pemberton's shop?'

Billy nodded.

'I'll visit her tomorrow to make sure she and the new baby are well.'

'Can they afford to pay?' Jim asked.

Billy shook his head.

'Then I will,' Jim said. He glanced at Renee. 'It's the least we can do after everything that's happened.' He sank back against the sofa and closed his eyes. He couldn't help but blame himself for the whole mess. If only he'd spoken up earlier. If only he'd told Renee the truth.

After the doctor had left, Billy locked the shop and returned to the living room. He found his mam topping up her glass of whisky. She sank heavily into an armchair with a desperate, sad look on her face. Billy had expected a tantrum, crying at least. He'd expected her to scream and shout, to lash out, even to throw him out on the street in the same way she'd done to Pearl. But she'd been stunned into silence by his news. He had never seen her like this before. All the anger he'd felt towards her meant nothing now the truth was out.

Renee looked up. 'I'll be a laughing stock,' she said. Her words came out in a whisper as she tried to make sense of all she'd been told. She knocked back her whisky in a single gulp.

Jim shifted his position on the sofa so that he could look his wife straight in the eyes.

'You're a grandmother,' he said. 'We've got a new bairn in our family and our son will finally be happy. We can't ask for more than that. If I told you once, I must have told you a thousand times not to force the lad into a marriage he didn't want.'

Silent tears began to roll down Renee's face, and Jim reached for her hand. She held his hand in her own, caressing his fingers, the first time in years she had shown such affection.

'When Billy came for the doctor earlier, I thought we'd lost you,' she said.

Jim squeezed her hand. 'You're not getting rid of me that easily,' he smiled. 'It'll take more than a fall and a gammy knee to get shot of me.'

Renee sniffed back her tears. 'All this time . . . all these months I've been organising a wedding, spending time trying to ingratiate myself into someone else's family, and I didn't notice what's been going on in my own. What if I'd lost you tonight? I can't bear to think about it.'

'You're in shock, Mam,' Billy said. 'We all are. What with Dad's fall and my news.'

'No, William,' she said firmly. 'I'm the one to blame for the mess we're in. I've been so eager to get in with the doctor's family I've forgotten what's important and real.' She looked from Jim to Billy and back again. 'My husband's health. My son's happiness. That's what matters. James, I'm going to nurse you hand and foot until you're back walking again. William . . . well, I can't say I approve of what you've gone and done with that colliery lass . . . '

'Pearl, Mam. Her name's Pearl.'

' . . . but if I promise to try with her, with

297

Pearl, will that do for now?'

'For now,' Billy said firmly. 'But I'll need help in the shop if Dad's not to work for a while.'

'I'll do what I can,' Renee said.

Billy saw how defenceless his mam looked, how shaken she was. It was time for him finally to step up and be a man. He felt ashamed for not having the courage before. 'No, Mam. You'll be looking after Dad. I'm not having you running up and down the stairs all day.'

Renee breathed a sigh of relief. Not working in the shop meant she wouldn't need to face the vultures who would come to pick over the news about the cancelled wedding. Gossip about the baby would spread too, and Ryhope folk would have a field day with the news. Keeping herself to herself, looking after James and tending to her family, a new baby too, would ensure Renee was kept out of the public eye until the storm passed. But before she hid away upstairs, she planned to visit Lil Mahone to tell her that she would no longer be entitled to free groceries. There was no need for blackmail and secrets any more, not now the truth of Pearl's baby was known. Though she still needed to keep Lil on side, for she never wanted it to come to light that she had known about the pregnancy the night she threw Pearl out. She would offer Lil a sweetener: a discount perhaps, or half a dozen free eggs once a week.

'Who will you get to help you instead?' Jim asked Billy.

'I know just the person to ask. She's smart, kind, a hard worker too.'

298

Jim laughed. 'And she's a bonny lass by the name of Pearl, I'd bet!'

At the mention of the girl's name, Renee forced a smile through pursed lips.

★ ★ ★

The next day, after the shop was locked up for the night, Billy drove the grocer's van up the colliery bank. He took with him a bag of potatoes and fruit for Pearl. And on the back seat of the car was a plank of wood salvaged from the yard to cover the hole in the floorboards.

Pearl was delighted to see him, but worried too when Billy told her what had happened to his dad.

'Dr Anderson came to see me today,' she said. 'He checked me over and said all was well. I didn't mention anything else; we didn't speak of Sylvia. Have you seen her yet?'

'I'm going tonight,' Billy replied. 'I wanted to come and see you and my little man first.'

Pearl was still in bed. 'Would you like to hold him?' she asked.

He looked at the tiny sleeping baby. He was wrapped in what looked like an old blanket, and his pink face peeked out. His rosebud lips moved as if singing a silent song.

'Is he dreaming?' Billy asked.

'He needs feeding, I think.'

Annie walked to them and lifted the baby from Pearl's arms. She told Billy how to position himself in his chair ready to receive his child.

'Support his head with your left hand,' she

299

advised as she gently handed over the baby. 'And hold his bottom with your right.'

The weight of the child surprised Billy. For such a tiny little thing, he was heavier than he looked. Pearl watched as he took in the sight of his child properly, for there had been little time for anything more than their reunion the previous night. She saw tears fill his eyes as he smiled down at the babe in his arms.

'Hello, little man,' he whispered. 'Hello, little baby Watson.'

'Watson? He's baby Edwards,' Pearl laughed.

'We could double-barrel his last name,' Billy teased. 'Or we could — '

He stopped short. He was going to suggest marriage; it was on the tip of his tongue to say it, to offer to marry Pearl. He wanted it more than anything. But he knew he couldn't propose yet, not until he'd spoken to Sylvia and called off their engagement. It wouldn't be right until then.

'We could what?' Pearl teased. A smile played around her lips as she guessed what Billy had intended to say.

'We could keep that question for another day,' Billy said, pulling his gaze from his baby's face and looking straight at Pearl. 'But let's say, if I was to ask the question?'

'And if I was to give you an answer?'

'What would it be?' asked Billy.

'Ooh, now then. It might be yes, it might be no.'

Billy's face dropped. 'It might be no?'

'No, silly. It would never, ever be no.'

There was a knocking at the back door and

300

Annie went to see who it was. She returned to the room with Joey and Boot.

'Keep the dog out; they get funny around new bairns,' Annie warned.

Boot slunk down the stairs to the yard.

When Joey saw Billy sitting by the side of Pearl's bed, he gave a wide smile. Still holding the baby in his arms, Billy moved from the chair to sit next to her on the bed.

'Take my seat, Joey,' he offered.

Joey whipped off his cap. 'Brought you this, for your bairn.'

He handed Pearl a piece of paper, and she saw immediately that it was another drawing. But it was different this time; it wasn't a drawing of Ned, the pit pony. This was a seascape, with calm waves licking the shoreline under high, rocky cliffs.

'It's Ryhope beach. Drew it this morning. I wanted to capture the day in the best way I knew how.'

'It's beautiful, Joey.'

She looked at her friend's face. She wanted desperately to ask him how he was doing, where he was working, but she didn't want to embarrass him in front of Billy. She was burning to know if he was still spending time with Jackson or if he'd had the nerve to cut free. She wondered if the police had caught up with Jackson yet, and whether they'd taken him in for questioning.

She showed the drawing to Billy, holding the page for him to admire the delicate lines.

'You've got a real talent there,' Billy said.

301

'You're almost as good an artist as you are a matchmaker. I can't thank you enough for what you did.'

Pearl looked at Billy and then at her friend. 'Joey? Can I ask you a favour?'

'Anything, you know that.'

'Would you like to be our baby's godfather?'

'What would I have to do, like?'

Pearl shrugged. 'I don't know, but all babies need godparents, isn't that right, Annie?'

Annie paused in her task of peeling the potatoes that Billy had brought with him.

'Well, godparents are supposed to make sure a bairn goes to church. But being a godfather, Joey, it really means you'll promise to look after the little 'un if anything happens to his parents.'

'You mean I'd be like a dad?' Joey asked, his eyes bright with excitement.

'More of a dad's assistant,' Pearl said, and she and Billy exchanged a smile.

'He's a ton weight, this baby,' Billy said.

Annie walked to him and lifted the child from his arms. 'Give him here, I'll lay him down on the bed for a while.' She placed the baby on the eiderdown between Pearl and Billy.

'What are you going to call him?' Joey asked.

'Haven't thought much about it yet,' Pearl replied.

'We could call him James, after my dad,' Billy suggested.

'I like that idea,' Pearl said. 'Little Jimmy Edwards.'

'Watson-Edwards,' Billy teased.

'Edwards-Watson.'

Joey watched them as they bantered back and forth about the surname. He was trying to make sense of the joke they were playing.

'Why does the baby need two names?' he asked at last. 'When you get married, it'll just be Watson, surely? You are getting married, aren't you?' It didn't occur to him that there'd be any question of it, not now they had a child. Would they really deny their baby its mam and dad?

Pearl and Billy fell silent, and then Billy stood to leave.

'I've got to go and see Sylvia, get this sorted once and for all. And when it's done, when I've said goodbye to the past, I'll be able to build our future.' He leaned across the bed and kissed Pearl softly on the lips.

'I'll see you out, lad,' Annie said.

She followed Billy to the yard, where Boot was sleeping. The dog opened a lazy eye when he heard footsteps.

'Good luck with Sylvia,' she said.

'I'll do right by Pearl, you know that.'

'I've no doubt you will. And thanks for bringing that bit of wood for the hole. It'll stop the draught coming in, although it's still a bit loose.'

'Annie?'

'What, lad?'

'If I was to ask for Pearl's hand, would you approve? I have to ask you; you're her only family.'

'Oh, I'd approve, Billy. I'd approve with all my heart.' Annie held her arms open. 'Come here, you daft lump.' She pulled him towards her in a

303

bear hug before sending him on his way to the doctor's house.

Back upstairs, she found the baby in Joey's arms, with Pearl instructing him on the right way to hold him.

'Support his head with your left hand and hold his bottom with your right. That's it, Joey, you've got him.'

The child began mewling, working his soundless lips into a cry that seemed to pierce Joey's soul.

'Crikey, he's loud,' Joey said. He glanced at Pearl with a worried look on his face. 'Can I really be his godfather?'

'Course you can.'

'Thanks for picking me, Pearl.'

Pearl smiled at him. 'And who else was I going to choose?'

The baby's cry became louder, more insistent.

'He's hungry,' Annie said. She shot Pearl a look.

'Look, Joey, I'm going to have to feed him now,' Pearl said.

'All right,' Joey said. But still he didn't move from his chair.

'No, Joey. I mean I'm going to feed him . . . ' She looked down at her chest. 'With my . . . you know.'

Joey's face dropped and he glanced from Pearl to Annie. 'Oh. Oh . . . I'm sorry, I didn't realise what you meant. Can I come back tomorrow and see him again?'

'Come back any time you like.'

Once Joey had left, Annie sat on the bed and

304

helped Pearl feed her new son. The baby suckled greedily at Pearl's breast, and when he was sated, Pearl laid him to sleep.

'I've just remembered, we had someone asking about your clippy mats today,' Annie said. 'Decent-looking woman she was. She's bought one from us before, the red and black one you made.'

'She wants another one making?' Pearl asked, surprised.

'Says she does. Same size as before, different colours. Do you think you're up to it, with the baby to care for?'

Pearl gave it less than a second's thought. 'I don't see why not. Baby will be sleeping most of the day, won't he? I think I could manage to get a new mat on the go, especially if someone's asked specially.'

'If you're sure, then I'll get you more scraps,' Annie said.

Pearl sat up straight in the bed. 'I'll be up and about in a day or two, won't I?'

'I think so, love. But Dorothy will tell you when.'

Annie turned back to the potatoes, giving silent thanks for Dorothy's wisdom and experience of bringing up her seven bairns.

★ ★ ★

Over the coming days, Pearl was indeed up and about. In fact, there was no stopping her. The tiredness she'd felt during her pregnancy seemed to give way to a burst of energy. She cleaned and tidied the room as best she could while Annie

305

was working in the shop. She fed the baby and watched him sleep, delighting in each tiny movement of his fingers and toes, every breath that he took. And when Billy asked if she would be interested in joining him behind the counter at Watson's again, she gave it serious thought. But first she needed some reassurance from Billy. As they sat together on the bed with their baby between them, she came straight out with it, asking the question that had been on her mind.

'Have you heard from Sylvia since you broke things off with her?'

Billy shook his head. 'No, and I don't expect to. Mind you, she wasn't as upset as I thought she would be. Oh, she cried, made a show of being jilted, left me in no doubt as to what a clown I was to have led her on like that. But then she started talking about her future. She said something about going to study at a medical school in Newcastle. But I don't want to sit here and talk about her. It's us I want to discuss, our future.'

Pearl picked up the baby and cradled him in her arms. Billy stood from the bed and Pearl looked up into his eyes.

'You're leaving so soon? But you've just got here.'

Billy shook his head. 'I'm not going anywhere.' He got down on one knee and took Pearl's free hand in his. 'Will you marry me, Pearl? After everything I've put you through, I know I hardly deserve you. But will you marry me and be my wife?'

A silence hung between them for a few seconds as Billy desperately waited for Pearl's reply.

'Yes,' she said. 'I'll marry you, Billy Watson.'

Billy thought his heart would burst with happiness. He kissed Pearl on the lips and sat down again at her side.

'I've been thinking of your other offer,' she said. 'Of coming back to work in the shop. And my answer to that is yes too.'

'I love you, Pearl Edwards,' Billy said. 'I always have.'

Pearl smiled. 'I've always known. Can I tell Annie we're engaged?'

'Course you can. I'm so happy, you can tell the whole world if you like. And when you come back to work, bring the baby,' he told her. 'It's time Mam and Dad met their grandson.'

'What about while I'm working?' Pearl asked. 'Who'd look after him then?'

'We could ask Mam,' he suggested, but from the look on Pearl's face he knew the idea hadn't gone down too well.

'We could, but she's got a lot of apologising to do first,' she said.

★   ★   ★

On her first day back at work, Pearl welcomed the familiar smells and sounds of the shop. It was almost as if she had never been away. But there was a sadness too, recalling all those months she'd been forced apart from Billy by his mam's lies. Oh, she'd heard from Billy that his mam was sorry for her actions, but she'd yet to hear the

307

words from Renee herself. And so her return to the shop was one of mixed feelings. She was happy to be back there, working with Billy, putting her busy hands to use tidying packets and tins. She was glad that the customers were happy to have her back. But she was surprised too that so many more of them than expected were aware of the news about her baby. But then gossip in Ryhope travelled fast. Annie had always told her so, and now Pearl was finding it out for herself.

As she worked with Billy, their baby lay between them, wrapped in a blanket in an old apple box that Billy had scrubbed clean. It sat behind the counter, tucked out of sight of the customers. But Pearl and Billy could see their son and keep their eye on him, singing to him, laughing and chatting as they worked.

When there was a lull in business Pearl knew she could no longer put off going up to see Renee. If she wanted a future with Billy, she had to make friends with his mam, for she could see no other way about it. It would be unthinkable to go through life not being on speaking terms. If she and Renee progressed further than just speaking, if they reached friendship and respect, then so much the better. But for now, Pearl knew she had to go and talk to the woman who would one day become her mother-in-law. Besides, Jim was upstairs too. She would face them together and take the support that Jim would offer if Renee had one of her turns.

She picked the baby up from the apple box and hugged him to her chest. She climbed the stairs slowly, keeping her breathing even. In her head, she armed herself with the words she would use against Renee if needed. She reached the landing, kissed the baby on his cheek then knocked lightly on the living room door. It swung open. Renee stood there, and Pearl was shocked at what she saw. How old the woman looked, how sallow and sunken her cheeks. Her hair, normally so carefully lifted and curled, was long, loose and unkempt. Her appearance rocked Pearl, this was a different Renee from the one she had last seen months ago, the one who had thrown her out on the street.

'Come in,' Renee said. She held the door open and Pearl stepped into the room.

Jim was sitting at one end of the sofa, with his legs up on cushions. As soon as he saw Pearl, he opened his arms to her and she went to him and kissed him on the cheek. Renee pulled a chair from the table so that Pearl could sit at his side. Pearl thought how unusual this act of kindness was; Renee would never have done it before. She sat and gently pulled back the blanket from around her baby's face. Jim reached out his hand and stroked the tiny cheek.

'What a little smasher. He looks just like our Billy did when he was born,' he said, his voice breaking with emotion. 'He's even got the Watson nose.'

Pearl turned to Renee. 'Would you like to hold your grandson?'

Renee sat stock still and Pearl saw tears fill her eyes. Without waiting for an answer, Pearl passed the child across, and Renee took him gently in her arms, looking deep into the baby's blue eyes. 'I'm sorry,' she whispered. 'So sorry.' She was talking to the baby, not daring to look at Pearl. 'Do you think . . . do you think you might ever forgive me?' This time, she turned her face towards Pearl, waiting for an answer, hoping it would be the one she needed to hear.

'All I ever wanted was Billy,' Pearl said. 'We loved each other from the start.'

'I always knew it,' Renee replied. 'And I'm ashamed of what I did.'

'So you should be,' Jim piped up.

'James, please,' Renee pleaded.

But her husband had no idea as to the real reason Renee was truly ashamed. The secret about knowing Pearl was pregnant when she threw her out would burn in Renee's soul for ever, driving her to make amends in every way she could.

'What do you say, lass?' Jim said to Pearl. 'Reckon we can put this behind us? Start again as a new family, a proper family?'

Pearl reached for his hand. 'I think so,' she said softly. She turned to Renee. 'Renee? What do you say?'

'Oh, I want nothing more, love,' Renee replied. 'Family is what matters, it's what always mattered. I wish I'd never let my stupid pride push me in the wrong direction. But I've learned my lesson the hard way and I know I will never do it again. I won't risk losing Billy. I won't risk losing you either, Pearl. And I will never, ever risk losing this bonny bairn here.'

'Thought of a name for him yet?' Jim asked.

'Billy hasn't told you?'

Jim shook his head.

'We're calling him James, after you.'

Jim laid his head against the pillow propped at his back and closed his eyes for a moment. When he finally spoke, his words took Pearl by surprise.

'And the wedding, when will it be?'

'Oh . . . we haven't really discussed it yet.'

She glanced at Renee, waiting for her to chip in, but Renee kept silent, focused entirely on the baby in her arms.

'If you need help with anything, you know where I am,' she said eventually. 'I'll be willing to help, but I won't be interfering, not this time around.'

'I should think not,' Jim muttered under his breath, but it wasn't quiet enough. Both Pearl and Renee heard it. Jim raised an eyebrow towards Pearl.

'Neither of us will do anything to jeopardise your happiness with Billy. You have my word on that.' He looked at his wife. 'Renee?'

'You have my word too,' she said.

'That's all settled then,' Jim said. 'But I've one more question to ask.' He gave a cheeky wink. 'Any chance of having Boot the rat-catcher back?'

★ ★ ★

That evening, Billy drove Pearl up the colliery back to her room. She told him what had happened with his mam and dad, and he was glad to hear her news.

'They were asking if we'd set a wedding date,'

311

she said. She thought for a moment. 'Will I move into your room above Watson's when we're wed?'

'I expect so. Would that be all right? It's not a big room, and there's Mam and Dad living in the flat too. But it'll do for now, won't it, until we can find somewhere of our own. And I don't see why we can't set a date. All we need to do is see the vicar and then invite those we want to come.'

'Says you, the expert in weddings,' Pearl teased.

Just then, the Colliery Inn loomed into view, and next door to it, Pemberton's Goods. Pearl cast a glance towards the shop as the van drove past and saw Annie in conversation with a customer, a smartly dressed man she didn't recognise. He didn't look like any local she'd seen, and he wasn't wearing the flat cap of the pit.

'Let me come up to help settle baby James,' Billy said. Pearl was happy to let him help with the baby as he was curious and eager to learn.

She was glad to return to the quiet of the room after the bustle of the shop. Once the baby was sleeping, Billy said his farewell and left, and Pearl got the fire going in the hearth to cook dinner for her and Annie. She knew Annie's routine off by heart after all the years she'd worked in the shop, and as she peeled and chopped potatoes and carrots, she knew her aunt would be heading home soon. But Annie was late tonight; what was keeping her?

As Pearl filled the kettle from the water jug by the fire and put it on the fire to boil, she heard Boot bark in the yard. It was unusual for him to bark; he was a placid dog unless he was chasing rats. She knew it wasn't Annie coming in; Boot would never bark at Annie. She walked to the landing and called out, 'Who's there?'

There was silence.

She crept slowly down the stairs, holding tight to the handrail. 'Dorothy? Joey?' she called, but once again there was just the sound of Boot barking. 'Who's there and what do you want?'

More silence. When she reached the bottom stair, she listened carefully. Perhaps whoever had been out there had gone? She dared herself to unlock the door but as soon as she did so, the door burst open, pulled by an unseen hand, almost knocking Pearl off her feet. Someone was there, a man with heavy stubble around his chin and his eyes paunchy from beer. A man she recognised immediately as Jackson.

She pulled at the door, trying to close it against the bulk of him, but she was no match for his strength. He'd been drinking; the stench of ale followed him into the stairwell as he forced his way in. Pearl fell backwards, her heel caught on the step, and Jackson's filthy arms grabbed her.

15

Whisky

'Rat on me to the police, would you? Get me locked up in the cells?' Jackson growled. 'Run to the coppers and don't think I'd find out? Well, you were wrong. I know folk in Ryhope, folk who tell me what's going on and who's snitching on who.'

Pearl kicked as hard as she could against Jackson's chest, arms and legs. She could tell he was drunk; he was clumsy in his movements, slow and awkward, but there was a bitterness to him that kept him focused in his attack. She kicked again; it was all she could do from where she'd fallen on the stair. Out in the yard, Boot was barking, but the door had swung shut against him. Pearl was on her own, with no one and nothing to help her. She kicked again, striking a blow against Jackson's shoulder that caught him hard. He stumbled back, leaving her enough time to stagger to her feet. She grabbed the handrail and pulled herself up the stairs fast. All she needed to do was reach the landing. Annie's sharp knife was in the pantry; she could use it to protect herself. If only she could make it to the top of the stairs before him . . .

'I'll get you for this!' Jackson yelled. Pearl didn't stop to pay his words any heed. All she

314

knew was that she needed to make herself safe, to get away from him as quickly as she could. She needed to protect her baby, lying sleeping in the room. She would not let Jackson near him. Little James was too young, too innocent, too beautiful to be caught up in such an ugly scene. She was terrified, afraid of what Jackson might do. Who knew what evil men were capable of when they were lost in drink? She'd heard horrors enough from Annie and Dorothy over the years.

Pearl pelted up the stairs, dragging herself up by the handrail, taking the steps two at a time. On the landing, she pulled the knife from the cutlery drawer. She didn't stop to look back to see what Jackson was doing, or where he was on the stairs. She had to make herself safe and keep her child from harm. She felt the knife handle in her palm, solid, reassuring. Her breath was coming out of her thick and fast. She heard Jackson on the stairs, swearing at her. She'd wounded him, and he wasn't prepared to let her go. He was cursing Annie too, cursing all women, using the worst kind of insults a man could ever use. She ran into the room and slammed the door shut, then stood with her back against it. Jackson was so close she could hear his breath rasping. He pushed hard against the door and Pearl pushed back with all her might. She twisted around and pressed against the door with both hands, holding the knife in her right hand. The anger in her rose, the need to protect her baby uppermost. She would do everything she could to keep Jackson out of the room and away from her newborn child.

He was hurling insults through the door, but Pearl didn't respond. She didn't waste energy on him. She kept her focus on the door, pushing it tight shut against him. She managed to keep him out on the landing for what seemed like an eternity. Where was Annie? Annie would save her, would throw Jackson out. Between the two of them they could see him off. But where was she?

Finally, though, Jackson's strength won and she couldn't keep him at bay any longer. The door flung open and he raged into the room. Pearl stumbled, the knife slipping from her hand and skittering across the floor. Jackson heard it as it fell and saw it come to rest by the fireplace. His eyes flashed, and Pearl felt a deep stab of fear. She moved backwards, edging away slowly, determined not to let him see her baby on the bed. With a quick movement, she flicked a corner of the eiderdown over the child, so that he was out of sight at least. She prayed he wouldn't cry, wouldn't give himself away. Jackson was too busy steadying himself against the fire-place wall to notice what had happened. He had no idea about the child and Pearl felt a victory of sorts.

The knife lay on the floor between them. Jackson lunged, and then it was in his hand. Pearl kept her breathing even as she backed away from the bed, from her baby, to the furthest corner of the room, where her clippy mat in its frame lay against the wall. Jackson jabbed at the air with the knife, an evil grin on his face.

'Think you can outfox me, do you?' he spat.

Pearl backed away further, slowly, deliberately. She needed to reach her bag of scraps. Jackson had no clue what she was doing, or what she was planning. Each time she took a step backwards, he followed her. He thought she was making it easy for him, backing herself into a corner of the room.

'They put you up to it, didn't they? Those tarts on the lane?' he hissed.

'No, I did it all on my own,' Pearl said with a touch of defiance. She refused to let Jackson get the better of her, even though she was terrified, unsure of what he'd do next. She needed to keep him talking.

'Was it Annie or Dorothy? Was it Peg? Who cares who it was? One of them must have put you up to turning me in to the police. They're all the bloody same, those women.'

He advanced another step. He was so close now Pearl could see grey stubble on his chin. She could go back no further; she was pinned against the wall. Quick as a flash, she reached down and pulled the progger from her bag, gripping it tight in her hand. She knew how best to hold it to give it the power she needed.

It happened fast. First she jabbed at Jackson's cheek with the progger, then she jabbed again, near his eye, and again. Jackson dropped the knife as he cried out in pain, cursing her once more. Pearl picked up the knife and held it in her left hand. In her right hand she kept tight hold of the progger. She was ready to attack him if he came towards her again.

'Get out,' she yelled.

Jackson didn't move.

'Get out,' she repeated. 'Get out or so help me I'll use these against you, and next time I'll be aiming for your eye. Go on, get out!'

Jackson moved unsteadily, the drink in him making him clownish. He wasn't looking where he was stepping, and didn't notice the hole in the floorboards. In all the commotion when he'd stormed into the room, the make-shift cover had moved, exposing the gap. Pearl was used to it; she'd lived with that hole, had grown up knowing its dangers, had been told often enough by Annie to watch where she stood. But Jackson didn't know. His foot caught in it and he fell flat on his face. This time he didn't move, didn't try to stand, didn't even curse or swear. He lay face down on the floor, moaning with pain.

Pearl dropped the progger and the knife and scooped her baby from the bed. He'd slept through it all, unaware of the evil that had unfolded around him. She stepped over Jackson's body and took the stairs as quickly and carefully as she could with the child in her arms. As she headed to the yard, the back gate swung open and Annie walked in. She was followed by a man Pearl had never seen before. And yet . . . and yet there was something about him she recognised, something that pulled at her. She was in too much of a state to give it any thought, though.

'What is it?' Annie asked the minute she saw Pearl. 'What's wrong? Is it the baby?'

'It's Jackson,' Pearl cried. 'He came for me,

318

tried to attack me. He wanted to get me back for telling on him to the police.'

'Oh, my darling girl,' Annie said. 'Are you all right?'

Before Pearl could answer, the man who had followed Annie into the yard stepped forward.

'Is he still up there?'

Pearl was dizzy with nerves after what had just gone on. She didn't fully take in the stranger's smart hat and clothes, his shiny shoes and expensive-looking coat. All she noticed was a clipped moustache and a friendly, open face.

'Jackson,' Annie began to explain to him. 'He's a drunkard, a villain.'

'And he tried to attack you, Pearl?' the man asked. Pearl was surprised to see the shock on his face. There was anger there too, she noticed. But how on earth did he know her name?

Without waiting for an answer, he bounded up the stairs, calling out, warning Jackson that he would call the police. Pearl hugged baby James to her chest.

'That man? Who is he?' she asked.

Annie laid her hands on Pearl's shoulders and looked deep into her eyes.

'That man, Pearl . . . that man is Edward Hawthorn.'

Pearl shook her head in confusion. The name meant nothing to her.

'Oh love,' Annie said, pulling her niece towards her. 'He's your dad. That man, Edward Hawthorn, is your dad.'

16

Dad

'What's going on?' a voice asked.

Pearl and Annie swung round to see Bobby Mac standing at the back gate. He was wearing a mucky white vest with braces holding up baggy trousers, a flat cap on his head.

'I heard noises, shouting, the dog barking. What on earth's going on?'

Dorothy appeared then too. 'Give the bairn here,' she said when she saw the state of Pearl.

Tears were running down Pearl's face as she tried to make sense of everything that had happened. She let Dorothy take the baby and fell into Annie's arms. Inside, she heard footsteps descending the stairs. Could it be true? Could that man really be her father? All these years she'd been told her dad was a man from the pit lane. All her life she'd believed he was just someone who'd paid her mam to spend time with him. She'd given him no thought. And now this smartly dressed stranger had arrived from nowhere.

The footsteps grew louder and Pearl turned, preparing herself. And then he was there, Edward Hawthorn, standing in the yard in front of her. Edward pinned Jackson's arms behind his back and forced him forward into the yard.

Pearl drank in the sight of Edward, noticing the tall, straight-backed way he had about him. The face that was so like her own. His hair, the colour of burnt copper, the same as hers too. Was he really her dad? So many questions flooded her mind. She couldn't speak, she could hardly breathe.

★ ★ ★

'Tart!' Jackson spat at Pearl, and then he spun towards Annie and Dorothy. 'And you two!'

Edward handled Jackson with precision and speed, forcing his arms further up his back so that Jackson cried out.

'Apologise,' Edward ordered.

'To these sluts?' Jackson laughed. 'Never.'

Edward twisted his arms harder. 'Apologise.'

Pearl saw Jackson's face contort with pain. He looked from Annie to Dorothy, and then he dropped his gaze to the ground.

'Sorry,' he whispered.

'Louder,' Edward ordered. 'And stand up straight, man. Say it like you mean it.'

Jackson almost choked on the word he was made to repeat. 'Sorry.'

Edward pushed Jackson out to the lane. He stumbled and tried to stand again but couldn't find his feet. He slumped against the wall. Boot followed and stood guard, baring his teeth.

'And who the hell do you think you are?' Bobby Mac asked when Edward returned to the yard.

Edward and Annie exchanged a look.

321

'Will I tell them or will you?' he said.

'Come on upstairs, everyone,' Annie said. 'We've got some explaining to do.'

Bobby Mac stepped forward. 'Annie? Can I suggest you come next door to the pub and I'll get everyone a drink. I think you could probably use one, by the look of you and Pearl.'

Annie locked the door at the bottom of the stairs and threw her arm around Pearl's shoulders. Dorothy held tight to baby James.

'Do you want me to come too?' she whispered to Annie.

'Of course I do, you're as good as family. You need to hear this,' Annie said.

In the poky back room of the Colliery Inn there was just one wooden table with a bench running around it. Bobby Mac placed a bottle of whisky on the table, then brought out five glasses and began filling each one.

'Annie, Dorothy,' he said, pushing their glasses toward them across the tabletop. Then he turned to Edward. 'Sir, will you take one?'

'Please,' Edward replied.

'What about you, Pearl?' Bobby asked, but without waiting for an answer he poured her a drink and pushed it towards her. 'My guess is you'll need this for the shock.'

Finally he poured himself a drink and pulled up a stool to sit next to Annie. She patted his hand. 'Thanks, pet.'

All eyes turned to Edward, waiting for him to explain. Pearl could hardly think straight after all that had happened. She toyed with her glass on the table, swirling the amber liquid, watching the way it clung to the inside of the glass. Then she lifted it to her lips and took the tiniest sip. It burned her mouth and throat and set fire to her chest. She took another sip, and a flame ignited within her, giving her the strength to speak up.

'Are you really my dad?'

Edward looked deep into Pearl's eyes. He saw Mary in the girl's features, the same pale skin, the same slim nose, the same smile. And he heard in her voice the same stubborn streak, the same directness that Mary once had. But there was a hint of steel in Pearl's eyes that he'd never seen in Mary. They were eyes that bored into him, demanding an explanation.

'Yes, I'm your dad.' He looked around the table, from Pearl to Annie, from Dorothy to Bobby Mac. 'You're Mary's family and friends, and I owe every one of you the truth.'

Dorothy shifted baby James in her arms and glared at him. 'Mary loved you, you know. You left her when you found out she was expecting. She never saw you after she told you; none of us did. And now you come back after all these years and the best you can do is say you owe us an explanation? You broke her heart, man! You just upped and left her in the lurch, pregnant with your bairn. And then she . . . ' Dorothy glanced at Pearl. 'Well, she didn't last much longer, God bless her.'

Edward lifted his glass and took a long sip. He removed his hat and placed it next to him. Then he straightened in his seat, all the while keeping his gaze towards Pearl. She reached for Annie's hand as she waited to hear what he had to say.

'I loved Mary,' he said at last. There was a softness to his voice. He looked at Annie. 'I always loved her. From the minute I met her, I knew she was special.'

'Oh, she was.' Annie smiled at the memory of her sister.

'We even talked of marriage,' he continued. 'We talked of love and of trying to find a way to be together. But it was no good in the end. My family . . . ' He paused and took another sip. 'My family would never allow it. I had to do as they told me. I was a young man, little older than Pearl is now. I couldn't stand up to my father and go against his wishes. My family wouldn't have understood. Their position . . . their standing would have been compromised.'

'A real man would have stood up for himself,' Bobby Mac said firmly.

'You're right,' Edward said. 'But I was no more than a boy, in love with a woman who worked the pit lane. My family would have been ruined if the truth had come out. I couldn't do it to them. I was a coward, a rotten, nasty coward, and I know I let Mary down. My parents forbade me to see her, forbade me to enter Ryhope. I was kept under constant watch. My father employed a chaperone; I was accompanied each time I left Roker.'

'And now?' Annie urged. 'Tell us. Pearl deserves to know the truth.'

'And now . . . ' Edward looked at Pearl and she saw tears in his eyes. 'And now it's too late to do anything to help your mother. But I have the means to help you as best I can.'

'How?' asked Pearl.

'I was away for four years at the front, and while I was fighting, my parents passed on.'

'Very sorry to hear that,' Bobby Mac said.

Edward shook his head. 'No. Don't be sorry. It was freedom at last. Coming home from the war, coming home to Sunderland, was liberating in more ways than one. With my parents gone, I am beholden to no one. For the first time in my life I am free.'

'But why have you sought me out?' Pearl asked. 'What am I to you other than a child of the pit lane?'

'You're *my* child of the pit lane,' Edward said. 'The child I have thought about for the last seventeen years. The child I always wanted but could never have while my parents were alive. They forbade me to see you, forbade me even to talk about you. My father beat me when I told him that Mary was pregnant. I had no choice but to join the army; it was either that or be chaperoned each time I left the house. He made sure I couldn't return to Ryhope. And in the army I made my way up the ranks, fought with the Durham Light Infantry.'

'You were marching in the Peace Parade. I saw you,' Pearl said, remembering the leader of the platoon smiling at her through the crowds.

'I saw you too,' he said softly.

A memory came to Pearl from the night she'd slept on the village green. 'Were you the one who left the money under my clippy mat frame?'

Edward nodded. 'I couldn't bear to see you sleeping rough.'

Having it said out loud, in public, sharing the news with her closest friends Dorothy and Bobby, turned Annie's stomach with guilt. Would they think she was really so dreadful that Pearl had chosen the life of a vagrant after she'd put her to work on the pit lane? She took a swig of whisky while Edward carried on.

'I didn't want to interfere; I knew I had to keep my distance. I couldn't make myself known to you until I felt sure there was a chance, no matter how small, that you might find it in you to forgive me. That night when I left money for you, it wasn't the first time I tried to help you.'

'It wasn't?'

'There was a time before, you were resting on the green with your eyes closed against the sun. I tried to help you then, but you had a dog at your side. It was intent on protecting you as best it could, and I was forced to walk away.'

'Now it's my turn to explain something,' Annie said. She squeezed Pearl's hand. 'Your dad here, he came to the shop some time ago. He bought your clippy mat, the first one. He begged me not to tell you he'd been looking for you.'

'You kept it a secret?' Pearl said. She was astonished that her aunt would have done this to her after everything they had been through.

'I made a promise,' Annie said. 'A promise I was determined to keep this time.'

'This time?'

Annie took a deep breath. Pearl deserved to know the truth, and what better time than now, when past secrets were being revealed?

'I've made promises before that I couldn't

keep. Promises to your mam.' Her voice wavered and Bobby Mac laid a supportive hand on her arm as she continued. 'Mary asked me three things as she lay dying. And I did my best, Pearl, I tried. She wanted me to look after you and give you a home.'

'And you have, Annie, you have,' Pearl said.

'I promised I'd love you as if you were my own. I know I haven't been the mam you deserve, just the one you ended up with, but always know I tried my best.' Annie took a sip of whisky to give her the courage to carry on. 'I got it wrong, didn't I? Sending you out to work the way I did? I should never have done it. Never.'

'You wouldn't have if you hadn't had to. We needed the money, Annie. I know why you did it but I also know I could never have done what you wanted me to do.'

'You had the courage to walk away, Pearl. That's more than I ever did. You see, there was something else your mam asked. She wanted me to take a real job, away from the pit lane. And I managed it, sort of, didn't I? With my job at Bernie's shop, even though I still had to work the pit lane when I was desperate.'

Annie and Dorothy exchanged a look.

'Mary always wanted more for herself, wanted better. But it's easier said than done,' Dorothy said.

'But you've done it now, Annie. You've paid your bills and cleared your debts,' Pearl said.

'All thanks to Bobby Mac here,' Annie said. She patted Bobby's knee. 'I'll pay you back every penny, you know that.'

Bobby laid his hand over hers. 'In your own time,' he said.

'What was the third thing Mam asked?' Pearl said.

Annie exchanged a look with Edward. 'That one day I'd tell you who your father was.'

Pearl gasped in surprise. All her life she had only ever known Annie, who had been both mam and dad to her, big sister and best friend rolled into one. She'd never imagined, not for one minute, that her mam had wanted her to know about Edward. And now here he was, larger than life and as handsome as could be, sitting at the table with them, a war hero back from the front.

'I gave you his name,' Annie said. 'Named you Pearl Edwards, for your mam always knew you were Edward's child.'

'But why didn't you tell me when he first came into the shop?'

'I didn't know if he was serious, didn't know if he would disappear again. I didn't want to get your hopes up in case he did a runner like before. And he made me promise, Pearl, me and the vicar both. We were both sworn to secrecy at first.'

'It's my turn to make a promise now,' Edward said. 'I promise I will never disappear again. I'll be here for you, Pearl. As long as you need me, as long as you want me, I'm here to help you and your child, my grandson. Along with my sister, you're the only family I've got.'

Pearl's mind whirled with questions, with doubts and anxieties, as she tried to take in the enormity of what she'd been told. As she attempted to make sense of Edward's words and of Annie's secrets from the past, there was one detail she focused on.

'But why would you buy my mat?' she asked.

'I wanted something of you in my home. I was hoping for a photograph from Annie, but being the wily sales-woman she is,' Edward smiled, 'I went home with a lighter wallet and your clippy mat under my arm. Then my sister Emily saw it and asked for another to decorate her rooms. She admired it greatly, as did many of her friends, who all wanted the same.'

'So that's why all my clippy mats have been bought?' Pearl said.

'It explains the new customers who've been coming into the shop,' Annie added.

'What do you say, Pearl? Do you think you could ever forgive me for all that has happened? Do you think you could allow me into your life?' Edward looked imploringly at Pearl, who had sunk back in her seat with the shock.

'I reckon he sounds on the level,' Bobby Mac said. 'You could do a lot worse for a dad.'

Dorothy had been silent up to now, holding the sleeping baby in her arms.

'You want to be in Pearl's life, you say?' she said at last. 'If you want her love and respect, you've got to earn it.'

'I'll do whatever it takes,' Edward said.

Dorothy shifted in her seat as the baby began to wake. She offered him to Pearl, who took him and held him to her chest. But then she stood and leaned across the table, holding the baby out to a surprised Edward.

'I'd like his grandad to hold him,' she said.

Bobby Mac erupted into peals of laughter as Edward awkwardly took the baby.

'Put one hand under his head, the other under his bum,' Pearl advised.

Once he was securely in his grandfather's arms, the child opened his eyes fully and looked up into Edward's face.

'What's his name?' Edward asked.

'James.'

'James what?'

'James . . . ' Pearl paused, and swallowed back the lump in her throat. 'James Edwards-Watson.'

'Nice name.' Edward smiled and glanced down at the baby's face.

'You know, I've held guns in these arms. I've held death. But this . . . this is the most beautiful thing I have known.'

Bobby Mac sniffed back a tear that threatened to fall.

'Another round of drinks, everyone?'

★ ★ ★

Over a second whisky for everyone but Pearl, who refused the burning drink this time, more confidences were shared. Edward raised a toast to Mary and spoke again of his love and admiration for the woman he'd met as a much younger man, and of the memories that haunted him after he'd learned from a friend that she'd died. He talked of joining the army as a way to free himself from Sunderland, and of the horrors of the Great War, before downing his whisky in a single gulp. He did not speak of war again. He had never married, he told Annie when she asked. His life had been dedicated to the Durham Light Infantry, to fighting for king and country.

When all the talking had been done and Bobby Mac said he'd need to make a move to prepare the pub for opening, the small group headed out. Jackson had gone and Boot was now sleeping. Dorothy went home, warmed by the spirit inside her and her memories of Mary, her friend. Pearl and Annie walked with Edward to their room. When they turned into the yard, Pearl was surprised to find Joey sitting on the doorstep. He opened his mouth in shock the minute he saw Edward.

'Get away from me!' he yelled. His eyes were wide, like a caged animal in the small yard.

'Joey, what on earth is it?' Pearl said. She'd never seen her friend so agitated before.

Joey stretched his arm towards Edward and pointed an accusing finger. 'It's him, Pearl! It's him! He's the ghost I was telling you about, the one who's been staring in our kitchen at night!'

Edward held up his hands in mock surrender. 'I'm sorry, lad. It's true. But I'm no ghost. I'm as real as anyone here.'

'He's my dad, Joey,' Pearl said.

Joey stood open-mouthed.

'I know, it's a lot to take in,' she told him. 'But it's true.' She spun round to face Edward. 'Why have you been spying on Joey?'

'When I found you, Pearl, I also found out how close you and Joey were. At first I wondered

331

if he was your brother. I could tell you meant a lot to each other and I wanted to do my best to keep him safe too.'

'You scared the living daylights out of me,' Joey said.

'I also saved you from that wretch of a man Jackson, more than once. He saw you as easy pickings, Joey, someone to do his stealing and thieving. I used to walk this back lane once, twice a week, remembering Mary, thinking about Pearl and watching out for you.'

'Would you like to come up to our room?' Pearl asked.

Edward nodded.

'You coming too, Joey?' she asked.

Joey kept his gaze fixed on Edward, as if he was ready to run as fast as his bad leg would take him. Annie led the way up the stairs with Pearl behind holding the baby. Joey stood at the back door and watched Edward head up, then followed, limping.

On the landing at the top of the stairs, Edward took in fully the ruinous state of the room where Annie and Pearl lived. He took in the sticks of furniture and the pile of blankets on the floor. Were his eyes deceiving him, or was that mould growing in the corner of the room? And then he saw the extent of the hole in the floor with its jagged wooden teeth that had snared Jackson's leg when he had entered the room to throw the fella out. He was shocked to the core. He'd heard of the Sunderland slum landlords, but it was the first time he'd seen such a hovel with his own eyes.

He stepped over the threshold and Annie pulled out a wooden chair for him to sit on. He refused, insisting that Pearl or Annie take it instead. Pearl sat on the bed with her baby in her arms and Joey perched next to her and cooed at baby James, letting the child take his little finger in his tiny fist.

'Can I make you some tea, Edward?' Annie offered. 'The fire won't take long to burn through.'

'No, thank you. I don't want to overstay my welcome. But I'll return, if I may. Later this week, perhaps?' He looked at Pearl, hoping she would give him the answer he longed to hear.

'That would be nice. I'll be working at Watson's Grocers. Maybe you could call there. You can meet Billy, too, he's my baby's dad. Watson's is down by the village.'

Edward smiled. 'I know where it is. And I've met Billy.'

'You have?'

'Have you been peering through the Watsons' kitchen window too?' Joey asked. The earnest way he spoke made Edward laugh.

'No, lad. But Billy and I have already talked, although he doesn't yet know who I am.'

'Oh, he will soon enough,' Pearl said.

Edward snapped his heels together and bowed his head slightly towards Pearl and Annie. 'I'll be off then, and I'll see you all soon.'

Pearl raised her baby's arm and waved it gently to Edward. He turned to leave, but stopped in his tracks when something caught his eye. He reached down to the floor to pick up a sheet of paper. It was a line drawing of what looked like a horse. He took in the craftsmanship of the work, then turned back to Pearl and Joey sitting on the bed. 'Is this yours, Pearl?'

'It's mine,' Joey said proudly. 'It's my drawing of my pit pony, Ned.'

Edward waved the sheet of paper. 'Can I take it with me?' he asked.

Joey shrugged. 'Course you can. I've got loads more at home.'

'Do you work, Joey?'

Joey sighed. 'I've been helping down the beach collecting sea coal, but there's not much money in it. And with my bad leg, it's hard walking all the way there each day.'

Edward said his final goodbyes and headed off down the stairs. After he'd gone, Annie stood from the fireplace, where she'd finally got the fire alight and the kettle on to boil. She stretched her arms and her back as if she was pushing a weight off her shoulders.

'Well, what do you make of all that, then?' she said.

'Looks to me like he's got money,' Joey said. 'Looks like a proper gentleman. Did you see his shoes? Real leather they were. He must be worth a fortune, I'd say.'

'Says he lives in Roker too. It's posh along there,' Annie said. 'What did you think of him, Pearl?'

Pearl began to reply, but her voice caught in her throat and she choked back her words. The emotion of the day had finally proved too much, and silent tears began to fall.

17

Edwards-Watson

Pearl found herself curious about Edward. Her feelings towards him surprised her, for she had never felt any lack in her life. As she'd often told Joey, she'd never thought of herself as an orphan. Annie had brought her up and Annie had been all she had known, or needed. Throughout her life the two of them had looked out for each other, taking care of one another. She had Annie to thank for feeding her and clothing her, for bringing her up as her own. But she also had Annie to blame for sending her out on the lane when she came of age.

Oh, Annie was flawed, everyone knew it, but was anyone qualified to judge what was right and what was wrong? Getting herself into so much debt in the first place had been what had led to such desperate measures. But Pearl knew she'd been right to dig her heels in and refuse to work the pit lane. In time she would forgive Annie for putting her out to the lane, just as she would forgive Renee for keeping her and Billy apart. For if she didn't forgive two of the most important women in her life, then she would live with a black, angry heart, and that was not what she wanted at all.

But now that she'd met Edward, her mind

buzzed with questions, and not just about him and his family, the home he shared with his sister on the other side of the River Wear at Roker. For the first time in her life, she found herself wanting to know more about her mam. Whenever she and Annie had talked about her, it had been Annie's account of Mary as her older sister that she had heard. Of their life growing up together in a crowded house on Scotland Street, a simple two up, two down in a terrace behind the cattle market. Its thin walls carried every noise from their parents' room next door and from their neighbours on either side.

Pearl knew little of her mam's life outside of these memories that Annie, and sometimes Dorothy, shared, and she had never felt the need to know more. Mary, Annie and Dorothy had forged a bond working on the pit lane. Their friendship had continued with Dorothy as welcome into their home as if she was family. Annie and Dorothy remained close, and Pearl had always felt their protection. But now, since Edward's arrival, secrets had finally been revealed. Pearl had learned of Annie's broken promise to her mam that she would never work again on the pit lane. Hearing of her mam's dying wishes had come as a shock, for Annie had never spoken of them before. Perhaps she'd been ashamed, too guilty to admit that she had failed. But at least there were promises that Annie *had* made good on. She had always looked after Pearl, making her feel as safe and secure as living in Bernie Pemberton's rotten flat had allowed. And now . . . well, now Pearl finally knew who her dad was, just as Mary had wished. Her surname finally made sense, after all those years she'd spent without a proper explanation of why she wasn't a Grafton, like Annie. She'd asked Annie many times about her surname of Edwards, and Annie had passed it off as an old family name.

She made a mental note to ask Reverend Daye if she could keep the Edwards name along with Watson when she married Billy. There was a lot to arrange. There was a date for the wedding to be set, and a date for baby James's christening. But first there were introductions to be made when Edward met Billy, Renee and Jim.

★ ★ ★

Pearl waited eagerly each morning in Watson's, hoping that the next person to come walking through the door would be her father. But it would be a while before she set eyes on him again.

No more did her heart leap and her gaze turn to the door each time she heard it open. No more did she dream about her dad walking into the shop. She felt a hardness build inside her. He'd promised her, hadn't he? He'd said he would see her again but after the first week passed with no sign of him, Pearl's heart began to grow heavy. Perhaps she was destined never to see him again. Now that he'd met her and had seen where she lived and what her circumstances were, had he been scared to return? Was she beneath him, not what he expected — or wanted? Doubts and anxiety filled her mind as the second week passed and still there was no sight of him.

By now, Boot was back living in the grocer's yard, and Jim's chalkboard once more stood proudly on the counter: *This shop rat free 14 days.*

Jim was up and about now. His knee was on the mend, but the pain still prevented him from walking downstairs. Pearl visited him each morning in the living room above the shop, bringing him news from the market. She carried the baby upstairs, and Jim adored seeing his grandson. Renee continued to fuss over her husband, and Jim made the most of it, revelling in the care and attention of the Renee he had fallen in love with all those years ago. She even ventured downstairs to face the customers now that gossip of Billy and Sylvia, of Pearl and her baby, had finally quietened down.

Slowly Pearl began to assert herself in the shop, arranging the fruit and vegetable boxes to her liking. Renee wasn't keen when she saw the chalkboard on the counter and suggested that it should be removed. But Pearl stood firm. She knew Jim wanted the board there and she was proud of Boot for keeping the rats away. In this way, she began to let Renee know she was in charge, downstairs in the shop, at least. Billy was happy to let Pearl have her way. And as they worked together at the counter, baby James lay between them, snuggled in a blanket tucked into the apple box.

Despite Renee's new-found kindness, which

everyone was still getting used to, flashes of the old Renee would appear when Pearl least expected. Although she was enamoured with little James, who put a smile on her face the likes of which Pearl had never seen before, she could be cutting with her criticism of Pearl's child-rearing skills. But no longer would Pearl take offence at or be upset by her words. Instead, she heeded the advice, for hadn't Renee brought up a son of her own? Billy was heartened to see the two women trying to get along, but he knew his mam still had a long way to go before Pearl would fully forgive her.

The past seemed a long time ago now. Memories of Sylvia disappeared and her name was never spoken. And then, one day, after the shop closed for the night, Renee and Jim announced their news.

'Your dad can't take the stairs any more,' Renee told Billy and Pearl. 'His knee won't get any better and he can't live a life upstairs. He doesn't see anyone or go anywhere. We've got no choice. We're going to have to move out.'

Billy had been expecting the news for a while. He'd seen how frustrated his dad was confined to the living room. Jim's only view from the window was the skyline and rooftops of Ryhope. He couldn't even wave to friends and neighbours walking by.

'Where will you go?' he asked.

Renee answered immediately; she and Jim had clearly given the idea much thought.

'There's rooms in the village, around the green.'

'But it's expensive there, Mam,' Billy said.

'We can afford it, son. It's just rooms that we'd rent, not a full house to buy. It's not as expensive as some. And it's on the ground floor, so it's perfect for your dad.'

'And there's a lovely little garden out the back,' Jim added.

He reached for Renee's hand and they both turned to look at Billy and Pearl.

'We want to offer you the rooms here,' Renee said.

'And the shop, of course, that goes without saying,' Jim said. 'Will you take it on, lad? I'd understand if you didn't want to, of course . . . '

'I'd love to,' Billy said.

' . . . young couple like you, you might have other ideas, don't want to get stuck in a tiny shop . . . '

'Dad, I said I'd love to take over the shop. It's what I've always wanted.'

Jim sank back against the sofa cushion. 'Thank you,' he said.

Billy turned to Pearl. 'What do you say, Pearl? Want to join the Watson family business?'

Pearl had never been more certain. 'There's nothing I'd like more.'

'Could I ask one thing?' Renee said. 'That you and Billy don't live here as man and wife until after the wedding? I don't think I could take being gossiped about any more.'

'Of course,' Pearl said. 'The baby and I are fine up at Annie's until then.'

'Speaking of which, I should drive you both home,' Billy said.

'Can we walk instead of going up in the car? It's such a nice evening out there.'

They were just about to head out when there was a banging at the front door.

'Not expecting anyone, are we?' Renee asked.

Billy and Jim both shook their heads.

'I'll go and see who it is,' Billy said.

Pearl stayed where she was, cradling the baby. She heard a man's voice, and strained to hear who Billy was speaking to; could it really be who she thought it was? Her heart quickened when she heard the voice again, louder this time. And then footsteps, two pairs of heavy footsteps making their way up. Billy walked into the room first.

'Is it true, Pearl? Is this man really who he says he is?'

'It's true,' Pearl replied. 'This is the man I've been telling you about.'

'Then, sir, you had better come in,' Billy said.

Edward stepped into the room, took off his hat and bowed his head slightly towards Renee and Jim. Pearl jumped up.

'Mr and Mrs Watson, this is my dad, Edward,' she said.

Edward thrust out his hand towards Jim first, then Renee. 'Edward Hawthorn,' he said. 'I'm very pleased to meet you both.' He reached for Billy's hand, and it took Billy a moment to gather his wits.

'I'm sorry. It's a lot to take in. I had no idea who you were when we met in the Albion Inn all those weeks ago.'

'It's I who should apologise,' Edward said. 'But I couldn't tell you back then that I was

341

Pearl's father, for I didn't know if she would want me in her life.'

'You two have met already?' Jim asked.

'It's a long story,' Edward said.

Billy pulled a chair out from the table. 'Where are my manners? Please, take a seat.'

Edward sat down, while Billy perched on the arm of the sofa next to his dad. Edward straightened in his chair and brushed the knee of his trousers. 'I'm sorry it's taken me so long to get away, Pearl,' he said at last. 'Work has been very busy and I was needed more than planned.'

Pearl saw Renee greedily take in the sight of Edward's shined shoes, his pressed trousers and his smart coat. And there was a scent about him too, a fresh citrus scent of cologne. Jim was also appraising the man sitting in front of him.

'What work do you do, Mr Hawthorn?'

'Oh, call me Edward, please. I've been in the army most of my life.' He cast a glance at Pearl before he carried on. 'And when I returned from the front, I found my circumstances changed, my family life altered. I was left with an inheritance and no plan of what to do. I decided, finally, that after living through the destruction of war, my desire was to create and build. I'm working on a project in Roker, building a small row of houses by the sea.'

This was something Pearl did not know. With the shock of Edward turning up in her life, she had not asked what he did for a living. She managed to hide her shock by letting her gaze fall to her baby in her arms.

'A builder, eh?' Jim said, impressed.

342

'I'm managing the build,' Edward asserted. 'I won't be getting my hands dirty. I run a team of men that I trust. Many of them are from my regiment, ex-soldiers, hard workers.'

'William?' Renee said. 'How about we have a little drink by way of welcoming Mr Hawthorn this evening? Could you do the honours and bring over the Scotch?' She turned to Edward. 'You will stay for a drink, Mr Hawthorn, won't you?' She hoped against hope that he would. She'd never had such a gentleman in her living room before. 'Do you know,' she said, 'the likeness between you and Pearl is uncanny: the same hair colour, the same eyes. I always said, from the minute I met her, that there was something special about Pearl. And now here you are, Mr Hawthorn. And to think we're to become related when these two are wed.'

'Mam, please don't embarrass our visitor,' Billy said as he poured the drinks. But Renee was in her element and carried on flattering Edward, her snobbery evident to all but herself.

'Can I say how much of an honour it is to welcome you into the family, Mr Hawthorn. A man who is building a row of houses, and in somewhere as prestigious as Roker.'

Edward was gracious and humoured her, but every now and then he glanced at Pearl and the two of them exchanged a secret smile. Pearl knew only too well that the old Renee was still there, under the surface. The Renee who had slapped Pearl when they'd first met, who had kept her and Billy apart because she thought her unworthy of her son. While the woman's caring

343

side had become evident since Jim's fall, Pearl knew she would do well to remember that under the calm and composed surface, the other side of her lived on.

Baby James began to cry, and Pearl shot Billy a worried look. 'I really must get him home,' she said. 'He needs feeding.'

Edward stood and offered Pearl a lift in his car.

'If you're sure you don't mind?' she said.

'It'd be my pleasure.' In truth, he was glad of the opportunity to speak to Pearl alone, for there was something on his mind.

Edward's car was waiting outside Watson's. From the living room window above the shop, Jim and Renee strained to see what model it was. They marvelled at its colour and size.

'Bet that cost a pretty penny,' Renee sniffed.

'It's none of our business,' Jim warned.

Billy helped Pearl into the passenger seat with the baby tight in her arms and waved them off. Pearl sank back in the seat. It was luxury compared to travelling in the noisy grocer's van. She looked out of the window and saw passers-by on the street staring at the car, straining to see who was driving and who the passenger was. It was an unusual car for Ryhope, too large and too showy by half. She felt uncomfortable being the object of so much attention.

★ ★ ★

Back in Dawdon Street, Edward followed Pearl upstairs. Annie had the fire burning and stottie

344

baking on the hearth. But despite the aroma of baking bread, the warmth of the day and the heat of the fire, the room still smelled damp from the mould.

'Take a seat, Edward,' Annie said. 'It's good to see you again.'

Edward stood firm. 'I won't stay; I don't want to intrude on your dinner.'

Annie was about to protest and insist that he was welcome to share the fresh bread and soup, but she was cut short as he continued, 'But I do have something to tell you both before I go.'

Pearl and Annie were curious about what he would say.

'The houses I'm building at Roker, I can let one of them go to you, if you wish to take it on. It's a small house, but a new one.' He looked around the room. 'In good condition, with its own netty in the yard.'

The two women exchanged a look.

'You're asking us to move away from Ryhope?' Pearl asked.

'The offer's there if you'd like it.'

Annie let a long sigh leave her lips and shook her head in disbelief. 'I can't say I've ever thought of leaving Ryhope. I wouldn't know what to do. I was born and brought up here. My workplace is downstairs, I've got Dorothy two minutes away if I need her — and I always need her. Who do I know in Roker?'

'I don't expect an answer straight away,' Edward said. Whatever he'd expected to hear, it hadn't been an outright refusal. Annie's words and tone made him feel as if he'd offered to put her out on the street instead of setting her up in a brick-built house with no hole in the floorboards and no mould on the walls. He turned to Pearl. 'What about you? Is it an offer you might consider for yourself, Billy and the child?'

He was shocked when Pearl shook her head too. 'If Annie doesn't want to move away from Ryhope, then neither do I. My family is here. Renee and Jim are moving to the village; they've offered us the rooms above the grocer's shop.'

'There are many delights to living in Roker,' Edward persisted. 'The beach there is safe to walk on, the sand is golden, and sometimes seals can be seen in the sea.'

'I dare say we'll visit some time,' Annie said. 'But I can't leave Ryhope. It's my home.'

'Pearl?' Edward asked.

'Ryhope's my home too.'

He joined his hands and put his fingertips to his chin. A plan was forming in his mind. 'Annie, if you are intent on staying here after Pearl moves to the grocer's, would you allow me to speak to your landlord about repairs?'

'Speak to Bernie Pemberton? Good luck with that,' Annie laughed. 'I've been on at him for years and he's never lifted a finger.'

'Oh, I think I may have a little influence there.' Edward smiled.

Annie's eyes grew wide. 'You'll threaten him?'

'No . . . no.' He had a lot to learn about the ways of Ryhope folk if this was how they settled disputes. 'But I do have contacts in the corporation planning and building office I can report him to. Would you have somewhere to

346

move into temporarily while repairs are being made to the room?'

'Well, I suppose I could move in with Dorothy for a bit,' Annie said.

'Or come to live with us at Watson's,' Pearl offered.

Annie thought for a moment. 'There's another option, of course.'

Pearl was intrigued; where on earth could Annie go?

'Bobby Mac's asked me to help clear some of Ella's things from the pub. He can't do it on his own; he's still struggling with the loss of her. And he said if I helped him there's a room up above, just a small one, but it'd be mine. I didn't want to tell you before, Pearl. I didn't want you to think I was leaving you on your own here, but if you're moving to Watson's, the time might be right for me to move on too. Taking up Bobby Mac's offer on a temporary basis while this place gets mended will give me time to see how I like it next door. And if it doesn't work out, I'll move back.'

'Renee's told me I can't move to Watson's until after Billy and I are wed,' Pearl said.

'I'll arrange the repair dates to suit everyone as best I can,' Edward said. 'Leave it to me.'

He swallowed hard, trying to hide his disappointment that Pearl and his grandchild wouldn't be living close to him in Roker. But he should have known better than to turn up out of nowhere and expect so much so soon. He made up his mind to visit her and Billy and the baby as often as Pearl would allow, and help his new family in any way he could.

'I'll arrange to visit Mr Pemberton as soon as I can. I'll offer him some of my men to carry out the repair work.'

'When will we see you again, Edward?' Annie asked as he headed out to the landing.

'Billy and I are meeting the vicar tomorrow to talk about the wedding,' Pearl said before he had a chance to descend the stairs. 'Annie's coming, Billy's parents too; even Joey. Would you like to come as well?'

Edward stopped dead in his tracks. 'I'd love to,' he said. 'Just tell me where and what time and I'll move heaven and earth to be there.'

With arrangements made to meet the next day, Edward left. Up in the room above Pemberton's Goods, Pearl and Annie heard the throaty hum of the car engine as it pulled away from the kerb and disappeared down the colliery bank.

★   ★   ★

The following evening, a small group huddled in the front pews at St Paul's church. Reverend Daye sat with his church diary in his hands. The pages lay open for the month of September. Pearl was on one side of the vicar, Billy on the other. Annie was sitting at Pearl's side and Renee and Jim beside their son. Renee had chosen to sit as far from Annie as she could. She might have mellowed towards Pearl, but there was a line that Renee refused to cross. She felt her reputation had been tarnished enough over the cancelled wedding to the doctor's daughter, not to mention having a grandson born out of wedlock. The last thing she wanted was to give the gossips another field day by being seen in the company of a woman who worked the pit lane.

Baby James was in Renee's arms, fast asleep. Behind them sat Joey, his first time inside the church. He couldn't keep his eyes off the stained-glass windows. He'd seen nothing like them before, the colours vivid, the craftsmanship pleasing to his eye.

As Reverend Daye flicked the pages of the diary, looking for a free Saturday for Pearl and Billy's wedding, a sound at the church door made the group turn. It was Edward. He removed his hat and made his way toward them, offering apologies for being late. Reverend Daye acknowledged him and carried on talking. No one noticed the walking cane in Edward's hand. As he slid into the pew next to Joey, he handed it to the boy.

'I had one of my men carve it from the picture you drew,' he whispered.

Joey gasped when he saw the handle of the cane carved in the exact image of his pony. 'For me, sir?' he asked.

Edward nodded. Joey ran his fingers across the dark wood, marvelling at the skill that had gone in to creating the handle.

'And I'd like to speak to you later about a job on my project. We could use your drawing skills.'

'Shh!' hissed Renee towards Joey.

'My fault, Mrs Watson. I apologise,' Edward said.

Reverend Daye rose and stood in front of the

group. 'Now, have you thought about a best man? And about who will give the bride away?'

Billy twisted around in his seat and looked at Joey. 'Would you do me the honour, Joey, of being my best man?'

'Me? Are you sure?'

'Course he's sure,' Pearl said. 'What do you say, Joey?'

Joey lifted his cane for Pearl to see, and she and Edward exchanged a smile. 'Yes, please,' he said. 'Thanks, Billy.'

'And Pearl, what about you? Who will walk you down the aisle?' Reverend Daye asked.

Pearl looked straight at the vicar. She had always known in her heart who she wanted to give her away. But would it be allowed? 'Can Annie do it?'

'Me?' Annie gasped. 'But I'm a woman. It has to be a man, surely? A father figure . . . ' She turned towards Edward. 'A dad.'

'Well . . . ' Reverend Daye began, 'it would be unusual for your aunt to give you away, Pearl, but not unheard of. And I like to think of myself as someone who moves with the times. If that's what you want, then that's who you shall have.' He scribbled a note in his diary.

'Can I have two people?' Pearl asked. 'Can I have Annie . . . and my dad?'

Edward thought his heart would burst with pride.

The vicar scratched his chin.

'Well now, let's think . . . ' He raised his eyes to the rafters, where a beam of sunlight shone red through the stained glass. 'I don't see why

350

not.' He added Edward's name to the diary and snapped the book shut. 'That's it, we're all done. If I don't see you before — and I sincerely hope I do — then I'll see you in September. I've never had three people walk down the aisle together; it's going to need some thinking about.'

The small group left the church and headed out into the sunshine. Renee walked ahead with her grandson in her arms. Jim and Annie strolled together slowly, deep in conversation, with Annie explaining all about her move into the Colliery Inn. Behind them came Edward, then Joey, who was learning how to walk with his cane. Following on at the back were Billy and Pearl. Before they left the church, they paused in the doorway. Pearl glanced at the stone steps where she'd hidden from Annie. Billy slipped his arm around her waist.

'Penny for your thoughts,' he said when he caught the faraway look in her eyes.

'I've come a long way,' she said softly.

'All the way from the colliery to the village?' Billy teased.

'All the way from the pit lane.' She reached up to kiss him on the lips.

'The next time we're in here, you'll become Mrs Watson at last,' he said.

'Mrs Edwards-Watson, you mean.'

And with that, they stepped from the church, holding hands, and ran to catch up with their family.

We do hope that you have enjoyed reading
this large print book.

Did you know that all of our titles
are available for purchase?

We publish a wide range of high quality
large print books including:
Romances, Mysteries, Classics
General Fiction
Non Fiction and Westerns

Special interest titles available in
large print are:
The Little Oxford Dictionary
Music Book
Song Book
Hymn Book
Service Book

Also available from us courtesy of
Oxford University Press:
Young Readers' Dictionary
(large print edition)
Young Readers' Thesaurus
(large print edition)

For further information or a free
brochure, please contact us at:
Ulverscroft Large Print Books Ltd.,
The Green, Bradgate Road, Anstey,
Leicester, LE7 7FU, England.
Tel: (00 44) 0116 236 4325
Fax: (00 44) 0116 234 0205

BELLE OF THE BACK STREETS

Glenda Young

'Any rag and bone!' Everyone recognises the cry of Meg Sutcliffe as she plies her trade along the back streets of Ryhope. She learnt the ropes from her dad when he returned from the War. But when tragedy struck, Meg had no choice but to continue alone. Now the meagre money she earns is the only thing that stands between her family's safety and a predatory rent collector . . . Many say it's no job for a woman — especially a beauty like Meg. When she catches the eye of charming Clarky it looks like she might have found a chance of happiness. But could Adam, Meg's loyal childhood friend, be the one who really deserves her heart?